THE

PELICAN

TREES

A Novel
Written by
Patrick Higgins
(A Grateful Believer)

THE PELICAN TREES

Published by
For His Glory Production Company
www.ThePelicanTrees.com

COPYRIGHT © 2010 Patrick Higgins
REVISED AND REFORMATTED 2018

All scripture quotations are taken from the Holy Bible, English Standard Version (ESV) © 2001 by Crossway Bibles, a publishing ministry of Good News Publishers.

Library of Congress
Cataloging in Publication Data
ISBN Paperback 978-0-9658978-7-7
ISBN E-book 978-0-9658978-8-4

Publisher's note: This is a work of fiction. All names, characters, organizations, and incidents portrayed in this novel are the product of the author's imagination or are used fictitiously. Any resemblance to actual persons, living or dead, events or locales is entirely coincidental.

Manufactured in the United States of America.

This book

is dedicated

to all

who are

diligently searching

for the Truth...

PROLOGUE

THROUGHOUT HISTORY SO MANY truths have been grossly misstated. One of the most misstated of all was that the visible world was more powerful than the invisible world. Most humans were taught to believe that all things seen with human eyes were more powerful than all things unseen.

This lie stretched far beyond mere sight only, to the extent that far too many believed if they couldn't see, hear, taste or touch it, it simply didn't exist. What began at the dawn of civilization had successfully stood the test of time, deceiving billions into believing this dangerous lie all the way up to this present age.

There were, however, a few exceptions to this man-made belief system. Two "invisibles" humanity believed in with absolute certainty were gravity and oxygen. There wasn't a person anywhere on the planet who didn't fully depend upon the two for survival.

Without them, everyone would stop breathing and float away.

Just as oxygen and gravity both existed in the world, a vast invisible spirit world also occupied the vast expanse of the universe. On one side were Satan's demons. Though totally unseen by human eyes, evil spirits patrolled Planet Earth 24 hours a day, 7 days a week, looking to torment, tempt, confuse, deceive, and ultimately destroy the human soul. On the other side were God's mighty warriors, sent by the Creator of the universe to combat Satan's demons and protect all who belonged to Him.

This world was always active and constantly on full alert. In short; the spirit world never rested. Every minute of every day, spiritual warfare was being waged in the world. The battlefield was the human soul. The sharpest of human eyes couldn't detect it, but it was there, nonetheless. And it was extremely intense!

Whereas oxygen and gravity were two invisibles created by the Most High God to silently protect humanity without ever judging anyone, when it came to the spirit world—especially the ways of God—most took mild interest because it challenged their beliefs, morals and lifestyles.

Most humans didn't deny the presence of God, they simply chose to ignore Him, wishing instead to live life on their own terms, without ever thinking if the choices they made were actually pleasing to their Maker or not.

Further, most humans believed in a literal place called Hell, but constantly deceived themselves into thinking they would somehow escape that horrifically dreadful place when death came to collect them at God's appointed time.

In short, most had no intention of ever going to that eternal place of torment.

At 33 years of age, Shelby McKinney was among the majority of those "unknowingly" living her life this way. She was about to get a serious wake-up call and be confronted by the spirit world like never before!

Only she didn't know it yet...

1

SHELBY MCKINNEY ARRIVED AT Charleston International Airport at 8:40 A.M., just as the fog was starting to lift.

What normally took 30 minutes took an hour and a half. Interstate 26 eastbound was a complete mess.

Shelby fully expected delays and left home two hours earlier than originally planned to ensure that she and her four-year-old daughter, Brooke, wouldn't be late getting there.

The airport was forced into a complete standstill due to the severe weather and dense fog. A strong front had muscled its way through the Carolina low country just before two in the morning, accompanied by strong winds, crackling thunder, vicious lightning and two inches of much needed rain.

It did little to quench the thirst of the extreme drought conditions that had pulverized much of the region for many months.

With so many downed trees, widespread power outages were being reported statewide. After reaching the mid-90's mark for twelve straight days—well above average for this time of year—temperatures dipped into the low 60's the night before, allowing for a more pleasant evening for Charleston residents.

As was always the case with dense fog, it disrupted rush hour for commuters throughout the historical port city and its surrounding areas. Traffic was bumper-to-bumper in most areas.

Battling rush hour traffic in pleasant weather conditions was already difficult for most drivers to cope with. Add dense fog into the mix and it was next to impossible to navigate the many crowded roadways without feeling a constant sense of imminent danger.

Many accidents had already been reported throughout the city.

Once the fog lifted, sunshine would dominate the skies above Charleston, returning the southern city to its "Chamber of Commerce" postcard-like fashion, very much resembling the way it looked when first discovered back in 1670, save for the many trappings of today's technology-driven society.

The forecast high was 82 degrees. Still a little on the humid side, but the 10-degree drop in temperature, along with the slightly lower humidity, would come to most as a welcome relief.

Shelby took Brooke by the hand and the two hurried inside the airport terminal. Searching the ARRIVALS/DEPARTURES screen, Shelby found the flight she was interested in: DELAYED. No big surprise there. All flights were delayed, with absolutely no timetable as to when things would once again resume.

They proceeded to the designated waiting area.

The moment the Mellon clan had been dreading for weeks—months actually—was now upon them. For the past 18 months, they'd awaited the call on a daily basis. Whenever the phone rang, they thought it was the inevitable; the death of the patriarch of the family, Shelby's beloved grandfather, Luther Mellon.

Though three days had passed since Luther had breathed his last breath, the fact that his casket was being delivered back from the state of Florida for burial made it seem more official, more real.

"Hi, sweetie," Shelby's mother said somberly, in her customary slow, seasoned Southern drawl. Trudy Ross's vowels were soft, her syllables long and slow. Wrapping her arms around her daughter, she kissed Shelby on the cheek. "Glad you made it safely."

"You too, Momma," Shelby said. "It's already hard enough driving in dense fog. Constantly brushing tears from my eyes certainly didn't help. But I can't stop crying. How are you holding up?"

"As good as can be expected, I suppose," Trudy replied, displaying the same tear-swollen eyes as her daughter. This was the first time they'd seen each other since hearing the devastating news. "One day at a time, right?"

Shelby nodded yes.

Trudy Ross was a petite woman with a petite face. Her short silver hair was always combed to perfection. Her hazel-green eyes were usually warm and friendly, but right now they lacked the sparkle she was always known for. She was too grief-stricken. She glanced downward.

Suddenly, as if a faucet was turned on, tears streamed down her face. Since hearing of her father's death, it was as if a typhoon had materialized inside her body and was violently trying to escape through her tear-ducts.

Shelby did her best to console her mother but she, too, needed comforting. Standing a full five inches taller than her mother, she tried hard not to rain teardrops on her hair or on her light blue cotton dress.

Instinctively, Brooke inched up as close to her mother and grandmother as she possibly could. Wrapping her little arms around both of their legs, she squeezed tightly and said, "Everything will be fine."

Shelby looked down at her precious daughter wearing her favorite pink dress and smiled. As quickly as it surfaced, it vanished just as fast.

7

Everyone was dressed casually. Shelby wore white jean shorts, a green t-shirt and her son Trevor's South Carolina Gamecock's baseball cap. Her long, wavy light brown hair was pulled into a ponytail and looped through the hole in the back of the cap. Because she was so long-limbed, she looked even taller than her 5'7" frame.

The eye-bags beneath her hazel-green eyes from too much crying and lack of sleep desperately needed covering. But Shelby wore no makeup. Tears and makeup weren't a good combination, especially when trying to navigate a vehicle through dense fog with a four-year-old in the backseat.

Shelby's father, John Ross, was in Birmingham, Alabama, on a week-long business trip, and wasn't expected back until the following night. He wanted to cut his trip short, so he could be there.

Knowing he would be back in plenty of time for the funeral, Trudy encouraged John to remain in Alabama. She took comfort knowing that her husband of 36 years would have walked all the way back from Alabama, if need be.

Shelby wiped this new onslaught of tears from her eyes and greeted Luther's sister, great aunt Bea and her husband, Sam. "How are you both?"

"We're fine, dear," great aunt Bea replied somberly, also displaying swollen eyes from mourning the loss of her brother.

"Hi, Uncle Jake," Brooke exclaimed, running into the arms of Shelby's older brother and only sibling. Her long, wavy brown hair flowed freely, bouncing up and down with each step she took.

At 35, Jake Ross was strikingly handsome and still single for the time being. To maintain his well-toned 6'3" physique, he hit the gym at least three times a week without fail. He had a full head of finely groomed, light brown wavy hair, hazel-green eyes resembling his kid sister's, a mouth full of near-perfect teeth, and a smile that instantly lured women in.

It was no secret that Jake was one of Summerville's most eligible bachelors. "How's my favorite niece today?"

"Fine."

"Still planning to marry me?"

"Uh-huh," Brooke replied softly, her deep blue puppy dog eyes adoringly probing her uncle's razor-stubble face.

"Thatta girl. You better not change your mind and break my heart."

"I won't, Uncle Jake."

Kissing his niece's forehead, Jake's gaze shifted to Shelby; "You okay, Sis?"

"I'll be okay," came the reply. "You?"

"As good as can be expected, I suppose."

"Hang in there, bro," Shelby said, kissing his left cheek. "We'll get through it just like when Grandma died two years ago."

Jake said nothing but flashed a weary smile.

"Hey, Charlotte. Hey, Morgan," Shelby said to her two cousins from Raleigh, North Carolina. "Nice to see y'all again. Any updates on when he'll be arriving?"

"I spoke to a woman at the Delta ticket counter a few moments ago," Morgan said, somberly. "She said Grandpa's flight was finally cleared for takeoff in Atlanta and should be airborne in a few minutes. If there aren't any more delays, he should be here in an hour or so."

"Very good then," Shelby replied. This was the first time she'd seen Charlotte and Morgan since their grandmother's funeral.

Delta flight #765 had originated in Fort Myers, Florida at the crack of dawn. The first leg of the flight went rather smoothly. It took off on time without a glitch, arriving in Atlanta 20 minutes ahead of schedule.

Then came the delays due to the intense fog in Charleston. The pilots expected to be grounded in Atlanta, but never imagined it would last three hours, and counting...

Finally, Delta flight #765 was on the runway at Hartsfield International Airport, third in line for takeoff. Once airborne, it would reach Charleston in less than an hour, along with Luther's remains.

Of course, old Luther didn't mind the long delays. Safely tucked away inside his coffin in the underbelly of the plane, amid all the baggage, he was totally unaware of any flight delays or that flight #765 was carrying his lifeless carcass back to his native South Carolina, for burial.

His old, sickly body may have been on that airplane, but Luther Mellon was nowhere near that casket. He was finally Home and would one day receive a new, incorruptible body, a heavenly body from God Almighty Himself. This new body would never be invaded by cancer or any other pain or sickness for that matter.

And what could be better than that?

2

LUTHER MELLON LIVED A very good life. He got to see 80, which he jokingly told anyone within earshot was one of his long-term goals in life.

That was almost three years ago. Luther never lived to see 83. He died two-and-a-half weeks shy of his birthday. The first 81 years of his life were lived in near-perfect health.

When Luther was 73, he and his wife, Eleanor, sold the house they'd shared for more than 40 years in Summerville, South Carolina, along with their successful lumber company, and retired to Florida. They purchased a condominium in Fort Myers, thus fulfilling a lifelong dream to spend their golden years together in a sub-tropical climate somewhere close to the Gulf of Mexico.

Though Summerville, South Carolina was generally nice in the winter it did get cold at times. It even snowed on occasion. As the years passed, the aging couple could no longer tolerate those inevitable, bone-chilling days like when they were younger, even if they were rare occurrences.

Before moving to the Sunshine State, the vibrant, elderly couple stressed to their offspring that when they died, both wanted to be buried in their native soil of South Carolina. It was where their parents and grandparents were buried. In fact, it was where all the Mellons were buried. At least the ones they knew of.

Eleanor joined them when she died of a massive heart attack in the middle of the night, a few months after Luther's 80th birthday. The couple was sleeping when Eleanor suddenly started pounding at her chest, gasping for air.

Luther was awakened and was horrified. Fear gripped him. He called 911, then held his wife's hand and prayed until the paramedics arrived. In no time the place was crawling with people.

After performing a battery of tests on her there was nothing they could do. Eleanor was gone.

When the grieving husband buried her back in Summerville, South Carolina three days later, he prepaid for his plot of earth alongside his beloved wife, fulfilling another lifelong promise they'd made to each other to be buried together, side by side, when death came to collect them both in the future.

Five months after Eleanor's death, Luther was diagnosed with prostate cancer. It was in the advanced stages. Everyone knew his days on earth were numbered. Some were surprised he'd made it this long.

When Mellon failed to show up for morning coffee poolside at the Flamingo Club Condominiums, for the second straight day, his neighbors and good friends knew something was wrong—especially Sophie Kellerman and Claire Montgomery.

They knew he hadn't taken a trip somewhere. Had he done so, especially if visiting his family back in South Carolina, it would have been the number one topic of discussion, as they sipped coffee or engaged in afternoon games of bridge, poker, or whatever activity was scheduled for that day. Visiting family, or having family members in for a visit, was what these seniors lived for.

Luther Mellon was no exception.

Besides, had he taken a trip back home to visit his family, or gone on another church retreat, he would have left his house key either with the Kellermans, the Montgomerys or Hank Cavanaugh—like he always did—so they could collect his mail, feed the fish and water his plants. But it never happened.

And then there was the car factor to consider; had Luther gone someplace, why was his car still neatly parked in his reserved parking space?

No, Luther wasn't away on a trip, they feared. And he certainly hadn't turned into a hermit or couch potato. No way! Not counting the few agonizing months he endured following his beloved wife's death, Luther Mellon was the most outgoing senior residing at Flamingo Club Condominiums.

When he was diagnosed with prostate cancer, oddly enough, he stopped feeling sorry for himself and started appreciating life again. This caused much of the boundless energy and enthusiasm he was known for to return.

And despite what some believed, it wasn't the fear of cancer that had sprung old Luther back to life, so to speak.

Realizing his time on earth was running short, he still had something of vital importance to complete before joining his beloved wife in Heaven.

Every detail needed to be carried out to near-perfection. His friends knew something was keeping him busy this past year and a half and that it was something important, because it took up so much of his free time.

In fact, it had grown into an obsession of sorts for him. But they never asked too many questions and Luther never offered any clues.

But despite his busy schedule, Luther never missed having morning coffee with them at the pool.

11

When he failed to show up for the second straight day, their collective fears were heightened to new extremes. Sheer panic set in, as they all felt their worst fears had come true.

Luther was gone alright. But where he went, there was no coming back.

With that justification, Sophie Kellerman and Claire Montgomery both placed frantic calls to the local paramedics for help. When questioned by Josh Hansen—the man in charge of the paramedic unit that day—they assured him it was serious this time. They'd banged on Mellon's front door several times and left countless voice and text messages on his cell phone, but still hadn't heard back from him.

Hansen reluctantly agreed to send a team over to Flamingo Club Condominiums to investigate. The skepticism on his part wasn't without foundation. Over the past six months, Flamingo Club residents had placed 19 calls for emergency help. All 19 turned out to be false alarms. The worse prognosis for the supposed victims was a bad case of heartburn.

Therefore, Hansen warned his colleagues not to jump too high when Flamingo Club residents called for assistance. Sure, their job was to respond whenever a call for help was made.

That went without saying. But if two calls came in at the same time, he usually sent his A-Team to check the other location, while the B-Team rushed off to Flamingo Club. If word ever got out about this, heads would surely roll, beginning with Hansen's!

But this time even he was convinced something was wrong. It felt different this time. Usually when Flamingo Club residents, an over fifties living community, called for help, they were seated alongside the supposed victim as they made their notorious mountains out of molehills. But not this time. Luther wasn't there among them. And each attempt to contact him had been fruitless.

When the first responders arrived, Mort and Sophie Kellerman, Jim and Claire Montgomery, and Hank Cavanaugh were already waiting for them. When the door to Luther's condominium was opened, the smell of death hit the paramedics square in the face.

Whoever or whatever was in there was dead alright.

Of that, there was no doubt.

Entering a place where a dead body was starting to decay wasn't a pleasant encounter; especially for the first person in. The stench alone could literally knock a person out, protective gear or not.

To the paramedics it was just another day at the office.

But to the loved ones they had to notify, it almost always came as tragic news.

12

Luther's friends did their best to catch a quick glimpse inside. Their shriveled-up bodies wouldn't allow the necessary height needed to secure a decent view.

Not that they wanted a good view; they just wanted to confirm that their good friend was no longer among them.

The seniors looked at each other with blank, faraway expressions on their faces and shrugged their shoulders, silently wondering who among them would be the next to go...

DELTA FLIGHT #765 TOUCHED down at Charleston International Airport, at 11:19 a.m., and slowly pulled up to the gate.

Shelby's brother, Jake, nervously paced the terminal floor. Everyone else sat patiently and waited. The moment was finally upon them. Luther was home, only to be buried in two days.

The two undertakers from Pollack Funeral Home rose from their seats, once again offered their sincerest condolences, and left to claim the casket housing Luther Mellon, so he could be prepared for burial.

The Mellon family held hands and looked out the window, as fond memories of Luther flooded their minds.

The fog outside had finally lifted, but the fog inside their heads would remain for quite some time; especially for Luther's beloved granddaughter, Shelby McKinney...

3

POLLACK FUNERAL HOME WAS situated on the southern outskirts of Summerville, South Carolina. The parking lot was completely full of cars, forcing some to park their vehicles elsewhere.

Colorful flowers of all sorts were carefully and thoughtfully arranged around Luther Mellon's casket. Even in death, the expression on his face was peaceful.

In Luther's right hand was a tattered old Bible he'd read every day the past 14 years, without fail. Following his deceased wife's lead, he clung to an old wedding picture in his left hand.

Draped around his neck was a Purple Heart medal he'd earned for his service in the Korean war, when he took a bullet in his right thigh for his country.

More than 300 of Luther's closest family members, friends, neighbors and acquaintances crammed the funeral home, including 70 members from the church he'd attended in Fort Myers, Florida.

They piled into the church bus at the crack of dawn and, save for two restroom stops, drove straight through, arriving in Summerville shortly before the funeral began.

Luther's neighbors from Flamingo Club Condominiums—Mort and Sophie Kellerman, Jim and Claire Montgomery and Hank Cavanaugh—also made the trip. Shelby's brother, Jake, fetched the five senior citizens at Charleston International Airport.

Luther's family and friends in the Palmetto State were deeply touched that so many had traveled all the way from the Sunshine State to pay their final respects to him.

Even eight years removed as one of its full-time residents, Luther Mellon remained one of Summerville's most popular citizens. When he and Eleanor moved to Florida, many joked back then that with one of its pillars about to be uprooted, the small town of just over 30,000 inhabitants was sure to collapse.

Somehow, they had managed...

To the surprise of many the mood was anything but melancholy, as one might expect at a funeral. Luther Mellon wouldn't want it that way. Along with his wish to be buried in his native South Carolina soil, next to his wife

14

of 59 years—a wish that would finally come to pass in a few short hours—he all but demanded that his funeral be a time of reflection and celebration.

Instead of mourning for him, he wanted everyone to reflect on the many great memories they'd created together in life. Most importantly, he wanted everyone to celebrate because he was in Heaven.

Luther often said, "When I die, if you feel the need to shed tears because you'll miss me, go right ahead. But please don't mourn for me, because I'll be in a much better place than you. I'll be at Home with Eleanor and Jesus!"

It was so like him to say things like that...

The memorial service was performed by lead pastor of Grace Bible Church, Paul Jamison. It lasted roughly an hour.

But three more hours were needed after the service, as many regaled the congregation with personal stories of precious time spent with the man whose life was being honored and celebrated.

Mayor Forrest Shipley called Luther Mellon a "genuine treasure for all Summervillians to cherish". Trying to lighten the mood he said, "As some of y'all know, Luther was urged to run for Mayor of Summerville on many occasions in the past. I'm just glad he never seriously considered running against me. If he did, we all know I wouldn't be Mayor right now!"

Everyone laughed.

The Summerville mayor grew more serious, "In all seriousness, Luther was one of the greatest men Summerville has ever known. It was my distinct honor and great privilege to call him my friend. May his memory always remain alive in each of our hearts."

When it was Shelby's turn to speak, she never made it through her little speech. Dressed all in black, with her light brown hair pulled straight back, she gripped the podium with both hands to keep them from trembling too much.

"I can't begin to tell y'all how much I'm gonna miss Grandpa. As many of you know, he was an amazing man..."

The grieving granddaughter took a deep breath and exhaled, then lowered her head and burst out in tears. The pain in her heart was palpable. Everyone felt it.

Her husband, Jesse, led her away from the podium, so he could console his grieving wife without so many onlookers gawking at them.

By the time it had ended, more than 20 of Luther's closest family members and friends had spoken.

Oftentimes at funerals, people said things about the deceased they normally wouldn't utter had that person still been alive. Knowing they'd never see that person again, at least not on this side of the grave, mourners tend to

15

wax poetic—sometimes to the point of sheer exaggeration—hoping to comfort the minds and hearts of those mourning the departed.

But each word spoken about Luther Mellon was genuinely heartfelt and full of deep emotion. There were many tears, yes, but mostly tears of joy. Everyone laughed. They cried.

Most importantly, they remembered...

Before heading out to the cemetery, Pastor Jamison closed the memorial service by saying, "Luther's many great achievements and lifelong friendships have been well documented. But if he was here now, I'm sure he would tell us his most significant moment in life occurred fourteen years ago. Not only was it something for which he could take no credit, it had nothing at all to do with personal achievement."

In a gentle voice the longtime pastor said, "Luther's greatest day was when God changed his heart and opened his spiritual eyes and ears to the Gospel of Jesus Christ. After reading the Word of God and coming to understand God's plan of salvation, our Lord saved his soul from eternal destruction. So, it does you no good to look for him in that casket. His earthly body may still be there, but he's in Glory where he'll remain with Eleanor, forever comforted by our Lord and Savior, Christ Jesus."

Pastor Jamison was a tall and slender man. By simply looking into the 60-year-old man's eyes, anyone could see he was a kind and gentle soul who loved sharing the love of Jesus and God's amazing grace with everyone with whom he made contact.

Pacing back and forth in even strides he said, "I'm beyond convinced that if our dear friend could speak to us now, after sincerely thanking us for coming out to celebrate his earthly life, each word spoken after that would be centered on Heaven and the importance of having eternal assurance through the Lord Jesus Christ. I'm sure he'd be happy to see us all again, but I also believe he'd be anxious to get back to his eternal Home with Jesus.

"Knowing him, he might end by saying, 'If y'all ever want to see me and Eleanor again, there's only one way—through a personal relationship with Christ Jesus! If you have Jesus, you have everything you will ever need in this world and in the world to come. If you don't have Jesus, you have nothing!'"

Pastor Jamison glanced out at Luther's family seated in the front rows. Some shifted uncomfortably in their seats. Most nodded thoughtfully, seemingly in total agreement with everything he had to say. But the veteran pastor sensed it was more from an intellectual standpoint than anything else.

He couldn't help but wonder who, if any of them, would end up being part of God's eternal family. All he could do was keep praying that God would soften their hearts, like He did with Luther and Eleanor way back when. Only

16

then could they have a soul-saving relationship with Jesus and be spared the horrific consequence of spending an eternity in hell, separated from God.

Pastor Simonton sighed, knowing only those whose eyes and ears were opened spiritually understood the seriousness of it all...

4

THE THREE HUNDRED MOURNERS gathered inside Pollack Funeral Home followed the hearse in single file for the short trip to the cemetery. Knowing this was the last step in the burial process and that they would never see Luther's body again, tears fell freely as six pallbearers slowly carried the casket to its final resting place alongside his beloved Eleanor.

At the behest of Luther Mellon, Mabel Saunders, one of his closest friends and one of Summerville's most cherished residents, was the last to speak. Most gathered were still mindful of her late husband Vernon Saunders' tragic death 14 years ago, when he was killed by a drunk driver.

At the time, the story gripped all of Summerville.

On the day of sentencing for her late husband's killer, the story quickly reached far beyond Summerville, ultimately impacting multitudes worldwide. It wasn't Vern's death itself that had created the fierce firestorm of publicity. Nor was it the many organizations camped outside the courtroom jockeying for position, in a hopeful attempt to use this tragic court case to garner more publicity and support for their respective organizations—Mothers Against Drunk Driving (MADD) topping the list.

Because Vern and Mabel Saunders were black, and Vern's killer was white, the race card became a huge factor, especially in the court of public opinion. In many circles, it was the hottest topic of debate for weeks leading up to Richard Klein's sentencing.

But in the end, what lit the fuse that launched the story into orbit, making it a "must-hear" for so many, was a single act of loving kindness orchestrated by Mabel Saunders herself.

The grieving widow went from being a complete unknown to highly sought after by many worldwide, literally overnight. Mabel eventually used this new spotlight to launch a new outreach ministry called *Operation Forgiveness*.

In the 14 years since that time, she was fortunate to travel the world many times over, sharing God's Word and winning souls to Jesus in the process. It was during this time that her friendship with the Mellons went from good to unbreakable.

Mabel Saunders was short and plump with dark skin and a lively expression on her face that made her look so much younger than her 79 years

18

of age. Beyond convinced that Luther and Eleanor were in Heaven along with her late husband, Vern, Mabel chose Heaven as her topic of discussion.

Dressed all in black, the godly woman with kind almond shaped eyes began, "As you can imagine, when my husband, Vern went Home to be with the Lord way back when, Heaven suddenly became my number one destination. I read everything I could get my hands on about Heaven and the afterlife.

"Even as a great lover of life, the more I learn about God's eternal Domain, the more I want to be there. Just knowing it's my final destination thrills me to no end. After all, it's where Jesus is. But Heaven is so much more than just being with Jesus. It's a real place with real people who have real duties to perform.

"I can assure you that we will not be turned into angels sitting on clouds playing harps all day, like some believe. Knowing Luther, he's undoubtedly made many new friends by now; friends he'll keep forever and ever."

Everyone circling Luther's coffin was comforted by her words. "From what I'm learning, everything looks, sounds, smells and tastes infinitely better up there than here on this fallen planet.

"Can you imagine food tasting a million times better and one-hundred percent pure? I get hungry just thinking about it. Just hope my new heavenly body's a whole lot thinner than this old overweight body I'm still stuck with..."

The way she said it caused many to chuckle politely, softly.

"And one thing is certain; no one battles boredom up there. Imagine never feeling bored or sad or lonely ever again. Heaven is so majestic that our frail earthly bodies could never handle being there for even a split second! And our futile earthly minds are far too limited to grasp the full magnitude of God's eternal Domain. I can't wait to experience everything Heaven has to offer.

"Anyone who would choose this life over Heaven should research the eternal Paradise for themselves in the Word of God. Think about it; if the earth is God's footstool, how much better will it be for all who step foot in Heaven and see firsthand just how majestic it really is? I don't know about you, but I can't wait to meet Jesus face to face. What a glorious moment it'll be!"

Tears formed in the corners of her eyes. "I guess the best way to explain Heaven is that it's simply perfect in all ways and never needs improvement! The only time it's ever enhanced is when another one of God's children leaves this fallen planet and steps into eternity in Paradise."

With her chronic heart condition worsening, it was difficult for Mabel to control her breathing at times, especially when she talked too much, which was often.

"I miss Luther so much," she said, breathing the labored breath of the out-of-shape. "He was my dear friend and brother in Christ. But just knowing I'll see him again someday comforts me greatly in my time of mourning," the Godly woman exclaimed with authority.

"Like Pastor Jamison said, Luther's not dead! He's more alive than any of us could ever hope to be, living in perfect health, peace and harmony where he'll remain forever and ever. Can I get an Amen?"

"Amen," came the reply of the majority.

"I rejoice knowing Heaven is also my final destination." Mabel let her gaze wander about. "Will it be yours? If so, I look forward to seeing you there someday. But if you're unsure where you'll spend your eternity, it'll be my honor to share the Word of God with you, as it clearly explains God's plan of salvation. My sincere hope is that everyone here chooses Jesus this side of the grave."

Mabel wasn't overly surprised that no one seemed interested. She received the same lukewarm response two years ago, when she spoke at Eleanor's memorial service. She knew they were listening, but were they really hearing her? She feared the answer was no.

Which is why the plan Luther had painstakingly set into motion—with her assistance—the past 18 months needed to work. If it did, it would ultimately bring each family member face to face with Jesus.

Just like a tiny seed ultimately grows into a mighty oak tree, the prayer was that the seed Luther hoped to plant inside the heart of his beloved granddaughter would take root and fully blossom into a mighty tree.

Once that happened, with God leading the way, the hope was that Shelby would impact the entire Mellon family tree, allowing them all to have a glorious reunion in Heaven someday.

Lord willing...

Before leaving the cemetery, everyone placed a white rose atop Luther's coffin. They reconvened at a nearby country club for a luncheon, compliments of Luther Mellon.

When the luncheon was finished, Martin Hightower, Luther's attorney in South Carolina and close family friend for more than 30 years, pulled John and Trudy Ross aside. They couldn't help but notice the unsettling concern in his eyes.

"Not to sound too indelicate," Hightower said, "but since we're all together, I think now would be a good time to decide when to meet for the reading of Luther's last will and testament."

"You're not being indelicate, Martin. After all, Terrence and Audrey," Trudy Ross said, referring to her brother-in-law and only sister, "will fly back

20

to Nashville three days from now. And Charlotte and Morgan have jobs to get back to. The sooner we get together, the better."

"Okay, so when?" Martin asked.

"Will tomorrow work for you?" Trudy's voice projected deep sadness and hurt.

"Hmm, no can do tomorrow. Booked solid all day. How about the following day?"

What Martin didn't say was he would be busy investigating the law firm in charge of Luther's business interests down in Florida, to see what had caused the glaring omission in his client's revised last will and testament.

Hightower feared something sinister had transpired down in the Sunshine State and was determined to get to the bottom of it. With the reading of the will just two days away, he only had 24 hours with which to work.

"I'll check with everyone," Trudy replied, "but I think that should be fine, Martin."

"Okay then, I'll plan to see y'all at my office two days from now. How's twelve noon sound?"

"Sounds good."

"In the meantime, if you need anything, please don't hesitate to call or text me." Martin sighed. "At least we know Luther's at peace now."

"Thanks for the encouraging words, Martin," John Ross said.

At 53 years of age, what little hair Hightower still had left on his head was light brown. He had a thin mustache and always wore glasses. Before heading back to his office, the rather plain-looking man made sure to hug each family member. When he got to Shelby he stiffened up, trying to avoid making eye contact with her.

Martin's unsettled demeanor didn't go unnoticed by anyone. They knew he was devastated over the loss of Luther. But there was more to it than that. He seemed deeply troubled, like he would soon be the bearer of even more tragic news, almost enough to rival Luther's death itself.

"What would we ever do without you, Martin?" Shelby said. The twinkle in her eye she was always known for appeared for a brief moment, then quickly vanished again. It was still too soon.

Martin didn't reply. He gazed into her eyes then looked away, fearing that if he didn't discover the reason for the glaring oversight in Luther's last will and testament in the next 24 hours, Shelby might never utter a kind word to him ever again, following the reading of the will.

For whatever reason, as Hightower slowly ambled to his car, he sensed the deep mourning Shelby McKinney felt was but a precursor of even more painful days to come...

21

5

TWO DAYS LATER, EVERYONE was gathered inside a large conference room adjoining Martin Hightower's office. Three-quarters of the walls boasted expensive-looking artwork. The other wall was converted to a giant bookshelf crammed with stacks of law books.

A nice luncheon spread was laid out on a long table, consisting of cold cuts, coleslaw, potato salad and all the fixins, compliments of Luther Mellon.

Even in death, Luther still managed to think of everything...

Everyone helped themselves then ate their lunches at the oval-shaped conference table.

Much like at Luther's funeral, Martin seemed fidgety, displaying the same anticipatory facial expressions. It was worse now. The story his eyes told was far beyond mourning his good friend.

Hightower was thankful Shelby wasn't seated directly across from him. She was four seats to his left. In between them were Shelby's parents and her brother, Jake. Jesse sat to Shelby's left. Next to him were Shelby's two cousins, Charlotte and Morgan.

To his right was Luther's youngest daughter, Audrey and her husband, Terrence Bannister. Great aunt Bea and her husband, Sam were seated next to them. Then came Pastors Paul Jamison, Mike Cantrell (from Luther's church in Fort Myers) and Mabel Saunders.

They were all there for one reason; to receive an inheritance.

Shelby's eyes wandered the room. She wondered why it usually took a wedding or funeral to finally bring everyone together. Sure, every now and then someone planned a family reunion. But too much time always passed in between events.

Who knew when they'd all meet up again? Would it take another funeral? After all, the last time Shelby saw Charlotte and Morgan was at their grandmother's funeral. They promised back then that they would maintain contact, which they did for a month or so, before eventually resettling back into their lives.

Shelby couldn't help but wonder if it would happen again this time...

After everyone had enough to eat, Martin Hightower coughed into his fisted left hand. "Shall we?"

Everyone stiffened up in their seats, suddenly anxious. It was time to see how much money and other assets Luther and Eleanor Mellon had accumulated in life, and how much would be bequeathed to each of them.

Hightower nervously retrieved Luther's will from the inside pocket of his suit jacket, doing his best to avoid making eye contact with anyone, which was so unlike him. Confidence wasn't something he lacked in the past.

Whatever was bothering him, everyone had a sinking feeling it had something to do with the will. Their minds raced with a million thoughts and questions. Was there a problem with the will? Had there been any discrepancies? Had any of Luther's offspring been intentionally left out? Had he shown slight or even full-blown favoritism toward anyone in particular?

They were about to find out...

Martin scanned his posh surroundings, cleared his throat and began in a professional tone, "I want to thank y'all for coming today. I just wish it was for a different occasion." *That goes double for you, Shelby*, Hightower thought lowering his head, suddenly wanting to be a million miles away. "I will now read for you the Last Will and Testament of Luther Mellon."

Martin spoke slowly and clearly so no one would misinterpret a single word he said. Forty-five minutes later he was finished. He carefully folded it up and placed it back inside his light brown sport jacket.

Looking up from his glasses, he bit his lower lip. "Any questions?" Beads of sweat formed on his forehead, as he waited in agony in total silence.

In less than an hour, more than $7M was bequeathed; $4.2M in cash, and another $3M in rare collectibles, property and stock market investments that were still earning dividends. There was also a million-dollar life insurance policy.

Of the $4.2M in cash assets, half was left to the Mellon family along with the $3M in other investments, for a total of $5.1M. It was divided proportionately among everyone gathered.

The other $2.1M in cash assets was divided into three equal portions; $700,000 was given to Grace Bible Church in Summerville. Another $700,000 went to the church Luther and Eleanor attended the past eight years in Florida, Grace Evangelical Church. The final $700,000 was left to Mabel Saunders' Christian outreach group, Operation Forgiveness.

What wasn't mentioned were the sealed envelopes that were recently mailed to three men; Martin Hightower and Luther's two friends in Florida, Bernie Finkel and Bob Schuster. Luther asked Pastor Cantrell to mail them the moment he learned of his death. He also asked his Florida pastor not to mention it to anyone else.

23

Bottom line: he wanted to keep it between himself and God. Each envelope had a cashier's check stuffed inside in the amount of $100,000. All three men were extremely appreciative of Luther's generosity. Honoring his wishes, each man kept it a private matter.

But right now, Martin Hightower wasn't thinking about Luther's generosity. He was too busy questioning his sanity.

Why was Shelby suddenly left out of the final draft of the will? Luther never once hinted of his intent to remove his granddaughter at any time, let alone at the last possible moment.

All Martin knew was Luther had asked him to mail the will to him in Florida last month, so he could officially certify it. Martin did as he was instructed. Luther then changed, signed and certified the will without Martin's knowledge.

That is until Hightower received the revised will in the mail after Luther's death. Even though everything seemed to be in perfect order, he still sensed foul play in Florida, because none of this made any sense to him.

Hightower refused to believe Luther had willfully done this to the one family member everyone knew he loved the most.

Pastor Paul Jamison was overjoyed to receive such a generous gift from Luther Mellon. After numerous discussions with church deacons regarding the need to make major renovations to the church, little ever got done mostly due to a lack of capital.

The $700K would sure come in handy. The South Carolina pastor was grateful to say the least. But knowing what was still to come, he kept his excitement level in check for now.

Pastor Mike Cantrell from Luther's church in Florida shared the same level of enthusiasm, but also managed to keep it in check, for the same reason.

Mabel Saunders looked up and said, "Praise God," in a hushed tone. She, too, was grateful to the Mellons for their very generous contribution. But right now, much like Pastors Jamison and Cantrell, Mabel braced herself for the firestorm about to ensue inside Martin Hightower's lofty conference room.

She closed her eyes and started praying for one person—Shelby McKinney.

At first, no one noticed what had just transpired. After slowly realizing Shelby had inauspiciously been left out of the will, the room grew eerily silent and icy still. Smiles faded, and conversations came to an abrupt halt. It's like they were suddenly attending another funeral. This time for Shelby.

Why was she left out of the will? They wondered in silence. Surely, a mistake must have been made. Then again, Luther seldom made mistakes. And certainly not one of this magnitude—not a chance!

Unless, of course, he really was losing his mind, like many in the family had come to believe the past few years. Perhaps the elevator inside his head no longer reached the top floors after all?

Then again, if Luther knew what he was doing when signing the final draft, what did Shelby do or say that was so horrible it forced her grandfather to remove her from the will?

Shelby blinked hard a few times, wondering if her mind was playing tricks on her. Realizing it wasn't, embarrassment and humiliation set in. She sensed she would take these horrific feelings to her grave with her, which is where she wanted to be right now; buried six feet under with her grandparents. She wanted to scream and run from this place as fast as she could.

Jesse wrapped his left arm around his wife. He could feel her trembling inside. Shelby started hyperventilating and gasping for every breath. She felt like vomiting. Everyone kept staring at her, burning holes in her, devastating her even more. She wondered what they could possibly be thinking.

They were wondering the same thing about her.

A lone tear escaped Shelby's eye. She brushed it aside hoping no one had noticed. During the reading of the will, each time another family member was mentioned, Shelby was thrilled to see their exuberant reactions, knowing her name would be mentioned at any moment. Toward the end, she even selfishly thought that perhaps her grandfather was saving the best for last.

Then Martin Hightower unceremoniously folded up the will and placed it back inside his coat pocket, without the slightest mention of her name.

Even surrounded by her family, Shelby McKinney felt terribly alone; cut off from the grandparents she'd loved and cherished with all her heart. One word kept surfacing in her mind: why?

Shelby's mother, Trudy, shot a desperate, sideways glance at Martin Hightower.

Martin shrugged his shoulders and mouthed the words, "I don't know."

Trudy was suddenly upset with her late father. *This isn't funny, Daddy! Why did you do it*, she thought to herself. New tears formed in her eyes.

Shelby's trembling increased. The room started spinning. She was losing all her strength. She could almost hear everyone laughing at her and silently mocking her.

"Everything will be okay," Jesse whispered in his wife's ear. "Try to remain calm. A big mistake was made, that's all. Everything will work itself out in time."

Unfortunately, Jesse's words did nothing to comfort her. Shelby had a sudden urge to grab the will from Martin's coat pocket and read it for herself, to see where the mistake had been made. *Why me, Grandpa? What did I do wrong?*

She covered her face with her hands doing her best to silence her sobs, but to no avail. Her body shook even more violently.

"I need to get out of here, Jesse."

"Where you going?"

"Ladies room," she said. "Is your phone turned on?"

"Yes, why?"

"Expect a text message soon."

Jesse grimaced, but understood how his wife felt. He removed his left arm from her shoulder, and Shelby stood to leave.

Trudy stood to comfort her daughter.

Shelby raised her right hand, "Not now, Momma."

Trudy sheepishly sat down again.

All eyes remained on Shelby until she left the conference room. They quickly volleyed back to Jesse.

"Restroom," was all Jesse could manage to spit out of his mouth. He, too, felt a full-blown anxiety attack brewing beneath the surface. "Breathe in, breathe out," he told himself, looking down at the conference table. He wanted to cry, if only for Shelby.

Martin removed his eyeglasses and covered his face with his hands. Elbows resting on the conference table, part of him felt like it was his fault. But all he did was read the will, not write it!

Jesse's phone vibrated: *I'm in the car. Will not return. Take your time.*

He promptly replied: *Be right there.*

Jesse stood to leave. At 5'10", he had short sandy-blond hair and a blunt chin that was usually covered with facial hair—usually in the form of a goatee—making him look even younger than 35. His eyes were deep blue and always active, always probing. He had a deep, cultured voice that resembled your basic disk jockey.

Clearing his throat, he said, "That was Shelby. I gotta go. As y'all can imagine, she's not in the mood to socialize right now." Jesse took a deep breath. "There must be some mistake. In time, we will know. Until then, let's not come to any unhealthy conclusions. Hope y'all have a pleasant afternoon."

At that, Jesse left.

"Why was Shelby left out of the will, Martin?" Trudy demanded to know, the moment Jesse left the room. She fought a strong urge to release another river of tears. Her husband, John Ross, wrapped his left arm around her, hoping to comfort his wife of 36 years.

26

But John, too, was on the verge of tears. Even at 33, in his eyes Shelby was still Daddy's little girl. And now that something awful had happened to his little girl, the pain in his heart was intense.

Hightower sighed, "I don't know, Trudy. Honest."

"Come on, Martin, you must know something! You were Grandpa's lawyer," Shelby's brother Jake barked. He was beyond feeling sad for his kid sister. What he felt now was full-blown anger.

Martin wasn't in the mood for a question-answer session. He was just as confused as everyone else. "The reason we didn't meet yesterday is that I spent all day investigating the law firm Luther recently hired down in Florida. When I sent the will for final certification last month, Shelby's name *was* in it.

"Now, why he changed it without my knowledge is beyond me. I honestly have no idea why she was suddenly removed. I really don't. The worst thing is, as far as I can tell, everything seems legitimate. Luther was of sound mind at the time of certification."

The concern in his eyes was unmistakable. "I'll certainly continue investigating this matter. But as much as I'd love to say I'll eventually get to the bottom of it and fix things, the will was certified by Luther, which means there isn't much I can do." Martin grimaced. "For now, we all need to be there for Shelby, and help her cope with this second tragedy to rock her world this week."

Hightower rubbed his throbbing head. "If I had the power to reinstate her into the will, I would have already done it. But these were Luther's final wishes and I don't have the power to change a single word of it, even if it doesn't make any sense to any of us."

Martin stood to leave. "Perhaps in time we'll have a better understanding. For now, I agree with Jesse; it's best not to rush to judgment. Sorry to leave so suddenly, but I have a splitting headache. Please stay as long as you'd like. There's no rush to leave."

"Thanks, Martin," Jake said, a little calmer this time. "Sorry for my outburst earlier."

"I understand, Jake. I feel like screaming myself."

"This is so crazy!" Jake pounded the conference table. "Why, Grandpa?"

Great aunt Bea nearly jumped out of her skin when she felt the table vibrating. She curled into her husband, Sam, and remained silent. What could she possibly say to provide comfort, when she was just as mystified herself? She hadn't the slightest idea why her brother did this to Shelby. It made no sense.

"Sorry, great aunt Bea," Jake said a little more softly, taking a moment to pull himself together.

"It's okay, Jakey," she said, and left it at that.

"I'll inform my secretary that y'all will be staying," Martin said, somberly. "Let yourselves out whenever you decide to leave."

"Thanks Martin," said Trudy somberly.

Martin removed a handkerchief from his sport coat and wiped the sweat build up from his brow.

Glancing at everyone through thick eyeglasses, he said, "I know it's bad timing and all, but I would be remiss if I didn't say I sincerely hope y'all enjoy what was bequeathed to you today. Have a pleasant day."

As it turned out, their premonition was right on the money; Martin did have the look of someone who would soon be the bearer of tragic news, almost rivaling Luther's death itself.

Now they knew...

Martin already knew sleep would come hard this night, just like the past three nights. Hopefully his wife, Maggie, would rub his throbbing head until he dozed off.

But even if she did, Hightower had an inner foreboding that he would never sleep soundly again until he finally had answers.

But one thing was certain: if any wrongdoings had taken place down in Florida, he would see to it that they—whoever they were—paid dearly for doing this to the Mellon family.

Poor Shelby!

6

MABEL SAUNDERS WATCHED IT all unfolding, and her heart sank deep in her chest. She knew great psychological damage had been done to Luther's granddaughter.

While Martin Hightower may have thought he was the only one to know in advance what was happening, it simply wasn't so. Not only did Mabel know, Pastors Paul Jamison and Mike Cantrell also knew what was going on. By being involved from the beginning and knowing every intimate detail of the plan, they fully expected this sort of reaction from Shelby.

For Mabel Saunders, it was difficult being one of God's faithful servants at a time like this. The elderly woman wanted to race outside and tell Shelby why it was happening, but with God's help she managed to remain seated.

This was all part of the plan. Part of the Mission. It was all being done with Shelby's best interests at heart.

In short: it needed to happen.

Still it hurt, especially knowing this was just the beginning of things to come. Until Shelby finally understood the reason behind this bizarre occurrence, life would be difficult for her.

"Would y'all mind if I prayed before we all went home?"

"Please do, Mabel. We could really use it," Trudy replied. The pain she felt for her daughter was immeasurable.

"Let us join hands." *Stay focused. This too shall pass*, Mabel thought closing her eyes. "Oh, great and wonderful Heavenly Father, we come before You this day with a full spectrum of emotions which need sorting through. But first and foremost, we rejoice again knowing that Luther and Eleanor have been reunited and are enjoying the full bounty of Heaven this very moment, in perfect peace and health. I can't wait for that day myself," she said. A euphoric glow formed on her face.

"Regarding the generous financial contribution the Mellons made to our respective ministries, I know I speak on behalf of Pastors Jamison and Cantrell when I say how grateful we are to You, Father, for their kind generosity. Help us to be faithful stewards of these proceeds, so we can better serve You and further Your Kingdom here on earth."

Mabel took a deep breath and the euphoric glow on her face vanished. "Lord, for each of us who received an inheritance today, may we all realize the things bequeathed to us are temporal and serve no eternal purpose in our lives. As Your Word states, Father God, what shall it profit a man to gain the whole world, but lose his soul? I pray this doesn't happen to anyone here.

"Finally, Lord, in the mighty name of Jesus, grant Shelby the strength she'll need to overcome this dark moment in her life. She was already devastated before coming here. Now she's completely shattered. Comfort her, Lord. Let her feel Your healing touch. Make Your presence real to her like a warm blanket would feel on a very cold day. I ask these things in Your sweet and precious name, Amen."

"Amen," everyone replied in unison, before heading home.

"IT'S TIME TO CHANGE our group name from '*Mellon's Mission Saints*' to '*Shelby's Saints*', and pray for our group's namesake like never before," Mabel Saunders declared, to the 139 believers on the conference line.

For the past 18 months, 70 members from Grace Bible Church in Summerville, South Carolina, and 70 from Grace Evangelical Church in Fort Myers, Florida, had participated in weekly conference calls to pray for the Mellon family.

These prayer sessions were clandestine, in that no one from the Mellon clan knew anything about them. Nor were they invited to listen in. But if God answered their prayers, Luther's offspring would be the ultimate beneficiaries. Lord willing...

"Just being there today was one of the most grueling challenges I've ever dealt with. Pastors Jamison and Cantrell were also there for the reading of the will. I'm sure they concur. We need to pray that Shelby has the strength to endure until the next phase of Luther's plan has finally been revealed to her."

Mabel wheezed heavily but was determined to finish. "By not being a true Christ follower, Shelby doesn't have God's full protection, which means Satan will do everything in his power to keep this plan from succeeding.

"And we mustn't be naive; though God is sovereign and in complete control of all things, the devil has undoubtedly assigned scores of demons to distract Shelby—physically, mentally, emotionally and psychologically—to keep her living in a constant state of confusion. Which is why, as *Shelby's Saints*, we need to pray for her without ceasing!"

They spent the next 90 minutes praying for each member of the Mellon family by name, that they would have the strength to endure what was headed their way. But mostly they prayed for Shelby.

Soon, very soon, she would need all the prayer she could get. Life was about to take yet another bizarre twist and test the family like never before. As of right now, Shelby was totally oblivious to it all...

7

SHELBY MCKINNEY SAT ON a Victorian-style canopy swing on her front porch, slowly rocking back and forth. The only sounds to be heard were a few passing cars in the distance, a steady chorus of birds singing, a few chirping crickets, and the clanking noise from the chains linking the swing she was seated on to its frame. They were in dire need of WD-40 lubricant.

It was another humid, sticky morning—early signs of a hot summer. The expected high was 90 degrees, with a good chance of a passing thunderstorm. It was already 83.

To help combat the hot temperatures, Shelby wore shorts and a sleeveless white shirt with colorful flowers splashed all over it. It was the only thing on, or inside, her body that resembled anything colorful.

The grieving mother of three was still in a stupor. Even three days after the reading of her grandfather's will, Shelby still couldn't overcome her deep depression.

Circling the top of her glass with her left pointer finger, a glass half-full of lemonade, she was comatose-like, totally unresponsive to her family's constant pleas to somehow find a way to snap out of it. Nothing was working.

Each time she came close to finally accepting her great misfortune, a fresh wave of sadness pulled her under again. The anguish in her heart was palpable.

She wasn't accepting phone calls or entertaining visitors, not even her mother. She just wanted to be left alone.

Even her plantation-style house wasn't so dreamy anymore. Situated just off U.S. Highway 17, it was a replica of the plantations that had sprung up all throughout the South for two centuries.

The moment Jesse and Shelby first laid eyes on it, it was love at first sight. When they finally saved enough money for a down payment, they were amazed it was still on the market.

As beautiful as it looked, it was in dire need of renovation.

The young couple spent every spare dollar they had making positive renovations. They even refurbished the two original antique chandeliers in the foyer and dining room.

Thick white Grecian-style pillars rose up 20-feet on either side of the front entryway to the four-bedroom, three and a half bath home. An outside porch made of solid oak wrapped around the house, along with an oak wooden fence.

Part of the porch was screened in to shield the family from bees and pesky mosquitoes whenever they ate outside or had morning coffee.

A dirt and gravel driveway, which started at the edge of U.S. 17, parted green grass straight down the middle, as it stretched and snaked its way up to the house and garage. In between the tire tracks—ruts forged by horse and buggy many years ago—grass, weeds and dandelions did their best to grow with moderate success.

The dirt road split into a "Y" roughly 50 feet from the front porch. On one side, it veered off to the right headed straight toward the two-car garage. The other side proceeded to the front of the house.

Massive live oak trees draped with Spanish moss lined much of the driveway offering enormous amounts of shade, which was crucial for summertime in the South.

In the back yard was another live oak, the granddaddy of them all. Its long, thick branches stretched out more than 100 feet in all directions. How the base of the tree supported the branches under all that weight was a wonder in itself? It made most other trees, save the ancient redwoods out West, look like mere bushes.

It was a major selling point for the McKinneys.

Especially Shelby!

Flowers of all varieties—including dozens of rose bushes—were spread about the property and were in full bloom. A few Palmetto palms littered the grounds, rising high above a carpet of finely manicured green grass. The countless hours Jesse spent maintaining the lawn over the years had really paid off. The McKinneys had one of the nicest and best manicured lawns in all of Summerville.

As diligently as Jesse worked on the lawn, Shelby worked equally as hard in the garden, growing tomatoes, cucumbers, lettuce, carrots, beans, radishes and corn. A four-foot high, white picket fence surrounded the garden, doing its best to protect the defenseless crops from deer, squirrels, and the like.

Whenever Shelby felt the pressures of life creeping up, everyone knew where to find her. But not now. Nothing was working.

Why would Grandpa just forget about me like that? Shelby wasn't mad at him. She was more hurt and disappointed than anything else. Try as she might, she still didn't know what she could have done to deserve this fate.

Each time she wracked her brain, she couldn't find a viable answer, which only added to her mounting anxiety.

Shelby rose from her seat and paced the front porch for the third time. *What could I have done to deserve this?* Not only was she left out of the will, her name wasn't even mentioned, not even as an afterthought! That was the real killer!

Shelby felt like an orphan—totally cut off from her own bloodline, as if she'd never existed. How would she explain it to her children? Whenever Luther's name was mentioned in the future, she'd be forced to relive it all over again, each replay filling her heart with even more anguish. *Not exactly something to look forward to*, she thought, reclaiming her seat on the front porch canopy swing.

Surely this noose around her thin neck would follow her to her grave. Up until now, each memory of her grandfather had been good, great even. Now this? Her last memory of him a nightmare?

The worst part was that she would never know why it happened.

The answer to that stirring question was buried six feet under with Luther.

"Good mawnin' Shelby."

Shelby snapped out of it and looked up. It was Charlie the mailman. "Good mawnin', Charlie," she said, somberly. "Wow! Is it 10:30 already?"

Charlie looked at the watch: "Ten-twenty-eight to be exact, ma'am." Charlie took pride knowing he was *always* on time; at least within 10 minutes. He often reminded his customers that he had a better on time percentage than even UPS and FedEx.

As a result, he received more money and gift cards at Christmastime than any other mail carrier in the region; in some cases, three times as much! If the longtime mail carrier wanted the Christmas gifts and money to keep flowing, he needed to remain on schedule. No exceptions. Even in June, when Christmas was six long months away.

Shelby often wondered how he did it. He was such a tiny man. Yet at 5'4", Charlie was in better shape than many who were half his age. In his early sixties, Jesse often joked that he was older than he weighed.

"Where does the time go, Charlie?" she asked, in her well-trained Southern drawl, trying her best to mask that she was on the verge of a nervous breakdown.

"I ask myself dat question all da time, ma'am," the mail carrier replied, noticing the dark circles beneath her eyes. He knew she'd been crying.

It suddenly dawned on her. "Why are you hand-delivering my mail, Charlie?" This was a rare occurrence. Normally, he stuffed it inside the mailbox at the front entryway of the property.

"Looks like someone tryin' to get your attention real bad," Charlie said, handing her a certified mail card.

Shelby squinted and gulped in some air. "Certified mail for me?"

"Yes ma'am."

33

Who could it be from?

Charlie handed her the rest of her mail. "Love to talk mo'," he said, "but you know I gots to keep my schedule. Besides, I wanna beat the rain."

"Anything good in here, Charlie? I could really use some good news."

"You know I don't look at no mail. I jus' deliver it."

"Hmm," was all Shelby could manage to say.

"Das the truth!" Charlie's dark skin was covered with perspiration. And his shirt was soaked all the way through.

"Okay, Charlie. I believe you." She wasn't in the mood to push the issue. It was too soon.

"By the way, sorry to hear 'bout your granddaddy. He was a good man."

"Thank you, Charlie."

"Everyone sure gonna miss 'im."

"You can say that again. Have a good day, Charlie," Shelby said, suddenly a million miles away, her attention focused on the certified notification in her hand. *Who in the world could it be from?* She didn't have a clue.

"You too, ma'am."

After doing her own sort of the mail, compiling the legitimate mail in one hand and the junk mail in the other, it could no longer wait. She needed to know what was so important it had to come by certified mail.

Taking one last gulp of her watered-down lemonade, Shelby went inside the house and slipped into her sandals by the front door where she always kept them. She grabbed the car keys, locked the kitchen door and left for the post office.

Sixth in line, the suddenly-energized woman wondered if she even wanted what she was here to collect. She always viewed certified mail as potentially bad news. Usually it was a creditor or a court date or something like that. Her credit was good, and she had no inclination of going to court for anything. She would just have to wait and see.

"Good mawnin', Sonny," she said to the postal clerk, handing him the card.

"Mawnin', Shelby. How ya holding up?"

"So-so…" Shelby wondered if Sonny knew she was excluded from the will. Probably. After all, news traveled fast in Summerville, especially bad news. And Sonny was a family acquaintance.

"Every word spoken about your granddaddy at the funeral was right on the money."

"Thanks, Sonny."

34

Sensing she wasn't in a talkative mood, Sonny excused himself and went to fetch the document. Before handing the manila envelope to her, signatures were needed to ensure the sending party it had been received by the recipient.

Shelby eyeballed the package and her heart throbbed. *Florida?* she thought, noticing the return address on the upper left-hand side of the package.

She was tempted to tear it open and search its contents in front of Sonny but thought better of it.

Remain calm. This was something that needed to be opened in private...

8

SHELBY MCKINNEY SPED HOME, her curiosity torturing her the entire way. She pulled her vehicle to a halting stop, ten feet from the garage, sending gravel flying from beneath her tires in all directions.

She went inside the house. A blast of cold air hit her square in the face. It felt good. She hung her car keys on the rack where they belonged, put her sandals back in their rightful place by the front door, and a minute later was back on the front porch swing with a fresh glass of homemade lemonade.

And the package...

Whatever was inside the manila envelope certainly wasn't junk mail. After all, who sent certified junk mail?

With a tinge of nervous excitement, Shelby opened the envelope and plucked out a four-page handwritten letter, a map of the state of Florida, and a tiny envelope containing a key or something. It was sealed. She read the first five words and her heart exploded within her:

My Dearest Shelby,

Greetings Pumpkin!

Could it be? "Grandpa?" Tears welled up in Shelby's eyes.

I hope this letter finds you in good health. As for my health, no need to worry. As you've undoubtedly heard Pastor Jamison and Mabel Saunders say at my funeral, I no longer have cancer, or any other pain or sickness for that matter!

I'm in Heaven where everyone lives in perfect peace and health all the time. Yes, Grandma's here too! You can rejoice knowing we've been reunited and will spend eternity together with the Lord Jesus Christ. Woo hoo!

"You didn't forget about me after all!" Shelby placed the letter on her lap as tears streamed down her cheeks one after the next. Her body quaked as her sobs grew louder. But for the first time in a long time, they were tears of relief. The weight of the world was suddenly lifted off her narrow shoulders.

Now she could explain everything to her family, and in so doing, redeem herself. Shelby dabbed at her moist eyes with a tissue, took a small gulp of lemonade, and read on.

But enough about us. Let's talk about you. I'll bet this letter has you a little confused, dumbfounded even. It pains me deeply to think how devastated you must have been after the reading of the will. Knowing the family the way I do, I'm sure some may be thinking the absolute worst of the situation.

Perhaps they think you did something awfully terrible in the past, and this was my way of paying you back by publicly humiliating you. Or perhaps they think I was upset because you didn't visit me enough in Florida, which, by the way, is a legitimate gripe. But that's not why I did it either.

You did nothing wrong to get on my bad side, so please stop torturing yourself! But I fear you did something God-awful terrible to yourself. But I'll come back to that...

What did I do to myself? Shelby was beyond puzzled. She read on.

I want to begin by sincerely apologizing for any pain I caused by excluding you from my will. I hope you know I would never willfully hurt you. That was never my intention. So why did I do it? Good question. I did it for several reasons, which I'll now share with you. All but one, that is. The last and most important reason will only be revealed if you succeed with this little journey of sorts.

*Journey? Hmmm...*thought Shelby.

I've concocted this bold and daring adventure solely with you in mind, sweetie. If anyone in the family would accept the challenge at hand, I knew it would be you. At least that's my prayer. Getting to the point: this letter serves to inform that you weren't excluded from my will after all.

Come on, Shelby, did you really think ol' Grandpa would do such a thing to his little girl? Never! As most of the family might have predicted, you will inherit your fair share of my possessions, and then some! That is, if you can find it...

Find it? Still clueless, Shelby read on.

I've taken the liberty of burying your inheritance somewhere in the sands of Florida; six feet under to be precise, just like me! At least my earthly body. But fear not, Pumpkin, I'm nowhere near that old grave site! I'm in the greatest place ever! There I go rambling on about myself again. Let's get back to your inheritance.

Now that it's been buried, your job is to find it with no outside help or interference from anyone else. I'm sure you're wondering why I'm doing such a cockamamie thing. A valid question, to be sure. Perhaps you think I've lost my mind or that Grandpa's playing some cruel joke on you. But please hear me out; this little project has been in the works for quite some time.

When you were a little girl, you were the most amazing child to behold. You were so alive and full of passion! The way you would get excited about the smallest of things was truly remarkable. You liked that you were unique, special, and precious even. No one ever needed to remind you of these things.

Just being with you made your grandmother and I feel as if we'd been dipped in magical waters. You made us feel young again. Yes, being with you was always therapeutic.

Simply put; you were one of the select few who lived life the way our Creator intended for us to live, like you were one in infinity! Even better, you always did your best to remind everyone else that they, too, were unique, special and precious.

"Oh, Grandpa." Once again tears streamed down Shelby's cheeks. She dabbed at her face with a new Kleenex tissue, and continued reading.

We were convinced you would never allow life, with its many ups and downs, to rob you of your childlike sense of wonderment. I guess we were wrong. By the time you graduated from college, a tragedy unfolded before our eyes. Your once boundless enthusiasm for life slowly faded away, replaced with a somber sense of reality.

Take it from someone who has allowed this way of living to rob me of so much precious time; it's next to impossible to be adventurous under such conditions. Life is a cup to be filled, my dearest Shelby, not drained!

Now that I'm gone, if there's one bit of advice I can offer you, it's this; regardless of circumstance, happiness is not a when, it's a now. It's a choice! And it's an inside job! You can't rely on others to make you happy in life.

Sure, being blessed with a great family and friends and doing the things you enjoy in life will certainly add to your overall contentment. But in order for true, genuine happiness to surface on a consistent basis, it must come from within.

You and Jesse have a nice life together. I'm proud of what you've been able to accomplish. Everyone in the family knows how dedicated you are as a wife and mother. But let's be honest; are you truly happy with yourself?

Relatively speaking, I think you are. But I'm a little concerned that you may be slowly losing your identity as an individual in the process of being Super Mom. Have you forgotten that aside from being a wife and mother, your life still matters on so many levels?

Sorry to say but I fear you've become a small fraction of who you once were. If your life were to end today, would you be completely satisfied with each choice you've made?

I may be dead now, but are you really alive? Or are you buried six feet under without even knowing it? Are you living passionately like you once did? Or have you resorted to trudging through the motions of life? Have you ever really given much thought to these questions before? I hope so, because I fear you are dying with your beautiful music still inside you.

One of my hopes with this great and daring adventure is that it will revive your weary spirit and reintroduce you to the most amazing person on the planet—YOURSELF!

I've learned the hard way that lasting happiness is the true measuring stick of success, not money! I know money isn't your vice like it was mine way back when. With that in mind, I'm convinced inheriting money isn't what you need right now.

What you do need, however, is to reinvigorate your sense of passion and live each day forward to the fullest! I believe this journey will allow you to do just that!

However, if you're completely satisfied and feel no need to embark on this adventure, simply discard this letter and carry on with your life. No harm, no foul.

On the other hand, if you're not satisfied deep down where it really matters, make Grandpa proud and go for it! Decide to take back your life and live each day from here on out to the fullest. You will never regret it no matter what happens; I guarantee it!

Which brings me to the map and key. I'm sure you've noticed there are no X-marks on the map. It was sent more for show than anything else. The key is to my safe-deposit box in Florida. I've transferred ownership over to you for the time being. But I will not reveal the name of the bank or location to you, except that it's somewhere in the state of Florida.

If you really want to know what's in my safe-deposit box, you must find it. But talk about an awesome adventure! It doesn't get any better than this!

Is he serious? Shelby thought.

Now for the time element; you have exactly three months from today to find the safe-deposit box and, consequently, the buried treasure. Why a time limit? Procrastination is a killer! Again, no pun intended. Inside the safe-deposit box are clues to further assist you, but extremely limited ones.

39

Other than that, it's up to you to do the rest. I love you, sweetheart, but I'm not going to make this easy for you. If I do, it will defeat the whole purpose and take all the fun out of it.

If you don't find it within the designated 90-day time-period, ownership will be transferred back to my estate. If that happens, your inheritance will be given to my church in Florida, and you'll never know what Grandpa has bequeathed to you.

My attorneys in Florida, who will remain nameless, have been given specific orders to follow and will fully comply. After three months have passed, they will have no choice but to adhere to my precise instructions. I hope it doesn't come to that.

By receiving this letter, the clock has started ticking. You now have three months and counting. If you decide to trust ol' Grandpa, and embark on this adventure, I believe it will be a major turning point in your life. Even when you're old and gray, you'll look back on it with a smile on your face, whether you find your inheritance or not! Imagine that...Naturally, I hope you find what legally belongs to you (for the next 90 days, that is).

Now that I am gone, I challenge you from this moment on to seize each day and live your life to the fullest. God created you to be one in infinity. Don't insult your Maker by being average or ordinary.

Embrace your uniqueness again, my dear granddaughter, and never settle for mediocrity on any level, ever again! Always strive diligently to accomplish the things you were created to do in life, regardless of opposition. Please don't leave this earth with your beautiful music still inside you.

God bless you, sweetie.

All my love,
Grandpa

P.S. Regarding the last reason for sending this letter—the one I said would only be revealed if you succeed in finding the buried treasure; all I'll say for now is those who find it live life to the fullest. Those who don't will always feel that something is missing. This one thing is the key to successful living.

Thankfully, Grandma and I were fortunate enough to figure it out while we were still alive. It literally saved our lives! My greatest wish is that you, too, will find it on your side of the grave. Happy digging!

Shelby sat in stunned silence. The knot in her stomach started loosening. Looking out at the driveway, everything looked greener again, brighter. It's amazing what a change of attitude could do to a person. As her thinking changed, so did her surroundings.

Ironically, she felt relieved and confused at the same time. The dark cloud of negativity was finally removed from her mind, but the constant weeping and lack of nourishment rendered her dizzy.

It wasn't easy constantly changing emotions on the roller coaster she was forced to ride these past few days. It was an unhealthy combination that zapped all the energy from her body.

Shelby sort of understood the premise of the letter. In short, she *was* going to inherit something from her grandfather after all. That was the good news. The bad news was that she first had to find it. There lay the problem.

To succeed, she needed to locate her grandfather's safe-deposit box in Florida. Then, and only then, would she be granted a few limited clues. If she didn't find the safe-deposit box and the buried treasure in the next three months, she'd be forced to surrender it altogether.

It was now the tenth of June, which meant she had until the tenth of September to find what was rightfully hers.

Jesse and the children had been so patient with her all week. To show her appreciation, she would cook their favorite dinner—Chicken Divan. After supper, she would do her best to explain what she received in the mail.

Shelby went inside. On a calendar hanging on the kitchen wall, she peeled back June, July and August. In big, bold strokes, she circled the tenth day of September, her deadline date for finding her inheritance.

It suddenly sounded so exciting.

"Thank you, Grandpa," she exclaimed, grateful for the sudden burst of energy.

41

9

"WHAT!? COME AGAIN," JESSE said mockingly, placing his two fingers inside his ears, as if to unclog them. "I must be hearing things!"

"I know it sounds crazy, honey. I felt the same way myself at first. That'll change once you finish reading the letter."

Jesse was visibly skeptical. Still reeling from the reading of the will three days ago, he wondered if this was Round Two.

The moment he came home from work he knew something was up. Shelby hurried the kids into the family room and inserted a Disney DVD for them to watch, then all but dragged him back to the kitchen. His first instinct was to lasso his wife and ask what had gotten into her. But she looked happy for a change, so he remained silent and played along.

Had the tide finally turned, he wondered. *If so, how?* Whatever the reason, Jesse was thrilled to see that his wife had returned from the abyss in which she'd been trapped. But never in a million years could he have guessed the source of her new-found excitement.

Trevor and BJ were the first ones to notice the radical change in her. When they stepped off the school bus, Shelby showered them both with hugs and kisses.

Shelby's mother was next to notice, when she dropped Brooke off after a day at the mall with Grandma. Seeing her daughter playing on the lawn with her two sons, Trudy rejoiced. After being trapped in mental purgatory all this week, Shelby looked happy for a change, blissful even. It was written all over her face.

"Wow! What's gotten into you?" Trudy had said.

"I heard from Grandpa today."

Mild shock filled Trudy's face, "What? How?"

"I received a letter."

"A letter?"

"He wrote it before he died. It came certified. I picked it up at the post office earlier."

"I can't tell you how relieved I am to hear that, sweetie. Can I read it?"

"Later, Momma." This was said in a near whisper. "I want Jesse to read it first before sharing it with anyone else, including the children."

"I see," came the reply. The expression on Trudy's petite face was evident: Momma was hurt.

"I promise you'll be the first to read it after Jesse. Then you'll understand. But for now, just know Grandpa didn't forget about me after all." Shelby smiled.

"Okay, dear." Trudy sighed. She wanted to protest more but decided to leave it at that. "Well, time for me to get home and cook supper for your Daddy. Don't forget to call me," came the reply, her curiosity already consuming her. "Curiosity's gnawing away at my insides."

Shelby laughed. "I won't."

Trudy drove off.

"Why are you so happy, Momma?" Trevor said, taking a seat on the couch, once they were inside the house.

"Wait until Daddy gets home!"

"Come on, Momma, tell us now," BJ replied, with a frown on his face.

"You'll find out soon enough." It took every ounce of strength she possessed to not spill her guts.

Brooke didn't ask questions. She was just glad Momma felt better again.

BJ and Trevor were scrawny boys, blessed with their mother's hazel-green eyes. Whereas Trevor was a spitting image of his father, BJ resembled his Uncle Jake. All three McKinney children had light brown hair which quickly turned blond during the summer months from constant exposure to the sun.

Though they differed on many levels, their overall looks were so inextricably woven together that it would be impossible to deny they were siblings.

Without even asking, Shelby knew Trevor, age seven, BJ, age five, and Brooke, age four, would all be up for an adventure like this, no questions asked! What child wouldn't; especially something of this magnitude?

Jesse, on the other hand, could pose a bit of a challenge. Shelby oftentimes teased him for having no sense of adventure. He was a practical man which, on the surface, was a good thing. But Jesse was a little too practical at times, to the extent that it drained him of so much of his childlike sense of awe and wonderment.

After reading the letter, Shelby realized she had become too practical herself, and far too complacent, especially of late. She and Jesse had become one and the same. That is, until her grandfather's words breathed new life into her, filling her mind with a boundless energy and enthusiasm she hadn't felt in far too long to admit.

Shelby hovered anxiously behind her husband seated at the kitchen table, as he read the last few paragraphs of the letter. She felt like a teenager again. It felt wonderful to be this excited.

Jesse finished, and placed the letter on the kitchen table.

Before he could speak, Shelby said, "I know it sounds crazy, honey, but I say we go for it. Personally, I need to. The kids'll be out of school in less than two weeks. We can leave then. Hopefully, I'll be able to zero in on the bank location before then. If not, I'm sure we'll find it once we get to Florida. It sounds so exciting."

"You sound so sure of yourself."

"Like Grandpa said, it will be fun for the whole family."

"I'm not so sure," Jesse said, craning his neck back to his wife. "For starters, we haven't the faintest idea where to even start digging. Do you know how big Florida is? Do you know how much sand we could dig up and still not find it? It could be buried anywhere. What happens if we don't find the safe-deposit box?"

Jesse paused to let his words sink in. "And even if we do find it, the letter clearly states clues will be limited. What if they're too vague to decipher? We could dig for many days and still find nothing. We only have three months to work with. What then?"

Shelby looked down at her feet. She was hoping for more of a positive response from her husband. "I don't know. But that's the fun part," she tried to reason, "we'll be like pirates searching for buried treasure, a map our only guide."

"If there even is another map," Jesse protested. He rubbed his hair-covered chin with his fingers, something he always did when deep in thought.

Shelby took a seat next to her husband. "You're right, Jesse, but even without a map, talk about a family adventure!"

"That letter really did something to you, hasn't it?"

"It made me realize just how much time I've wasted. I'm so ready to do something bold and daring. Grandpa's right; part of me feels like I am dying with my music still inside me. Remember when we first got married? All the things we planned on doing together? Have we done any of them?"

Jesse didn't respond. But she knew he was seriously mulling it over inside his mind. His blue eyes told that much.

"No, we haven't. After the kids were born, it all faded away." She sighed. "Though I don't talk about it much, I still think of the many 'What if' scenarios on occasion."

"Are you unhappy with our life together?"

44

"Of course not, Jesse. I wouldn't trade what we have for anything in the world. But let's be honest; we could use a little more fun and adventure. I know we're getting older and all, but we're not that old. The kids are growing so fast. If we think the first ten years flew by, we ain't seen nothing yet. The next ten will fly by like that!" Shelby snapped her fingers to further demonstrate her point.

Gazing into Jesse's aqua-blue eyes, she went on, "Grandpa just presented us with an awesome family adventure. Even if we don't find what we're looking for, it'll still be great fun."

"You know you don't mean that."

"You're right," she said. "I don't think I'd be able to ever accept not finding what Grandpa left for me. But I'll feel a million times worse if I never try."

Jesse grimaced, but also understood how his wife felt.

"Naturally, once we're there, I'll do everything in my power to find my inheritance. Our inheritance!" she corrected herself. Shelby could no longer sit still. She got up and paced the kitchen floor for the second time. "We haven't planned a vacation for this summer. This can be it. We can live without Myrtle Beach, Hilton Head or Kiawah Island for one year.

"And we can finally take the kids to Disney World like we've been promising for years. Personally, I'd like to visit the Magic Kingdom on June twenty-first to celebrate Grandpa's birthday in his honor. If we stay at a hotel outside the park, it won't be too expensive."

"Do the kids know?"

Shelby shook her head. "I wanted to tell you first. You know they'd leave right now if we could."

"You're probably right about that."

There was an awkward silence. She knew her husband of 10 years like a book. By simply observing him, she knew he was seriously considering it.

"Okay, let's do it," Jesse said, throwing in the towel.

Shelby wrapped her arms around her husband and kissed his right cheek. "Thank you, honey. You'll never know what this means to me."

45

10

EVERYONE WAS GATHERED AT the dinner table. The Chicken Divan tasted as good as it looked and smelled.

Jesse was already on his second helping. The kids, on the other hand, were too anxious to eat. They picked at their food wondering what was going on, knowing it was something good. Momma's upbeat demeanor dictated that much.

Minutes passed like hours until Shelby finally said, "Kids, your father and I have something to tell you after dinner."

"Tell us now, Momma," BJ replied.

"Patience, son," Jesse said. "You'll find out soon enough. Now finish your dinner."

"Oh, all right," came the reply.

After dinner, everyone was gathered in the family room. Shelby held the manila envelope in her hand. She turned off the television and dropped the envelope onto the coffee table. "I received this in the mail today."

"What is it?" asked Trevor, reaching for it.

"A letter from GG." GG was the nickname Trevor, BJ and Brooke, had given to Luther, short for "great grandfather."

"What's it say?" asked Brooke.

"Well, as you know, sweetheart, Mommy's been feeling sad the past few days over GG's death. But there's more to it than just that." She took a deep breath. "GG left behind a will…"

"What's a will?" Brooke inquired, her eyes resting upon her mother as if being told a bedtime story. The boys listened just as intently.

Jesse answered. "Basically, it's a list GG made of everything he and great Grandma owned. Since great Grandma went to Heaven first, it was GG's job to divide everything equally among the family before he joined her there. They no longer need it where they are."

"Did he leave anything for me?" Brooke pressed on. The deep aqua-blue eyes she inherited from her father were aglow.

"That's just it, honey," Shelby said, regaining control. "Daddy and I didn't tell you earlier, but for whatever reason, it seemed GG forgot all about us. Until today, I had no idea why. This upset me almost as much as his death."

"Why did he forget us, Momma?" Brooke was on the verge of tears.

"It's okay, sweetie." Shelby took her little girl into her arms. "GG left something for us after all."

"What is it? What is it? What is it?" all three children said in order.

"That's just it. I, we, don't know yet." Shelby glanced at Jesse. He gave her an affirmative nod of the head. "How would you kids like to go to Florida?"

"Florida?" asked BJ. "Yes!"

"Yes!"

"Yes, Momma!"

"Whatever was left for us is buried somewhere on a beach in Florida."

"You mean we're going on a treasure hunt?" said Trevor, the oldest sibling.

"I guess you could say that." Shelby felt as excited as her three children looked.

Jesse weighed in; "We were thinking of going to Disney World while we're there."

"Awesomeeeeeeeeeeee!" said BJ.

"Really?" said Trevor.

"Yup," said Jesse.

"When we leaving?"

"We were thinking the first Monday after school's out." What Jesse saw on his kids' faces made it seem more real, elevating his excitement level to heights not visited in ages. "But only if the grades are good. Is there anything we should know before booking this trip?"

"My grades are fine, Daddy," Trevor said.

"BJ?"

"My grades are fine, too."

"Brooke?"

"My grades are fine, too, Daddy."

BJ and Trevor both chuckled. Still in pre-K, Brooke didn't get a report card. Whenever her two brothers came home with theirs, she would get upset. To keep her happy, Shelby would give her daughter a report card on the same day the boys came home with theirs, grading her on the things she did around the house.

"Okay then, looks like we're going to Florida."

"Hooray!" said Brooke.

"Woo hoo," Trevor and BJ both said at the same time, fist bumping each other. It was difficult to discern whether they were more excited about finally going to Disney World, or digging up a buried treasure in the sands of Florida. It was probably too close to call.

"Settle down a moment, kids," Shelby said, "we haven't told you everything yet."

All three sat on the floor.

"Here comes the tricky part. The only thing we know so far is that the treasure chest is buried somewhere in Florida. Actually, there's another clue. See this key?"

All three nodded yes.

"It's to GG's safe-deposit box. The only problem is he didn't tell us which bank. We may need to drive to a few banks until we find the right one, okay?"

All three nodded approval.

"Well, okay then, it's settled. We'll leave the Monday after school lets out."

The kids did a celebration dance without being ordered to settle down this time.

Jesse watched with a smile on his face. It was great being a parent at times like this. Getting time off from work wouldn't be a problem. He had more vacation time than he would ever use. *They can manage without me for one week.*

Shelby looked up at the ceiling and mumbled another "thank you" to her late grandfather. His letter served to rescue her from the doldrums of self-pity and despair, instantly reinstating her desire to want to be happy again. *Life is perfect!*

Or so she thought...

Shelby was unaware of the consequences she would face by going on this journey. Her decision to proceed created a vicious firestorm in the invisible world, between God's mighty warriors and Satan's fallen demons—the very ones the Most High cast down from Heaven long ago, along with Satan himself.

Having been in God's presence and tasting the fullness of Heaven, only to be forever vanquished still incensed Satan and his vast army of condemned imps to this day. By ultimately choosing Satan over God, in God's very presence, they knew the Most High's decision to banish them was a permanent one; meaning Heaven was a place in which they would never step foot again; a place where its inhabitants would never again fellowship with their kind.

If they couldn't go back there, why should anyone else be able to, especially lowly humans? With this unholy mindset, their mission was to do all they could to stop anyone else from stepping foot inside God's bountiful domain.

"Eternal condemnation for all!" was their constant battle cry. Those four words provided all the necessary fuel to drive their fierce, global mission. Nothing else mattered to them!

The fact that Satan knew God's Word so much better than humans made his mission so much easier to carry out. All demons under Satan's command knew an eternity spent in Heaven with God Almighty, versus an eternity spent in hell with them, was predicated on a single decision; either receive or reject God's plan of redemption for humanity, which was only possible through a personal relationship with His Son, the Lord Jesus Christ.

Satan's demons knew humanity needed to make this decision while still alive in human form. Advantage Satan!

Fully mindful of this, the Master Deceiver assigned demons to all who weren't true children of the Most High God. Their task was constant: torment, tempt and deceive without ceasing, to keep their assignees living in spiritual bondage and darkness until death finally came to collect them.

Knowing the great potential danger this little treasure hunt had just created in the spirit world, both sides were gearing up for yet another fierce battle.

Just because humanity couldn't see it didn't mean it wasn't there. It was there, and it was extremely intense!

11

LUTHER MELLON WAS REUNITED with his beloved wife, Eleanor, living in perfect peace and health. Perfect as it was, he would rejoice even more knowing his granddaughter had decided to proceed with the adventure that took so much time, effort and prayer to set in motion before his death.

Even with the many built-in peaks and valleys he knew Shelby would face along the way, his prayer each night was that she would endure it all with the same level of enthusiasm and vigor he himself had exuded in the 18 months he spent obsessing over each detail. There was too much at stake, spiritually speaking, to leave something important out.

It took Luther most of his life to finally learn that anyone who thought they deserved Heaven for doing good deeds or by honoring man-made religious traditions had zero understanding of the Gospel. What he came to realize was the only thing a person could bring to their salvation was their sin which needed forgiving from God.

Tragically, mostly thanks to Luther himself, his family had little understanding of the ways of God. All were kind and generous souls who took great pleasure in helping others in need. But they failed to realize these things didn't bring them closer to God.

Prior to his conversion, Luther thought the very same things. Sadly, his greatest student was Shelby. She absorbed his words of wisdom like a sponge absorbed water.

Luther often told her, "You are the master of your own universe. Everything starts and ends with you!"

It was a philosophy he believed most of his adult life. Everything changed when God got his attention and Luther realized how shallow that philosophy really was, because the most important element was clearly amiss in that way of thinking—the Most High God!

Prior to his conversion, Luther acknowledged there was a God, but said He was too busy meting out judgment to all the evildoers in the world to be intimately concerned with everyone else. The benefit to this was that it allowed the good citizens of Planet Earth to pursue their dreams in relative peace and harmony.

The guilt he felt for preaching the wrong message to his family all those years was all the motivation he needed to find a way to somehow right the ship before death came to collect his soul.

But how could he change his message and convince them that it really wasn't about "self" after all? That God wasn't some far away Being who was too busy dealing with everyone else that He had no time left for them? Why would they even listen?

After all, his "success" message had taken full root, to the extent that all were productive citizens in life. By changing his message now, perhaps they'd think senility had finally set in when nothing could be further from the truth.

Though God had forgiven him for "unknowingly" misleading them for so many years, by being the patriarch of the family, Luther sometimes felt their blood on his hands. Everyone in the family knew *of* Jesus, but he seriously doubted if they knew Him personally, deeply, intimately.

Which is why Shelby needed to find her inheritance at all costs! She was the key to making his plan work. By finding the buried treasure chest, she would find the key to the second safe-deposit box stashed inside, which would allow her to discover the most important element of this little adventure—her salvation.

Luther firmly believed once she came to faith in Christ, no one else had the ability to rouse everyone's curiosity, regardless of topic, better than Shelby. And what better way than to throw a little adventure into the mix?

Ironically, while everyone in the family firmly believed he and Eleanor were in Heaven, they didn't know *why* they were there, only that they *were* there. Most would be shocked knowing it wasn't because they were good people, or because they helped so many in life by giving large sums of money to various good causes. Nor was it because they'd left a sizable inheritance to their family.

Those things, while noble, had absolutely nothing to do with it. They were in Heaven for one reason and one reason only; they understood and received God's plan of redemption.

It tragically took losing a lifelong friend for Luther to seriously contemplate eternity and the afterlife for the first time. It happened 14 years ago when Vernon Saunders was killed in a car wreck. He was hit by a drunk driver who'd failed to stop at a red light early one evening in Summerville, South Carolina. He plowed straight into Vern's vehicle, hitting it head on. He was killed instantly.

Vern was survived by his wife of 43 years, their five children and 14 grandchildren. After 40 plus years of wedded bliss, Mabel Saunders was suddenly alone. Luther wanted justice at all costs!

51

The Mellons did all they could to comfort Mabel in her time of grief. The more time they spent with her, the more angered Luther became toward Vern's killer. He couldn't understand why God would allow this to happen to a dedicated family man and church deacon for more than 30 years.

According to most, Vernon Saunders was one of God's most faithful servants and was desperately needed in their tightly-knit community.

In private, Luther wondered if Vern really was on God's good side or not. Was he secretly hiding some dark secret no one knew about, including Mabel?

Luther did not know. All he knew was if God allowed something so tragic to happen to one of His most faithful servants, what assurance did he have of ever seeing 80, which everyone knew was one of his long-term goals in life?

Luther quickly concluded there were none.

Vern and Mabel Saunders valued their friendship with the Mellons, but they were always concerned for their spiritual well-being. On the few occasions they got to share the Gospel with them, Luther and Eleanor never disagreed with anything they heard.

But agreeing with the Bible without applying its life-altering message to one's life was not only a slippery slope, but a dangerous trap set by Satan himself. What made this trap more dangerous than all others—drugs, alcohol, gambling and pornography—was that everyone ensnared in those addictions were fully mindful of them.

On the other hand, those stuck in the "agreeing only or good works equals salvation" traps were totally unaware of it.

Most wouldn't think to call it a trap. The proof was that millions were presently confined there. Even more tragic was that billions had already perished while ensnared in this deadly trap and were currently in Hades awaiting God's great judgment.

Fully mindful of this, the Saunders constantly prayed that God would rescue Luther and Eleanor from this—and all other salvation-blocking traps in which they might be stuck—and open their eyes and hearts to the Gospel of Jesus Christ before it was too late!

When Vern died, the responsibility of praying for the Mellons fell squarely on Mabel's suddenly frail shoulders.

Less than a year after Vern's death, Luther's curiosity regarding eternity and the afterlife was heightened considerably, after witnessing something truly remarkable transpire inside a crowded courtroom.

The way Mabel Saunders conducted herself during the emotionally-charged court proceedings is what eventually pushed the Mellons over the edge into the loving arms of Jesus.

Richard Klein, the man responsible for killing Vern Saunders, and making Mabel Saunders a widow, pleaded no contest and was found guilty of vehicular manslaughter. Klein was sentenced to 10 years behind bars with the possibility of parole after serving seven years with good behavior.

At Klein's sentencing, the judge granted Mabel permission to address her husband's killer.

Everyone braced themselves.

Inching as close to her husband's killer as she possibly could, Mabel Saunders looked Klein in the eyes and said; "When I first heard this was your third DUI, I was shocked, then furious for the longest time. Your irresponsible actions last year forever altered my life and the lives of so many others, including my five children and fourteen grandchildren." Tears welled up in her eyes. "You robbed me of so much precious time with my beloved husband and rid the world of a man who made such a huge difference in the lives of so many. Because of you, he's gone."

Mabel paused and took a deep breath. "I've been a God-fearing woman all my life. I'm mindful that Jesus often spoke on love and forgiveness, more than most other things, in fact. I can't tell you how many times I wrestled with God regarding forgiving you, Richard. My Maker kept prompting me in my spirit to forgive you, but I couldn't bring myself to do it.

"Truth is, I didn't want to forgive you. I was too angry and too devastated! I blamed you and you alone for ruining my life. Everything that was wrong in my life suddenly became your fault!

"Playing the role of the grieving widow-slash-victim, gave me a certain level of comfort." Mabel paused. "But like all things that aren't from God, it never lasted. Funny thing is, the more I openly attacked you, the more your face haunted my dreams at night. I went from being a victor in Christ to victim, practically overnight. Well, I'm tired of playing the role of victim. It's time for me to become a victor again! And it begins today!"

Without the slightest trace of anger or malice, Mabel looked the 26-year-old man square in the eye and said, "Richard, from the bottom of my heart, please know that I forgive you for killing my husband." She paused to let her words hang thick in the air. "And I hope you can forgive me for speaking so badly about you in public all this time. It was wrong of me and I'm sorry. I needed to be reminded that great minds talk about ideas, average minds talk about events, and small minds talk about other people!"

You could hear a pin drop inside the courtroom that day.

Richard Klein lowered his head in shame and started sniffling, totally blown away by Mabel's loving kindness. It was the last thing he expected that day!

53

Fully mindful of the race factor this court case had generated, which, in Mabel's opinion, had been blown out of proportion by the media—because Vern Saunders was black, and Richard Klein was white—she nipped it in the bud, so to speak, by focusing on the much larger issue at hand: forgiveness!

Shifting her gaze to her children and grandchildren, all of whom were still too angry to offer Richard Klein their forgiveness, she said, "Jesus commanded us to love thy neighbor. He didn't say love thy next-door neighbor only, or thy black or white neighbor only. He commanded us to love all our neighbors to the best of our ability, without malice, prejudice or geographical parameters! I intend to do my part today."

Her gaze turned back to Richard. "I've come to realize the animosity I've harbored toward you all this time put great distance between me and God. Of course, God never moved. I did all the moving myself. Whenever I wavered about possibly forgiving you, God kept bringing me back to the most important event in all of world history—the death of His Son on the cross. Each time I did an inner-voice kept saying, 'It was your sins that put Him there, Mabel, yet He freely forgave you!'"

Mabel looked up at the ceiling. A stray tear rode down her right cheek. "I felt so ashamed and was completely broken before God. With fellowship between us restored, God kept reminding me in my spirit, and in His Word, that He was mindful of my pain, anger, and even my loneliness. So long as these emotions didn't become crutches, they would eventually serve to strengthen me.

"I realized I had overstayed my welcome at those dreadful places and it was time for me to move on. Gosh, I not only parked there, I practically moved in and was turned into a full-blown victim as a result. I was reminded that it's next to impossible to make sound, logical decisions when overly emotional. This is especially true for us women," she said jokingly, hoping to ease the tension inside the courtroom.

It worked. Light laughter permeated all throughout.

"Thankfully God made me see just how selfish I was being, by allowing my personal feelings and emotions to triumph over what He was trying to accomplish for His glory. He commanded me in my spirit to get out of the way and just trust that He knows what He's doing at all times! The Most High promised if I would remain obedient and take the first step in faith, He would do the rest. I'm convinced that first step is forgiving you."

Taking a deep breath, Mabel said, "I know you didn't mean to kill Vern. So please stop torturing yourself." Her voice was warm and caring.

Klein's sobs grew louder and more pronounced.

Dabbing at her eyes with a handkerchief, she continued, "After God challenged me to shift my focus from my needs to yours, I realized you weren't a cold-blooded killer. You're just an alcoholic who needs help. I tried to imagine the mental anguish you must battle each day. I'm sure the many nightmares I've had this past year are nothing compared to what you've been forced to endure."

Klein's head remained down. His long, dark brown hair covered much of his face like a curtain. There was an awkward pause inside the courtroom, as many wiped tears from their eyes and quietly sniffled.

Mabel took a few moments to collect herself, then went on, "I've been observing you throughout the court proceedings. I truly believe you are remorseful and that you never meant for any of this to happen. You don't want to be here anymore than I do. I believe you really are a nice young man. You just happen to have a major addiction, which, sadly, has cost both of us so very dearly.

"Now that I'm back on the road to recovery, the healing process has finally begun. It's time for it to begin in your heart too. Fair enough?" Mabel flashed the most magnificent smile Richard Klein had ever seen before. Her eyes sparkled like diamonds, her warmth felt like a sunbeam on his face. For a moment he let himself bask in it.

Finally, in between sniffles, Klein looked up and gazed into Mabel's almond-shaped eyes, "I'm so sorry for the great pain and heartache I've caused you. Thanks, so much, for your kindness and forgiveness. You'll never know what it means to me. You truly are a remarkable woman, and whatever it is you have, I want it too."

"It's not me, but He who lives in me. Your life matters to God, Richard. You matter to me, too. If you ever need anything, like reading materials or clothing, just let me know. My door will always be open to you. Always know there's someone on the outside praying for you daily. Let's be friends, okay?"

Richard half-smiled. He was too numb to speak.

"I only wish you could have met Vern. After all, it's because of him that we're now connected. I can assure you if he was here right now, he would also forgive you. With that in mind, can I ask something from you?"

Klein nodded yes.

"Can you honor Vern's memory by making something good of your life? You can do this by reaching out to those in need and by loving your neighbors, even your fellow prison inmates."

Klein nodded yes again.

"I know the next ten years will be difficult for you. But with God's help, you can flourish despite your surroundings. You're still young. Hopefully,

55

when you get out, you'll be a major contributor to society. For now, hang in there, Richard. Never forget that Jesus loves you and so do I."

At that, the older Godly woman turned and sat down.

Once again, you could hear a pin drop inside the overcrowded courtroom.

Luther and Eleanor Mellon were among the angry mob of citizens gathered there on that rainy afternoon.

Like everyone else, they expected Mabel to blast him. But it never happened. Instead, with their own two eyes, they witnessed true Christian love and forgiveness in motion.

Growing up in the Bible belt, Luther had heard the message of forgiveness preached on numerous occasions, and the need to "Love thy neighbor". But nothing penetrated his hardened heart like what transpired that day. Luther was 67 at the time.

Richard Klein was right; Mabel Saunders really did have something no one else had...

12

IN THE DAYS FOLLOWING Klein's sentencing, God fulfilled His promise, moving miraculously for all to see.

Mabel left the courtroom that day forever changed. Her courtroom "sermon" was shown repeatedly on local TV news stations. Sound-bites were aired on several radio stations. More than 100,000 viewers watched it on *YouTube, God Tube, Facebook, Twitter* and various other social media sites the first month alone.

One global television conglomerate even featured it as their human interest "feel-good" story of the week.

Mabel was flooded with requests from churches worldwide to post her courtroom video clip on their web sites. She received thousands of cards and letters, and hundreds of thousands of e-mails and text messages from strangers worldwide. Four months had to pass before she could personally respond to each correspondence.

To her great joy, she got to pray with many of her well-wishers in person, on the phone and online. Hundreds became Christ followers practically overnight. It quickly turned into thousands, and a new chapter was opened in her life.

At 64 years of age, Mabel Saunders launched a new outreach ministry called *Operation Forgiveness.*

Her life became a nonstop whirlwind of appearances and speaking engagements. By focusing more on the needs of others and less on herself, God used that time to remove all pain, anger, sadness and loneliness from her heart, supernaturally replacing it with an inner-peace and joy that knew no bounds! And it showed! Everyone could see and feel it. They could almost touch it.

And it all started with something as simple as forgiving Richard Klein...

Though she missed Vern terribly, knowing they would one day be reunited in Heaven, she considered all her suffering more than a fair trade off; especially since many had trusted in Christ as a result.

Despite her busy schedule, Mabel kept her promise to keep in touch with Richard Klein, even visiting him in prison at least once a month, without fail. On her third visit there, they made the news in Heaven, when Richard committed his life to Jesus.

Even from behind prison bars, it was the happiest day of his life.

It was Mabel's unconditional love for Vern's killer at every turn that finally forced Luther Mellon to realize just how poorly he would have handled the situation, had it been Eleanor instead of Vern.

He never would have confronted Richard Klein with the same level of grace Mabel had shown that day. His words would have been full of venomous hatred, without the slightest hint of grace, compassion or forgiveness. Yes, it had to be God working through her, Luther remembered thinking back then.

People simply weren't that nice, especially to those who killed cherished loved ones! Mabel's angelic behavior—that's what Luther had called it—forced him to seek new answers to his many "life" questions, especially those regarding death and the afterlife.

By so doing, he and Eleanor realized they had no true eternal assurance. They were simply hovering between two eternities.

A few weeks after the trial had ended, the Mellons invited Mabel to accompany them to their timeshare on Sanibel Beach, Florida. Mabel needed a break and gladly accepted their kind offer.

It turned out to be the two most significant weeks of their lives. Mabel shared God's Word with them every day. The more she read to them, the more the vibrant seniors felt the Most High softening their hearts and drawing them to Him. They started hungering and thirsting for it more and more. It was the most amazing sensation.

Once they finally understood God's plan of redemption, it could wait no longer. Standing underneath a huge banyan tree on the beach fronting their timeshare, with two tall pine trees on either side of it, Luther and Eleanor both received Christ as Lord and Savior.

The "pelican trees", as Luther had affectionately dubbed them, because of the hundreds of pelicans always perched on their many branches, very quickly became their favorite place on earth.

Luther felt so transformed that day and made a solid commitment to do whatever it took to get his family on track, spiritually speaking. That commitment was greatly accelerated after Eleanor died, then turbo-charged when he was diagnosed with prostate cancer.

He needed to formulate a plan to get his family to see the Light for themselves and sought Mabel Saunders' advice on the matter.

After a lengthy phone call, it became apparent to them both that whatever plan was ultimately set in motion, Shelby needed to be the focal point of it all.

Before ending the call, Mabel said, "You always said Shelby was an adventurous woman, right?"

"She used to be, why?"

"Why not reinvigorate her senses by sending her on a great and daring adventure? Something that will heighten her senses in such a way that it will force her to think outside the grain of sand which is her life and allow her to exist on a much higher plane!"

"What kind of adventure are you suggesting?"

"That's for you to figure out, Luther," Mabel had said. "But whatever you choose, just make sure it ultimately leads straight into the arms of our beloved Savior! Once you figure it out, call me and I'll do anything I can to help bring it to life, to the best of my ability."

Many weeks passed before Luther finally had what he thought was the perfect plan. He called Mabel. "I think I got it!" He was so excited, he forgot to say hello.

"I'm all ears, Luther."

"I was going over my last will and testament and it suddenly struck me; instead of bequeathing Shelby's portion of my possessions to her at the reading of the will, why not bury it somewhere here in Florida and send her on a buried treasure hunt? I'm talking about a real wild goose chase. Something that will challenge her mightily. But at the end of the journey will be Jesus."

Mabel bubbled over with excitement, "What a terrific idea, Luther. I love it!"

And that's how it all started...

The moment Luther set the treasure hunt idea in motion, the spiritual attacks began. Initially, he didn't put one and one together. He thought his old mind was playing tricks on him.

After a month had passed, it dawned on him that the attacks—including constant bouts of dizziness—were most intense when working on this project.

As the spiritual attacks intensified, Luther and Mabel increased their prayer time together. The more they prayed, the more the pieces continued falling into place, despite Satan's ongoing attacks.

Then Mabel Saunders was diagnosed with chronic heart disease. She knew she needed to start grooming her replacement at *Operation Forgiveness,* to carry on her legacy when death came to collect her.

With a handful of possible replacements in mind, including two of her own children, Luther and Mabel prayed for each person nightly, but God never gave her a clear-cut answer. It was no secret that she wanted one of her own children or grandchildren to oversee operations when she was gone. But they all led very busy lives and careers, and only expressed mild interest at best.

Suddenly Shelby McKinney popped up on her radar screen...

At first, Mabel dismissed the notion altogether, thinking it was because she and Luther were working so closely together on Shelby's behalf. Besides, she wasn't even a Christ follower.

Nevertheless, her face continued to burn in Mabel's mind. After many months of praying, God finally confirmed that Shelby was the one. But not until she became a born-again believer.

Luther rejoiced when Mabel shared this wonderful news with him. "All the more reason for me to get busy!" he had said.

It was then that Luther contacted many of his closest brothers and sisters in Christ, both in South Carolina and in Florida, seeking prayer for his plan to succeed. This was the group Mabel Saunders originally named *Mellon's Mission Saints.* She changed it to *Shelby's Saints* the day Luther was buried.

Thankfully, God had allowed Luther to live long enough to complete his last Mission in life. If successful, it would lead to a joyous family reunion in Heaven someday for the entire Mellon clan.

Now that he was gone, it was up to Shelby to make it happen...

13

JUNE 14 - DAY 4

SHELBY WAS SEATED AT her desk in the family room online, researching various bank locations in Florida. This had become her combat room, so to speak.

Jesse was at work. The boys were at school. Brooke was still in her pajamas playing with her Barbie dolls.

Hovering inside the house were the demons Mabel Saunders' feared Satan had assigned to her. Though totally unseen, they were there in full force. Their faces were grossly misshapen and hideously marred, projecting an image of evil incarnate.

They cackled and hissed among themselves. They shrieked and moaned, cursing God Almighty, filling the air with unspeakable blasphemies. Only no one in human form heard or saw any of it.

Not only did these uninvited visitors know about the buried treasure, they were also aware of the constant prayers being offered up to the Most High God by *Shelby's Saints*, as evidenced by the brilliant white Light hovering high above them. The more they prayed on their namesake's behalf, the more brilliantly the Heavenly Light intensified.

The demons assigned to Shelby didn't need to be outside the McKinney household to see the Light. Concrete, wood, tiles and tar did nothing to obstruct their view. Even in a fierce hurricane, they still saw the Light ever so clearly. There wasn't a place in all the universe in which Satan's demons could hide to escape it.

The more it pulsated, the more frantic and terrified they became.

The task of each demon assigned to Shelby McKinney was a never ending one; to continually confuse her mind and keep her off track, spiritually speaking. Temptation, torment, doubt, deceit and despair would invade her life later. For now, their focus was to keep her living in a constant state of confusion.

Regarding the buried treasure, they weren't the slightest bit concerned about the money their assignee stood to inherit if she found it. It was the least of their concerns.

In truth, they wanted her to find it. If she did, chances were good it would keep her rooted in the world in which their fallen commander always had his filthy talons deeply entrenched.

What they didn't want, however, was for Shelby to find the contents stashed inside the second safe-deposit box. The stakes were just too high! Just knowing *Shelby's Saints* were offering up constant prayers on their assignee's behalf was all the confirmation needed that the spiritual warfare would soon be intense.

Both sides would burn with the heat of battle—one side hell-bent to destroy her soul for all eternity. The other side would burn with the fervor of God's sovereign righteousness!

Totally oblivious to it all, Shelby's goal for today was to finish compiling a list of the 100 banks within the closest proximity to her grandfather's condominium. She already had 73 locations mapped out.

Earlier in the week she hung the map her grandfather had sent on the wall above the computer desk. Whenever she obtained a new bank address online, she placed a green stick pin on the map. Green was everywhere.

Hopefully the safe-deposit box would be housed in one of the first 100 banks. If not, Shelby was determined to visit every bank in the state of Florida, if need be, to find her inheritance.

It didn't seem plausible that her grandfather would do his banking too far from his home. He was always a simple man in life. Banking far from home would have been very un-Luther like, especially at his age.

Then again, perhaps to keep her on her toes, he purposely chose a bank far from his residence. Perhaps the bank she was looking for was located clear across the state? The letter did state he wasn't going to make it easy for her.

So many questions...

For whatever reason, Shelby believed locating the bank would be the easiest part of the job. Nevertheless, it was the most crucial part. Simply put; no bank, no safe-deposit box. No safe-deposit box, no additional clues. No clues (limited as they would be), no treasure chest. No treasure chest, no inheritance!

Once located, however, everything else would probably prove more difficult. But she wasn't too concerned. It was all part of the journey. All part of the fun.

Mapping out the 100 closest bank locations beforehand was a good move on more than just one level. Not only did it give her a sense of accomplishment, it also served to ease Jesse's mind a bit. Despite his many protests to the contrary, Shelby knew he was still iffy about the whole idea.

He wasn't the only one. Her brother Jake was equally skeptical. No one loved, admired and respected Luther more than Jake. But he feared his grandfather had indeed lost his mind for doing this to Shelby. Sure, it sounded exciting to embark on a buried treasure hunt, but to Jake, it also sounded a bit childish.

Jake believed Shelby was just as crazy for accepting the challenge. But he also knew how badly his kid sister needed this. The one good thing was that everyone could finally move on with their lives, no longer trapped beneath the huge canopy of guilt the reading of the will had created for all involved.

It wasn't their fault Shelby was left out of the will.

Still, the guilt lingered.

Shelby was taking a sip of lemonade when the phone rang. "Hello?"

"Shelby?"

"Yes?"

"It's Martin."

"Hi, Martin. How are you?" At first, his voice brought her back to last week, when he momentarily shattered her life. She pushed it out of her mind.

"I'm okay, thanks. How are things coming along?"

"Much better now, thank you."

"Would it be okay if I dropped by?" Hightower asked.

"Sure. Is everything okay?"

"There's something I really need to discuss with you."

"Can you tell me on the phone?"

"I'd rather not."

"Well, alright then, sure, come on over."

"I'll be there in a jiffy."

When Jake told Martin that Shelby hadn't been excluded from the will after all, relief flooded over him. But when he said it would be easier to find a needle in ten haystacks than to find her inheritance, his concern for her only escalated.

How could she possibly find the buried treasure with only an unmarked map and a key to a safe-deposit box to work with? She could easily visit a thousand banks in Florida and still not find it.

Shelby was bright, but she was no Sherlock Holmes. If she had any shot at finding the buried treasure, Martin believed she would need all the help she could get.

Martin Hightower still couldn't fathom why his good friend of 30 years had done this to his granddaughter. As chief executor of numerous wills over the years, it wasn't uncommon for a client to remove certain family members from their will. It happened quite frequently. Martin never lost an ounce of sleep over it in the past.

But this case was different. If anyone deserved an inheritance, he firmly believed it was Shelby. Which is why he finally decided to call her.

Always one to play by the rules, this was so out of character of him. Sure, he applied the "bend not break" rule to his practice whenever he felt it might help a deserving client in the end.

Was this case applicable to this rule? He was still unsure.

Was it unethical? It certainly felt like it.

In any event, if Shelby only agreed, he would break an oath he was sworn to uphold by going against a client's wishes and disclosing personal information. The fact that he was disrespecting a good friend's last wishes tore him up inside. But if it brought Shelby a little closer to finding her inheritance, it would be worth it.

In the end, it was all about helping Shelby.

A few moments later, Shelby heard Martin's car pull into the driveway. She and Brooke greeted him at the kitchen door. This was their first-time meeting since the reading of the will.

Martin still looked a little disheveled. "Hello, Shelby," he said, rather glumly.

"Hi, Martin."

"I can't tell you how awful I felt last week at my office."

"Let's just try and move on, okay?" Shelby said, doing her best to keep her smile in place.

"Fair enough," he said.

"Hi, Mister Hightower," said Brooke.

"Hi, sweetie." Martin bent down and gave Brooke a kiss on the forehead. "Would you like something to drink?"

"No, thanks," he said, "I won't be staying."

Shelby eyeballed him, suddenly suspicious, "Are you sure you're okay?"

Martin gulped hard. He was still unsure if he wanted to go through with it or not.

Shelby nodded, and Martin unhesitatingly spit it out, "I have something in my possession that I'm not sure your grandfather would want you to have."

"What is it?" Shelby immediately regretted saying it. Just having this conversation made her feel like she was betraying the one man she'd deeply loved and admired all her life.

Sensing Martin's growing discomfort, she took Brooke into the family room. Her favorite cartoon was about to come on.

When Shelby returned, Martin proceeded with caution, "Before I spill my guts, are you sure you want me to tell you?"

"No, I'm not sure!" Shelby gave Martin a sideways look, "Is it about my inheritance?"

"Yes."

"What about it?"

"I have in my pocket the names of two men in Florida. They will remain nameless for the time being." Shelby raised an eyebrow. Not knowing how to gauge her reaction, Martin proceeded with caution. "Apparently, they were friends of your grandfather. They did business together."

Are they the ones in charge of my inheritance? she thought.

"Luther, excuse me, your grandfather, advised me shortly after your grandmother's death that when he died, some of his business interests in Florida would be handled by another firm instead of me. At the time, I didn't think much of it.

"But when you were suddenly removed from the will, it made me question why your grandfather put me in charge of his entire estate, except for whatever business he was doing with this two-man law firm in the Sunshine State. No matter how hard I tried, I couldn't come up with a logical answer."

Martin sighed. "That is, until Jake mentioned the letter..." His voice trailed off.

"And?" Shelby said, tilting her head one way then another.

"Using various legal channels on the day before the reading of your grandfather's will, I was able to locate the firm representing him down in Florida." Martin took a deep breath, cleared his throat and shifted his weight. "Before I continue, would you mind if I ask you a few questions?"

"What kind of questions?"

"Look Shelby, I know you're excited about digging in the sand and finding your inheritance and all, but some of your family members, whom I won't mention, think you're being sent on a wild goose chase.

"I'm not gonna lie, I agree with them. No one knows these two men in Florida or how long they knew your grandfather. How do we know they haven't made certain revisions to the will, then forced or even tricked your grandfather into signing it against his will?

"How do we know they aren't the church or charity to be named later? We all know how religious your grandfather was. If these two men are the church or charity to be named later, believe me, you'll never see a dime of what's legally yours."

Shelby looked like she wanted to say something but remained silent.

Martin sighed, "There are too many questions without answers, Shelby. Too many for comfort. I'd hate to see you go all the way down there, only to have your hopes extinguished when you never had a chance in the first place.

"The names on the piece of paper in my pocket are the two men running things down there. It's only their names. No addresses or phone numbers. No e-mail addresses or web sites. Do what you want with it. At the very least, perhaps you can do some snooping into their pasts to see if they're honest businessmen."

Shelby remained silent, but her mind raced. *What could it hurt to do a little research, to see if they're on the up and up...*

"Perhaps it'll amount to nothing," Martin continued, "but maybe it will prove helpful. So, what do you say?"

"Wow! I don't know, Martin. I mean, if they are the men in charge, according to Grandpa's letter, they were sworn to secrecy. And if they are the 'charity to be named later', why would they even want to help? I think if Grandpa wanted me to know their names, he would have included it in his letter."

That statement heaped a huge pile of guilt upon Martin's head. He felt like Benedict Arnold. "I see."

Deep down inside Shelby didn't want to know their names. Sure, it was a challenging task, but for the first time in a long time, she was enjoying herself. "Are you aware of the time factor?"

"I am," Martin replied, skeptically.

"Who told you?"

"Jake. It was the straw that finally broke my back. Listen Shelby, I don't want to disrespect your grandfather by doing something I'm not supposed to. No one respected Luther more than me."

"I know that, Martin."

"But I'm having a hard time figuring out why he did this to you. I know you're determined to find the buried treasure, but there's plenty of evidence to the contrary. Or should I say lack thereof. You'll probably need every one of those ninety days, if you are ever to succeed."

"Eighty-six days, actually," Shelby replied with a sigh. "The clock started ticking upon receipt of the letter."

"Even more reason for me to help you then."

"I appreciate your concern, Martin, I really do."

"But..."

"I don't know what to do. On one hand, if I accept it, I might feel like I'm cheating, which would take all the fun out of it. On the other hand, perhaps I really am looking for a needle in a haystack."

"Ten haystacks, according to Jake," said Martin, with a slight humorless chuckle. "Let's face it, Shelby, the odds aren't exactly as we'd like them to be."

Shelby ignored the comment. "Having their names might be a good insurance policy, especially for Jake and Jesse. And besides, it's not like you're giving me their phone numbers or addresses. If I want more info, I'll have to do my own research, right?"

"Exactly." Martin had been thinking similar thoughts all day.

"Well then, sure, leave their names. I'll think about it and discuss the matter with Jesse. If I decide not to go through with it, I'll throw the paper in the trash can without ever looking at it. But if I do decide to look them up, there will be no need for us to meet again."

"Are you sure?"

Shelby nodded yes, and Martin placed the piece of paper on the table, then left without saying another word.

14

JUNE 17 - DAY 7

"THAT'S RIGHT, SHELBY...YES...Everything your grandfather thought you might need will be found inside the safe-deposit box...What?...That's correct...What's inside the box?...You know I can't answer that...What?...You know I can't answer that, either."

Bernie Finkel shook his head in utter amazement, unable to fathom how Shelby McKinney had tracked him down. His phone numbers were all unlisted, had been for many years. And how in the world did she know who he was anyway? He was specifically told that no one from Luther's family knew anything about him or his partner, Bob Schuster.

Three days had passed since Martin Hightower left the piece of paper on her kitchen table, leaving her 83 days to go, and counting.

Seven days came and went so fast, and she hadn't even stepped foot in the Sunshine State yet. The clock inside Shelby's head was already taunting her. Add the dark cloud of negativity created by Jake and Martin Hightower into the mix, and it was easy to see why her head had become so full of uncertainty.

Thanks to them, there were too many questions without answers to have a peaceful feeling inside.

Finally, with Jesse's insistence, Shelby did a little poking around to make sure they—whoever *they* were—weren't out to steal what was rightfully hers.

In short, she wanted to make sure they were honorable businessmen. Since Bernie Finkel's name topped the short list of two, she called him first.

Per Luther Mellon's precise instructions, all Bernie Finkel knew about this little escapade was that Shelby needed to find Sunrise Savings and Loan on her own, with no outside help from others. How she'd succeeded in tracking him down was totally beyond him. *Had she hired a PI?*

"Uh, Shelby, how did you get my phone number?"

"I have my sources, Mister Finkel." A smile broke across her face. She was turning out to be a pretty good sleuth after all. *Grandpa was right. This is fun!*

"I see," said Bernie, feeling slightly insulted. And violated! "Do you care to share your sources with me?"

68

"Why would I do that, Mister Finkel," she said in her rich, Southern cultured voice.

Bernie pressed once more for details, but Shelby clammed up. He had no choice but to let it go at that. Deep down inside, the Florida lawyer sympathized with her.

The poor woman had been through such a traumatic experience. First to lose her grandfather. Then to not be mentioned in his will, only to receive a letter a few days later stating if she wanted her inheritance, she had to find it two states south of hers.

In Bernie Finkel's mind, Luther was playing a cruel, childish game with his beloved granddaughter. Yet, Shelby sounded so jubilant on the phone, which, to him, was rather odd. Had he been in her shoes he would be beyond frantic.

Part of him wanted to just cut to the chase and, if nothing else, at least tell her where the bank was located. But he couldn't. His hands were tied. He had to stick to the rules. No exceptions!

"While I can't furnish you with any information, I will say this: your grandfather went over his will once a year with a fine-tooth comb to see if any changes or revisions needed to be made.

"Not counting when he removed your name, which thankfully you now know the reason behind it all, I don't believe he ever changed anything else. He did, however, make numerous changes to the letter he wrote you."

"What do you mean?" A confused expression formed on Shelby's face.

Poor woman, Bernie Finkel thought. "The letter you received wasn't as fresh as you might think. Your grandfather started writing it a few months after your grandmother died, when he was diagnosed with prostate cancer. He made a dozen or so revisions since that time. Guess you could say he wanted it to be fresh when you received it, as if he wrote it the day he died. I believe his last revision was a little more than a month ago."

"Aw, that's so nice to hear," she replied. Bernie seemed like such a nice man. Surely, he wasn't out to steal from her.

"Your grandfather loved you deeply, Shelby. You held a very special place in his heart."

Bernie Finkel's head started throbbing. The 67-year-old Florida lawyer stood an even 6'0". He wasn't bald, but upon reaching 50, his salt and pepper colored hair started thinning out a little more each year. He had a large nose, long sideburns, and a long thin face.

He wore bifocal glasses which did nothing to hide his bushy eyebrows. For whatever reason, his mouth was always open, even when he wasn't talking.

Bernie took a deep breath, "I wish I could further assist you, young lady, I really do, but I'm under strict orders. I hope you can appreciate that."

"Yes, I can. And besides, you've already helped me more than you know."

"Oh yeah, how's that?" Bernie replied, totally unaware that her questions were merely a diversion to keep him on the phone long enough to see if he was trustworthy or not. Jesse listened on the phone in the kitchen and gave his wife a thumbs-up gesture. He, too, sensed Bernie Finkel was a trustworthy man.

"I'd rather not say," Shelby said, "but I can assure you that you've put my mind at ease. Thank you, Mister Finkel."

"You're welcome, dear. Hey, you found me; you should have no trouble finding the buried treasure, I mean your inheritance, even if it is buried two states south of South Carolina." This was said with as much conviction as Bernie Finkel could muster, which wasn't much.

Treasure? Inheritance? Interesting! thought Stuart Finkel, Bernie's 31-year-old grandson. *Very interesting!*

"Yes, okay. You too, Shelby. Bye." Bernie replaced the phone and stared at the wall in front of him. Why Luther had done this to the one family member he seemed to cherish the most was totally beyond him. He hadn't the faintest clue.

Then again, Bernie Finkel wasn't an adventurer by any stretch of the imagination, and never would be. He was anything but a risk-taker. He was as practical as they came.

Stuart Finkel was seated at the kitchen table finishing his third cup of coffee. Bernie excused himself from his grandson to call his partner, Bob Schuster. Bob was the one who brought the "Mellon Project," in-house so to speak, and was the chief executor.

Whereas Bernie didn't know Luther Mellon personally, Bob and Luther were close friends in life. They even attended the same church in Fort Myers. Bob was also one of *Shelby's Saints.*

On the third ring, Bob picked up his cell phone by the pool. "Hello?"

"Yeah Bob, it's me."

"Well, hey, Bernie, what can I do for you, old pal?"

"Am I calling at a bad time?"

"Not at all. Ruth and I are barbecuing chicken and ribs in the backyard."

There was a brief pause as Bernie cleared his throat. "Did you happen to receive a strange phone call?"

"No, why?"

"You'll never guess who called me..."

70

"Who?"

"Shelby McKinney."

At first, Bob Schuster couldn't place the name. Then it hit him like a sledgehammer to the head; "Shelby McKinney? As in Luther Mellon's granddaughter?!"

"That's the one."

"How did she get your number?" Bob Schuster sat up in his lounge chair, unable to contain his excitement. The game had finally begun. *Yes!*

At 68, Bob Schuster looked like a TV game show host, with a full head of salt and pepper hair, warm gray eyes and a near-perfect smile that instantly impacted everyone fortunate enough to be on the receiving end of it. He was an eloquent man, humble and gracious. He was passionate for God and compassionate for His people which, in today's self-centered world, was quite rare.

"I thought perhaps you knew, Bob."

"I haven't the faintest." Cupping the phone, Bob whispered to his wife, Ruth, "Shelby McKinney just called Bernie."

"Really? How?" Ruth's small ears perked up and her soft brown eyes were aglow.

"Bernie doesn't know," Bob whispered again.

"Isn't that strange," Bernie said more to himself than to Bob.

"What did she want?"

"You know, the usual; the location of the safe-deposit box. What's in it. Stuff like that."

Safe-deposit box? Stuart Finkel thought, a greedy glint in his eye. Bernie's grandson was doing all he could to eavesdrop on the conversation. Thanks to his grandfather's deep voice, he was able to pick up important bits and pieces here and there, even when he spoke in hushed tones.

Stuart Finkel was 5'10". He had a head full of curly brown hair and a long, thin nose that resembled his grandfather's. His face was long and thin. His teeth were severely stained from too much coffee and nicotine. If he could afford it, he would smoke four packs of cigarettes a day. His beady brown eyes were always angry and full of malice and deceit. It had been said by some that he projected the look of someone who didn't know he possessed a soul.

"Did you tell her?" asked Bob.

"Of course not, Bob. You know me better than that."

Bob chuckled. "Just kidding, pal. I know you would never disclose private information to someone else."

Bob Schuster trusted his good friend and partner of 37 years with his life. But Bernie was always so serious. Too serious, in fact! He had absolutely no sense of humor. Because of this, Bob liked to prod him on each chance he got.

"What a feisty woman she is."

"I'll bet. Especially if she's anything like Luther. What does she know?" Bob's excitement level kept rising.

"As far as I can tell, nothing. Except that she's inherited something from Luther and, whatever it is, it's buried in a treasure chest here in Florida. And there are more clues awaiting her once she locates the safe-deposit box. I don't believe she knows anything else. If she does, she didn't tell me."

Stuart Finkel strained hard to hear anything else that might help him with this new opportunity of sorts. The little he heard sounded exciting. And potentially profitable.

"I hope she finds what she's looking for."

"Me too, Bob."

"If you hear anything, get back to me."

"Likewise."

"Sure thing." At that, they said their good-byes.

Bernie Finkel had no clue where Luther Mellon was going with all this running around nonsense, but Bob Schuster knew exactly what was happening. In fact, while the idea to bury Shelby's inheritance in a treasure chest in Florida was all Luther's, Bob helped him bury it on Sanibel Island twice last year, as test-runs.

The first time was roughly a year ago at 3 a.m., on a clear moonlit night when the beach was completely deserted.

The two men dug a three-foot hole in the sand and placed the chest inside, then filled the hole with sand.

The only thing inside the chest was a GPS locator, in case it became dislodged. Before leaving Sanibel Beach that night, they prayed for God's full hedge of protection around the chest.

A week later, once again at three in the morning, Bob and Luther rejoiced to find the buried chest exactly where they'd buried. God had indeed protected it for them. Never once did they need to activate the GPS locator.

A month later they buried the chest again, also three-feet beneath the surface on Sanibel Beach, this time loaded with worthless metals. The reason they dug three-foot holes in the sand—instead of six as stated in Luther's letter to Shelby—was to see if the chest could be detected by beachcombers out scouring Sanibel Beach using metal detectors.

Even three feet beneath the surface, weighted down with metal, no one discovered it. Bob and Luther became even more confident that the chest would be perfectly safe six feet under when it came time to burying it for real.

The one thing that did concern them was the ocean's tide. It was so unpredictable at times. With hurricane season fast approaching, if Shelby needed 90 days to find the buried treasure, that would take her deep into hurricane season.

Even without a hurricane, any fierce sustaining storm could potentially erode part of the coastline enough to dislodge the chest, lifting it to the surface for all to see. Or perhaps even out to sea. If that happened, chances were better than good that she would lose her inheritance altogether.

No one had to remind Luther that he was taking a huge risk by doing all this. But it was a risk he was willing to take if it led to what *Shelby's Saints* had fervently been praying for since setting this crazy plan into motion— Shelby's salvation!

This was the first time Bob had ever left Bernie out of the loop in their 37-year partnership. But because Bernie wasn't a Christian, it needed to be this way. Totally oblivious to the master plan behind it all, the little Bernie Finkel knew about the *Mellon Project* made no sense to him.

But it made perfect sense to Bob Schuster. If, and when, Shelby found her buried inheritance, it wouldn't mark the end of a great and daring adventure, but the beginning of one. Bob just hoped she'd eventually come to realize it for herself.

It was almost Showtime, which meant he'd soon place $100,000 in stacks of hundred-dollar bills inside the treasure chest, along with rare coins, jewelry, and a cashier's check in the amount of $400,000, before burying it in the exact location of Luther's choosing on Sanibel Island.

As much as Luther wanted his granddaughter to find what was rightfully hers, the material items stashed inside the treasure chest weren't the most important part of the plan. That distinction was reserved for a one-paragraph letter and key to a second safe-deposit box. The items stored inside safe-deposit box number two is what had spawned this daring adventure in the first place.

If Shelby found the treasure chest, but ignored the contents housed inside the second safe-deposit box, it would be a tragic disappointment to everyone praying for her success.

Bernie Finkel rejoined his grandson in the kitchen.

"Everything okay Pops?" Stuart said.

"Yes, it was only Bob."

"What did he want?"

"Oh, just business, that's all."

"What kind of business?" Stuart listened with mock interest, as Bernie danced around the question.

Sensing his grandson might be playing him again, Bernie backpedaled and revisited the subject they were discussing before Shelby McKinney called; deep-sea fishing.

Stuart did all he could to seem interested, but thanks to this new potential windfall, he was totally disinterested in anything else his grandfather had to say that wasn't directly related to the buried treasure.

If there was a treasure to be found, it would be found by him, and not this Shelby woman!

Bernie Finkel didn't know it but wouldn't be surprised to learn his grandson didn't come to talk about deep-sea fishing, or baseball, or anything else discussed the past hour and a half.

Stuart was simply biding his time, waiting for the right moment to hit ol' Grandpa up for yet another loan—just $3K this time—even though Bernie had already cut him off last year.

Everyone knew Stuart Finkel had a serious gambling addiction, especially when it came to wagering on sports and horses.

Now he owed money to the wrong people. If he didn't have the $3K interest payment on the $10K principal due next Friday, Vinnie and Carlos— the two money collectors working for Finkel's bookie—would be out looking for him again. And when they found him, it could get ugly.

Stuart had already borrowed more than $50K from his grandfather the past few years, without paying back a single dime of it. Finally, last year, Bernie decided enough was enough.

Maybe I won't have to beg ol' Gramps for money after all, he thought. *Maybe I can inherit someone else's money. This could be the big break I've been waiting for all my life!* Thoughts were popping in Stuart's head like popcorn in a popper. *All I gotta do is find the location of the buried chest then beat Shelby to it.*

Bernie Finkel rambled on about deep-sea fishing, but Stuart was already a million miles away, shrewdly devising a plan of attack. He didn't have much to go on, but from what he'd heard so far, he knew more than this Shelby woman knew, including the name or location of the bank housing the safe-deposit box.

Advantage Stuart. And a huge one at that. If there was one thing he knew about his grandfather, it was that he didn't trust banks or bankers. Once he found a good lending institution, he plugged all his clients into it.

And that bank was none other than Sunrise Savings and Loan. Of that, Stuart was 100-percent certain. This was extremely valuable information. The problem was they had four branch locations in the Fort Myers vicinity. Surely, one of them housed the safe-deposit box that stored the clues leading straight to the buried treasure chest.

But which one was the lucky recipient?

It was the million-dollar question...

It was time to go. Stuart suddenly had more important things to do. For starters, he needed to set up a meeting with his three friends, Jed Ashford, Chris Watkins and best friend, Ricky Clemmons. He would summon all three to Bubba's Bar and Grill for happy hour, then blow their minds with his earth-shattering plan.

As Stuart stood to leave, Bernie was amazed he didn't ask for money again, which was a miracle in itself. But what did concern him was how his grandson went from being totally downtrodden before the phone calls with Shelby McKinney and Bob Schuster, to suddenly exuberant, just like that.

Bernie Finkel scratched his chin. No, something wasn't right.

Once outside, Stuart pulled a cigarette from behind his left ear, stuck it inside his mouth and lit up, a wry grin on his face and dollar signs in his eyes.

Bernie Finkel said nothing, but watched his grandson leave with growing contempt. Whatever had gotten into him, it wasn't good. Stuart was up to no good again.

Stuart slid behind the wheel of his truck, put the key in the ignition and drove off without even waving goodbye.

SHELBY MCCKINNEY STARED AT her computer screen with a satisfied smile on her face. There was no need to call Bob Schuster. Bernie Finkel removed all remaining skepticism from her mind, mostly planted there by Martin Hightower, her brother Jake, and to a lesser extent, her husband, Jesse.

But if she only knew the potential danger she'd just invited into her life by simply calling Bernie Finkel, the smile on her face would quickly evaporate, replaced with unbridled fear.

Shelby had no idea that Bernie Finkel's grandson was a ruthless, desperate man, who'd eavesdropped on much of the conversation, unknowingly placing her family in jeopardy.

Sometimes the most innocent of tasks—like calling a total stranger on the phone—turned into the most lethal of outcomes. Shelby McKinney was about to find out in the worst way.

The demons assigned to her were already preparing for battle...

15

STUART FINKEL AND HIS three friends, Jed Ashford, Chris Watkins and Ricky Clemmons, crowded a small table on the outside deck at Bubba's Bar and Grill, totally unaware that they were surrounded by scores of frighteningly evil, invisible beings.

Almost half were assigned to Stuart Finkel alone. They knew exactly what he was up to and what he was about to propose to the others. Though Finkel couldn't see them, they'd been part of his life for many years. Their job, as was the task of all demons under Satan's powerful command, was to constantly torment and tempt each victim, to stir each conscience with wild, sinful thoughts that would keep them living in darkness, fully enveloped in the bondage of sin—anything to keep them from seeking the face of God!

Stuart Finkel was no exception...

But the grim spirit world hovering above the crowd didn't revolve around Stuart Finkel and his three friends only. There were many souls to torment this night. Many missions to carry out. Many lives to destroy. Only human eyes couldn't see them. Nor could human minds detect their presence.

Bubba's was a popular watering hole in Fort Myers. With happy hour now upon them, the place was completely packed with hundreds of customers all wanting to take a load off. Many came straight from work, as evidenced by their attire.

Every seat and table were taken, forcing many to enjoy their drinks in the stand-up position. Since it was Friday, most had a little extra spending money in their pockets to burn.

The bartenders and cocktail waitresses at Bubba's were eager to squeeze as much of it out of their customers as they possibly could.

Offering free hors d'oeuvres helped sweeten the pot a little.

The demons stationed outside Bubba's flapped and clawed, their razor-sharp talons stabbing at the humid air. Their midnight black, calloused, wings were long and fierce.

The demons inside Bubba's whirred in place. All were wildly rambunctious, always edgy, never calm, never comforted.

Whenever they cursed God, which was constantly, their jaundice yellow eyes turned a horrific blood red, and brownish-green smoke protruded past rows of venomous fangs, as they filled the air with wickedly frightening moans and shrieks. If they could materialize for all to see, everyone would run from this place in an instant; or fall prostrate to the ground fearing for their lives.

Totally blinded to the evil presence all around them, many drank heavily and sang their favorite songs screaming from the jukebox, mostly country songs.

Drinks of all kinds were being mixed and poured. Beer flowed out of several taps like water into frosted mugs and pitchers before being served to the clientele in mass quantities, including to those on the outside deck, where smoking was still permitted.

Stuart and Company had 57 dollars between them. Every cent would be spent on beer, maybe a shot or two of tequila each, and on cigarettes. If there was anything left over, they'd leave a tip for the waitress.

The cocktail waitresses at Bubba's loathed Stuart Finkel and grimaced at the mention of his name. Painfully aware of his lewd and crude tendencies, they frequently begged J.T.—the manager of Bubba's—to ban him from this place, often telling him, "We're cocktail waitresses, not slaves!"

While Jed, Chris and Ricky were all seen as undesirables, no one was more detested than Stuart. But Finkel wore his loathsome reputation as a badge of honor. Being dubbed a "bad boy" gave him a deep sense of pride.

This place wasn't exactly the best place to hold a business meeting. But happy hour served two purposes; the drinks were cheap and there was plenty of free food to munch on.

Dozens of empty hors d'oeuvres plates crowded just about every table, especially Finkel's. They were piled high atop one another, along with dozens of messy cocktail napkins.

Whenever a new tray of food was brought out from the kitchen—chicken wings, fried mushrooms, French fries, whatever—Stuart and his three friends were usually the first to invade, leaving little leftover for the others.

"Stop hogging all the food, guys! Do it again, and y'all are gone for good," barked J.T., the last time it happened. "I ain't kidding!"

But nothing would upset Stuart's mood this night, especially J.T. Already on their third pitcher of the amber liquid, Finkel kept filling his friends' heads with thoughts of good fortune.

The jukebox played an old country song, and many shouted out the lyrics. Even outside, Stuart practically had to scream just to be heard. When the music stopped, he spoke in a near whisper, as if trying to conceal details which would somehow compromise national security if anyone else heard it.

Then another song started playing, and Finkel had to yell again to be heard. Despite the many distractions, he was quite animated in his deliberation, frequently using his hands to accentuate certain points of importance.

He even pounded the messy table with his fists when necessary. Each time he did silverware rattled along with the empty plates and beer glasses, and ashes from cigarettes hanging in the corner of his mouth—seemingly one after another—broke off and fell to the table.

Stuart brushed the ashes aside without ever losing eye contact with his three buddies. "This is it," he declared, "the big payoff!"

His three friends nodded skeptically. Whenever it came to Stuart Finkel, it was always hard to decipher truth from fiction. He was a notorious liar. Jed, Chris and Ricky had fallen victim to his many lies in the past. They didn't want to see history repeat itself again.

"How do you know for sure there's cash inside, Stu?" Ricky Clemmons' asked. His chair was a good two feet away from the table. Twenty-nine, he was 6'4" and weighed 320 pounds. His face was round. He had a small nose and crooked teeth. He was almost completely bald. Because of his increasingly expanding beer belly, his legs no longer fit under the table.

"Oh, there's cash inside, alright," Finkel lied, "Already been verified, boys."

"Yeah, by who?" asked Jed Ashford.

"Who do you think, bonehead, my grandfather!"

"Why would he tell you," Chris Watkins replied, even more suspiciously. He hated Stuart and didn't trust him as far as he could throw the man. Chris was still mildly amazed that he agreed to the meeting in the first place.

"He didn't, Chris. I heard him talking to his business partner on the phone, okay?"

"What did he say?"

"I couldn't hear everything, but I heard all the important stuff."

"And."

"There's a huge bundle of cash inside just waiting to be had." Finkel smiled awkwardly, exposing his coffee and nicotine-stained front teeth.

"And just how do you know that, Stu?"

"Because the grandfather was a very wealthy man, Chris. Which means there could be millions stashed inside the treasure chest."

It was hot and humid, and Stuart's long wavy brown hair was soaked with sweat. It slowly but steadily trickled down his forehead, sometimes dripping in his eyes, stinging them, causing him to squint. The rest trickled down his long thin nose and red, pock-marked cheeks. But he remained focused despite it.

After a prolonged stare down, Chris Watkins backed off. Even he had to admit this scam seemed doable; almost like taking candy from a baby. But he needed to hear more.

Jed and Ricky were already hooked. From what they'd heard so far, it was almost too good to be true and certainly too good to walk away from! The more Stuart spoke, the more they felt a big payoff coming. And for what? Staking out four bank locations until this Shelby woman showed up, then following her to the buried treasure and stealing it from her the moment she unearthed it? No big challenge there!

"If we do commit, what's the plan of attack," Ricky Clemmons said, downing half the beer in his glass.

"Well, for starters, we have three clues at our disposal, fellas, four actually. We know the woman's first name is Shelby. We know she's from South Carolina and that she's someone's granddaughter, which means we won't be looking for an old geezer."

Stuart took a long drag from his cigarette and blew it skyward. "Most importantly, we know something this woman doesn't know."

"Oh yeah, what's that?" Chris Watkins aid.

"The bank housing the safe-deposit box. I'm one-hundred percent certain it's Sunrise Savings and Loan. I just don't know which location. But there are four of them here in Fort Myers and four of us. Do the math yourself, fellas."

Stuart took another long drag from his cigarette. "All we need to do is stake out all four banks until Shelby shows up. Then follow her straight to the buried treasure. This is an easy score."

"How will we know it's her, Stu?" asked Jed Ashford.

"The way I see it, her being from South Carolina is our best chance of spotting her."

"Why's that?" asked Ricky Clemmons, his beefy right paw raising his beer glass to his mouth again. If this could ever be considered exercise, Ricky would be in perfect shape.

"Because we'll only be looking for women driving cars with South Carolina license plates, dummy."

"Makes sense," Ricky replied, ignoring Finkel's condescending comment.

"Of course, if she takes an airplane instead, it'll be more difficult to find her."

"What will we do if that happens?"

"I'm still mulling things over in my mind." Finkel took a moment to down the rest of the beer in his glass. "But don't worry, fellas, I'll have a solid game plan come Monday morning."

79

"But..." said Chris Watkins.

"Like I said, Chris," Stuart snapped, cutting him off, "I'll have a better game plan come Monday, okay? Give me a break, man, I just found out about it a few hours ago."

Finkel paused. *Stay calm*, he thought to himself. "Now's not the time to worry about the small details, boys," he said, in a more reassuring voice, "Tonight we celebrate!"

It was the icing on the cake. "Here, here!" Ricky Clemmons declared with authority. Jed Ashford raised his beer glass. Chris Watkins was still visibly skeptical.

Stuart knew Jed, Chris and Ricky weren't exactly the sharpest knives in the drawer. They couldn't see the many potential barriers they stood to encounter, which, of course, was a good thing.

But Stuart Finkel wasn't the sharpest knife in the drawer either. But what he lacked in intelligence, he more than made up for with sheer determination and ruthlessness. If he had to hurt someone, even badly, to get what he wanted, so be it.

Finkel felt a huge payoff coming this time. If...no, not if, when he found the money, he corrected himself in his mind, and paid Vinnie and Carlos the $13K—including the $3K interest—he owed, he would clear his debt to them and would never use their services again. *Thirty percent interest a month! They really were sharks!*

While Chris, Jed and Ricky were under the impression that they were full-fledged partners in this scam, they were nothing more than his lowly helpers. Perhaps he'd let them split 10-percent between them; if that.

Finkel would keep the rest for himself and totally disassociate himself from his three loser friends and move on to greener pastures. He would go straight to the racetrack and bet wisely, only on the favorites, and turn big money into huge money, setting himself up for life. He could almost feel the money in his hands now.

If he didn't find it, well, he didn't want to think along those lines. It pained him too much.

"What happens if they decide at the last moment to place a cashier's check inside the chest instead of cash?" Ricky Clemmons said, suddenly serious again. He was trying to sound intelligent. "If so, we're beat."

Stuart downed another glass of beer. "Come on, Ricky, use your brain! Have you ever heard of check washing?"

"Of course, I have," Ricky said, brushing the correction off.

"Fear not, fellas, if there's a check inside we'll find a way to cash it. We'll hire someone to remove the ink from the check using a special solvent that won't compromise the overall clarity or vital details."

"Hmm," said Chris Watkins, with an inner-foreboding that the bottom would eventually fall out of this scam, like all others Stuart had run by them in the past.

There was a pause, as everyone silently weighed all the options, deciding if they wanted in or not. Finkel studied their faces, knowing all along that Chris Watkins would be the hardest to sell.

But even he couldn't deny the extremely favorable risk-reward factor this heist presented. No matter how he sliced it inside his mind, the risk factor was minimal. The payoff, on the other hand, was potentially huge. Watkins' mental "wish list" was growing by the minute. *A million bucks, huh?*

But Finkel's mind raced even faster. He wondered how much cash was stashed inside the buried chest. Would it be full of rare coins and fine jewelry valuing in the millions, like he'd seen in various pirate movies on TV? Perhaps there would be deeds to fine collectibles and expensive artwork inside?

The possibilities were seemingly endless...

If there were valuable collectibles in the chest in lieu of cash, Stuart would be forced to liquidate $13K and turn it into quick cash. Even if it meant getting pennies on the dollar, he would likely do it. Once his debt was paid to Vinnie and Carlos, he would play hardball with the rest of the merchandise until the right buyers came along.

Even if it meant going to Naples, Miami or West Palm Beach to get the right price, he would do it. Of course, if the chest was full of cash like he hoped, all that running around could be avoided. He would pay off Vinnie and Carlos, throw a few bucks at Jed, Chris and Ricky, and get out of Dodge.

But none of this could happen until they first found Shelby!

The alcohol was starting to kick in. Finkel tried to refocus. "Like I said, fellas, my grandfather sends all his clients to Sunrise Savings and Loan. Which means our formula for success isn't exactly rocket science: four banks, one man at each location!

"With that in mind, come Monday morning, our job will be to look for South Carolina license plates at each location. Once we find the girl, she'll lead us straight to the buried treasure. Even you three morons can understand something this simple."

If Finkel could do this job without them, he wouldn't have called this meeting in the first place. But he did need them. For how long, it was too soon to tell. Therefore, he had to treat them like the full-fledged partners he promised they would be. At least for now.

81

Taking one last drag from his cigarette, Stuart squashed it out in the tiny shot glass that was full of Tequila a few seconds ago.

Pointing his long, bony forefinger at each of them, poking holes through the clouds of cigarette smoke he'd just created, Finkel's eyes narrowed. "Are you with me or not?"

Jed, Chris and Ricky each nodded yes; they were completely mesmerized, as if under the ether.

Chris Watkins snapped out of it. "What about our jobs, Stu?" Jed and Chris both worked the day shift at a local supermarket, as stock-persons. "How can we stakeout a bank and work at the same time?"

"Yeah," Jed Ashford said, weighing in rather pathetically. He should have kept his mouth shut.

Stuart rolled his eyes, "Come on, fellas. Get real! Quit your jobs! I already quit mine! Why work at that dump when you'll soon have enough money to last the summer. Maybe longer. You're only twenty-eight. If you wanna find another dead-end job when the money runs out, go right ahead."

Both men relaxed. Stuart Finkel was a very good liar.

Jed looked at Chris and both men shrugged their shoulders. "We're gone," they said, raising their beer glasses.

Ricky Clemmons didn't need to quit his job. He was unemployed the past three years, while holding out for a good paying job, with no success. During that time, his bank account shrunk to zero and his belly grew to unbelievable proportions. Ricky was a big, sloppy fellow. It looked like he drank a whole keg of beer all by himself, then swallowed the keg for good measure. But even he agreed this was something worthy of his precious time and effort.

Stuart raised a shot glass. "To striking it rich!" he declared proudly.

"To striking it rich," all three said in unison.

The demons assigned to Finkel hovered above, slobbering black foam all over themselves, knowing full well their assignee was lying to his three friends. This didn't concern them one way or the other.

"There's one other thing I haven't told you, fellas. With time being of the essence, if we're unable to find Shelby within a week or so, I still have one last rock-bottom option to exercise. Been mulling it over in my mind the past couple hours. But I'll only share it with you if we need to act on it. If we find her, it can all be avoided."

"Sure, Stuart, whatever you say," Ricky Clemmons replied.

Jed Ashford and Chris Watkins nodded cautiously.

"For now, let's relax and enjoy the weekend," Finkel said. "Come Monday morning, the real work begins. We'll meet at the seven-eleven convenience store on Ford Street, at seven-forty-five sharp, for coffee before heading off to our assigned posts.

"Once we're on the job, the only time we can ever leave our posts will be to use the restroom. And don't forget to pack lunches of a non-alcoholic nature."

The fifty-seven dollars they came with was gone. It was time to leave. The waitress received a 75-cent tip. She was just glad they were finally leaving.

Stuart, Ricky, Jed and Chris were three sheets to the wind, four sheets, actually. They strolled out of Bubba's with a certain air of supremacy in their collective strides, as if they were wounded war heroes coming home after a fierce battle, or astronauts heading to outer space for some great earth-saving mission. *Yeah right!*

Except for the waitresses' loathsome glances, few others noticed them leaving.

At least in the human world...

The demons assigned to the four men broke free of their vicious jostling with the other demons and followed them outside.

Their razor-sharp talons stabbed at the darkness as they took to flight, once again releasing deafening shrieks which vibrated all throughout the always-active spirit world! Each time they blasphemed God, acrid brownish-green sulfurous smoke slobbered from their mouths and nostrils.

"Maybe we'll buy this place with some of the money," Ricky Clemmons declared with authority.

They all laughed.

"Yeah!" said Stuart. "First thing we'll do is fire J.T."

They laughed harder.

16

JUNE 20 - DAY 10

IT WAS MONDAY MORNING. School was out and the McKinneys were just finishing breakfast.

Sipping his morning coffee, Jesse took one last look at the map. If they took the easiest and quickest route to Orlando, there would be no need for a map or GPS, which Jesse hated using anyway. All they'd have to do is take Interstate 26 West to I-95 South, then take it all the way to Daytona Beach, Florida, before connecting to I-4 West and taking it straight to Orlando.

Jesse didn't need a map or GPS for that.

The problem was Shelby had other plans. She wanted to take U.S. 17, not I-26 and I-95, at least until they reached the state of Georgia. According to Shelby, not only did U.S. 17 offer better scenery, it passed straight through Beaufort, South Carolina, one of her favorite places growing up. Sure, it would take longer, but they were officially on vacation. So why not relax and enjoy the ride?

Jesse reluctantly agreed to her wishes.

The minivan was loaded with suitcases, a bag full of snacks, a cooler full of cold drinks, and shovels for digging sand.

Jesse went outside with the children, as Shelby took one last glance at the Weather Channel. The Carolinas, Georgia, Alabama, and Florida were all shaded in dark green, which meant driving could be treacherous at times along the way. Hopefully the rain would cool things off a bit. It was stifling hot outside; already 90.

But the McKinneys were appropriately dressed for the elements. They had no plans of getting dressed up this week, unless shorts, T-shirts and swimsuits could be considered dressing up.

Shelby locked the front door behind her and climbed into the minivan.

Scanning the property, Jesse was satisfied that his mental checklist was complete. The trash was curbside ready for collection. His pick-up truck was neatly parked inside the two-car garage. All the lights inside the house were turned off. All the doors were locked, and the alarm system was activated.

With everyone buckled in, Jesse turned the minivan south on U.S. 17, and the McKinney family adventure began in earnest.

What made U.S. 17 so unique in the Carolinas was—unlike most parts of the country—it offered a neutral breeding ground of sorts, allowing plants, trees and other foliage predominantly grown in the northern regions, to coexist with plants, trees and foliage grown in the southern regions of the country.

In the blink of an eye, one could see maples, weeping willows, pine trees, palm trees, crepe myrtles, and Spanish moss-covered oak trees all on the same property, uniquely showcasing the many beautiful Carolina homes of all colors, shapes and sizes.

It was magnificent to see.

While most drivers crowded the nation's many major interstates, freeways and turnpikes, country folk knew the real driving took place on America's back roads. It was where the real scenery greeted each driver and passenger, especially in South Carolina.

On many levels, it was where the America of old met up with the America of new, where history clashed with the present.

Remarkably, the two complemented each other nicely.

To Shelby, this was a *must* drive. Jesse, on the other hand, had driven U.S. 17 on numerous occasions and didn't feel the need to drive it again. He just wanted to get to Orlando.

The children were in total agreement with their father. They couldn't care less about all the nostalgia. Trevor, BJ and Brooke tossed and turned in bed much of the night, knowing once the sun came up, their adventure, their journey, would finally begin.

It was as exhilarating as Christmas Eve.

Most families only dreamed of going in search of a real live buried treasure. But for the McKinneys it was now a reality.

This would be the boys' third time going to Florida, Brooke's second. But in many respects, it was the first time for all three, because they never went to Disney World in the past.

Thanks to her late grandfather, Shelby felt like a little girl again. She rediscovered that it was okay to be a mother while still possessing a childlike spirit. This allowed her to cherish the little things in life again—things she'd all but forgotten about of late. They loomed large in her mind again.

Even Jesse's excitement level was on the increase. He knew the buried treasure hunt was designed specifically with Shelby's best interests at heart. Even if no one else in the family had to jump through hoops to get their inheritance, the kids were enjoying themselves, and it wouldn't be all about business.

With that justification, Jesse was determined to enjoy this quality time with his family. If they found the buried treasure chest, it would only add to the overall experience.

When they passed the first mile marker sign for Beaufort, Shelby said, "My grandparents never passed through Beaufort without stopping to eat at their favorite restaurant, the Southern Mansion Inn."

"Can we try to keep it under an hour?" Jesse said in his deep, country voice. He would do his best to make up the time once they were back on the road and the kids finally dozed off.

"Absolutely!" Shelby declared.

"Hmm, we'll see. So, what's the plan?"

"Let's just park and see what happens."

Jesse stuck out his tongue, then smiled. Finding a vacant parking space, he eased the van into place.

Beaufort, South Carolina, was a city steeped in rich history and tradition. It very much looked like a city that had no idea it was even in the 21st century. Nor did it care to know. Its slow, peaceful pace was soothing to most living and visiting here.

Horse-drawn carriages full of tourists moseyed down U.S. 17 at a leisurely pace, passing cozy little shops, restaurants, mansions and plantations along the way.

Shelby could almost envision Mark Twain sitting on a wooden rocking chair on a front porch sipping iced tea or lemonade, waving to all who passed by.

Shelby's last visit to this place was many years ago, when she was still too young to fully appreciate it. In many respects, it looked a lot like home. But the fact that it *wasn't* home made it all the more intriguing.

They strolled Main Street doing a little window shopping. Shelby noticed the Southern Mansion Inn and it all came rushing back. The plantation house, turned restaurant, was an architectural masterpiece.

Though a little on the expensive side, the ambiance alone all but demanded your patronage. The huge screened-in porch was converted into a dining area at the turn of the twentieth century.

Jesse beat Shelby to the punch, "Shall we?"

"Really?"

"Sure, why not. Looks like a nice place."

"Thank you, Jesse," she said sweetly, in a youthful voice that sounded 10 years younger than her actual age.

Once seated, Shelby perused the lunch menu and was thankful it wasn't too overpriced. The boys ordered cheeseburgers and fries from the kid's

86

menu. Brooke ordered chicken tenders. Shelby and Jesse both ordered Chicken Marsala.

Waiting for the food to arrive, Shelby couldn't erase the smile from her face. It was a surefire reaction of someone who'd just been given a new lease on life. Finishing her second cup of the best coffee she'd ever remembered tasting, the mother of three was still totally oblivious to the hornet's nest she would find herself in upon arriving in Fort Myers, Florida two days from now.

She had no idea there were four extremely dangerous men awaiting her arrival.

Shelby McKinney would soon be tested in a mighty way...

STUART FINKEL WAS PARKED outside Sunrise Savings and Loan on North Tamiami, smoking one cigarette after another, closely monitoring each car that pulled into the bank parking lot, always hoping the next one would be the woman from South Carolina.

As of yet, there hadn't been any "Shelby" sightings by anyone. Though only four hours into the first day of bank parking lot surveillance, Ricky Clemmons, Jed Ashford and Chris Watkins were already complaining, mostly about the oppressive heat.

The four men began their day at the 7-11 parking lot on Colonial at 7:45 a.m., each under a canopy of demons. They taunted one another and jostled and sparred in midair. Each time a demon was struck by the razor-sharp talons of another demon, brownish-green smoke poured out of their nostrils, along with loud deafening shrieks and moans which echoed ever so loudly throughout the spirit world.

But no one in human form heard or saw a thing...

When their assignees left the 7-11 parking lot with their morning coffees, they stopped fighting and followed. Upon reaching their destination, the demons resumed their sparring and jostling, always cursing God, never ceasing to fill the air with hideous blasphemies.

When dealing with humans, Satan's demons knew the only certainty was that there was always great uncertainty. But Stuart's demons had it so much easier than most others under Satan's command. Finkel rarely, if ever, needed prodding from them to remain off track.

Of Jewish descent, he was a typical pagan American, totally oblivious to the "straight and narrow" teachings of God. He was one of the demons' better students. He rarely gave God or eternity a passing thought. When he did, it was always for the wrong reasons.

The demons assigned to him didn't anticipate their subject changing sides anytime soon. Not only did they know the exact location of the safe-deposit box, they also knew where the treasure chest was buried, not to mention everything stored inside. They were determined to do all they could to help Stuart succeed with his devious plan.

If Finkel somehow managed to gain possession of the buried chest, they knew he'd be greatly pleased with everything inside it. But the material items stashed inside the chest meant absolutely nothing in the spirit world. To Satan's demons, they were completely worthless items. The only purpose they served was to continually tempt and deceive humanity, to blind and ensnare them with their luring glitz and glimmer. Nothing more.

In the spirit world, it all came down to words, actions and convictions. In this case, the only two things Satan's demons were remotely interested in was a very bland looking, glitter-less, one paragraph letter and key to a second safe-deposit box. Those two things presented grave spiritual danger for their side, because they led straight to the ultimate Message itself—God's Holy Word!

All demons under Satan's rule knew their leader stood ready to pounce on the wicked and claim them as his own the moment God allowed it. Like greedy, hungry lions waiting for the opportune time to devour their prey, they stood watching and waiting, knowing the only thing holding them back was God's restraining power.

The moment the Most High withdrew His hand of protection from someone, Satan's demons attacked at once, dragging their souls straight to the bottomless pits of hell.

The demons assigned to Stuart Finkel longed for that moment. Nothing would please them more than to shred their assignee into a million pieces with their jagged fangs or razor-sharp talons, condemning his soul to hell for all eternity.

But they didn't have that power. Not yet, anyway.

And this meant, for now, that they had to remain focused on the task at hand. The demonic beings assigned to Jed Ashford, Chris Watkins and Ricky Clemmons, knew Finkel's promises of good fortune made to their assignees were nothing more than well-crafted lies. If he found the money, he would quickly ditch them. That was Finkel's trademark—his legacy.

But they weren't at all concerned with his disloyalty to those they were ordered to follow. Trust and loyalty were unimportant to them. To live in a world of total distrust and disloyalty for all eternity was a heavy burden for anyone to carry, demon or not!

In that light, whether Finkel honored his commitment to equally portion the stolen treasure with his three so-called partners mattered not to them. What did matter was keeping their subjects off track, spiritually speaking, and keeping Shelby McKinney from finding what was stored inside the second safe-deposit box.

As much as the Lord Jesus longed to save sinners, Satan longed to destroy them. Both sides used humanity to help spread their messages and carry out missions, whether good or evil.

The biggest difference was, unlike God's people, who got to store up treasures in Heaven, Satan's demons never received rewards for their heinous efforts. Unless eternal torment could be considered a reward...

17

AFTER ENJOYING A SCRUMPTIOUS meal, the McKinneys were back en route to Florida. Jesse was amazed that they'd kept their visit to Beaufort to under 90 minutes.

The short ride to Savannah was smooth and uneventful. The kids started getting sleepy 30 minutes south of Savannah. They dozed off within five minutes of each other, shortly before the skies darkened and the rain came down in typical Southern fashion, in buckets.

It pelted the minivan so fiercely that Jesse was forced to pull over at a tiny produce hut until the rain subsided.

Shelby wasted no time grabbing an umbrella from underneath her seat and going inside looking for fresh fruit.

Jesse whispered, "As soon as it stops raining, even a little bit, we're outta here."

"Okay, sweetie," said Shelby, quietly.

Twenty minutes later the rain slowed to a near drizzle, and Shelby walked back to the van carrying a bag full of bananas, peaches and mangoes. She danced in the light drizzle, doing her best to avoid the puddles in the dirt and gravel parking lot. The warm rain felt good on her skin.

"The woman inside was kind enough to slice open a mango for us. It's perfectly ripened."

"How nice of her," said Jesse.

Shelby sunk her teeth into the fruit. "M-m-m yummy!"

Jesse then dug in. "Best mango I've ever tasted."

The kids were snoring away in the back seats, totally oblivious to their surroundings. Even the occasional loud peals of thunder couldn't rouse them, making this near-perfect husband and wife moment possible.

A few moments later, Jesse proceeded south on U.S. 17.

Shelby closed her eyes and sniffed in the many beautiful aromas which typically followed a southern rainfall. There was nothing like it. A smile broke across her face. *What a terrific day!*

Halfway through the state of Georgia, U.S. 17 met up with Interstate 95, roughly 250 miles northeast of Orlando. Jesse silently rejoiced. *Time to hit the interstate and make up for lost time!*

Less than an hour later, the proud father shouted, "Wake up sleepy heads, we're a mile from the Florida border!"

The minivan came back to life with extremely jubilant passengers. Shelby fumbled in her handbag for her phone.

Jesse slowed down just enough for his wife to take two snapshots of the *Welcome to Florida* sign.

A mile or so later, he pulled into the *Florida Welcome Center* for a few selfies and complimentary orange juice.

"Don't get too excited, kids," said Jesse, in between sips of juice, "we still have two and a half hours to go."

At least they were in Florida. Trevor, BJ and Brooke stayed awake for the remainder of the ride. They passed the time counting Disney billboard signs, out-of-state license plates, singing songs, quarreling among themselves, making up and doing it all over again.

It made the time go a little faster.

At 7:40 p.m., the McKinneys reached the Orlando City limits.

At 8:15 p.m., they pulled into the resort parking lot in Lake Buena Vista, 15 minutes behind Jesse's target time. He was mildly impressed, three kids and all. The hotel was a stone's throw from Disney Springs, formally known as "Downtown Disney".

Shelby pulled back the curtain in their hotel room exposing a stunning view of the shopping and entertainment district.

The kids didn't know how much Mom and Dad had paid for the room. It could have been a million dollars for all they knew.

The view alone was worth every penny.

Jesse ordered two pizzas and had them delivered poolside. They swam until 10 p.m., then went up to the room.

Jesse showered and climbed into bed. He was exhausted from a full day of driving.

Shelby was still energized and wasn't yet ready to call it a night. She took the children to Disney Springs for a late evening stroll.

Chock full of ambiance, Disney Springs was situated smack dab in the middle of the Disney empire in Orlando. Remarkably, admission was free, which wasn't very Disneyesque. But shoppers paid premium prices for everything else.

Shelby, Trevor, BJ and Brooke held hands to avoid getting lost in the humongous sea of mixed humanity, consisting of thousands of people journeying from every corner of the globe.

It presented a nice ethnic mixture.

Shelby got ice cream cones for the kids, a passion fruit smoothie for herself, and they wandered into the largest Disney Store on the planet. After visiting a few more stores, Trevor noticed a bunch of kids splashing around in a dancing fountain where water shot up out of the sidewalk.

"Look BJ," Trevor shouted to his younger brother.

"Can we go in, Momma?" asked BJ.

"I wanna go, too, Momma," Brooke exclaimed excitedly.

"You're not wearing swimsuits," came the reply.

"Come on, Momma, some of the other kids aren't either!" Trevor said.

"Oh, alright," Shelby finally said in surrender. "But not until y'all finish eating your ice cream."

"Yes!" Trevor and BJ both said at the same time.

Shelby found a vacant bench near the fountain. Trevor and BJ practically inhaled their ice cream cones, removed their shirts and within seconds were completely drenched. Brooke joined them.

Trevor and BJ did their best to keep an eye on their little sister, but Brooke posed a serious challenge at times running here and there with a reckless abandon only a child her age possessed.

One of Shelby's favorite past-times was people-watching. *What better place than here.* She sipped her passion fruit smoothie with one eye on her kids, the other on everyone else, taking many pictures of these priceless family memories now being created. The looks on her kids' faces said it all; this was their heaven on earth.

Though thrilled to be in Orlando, Shelby's thoughts kept drifting to why they were in Florida in the first place; to find the buried treasure. *How many other families here are searching for a buried treasure chest full of real money?* Taking the final sip of her smoothie, she concluded there were none.

"Five more minutes, kids."

Judging by the exhausted looks on the many faces passing by, Shelby knew they would look and feel the same way 24 hours from now, after a full day at the Magic Kingdom. Which meant they needed all the rest they could get now.

"Okay, Momma," said BJ. He was the only one close enough to hear her command.

Five minutes later, Shelby pulled her children away from their newest best friends. She couldn't help but marvel at the way children interacted and coexisted so beautifully together. Parents could learn so much from them by simply observing, including how to become better human beings.

92

They arrived back at the hotel shortly before midnight. Opening the door, Shelby once again cautioned Trevor, BJ and Brooke to be quiet. In short, don't wake Daddy!

Within minutes, the McKinneys were sound asleep. If Shelby knew there were four extremely dangerous men waiting for her in Fort Myers, scheming to steal her inheritance the moment it was unearthed, the exuberance she felt all day would be replaced with unbridled fear...

18

JUNE 21 - DAY 11

SHELBY LAY IN BED next to her husband wide awake, thrilled to be in Florida, far away from home and her ordinary life of late. Everyone was still sleeping.

Shelby looked at the clock: 6:53 a.m. *Time for coffee.*

There was a coffee maker in the room, but if she brewed a pot the aroma would surely wake everyone. Time for Plan B.

Shelby quietly climbed out of bed, changed into her swimsuit, threw on a pair of shorts, grabbed Trevor's University of South Carolina Gamecock's baseball cap and rode the elevator down to the lobby.

She felt hungry and purchased an apple danish pastry and a large coffee from the deli in the hotel's massive lobby. She also grabbed a complimentary *USA Today* newspaper and went to the pool.

Shelby found a reclining lounge chair and small drink table and claimed both as her own.

Looking skyward, she said, "Happy birthday, Grandpa! I love you!"

Only a handful of people were poolside now. That would soon change. Today promised to be another hot one. Once the sun steadied itself over Orlando, the heat and humidity would be unbearable. Those not going to theme parks or to the many other tourist destinations Orlando was famous for, would turn into all-day swimmers or hibernate inside their air-conditioned hotel rooms until dusk.

Showers were forecast for later, but currently there was no sign of rain. This was typical for this time of year in Florida.

On any given day in the Sunshine State—especially during summer months—the sun would dominate the cloudless sky above painted crystal blue by God Almighty Himself, much like now. Then out of nowhere, clear skies would give way to cumulus clouds, massive enough to absorb hundreds of buildings the size of the Empire State Building in just one cloud.

Watching airplanes flying through those monstrosities made it difficult to fathom that they weighed several tons and were carrying hundreds of passengers. They looked more like model airplanes being shot out of a cannon, totally incapable of posing the slightest threat to the menacing clouds.

94

In just minutes these clouds, bleached a brilliant white by the sun, would give way to dark, angry, ominous clouds, and peace and tranquility would be replaced with fierce storms of a monsoonal nature. They were amazing to encounter, but never to be taken for granted. Some storms were so fierce that one might think the clouds had sucked up the entire Atlantic Ocean and Gulf of Mexico, before violently spewing them out on the state of Florida.

Oftentimes they lasted 30 minutes or so before the skies cleared, allowing tourists, locals, and the Florida wildlife—also forced to seek shelter from the dangerous elements—to move on with their day.

But for now, it was simply perfect. A warm, gentle breeze intoxicated Shelby's senses, filling the air with magnificent aromas from plants, residual suntan lotion and chlorine in the pool.

It smelled like vacation time.

Shelby removed the lid from her coffee cup and blew into the steamy foam cup before venturing a sip.

This was the kids' big day. They would remember going to the Magic Kingdom for the rest of their lives.

Shelby was just as excited but couldn't stop thinking about her buried inheritance. Even if she didn't have much to go on, she couldn't wait to start digging holes in the sand and find what was buried six feet beneath the sand for her to discover.

If she didn't find it, her mind would torment her until the day she died. She blinked that thought away and fingered through the *USA Today* newspaper, hoping for a possible mental distraction. It didn't work. She was too anxious to read.

At 7:30 a.m., Jesse and the kids joined her at the pool.

"Mommyyyyyy!" shouted Brooke, running to her mother.

"Hello, Sunshine!" Shelby chuckled seeing Brooke's swimsuit was on backwards. It was also inside out. The boys were properly dressed, but their hair stood straight up in the air, including Jesse's.

"What a motley crew y'all are!"

Jesse chuckled. "Give us a break. We're on vacation!"

"Yeah," said BJ.

Shelby just smiled.

"There's my hat! Grrrrr, Momma! I looked everywhere for it."

"Sorry, Trev. It's here, safe and sound."

"It's okay, Momma."

The boys wasted no time jumping into the pool. Shelby grabbed Brooke by the arm. First things first. It was time to fix her swimsuit.

They returned from the restroom a few moments later. "Well, honey, what do ya think?" Shelby said, showing off her new swimsuit to Jesse.

"Looking good, honey!"

"Not bad for three kids, huh?"

"Not bad at all!"

"You look so pretty, Momma."

"Thanks, Trev." Shelby jumped into the pool hand in hand with Brooke. The McKinneys swam together for an hour or so, before heading back to the room to get ready for breakfast.

Then it was off to the Magic Kingdom.

AT 7:45 A.M., THREE hours southwest of Orlando, Florida, Stuart Finkel pulled into the 7-11 parking lot. Ricky Clemmons was right behind him. Jed and Chris were already there sitting on the curb outside the convenience store waiting, which was rather surprising. Both were notorious for being late.

"Good morning, fellas," Ricky said, exiting his vehicle.

"Hey," said Jed.

Chris looked up and nodded but said nothing.

"Ready for day two in the hot sun," Stuart exclaimed, climbing out of his red pick-up truck.

"Yeah right," said Chris.

Finkel slammed his car door shut, "C'mon fellas, look alive. It's gonna be a great day. I can feel it." Getting no response, he said, "Who wants coffee?"

Chris Watkins was too busy yawning to utter a reply. Stuart took one last drag from his cigarette and flicked it at Watkins' head, just missing his face. "Wake up, sleepy head. It's showtime!"

"What's wrong with you, man," Chris snapped angrily, running his fingers through his hair to make sure he wasn't on fire. "You could've singed my hair, you maniac!"

"Yeah, but did I?"

"No."

"Then quit complaining!"

Chris Watkins stood as if to retaliate. At 5'11", he was a full inch taller than Finkel. But Stuart's long, wavy hair made him appear a little taller than Chris. At the last moment Watkins backed down sheepishly. Finkel wasn't worth the effort.

"That's what I thought!" Stuart snapped. "Wimp!" He went inside the store for coffee, donuts and cigarettes. When he returned, Chris was still visibly upset. "Take it easy, man. I was just messin' with you."

"It wasn't funny, Stu."

Finkel thought of working Chris into another lather—he was so easy to spur on—but with four bank parking lots to monitor, he needed him. He shrugged his shoulders, "You're right. I'm sorry, man."

Watkins looked deep into Stuart's beady brown eyes and actually believed him, a rarity to be sure. "Okay."

They shook hands. Stuart handed his partners their coffees. Taking a small sip, he said, "What location you going to again, Ricky?"

"Edwards Street," Clemmons said.

"Good."

"Jed?"

"South Tamiami."

"Chris?"

"North Tamiami," Watkins said glumly.

"I'll be at the location on Ford Street. Any questions?"

"No."

"Okay then, let's get busy. See you back here at four-thirty."

"Aye-aye, captain," said Ricky.

Jed and Chris said nothing. Both were long-faced.

"Wait! Before y'all go," Stuart said, retrieving three empty milk gallons from inside his truck. "These are for bathroom breaks in case it gets too busy to leave your posts." He handed one to each man. "When traffic gets too busy, if you gotta go, this is better than nothing. Just don't leave your posts! Never lose sight of the big picture; more money than we can possibly spend!"

"Yeppers," said Ricky evenly, with a growing tinge of excitement.

"Good." *Hopefully more than I can spend, that is!* Stuart climbed into his truck and rolled down the window. "Oh, and by the way...," With a full day of surveillance under his belt, Finkel learned something useful. "...if you see a car with South Carolina plates pull into the drive-thru section, pay it no mind."

"Why's that?" asked Jed Ashford.

Stuart looked at Jed like a frustrated teacher would look at an underachieving student. "Come on, Jed! Who looks for a safe-deposit box at the drive-thru window? The person we're looking for will surely be going inside the bank. Dummy!"

"Good thinking, Stu." Ricky Clemmons gawked at Stuart as if he were the Dean at the University of Limitless Intelligence.

"I know, Ricky," Stuart said confidently. "That's why I'm the leader."

Jed and Chris weren't nearly as impressed.

"Let's get to work." Stuart lit a cigarette, revved up his truck engine and drove off to his designated bank location.

Jed, Chris and Ricky did the same.

The demons assigned to all four men followed closely behind...

19

"NEXT STOP, DISNEY'S MAGIC Kingdom," said the friendly voice over the intercom speakers, causing the faces of every child on board the monorail train to light up. The monorail came to a stop. The doors opened, and the mass of humanity crammed inside disembarked all at once. Then the foot race to the turnstiles began.

Once inside the theme park, the McKinneys strolled along *Main Street USA*. Much like Beaufort, South Carolina, *Main Street USA* was reminiscent of a bygone era, with its quaint shops and horse-pulled trolleys full of people.

Off to the left, they spotted a singing barbershop quartet, gleefully serenading its audience in perfect harmony. Large balloons of all colors bearing the shape of Mickey Mouse's head stood at full attention in bunches ready for purchase.

Every little nook and cranny on this world-famous landmark street was used for something.

"Look Mommy!" Brooke exclaimed, totally awestruck seeing Cinderella's Castle ahead in the distance. Her jaw dropped open and her eyes widened, as if her last breath had been sucked out of her lungs. Then she broke into the most beautiful of smiles.

The McKinneys inched as close as they could get to Cinderella's castle. Jesse took video using his phone, as Shelby took pictures with hers. They had "tourists" written all over them.

"There are two parades today," Jesse said, perusing the map of the park to whoever in the family was listening, "one at three, and another one at nine. And the fireworks begin at ten."

"Why don't we spend the morning and afternoon going on as many rides and attractions as we possibly can," Shelby said, "After dinner, we can slow the pace a bit and watch the light parade and the fireworks."

"Sounds like a plan," Jesse replied, knowing it would be up to him to keep the family on schedule. "Okay, kids, where to first?"

"Pirates of the Caribbean!" said BJ.

"Yeah," said Trevor.

"Okay, Pirates of the Caribbean it is!"

After waiting 30 minutes in line, the McKinneys filled the third row of the boat designated to take them on their pirate adventure.

Jesse took more video using his cell phone. His steady hand swept back and forth, capturing both the attraction itself and the euphoric expressions on his kids' faces, especially BJ and Trevor.

It was priceless!

All riders exiting the *Pirates of the Caribbean* attraction were forced to walk through a souvenir shop before being released back to civilization. Pirate's paraphernalia was displayed everywhere—eye patches, treasure chests loaded with fake loot and jewelry, pirate's drinking cups, and clothing—to fit all shapes and sizes.

"I hope our buried treasure looks like this, Momma," Trevor exclaimed, showing his mother a toy treasure chest.

"Me too, sweetie. I just hope ours is much bigger."

Trevor rolled his eyes, "Of course, Momma."

It didn't take long for the begging to begin. "Can we have pirate swords and eye patches, Daddy?" said BJ.

"Yeah, Daddy, please?" said Trevor excitedly.

"Please, Daddy," BJ persisted.

Jesse finally weakened and pulled out his wallet, already knowing that Brooke would want something next. For now, she was simply biding her time. But it wouldn't last.

From there, the McKinneys rode *Big Thunder Mountain Railroad*, which was more of a roller coaster than a train ride. They liked it so much they waited in line another 20 minutes to ride it again.

After that, Shelby rode *Splash Mountain* with Trevor and BJ. Brooke wanted to ride it, too, but didn't meet the 44" height requirement. She was greatly disappointed.

Jesse and Brooke stood on an elevated bridge offering the best view of the water ride, watching boats drop 50 feet straight down. The splash it created soaked everyone inside.

When it was time for Shelby and the boys to make their big splash, even without looking, Jesse knew it was them. He heard BJ shouting, "Awesomeee," all the way down, his new word of late.

As the noontime hour approached they ventured over to *Fantasyland*. The air was noticeably hotter and more humid, and the lines were much longer. But the kids didn't seem to mind.

To help combat the heat, air conditioners were turned on full-blast inside restaurants, stores and attractions.

Jesse wondered how high the monthly electric bill was. *At least a million bucks*, he finally concluded.

The one attraction in *Fantasyland* with little wait time was *Mickey's PhilharMagic*—a 3-D movie adventure spectacular that recreated scenes from select classic Disney films. It was just as advertised—spectacular!

When the McKinneys exited the attraction, they heard thunder breaking a short distance away, followed by strong winds. Before Shelby could retrieve the three disposable raincoats she kept in her bag for the children, they were caught up in fierce downpour.

A loud rumble of thunder shook the air above them. Brooke nearly jumped out of her skin. "I'm scared, Daddy!"

"I think now would be the perfect time to eat lunch," Jesse said, gathering Brooke into his arms.

Shelby reached for Trevor's and BJ's hands, and the McKinneys went inside the first restaurant they could find. Hundreds of people were crammed inside. With the air conditioning turned on full blast, many who were soaked with rainwater shivered while eating their meals. They were desperate for the sun to return.

After lunch, the rain stopped and the McKinneys trekked to the other side of the park, to *Tomorrow Land.*

Thrilling as it was, not even riding *Space Mountain* could keep Shelby's mind from drifting back to the buried treasure hunt. As the minutes passed, she grew more and more consumed by it.

AT 4:30 P.M., STUART Finkel pulled into the 7-11 convenience store parking lot.

His three downtrodden partners were already there waiting for him. There was no need to ask how their day had gone. It was written all over their miserable faces.

Jed Ashford and Chris Watkins looked like they wanted to quit. Shortly before Stuart arrived, Ricky overheard Chris saying something to Jed about begging for their jobs back at the supermarket.

Even Ricky Clemmons was starting to lose hope. Overweight by at least a hundred pounds, baking in the hot sun all day was wearing him out.

"Who wants beer?" Finkel said, lighting a cigarette. "On me."

"Me," Ricky replied, taking a deep breath.

"Let's forget about business for now and chill out," Stuart said, taking a long drag from his cigarette.

"Sounds like a winner," Chris said, yawning.

"Whaddya say we head to your place, Jed? I'll go inside and get a case of beer. See ya there."

"Sounds good," Jed replied.

101

At that, Finkel went inside the 7-11, knowing if they didn't find this Shelby woman soon, he would lose Jed and Chris within a day or two. Perhaps Ricky, too.

Even worse, if he didn't have the $3K interest payment in three days, he'd be forced to dodge Vinnie and Carlos again.

"Where are you, Shelby?" Finkel said under his breath, pounding the steering wheel hard enough that it vibrated.

AT FIVE O'CLOCK JESSE announced that he was taking his family to Disney's Spirit of Aloha dinner show, located at the *Polynesian Resort*. Before reaching the *Polynesian Resort*, the monorail train made two brief stops; one at *Disney's Contemporary Resort*; the other at the main ticket and transportation center.

When Walt Disney purchased this vast expanse of land in Central Florida, no one imagined how massive it would eventually become. To watch him single-handedly transform Orlando, Florida, from nothing but swampland, into the "Vacation Capital of the World," virtually overnight, was remarkable!

Thanks to him, Orlando was a "must-visit" destination for countless millions each year. Few would argue that Walt Disney put Central Florida on the map. While many had since followed in his footsteps—*Universal Studios and Sea World* chief among them—he started it all.

Sadly, Walt Disney never got to see his dream come to pass. He died on December 15th, 1966. He would be thrilled to see how his imagination had so brilliantly captured the minds and hearts of so many worldwide.

The monorail pulled up to the *Polynesian Resort* and came to a halting stop. It was as if the McKinneys had taken an airplane—not a monorail—and landed in Hawaii, Tahiti or even Fiji.

They went inside the hotel's main building, aptly named the "Great Celebration House".

A few moments later, everyone attending the luau were led down a torch-lit pathway for the relatively short walk to the luau facility. Lush vegetation and tropical foliage dotted the landscape.

From an aesthetic viewpoint, for being so far away from the South Pacific, Disney did a magnificent job of recreating Polynesia at its finest, even down to the thatched-roof buildings housing those fortunate enough to vacation there.

Once seated, everyone was treated to an entertaining spectacle of Polynesian song and dance for all age groups.

"M-m-m, delicious," Jesse declared in between bites of pork. "The food alone's worth the price of admission!"

102

When the luau was over, the McKinneys rushed back to the Great Celebration House to board the monorail back to the *Magic Kingdom*. The monorail made a brief stop at the *Grand Floridian Resort and Spa*—to drop off passengers and pick more up—before arriving at the Magic Kingdom. Then the footrace to the turnstiles was on again.

"It's like deja vu all over again," said Jesse.

Shelby nodded, then sighed.

With darkness setting in, bright colorful lights transformed the world-famous theme park into an enchanted fantasy playground. Cinderella's Castle, especially, looked spectacular drenched in bright colorful lights which continually changed colors. As beautiful as everything looked earlier, it couldn't compare to now.

At 8:45 p.m., the McKinneys got ice cream cones, found a good spot on *Main Street USA,* and waited for the light parade to begin.

Just when the grownups thought they could keep their purse strings tied and wallets safely secured inside their back pockets, hucksters—dressed in Disney uniforms—peddled all sorts of Disney souvenirs and glow toys for kids to take home.

"Man, oh man. Wonder how much money Mickey and Minnie raked in today?" Jesse said, wondering if it could even be counted. He thought not.

At 9:00 p.m., the parade began right on time. Trevor, BJ and Brooke were totally awestruck, watching their favorite Disney characters slowly passing by on brightly illuminated theme floats.

Jesse held his ice cream cone in one hand, and his cell phone in the other, capturing footage of the parade.

When the parade ended, the McKinneys remained where they were and waited for *Wishes Firework Spectacular* to begin.

At 10:00 p.m. sharp, brilliant colors and images from Disney movies washed over Cinderella's Castle, synchronized to an unforgettable musical score, narrated by some of Disney's most endeared characters.

"Look Momma!" Brooke said, seeing Tinkerbell appear in a window high up on Cinderella's Castle. She was all aglow.

Brooke's little jaw nearly touched the ground when Tinkerbell flew above on a steel cable, as fireworks lit up the sky above her.

Jesse made sure it was all captured on his cell phone.

After the last firework flickered in the evening sky, even though the park was still open for another hour and a half, most made a beeline for the exits, including the McKinneys.

Brooke was suddenly sleepy and didn't feel like walking. Jesse hoisted his daughter up onto his shoulders.

Thankfully, Trevor and BJ were still energized, fully capable of walking back to the car without parental assistance.

One of the tourists' many creeds at Disney World was, "Lines, lines, everywhere lines!"

Jesse and Shelby knew this well in advance. But just to leave the park? When Jesse saw the massive lines for the monorail, he wanted to switch places with Brooke and sit on her shoulders instead.

Hadn't everyone already waited long enough in lines? Jesse was tempted to strong-arm his way through the massive crowd and create a pathway to the monorail for his family, but he refrained. He was certain he wasn't the only parent thinking these thoughts.

Five monorail trains came and went before the McKinneys were finally able to secure a seat inside.

Once in motion, the steady whooshing sound the monorail made gently rocked many children riding inside the car to sleep. It was the Magic Kingdom's goodnight lullaby to all their younger guests. Not even the voice on the intercom announcing the next stop could wake most children.

Come morning, while most parents woke with stiff necks and sore backs from too much walking, lifting and carrying, their children woke feeling completely rejuvenated and ready for Round Two.

THE FIFTY THOUSAND GUESTS visiting the Magic Kingdom got to see many wonderful things in the few hours spent there.

But what they didn't see, couldn't see, were the countless thousands of demons hovering high above the world-class theme park, following those whose names weren't found written in the Lamb's Book of Life everywhere they went.

Even without purchasing admission tickets, Satan's demons flapped and clawed high above Walt Disney World, before gliding down to the surface, sweeping just above the landscape at blinding speed, mere inches above the Magic Kingdom's most popular rides and attractions, just above the heads of those they were assigned to tempt, torment, deceive and destroy.

Not even the "Happiest Place on Earth" could prevent it from happening...

20

WEDNESDAY JUNE 22 - DAY 12

THE NEXT MORNING THE McKinneys were traveling west on Interstate 4 toward Tampa, en route to Fort Myers, Florida.

Exhausted after a full day at the Magic Kingdom, Shelby was, nevertheless, raring to go. The makeshift map she'd made at home was spread out before her, partly on her lap and partly on the dashboard. According to her timetable, they were already two hours behind schedule, mostly because of the Disney character breakfast that was part of their reservation package.

Shelby took dozens of pictures, as Trevor, BJ and Brooke proudly posed with some of their favorite characters.

It mattered not that the characters gracing their breakfast table were the same ones they saw prancing around the Magic Kingdom the day before. The kids were just as awestruck. Shelby likened it to adults seeing their favorite artists performing live in concert, then being awarded backstage passes after the show.

Shelby enjoyed it, too, but with only five days left with which to work, she just wanted to get to Fort Myers and start searching for her buried inheritance. In the back of her mind, she wondered if the bank she was looking for was back in Orlando.

After all, it was part of the Sunshine State. She seriously doubted it. Orlando just didn't feel right to her.

With time so limited, she hoped it was in the Fort Myers area instead of elsewhere. The clock inside her head kept ticking a little louder with each passing day, but Shelby managed to keep her growing anxiety in check for the time being.

With Orlando an hour behind them, the elation Trevor, BJ and Brooke felt at breakfast was replaced with sheer melancholy. Buried treasure or not, none of them wanted to leave Orlando.

Everything they ever wanted, needed was there; Disney World, a great hotel with three pools and jacuzzi, and a million other activities to keep them occupied day and night.

Why would any child want to leave that new-found paradise?

But this was just the calm before phase two of their awesome family vacation kicked in. Once they smelled the salty sea air blowing off the Gulf of Mexico and swam in the hotel pool on Fort Myers Beach, they'd be reinvigorated again.

"Wasn't Space Mountain awesome, boys!" Jesse said, hoping to break the sadness on the three faces he saw in the rear-view mirror.

"Awesomeeeeeeeeee!" BJ exclaimed.

"I liked Splash Mountain better," said Trevor.

"I can't decide which was better," Jesse replied. "Both were awesome."

"I wanted to go on Space Mountain and Splash Mountain, too, Daddy," Brooke said, long faced. Her baby blues looked ever so sad.

"Next time we go there, you'll be big enough, sweetheart," Jesse replied.

"Really?"

"Absolutely!" Jesse flashed a reassuring smile that Brooke saw in the rear-view mirror. She smiled back.

"Don't look so sad, boys! Before you know it, we'll be digging for buried treasure!"

"Yes!" BJ exclaimed, reaching for his pirate sword. It suddenly sounded exciting again.

They reached I-75 a few miles east of the Tampa city limits, and Jesse steadied the minivan southbound.

"Woo hoo!" Shelby shouted, her excitement level climbing to a whole new level...

STUART FINKEL WAS INSIDE his old pick-up truck, smoking one cigarette after another. It was just before 2:00 p.m., and still no sign of Shelby. Bank traffic was slow.

Finkel felt nauseous and dizzy from the oppressive heat, from too much alcohol in his system, and from staring at so many license plates the past three days.

Taking a bite of his turkey and cheese sandwich—which more resembled a turkey and cheese melt due to the intense heat inside his truck—Stuart thought how much easier this job would have been 20 years ago, when each state offered a single template for licensed drivers to display on the backs of their vehicles.

These days, with each state offering numerous templates from which to choose, covering a multitude of causes worth championing, it was difficult identifying one state from the next.

Whenever the heat became too oppressive, Finkel would start the engine to generate a quick blast of air conditioning, before turning it off again to conserve gasoline. Each time he rolled his window down, cigarette smoke poured out of the truck as if coming from a chimney.

106

For someone trying to look so inconspicuous, Stuart Finkel was doing a lousy job. The constant revving up of his engine made him stick out like a sore thumb being illuminated by massive floodlights.

He already received a few menacing looks from security guards and bank customers, but as of yet, he'd done no wrong. All they could do was ask him to leave.

"Where are you, Shelby?"

Stuart retrieved the smut magazine he kept under the seat for moments like this. His eyes volleyed back and forth from the foul images inside the raunchy magazine to each car pulling into the bank parking lot.

This was only day three, but it already felt like a month. Despite his growing desperation, each time his three partners called his cell phone, Stuart remained upbeat.

"We'll find her soon enough, boys. Stay focused! Never forget, more money than we can possibly spend!" he told them each time.

And each time it seemed to do the trick. But Finkel was growing weary of always feeling the need to drop little tidbits of wisdom on Ricky, Jed and Chris to keep them motivated. It was getting old.

"Soon, I'll no longer need them," Finkel said, eating the last of the potato chips.

Wimps!

21

THE MCKINNEYS ARRIVED IN Fort Myers, Florida at half-past two that afternoon.

Before reaching their hotel, Shelby spotted a bank a mile or so off the I-75 exit. "Pull inside, Jesse, hurry!"

Jesse shot a confused look at his wife but obeyed.

"Okay. Here goes nothing!" Shelby smiled brightly. Excitement oozed out of her.

"I wanna come, Momma?" said Brooke, excitedly.

"Why don't we all go in?"

The McKinneys went inside. If they expected a welcoming committee or marching band or confetti falling from the ceiling announcing their arrival, it never happened.

"May I help you?" said a heavyset middle-aged woman with bleached blonde hair. She was stationed at the information desk.

"I sure hope so." Shelby took a deep breath and her mind went blank. For the first time since accepting her grandfather's challenge, she realized she might face a few unpleasant encounters along the way. "Hmm, how can I say this? I'm here to see if I'm even at the right bank or not."

The woman gazed at her skeptically. *Tourists!* "Well, ma'am, we have several branches in the area. Which location are you looking for?"

"That's just it." Shelby sighed. "Quite frankly, I don't know the name of the bank I'm looking for, let alone the branch location."

"Are you okay, ma'am?"

Jesse wanted to run from this place as quickly as he could and wait for them back inside the van.

Shelby chuckled nervously. "I know it sounds crazy. Believe me, if I told you everything, you'd see just how bizarre it really is."

"Why don't you state exactly what it is you're looking for, and I'll see what I can do to assist you."

Shelby took her time explaining everything in great detail. The more she continued her gum-flapping, the more impatient the three customers standing behind her became.

The bank employee shot them a quick glance as if to say, "Hey, don't look at me like that. It's not my fault!" but remained silent and listened to her customer's far-fetched ranting and raving about some buried treasure.

"You're right, it is bizarre. Let me check with the branch manager. Be right back" The woman excused herself.

Shelby glanced at Jesse. He was giggling under his breath, shaking his head from side to side.

"What's so funny?"

"Man, oh man," Jesse said, "this is crazy!"

"Oh, shush," she said, slapping his arm. "I'm trying to enjoy the moment."

"Good luck," he said, giggling again.

"Grrrrr, Jesse!" Shelby replied, trying not to laugh.

"Just glad you're doing all the talking."

Shelby was about to reply, but the woman with the bleached-blonde hair returned. Without uttering a word, the answer was written all over her face.

"They never heard of Luther Mellon, right?"

"Correct," came the reply, evenly.

"Can you please point us in the direction of the nearest bank? We're from South Carolina, so we're not really familiar with the area."

"Which way are you headed?"

"Westbound," Jesse blurted out. He just wanted to leave this place.

"There's a bank a half-mile down the road on the right," said the kind, middle-aged woman.

"Thanks for trying to understand me," Shelby said. "I can't tell you how much I appreciate it."

"You're welcome, ma'am. Good luck with your search. I hope you find what you're looking for."

"Me too." Shelby said.

"Glad that's over with," said Jesse, walking back to the van. "You should have seen the looks on the faces of the people behind you. It was brutal."

"I'm sure it wasn't that bad," Shelby replied, doing her best to make light of an awkward situation.

"If you say so, dear." Jesse put the key into the ignition. "Where to next?"

"You heard the woman. There's a bank a half-mile down the road on the right."

"Would it be okay if I waited in the car this time?"

"Sure, if that's what you want."

Whereas Shelby was good at improvising, Jesse tended to clam up when placed in uncomfortable situations. He sensed his wife would be improvising herself into total oblivion the next couple of days.

A few moments later, Jesse watched Shelby and the kids leaving the second bank. It was evident they'd struck out again. At least the kids got lollipops this time.

Shelby fastened her kids securely into their seats and climbed into the front passenger seat.

Reaching for the makeshift map, she crossed off this bank location, no longer counting it a possible suspect. "Two down, ninety-eight to go!"

"Just hope it's not nine-hundred and ninety-eight," Jesse joked. At least he hoped it was a joke.

They ended up going to eleven banks before finally checking in to the hotel. It was 4:45 p.m. For their good behavior, Jesse let the kids take a short swim in the pool before dinner.

"Best to let them swim to release all that stored-up humiliation from listening to you trying to explain yourself."

"Ha ha ha, Jesse. Very funny."

"I thought so. Besides, letting them swim is much cheaper than paying for counseling sessions."

"The only one who needs counseling, dear, is you," Shelby declared, sticking out her tongue.

"Hey, I won't deny it. I'm still shell-shocked. But I'll be fine after five to seven years of intensive psychotherapy." Jesse burst out in laughter again.

"You only went inside one bank, you wimp!"

"Sometimes one's all it takes, honey," came the reply. "But at least I still have my sense of humor."

Shelby sat on the edge of the bed staring at the map, "Shhhhhhh. I'm trying to concentrate."

"Yes, dear," Jesse said. "Why don't you write a little speech and memorize it. This way, you'll be better prepared tomorrow."

"Was thinking the same thing…" Shelby said.

"After dinner, I'll take the kids to the pool. This way, you can get better organized. Once you're finished, we can stroll the beach before sunset, okay?"

"Sounds perfect."

BEFORE MEETING UP WITH Jed, Chris and Ricky, Stuart Finkel stopped by his grandfather's office, to see if he could somehow pry anything worthwhile out of him, or better yet, gain access to his client list—whether in a filing cabinet or on his computer—when no one was looking.

Anything he could dig up on this Shelby woman and the buried treasure hunt would be most helpful.

By the time he arrived, his grandfather was already gone for the day. But his business partner of 35 years was still there.

"Where's my grandfather?"

"Nice to see you too, Stuart," Bob Schuster said, with a frown.

"Oh yeah, sorry. Hi, Bob."

"Is there something I can do for you?"

Bob Schuster eyeballed his visitor suspiciously, trying not to gag from the stale smell of cigarettes. He was soaked with sweat. As always, Stuart had that no-good look about him.

One thing was certain; just by looking at him, Bob knew he hadn't done anything productive, including shower. He was merely wasting his life away, waiting for the next scam to come along.

"Just need to talk to Gramps," Stuart said, nonchalantly.

"You just missed him. He left a few minutes ago."

Bob was determined not to let Stuart leave his sight. He'd done too much harm over the years and hurt too many people—especially his grandfather—without the slightest remorse or repentance on his part.

Bob looked at his watch. He didn't have time for this nonsense. He was taking his wife, Ruth, out to dinner and needed to get going.

Sensing Stuart was there because he needed money again, Bob wanted to say, "Get a job, you bum! Stop leeching off your grandfather! Go out and do something with your life!"

Instead, he said, "If you really need to see him, you know where he lives. I'm sure that's where you'll find him."

"So, you're saying he won't be back for the rest of the day?"

"That's correct." *Man, oh man*, thought Bob! *Talking to him is like talking to a brick wall.* "Only the security guard will be here," Bob said glaring at Stuart angrily. "All night!"

Stuart grimaced. He let out a loud sigh and left without even having the decency to say bye.

Bob Schuster was just happy to see him leave. Locking the door behind him, the longtime lawyer was totally unaware of just how low his partner's grandson was about to stoop this time...

22

THURSDAY JUNE 23 - DAY 13

SHELBY ROSE WITH THE sun at 6:05 a.m. Physically, she still felt tired and wanted to sleep a little longer, but her mind wouldn't allow it. She was too fidgety.

After devising what she thought to be the least embarrassing approach when entering inside a new bank, she was fired-up again.

Shelby slipped into a colorful one-piece swimsuit, threw on a pair of denim shorts and quietly left the hotel room, hoping not to wake her family.

Down in the hotel lobby, she poured herself a cup of coffee, added the right mixture of cream and sugar and set out for the pool. The sun was slowly rising, but not enough to feel its heat yet.

By no means was this a vacation day for Shelby. It was all about business. If it was up to her, she'd already be out visiting banks, but they weren't open yet. She had no choice but to remain patient a little while longer.

Shelby tried relaxing at the pool but couldn't sit still. She decided to take a stroll on the beach. For so early in the morning, many were out walking and jogging the beach. Surf fishermen lined the shoreline, casting their lines into the Gulf of Mexico, hoping to catch something tasty for lunch or dinner.

Shelby watched one man wrestling fiercely with his fishing line, doing all he could to pull in whatever had just taken his bait. Whatever was on the other end of the line must have been massive because it was putting up quite a struggle, fully prepared to give the man everything it had, one way or the other.

The chirping of seagulls hovering above patrolling the salty sea air looking for breakfast was soothing. They were forced to share this strategic part of coastline with many other birds, namely pelicans. Hundreds of the long-beaked birds glided gracefully over the water looking for fish to eat, sushi-style.

Shelby stopped walking to observe one pelican nosedive down into the water at full-speed, like an air-to-surface missile after finally locating its target. Whereas man-made missiles occasionally missed their targets, once a pelican spotted its prey, it almost always came away with a tasty snack. They were amazing hunters.

In a perfect world, the McKinneys would locate the safe-deposit box and buried treasure within the next 24 hours, then celebrate by going back to Orlando and going to another theme park or two.

There were so many to choose from...

While this was a distinct possibility, for whatever reason, Shelby seriously doubted it would end so easily.

After all, once the safe-deposit box was located, they still had to decipher all clues, limited as they might be, before knowing where to start digging for buried treasure.

Shelby couldn't help but wonder if perhaps they'd unknowingly walked over top of it on their early evening stroll last night.

For whatever reason, just like Orlando, Fort Myers Beach didn't feel right to her. In her mind's eye, she envisioned unearthing her inheritance on some secluded hidden beach. Her gut told her this wasn't the place.

After walking a mile or so south, Shelby ambled back toward the hotel, coffee in-hand, feet splashing in the shallow gentle waves. The beauty of this place never ceased to amaze her.

Her late grandfather was right; she really did need to visit here more often. *What a great way to start the day*, she thought. *This was a great way to start any day!*

But with only four days left with which to work, the only way the South Carolina native would consider calling this day "productive" would be to locate the bank housing the safe-deposit box. Anything less would be deemed a total failure.

Shelby arrived back at the hotel to find everyone lying in bed watching the tourist channel on TV. Either they were still exhausted from Orlando or not overly thrilled with today's itinerary.

Shelby believed the latter to be true. Who in their right mind would want to drive from one bank location to the next in this heat until finally hitting pay dirt? *Apparently only me!*

Shelby spread the map across the small table. There were plenty of banks in the region to keep her busy for weeks on end. If forced to travel clear across the state to find it, Shelby feared they'd never locate the safe-deposit box in the next four days, which meant they'd never find what her grandfather had buried just for her.

Shelby pushed this debilitating thought from her mind and refocused. To keep from becoming totally overwhelmed, she would stick to the original plan and start with the banks closest to her grandfather's condominium, then spread out from there.

Perhaps they'd strike gold with the first handful of banks visited.

Wouldn't that be great...

AT 7:45 A.M., STUART Finkel pulled into the 7-11 parking lot to find Ricky Clemmons already there.

Eight minutes later, Jed Ashford and Chris Watkins showed up.

Finkel was mildly surprised they showed up at all. Handing both men their coffees, he said, "Jed, you really need to stay focused today. The Edwards Street location can be a little tricky. You need to be on your toes at all times."

"I got it covered, man," Watkins barked. As the days passed, he was growing increasingly impatient with Stuart's bogus commands.

It was day four on the job and they were still stuck at zero. Not only had they not found Shelby, they had no idea what she even looked like. There was no composite from which to work. All they knew was she was from South Carolina and she was someone's granddaughter. Nothing more.

They didn't know if she was Black, Caucasian, Hispanic, Indian or Asian. For all they knew, she was anywhere from 18 to 50 years of age. Maybe a little younger. Maybe a little older.

Certainly not much to go on...

Even if they knew what she looked like, how could Stuart know for certain the safe-deposit box was inside one of those four banks? This job was turning out to be more difficult than originally thought.

"We quit good-paying jobs for this?" was something Jed and Chris had both uttered numerous times the past four days.

Both men had a sinking feeling that Stuart had deceived them yet again, that at the end of this rainbow was another failure at the hands of their so-called leader.

With day five fast approaching, everyone dreaded the thought of rotating back to the bank they originally staked out on day one. Monitoring the same bank twice in the same week wasn't smart. But it was totally unavoidable at this point.

By playing with fire twice in the same week, the fear was that one of them would get burnt at some point.

In a hopeful attempt to keep everyone motivated, Stuart purchased four packets of play money at a local *Dollar General Store*—million-dollar bills to be exact.

"Whenever you feel tired or bored," Finkel said, handing one to each man, "just look at these million-dollar bills to constantly remind you of why we're doing this in the first place; to get rich boys!"

114

The fake money routine worked for an hour or so, before the three men reverted back to their negative thinking.

But Stuart Finkel wasn't fooling himself. If they were going to find this Shelby woman, they would need a huge break. A miracle, really. The very thought caused a lump to form in his throat.

Where are you, Shelby?

SHELBY MCKINNEY LEFT THE next bank and walked back to the minivan. She was perspiring. A cold blast of air conditioning hit her in the face. It felt good.

"Well?" asked Jesse, evenly.

Without replying, Shelby reached for the list and crossed this location off. This was the sixteenth bank visited. After the fourth one, the children gave up and remained in the van with their father.

Trevor said, "Why can't we call the banks instead of doing all this driving around? This is boring!"

Taking a moment to consider her son's idea, Shelby dismissed it. If they treated her this suspiciously in person, how much worse would it be on the phone? The moment she started explaining herself, most would probably slam the phone down in her ear.

"Trevor's right, Momma. This is boring!"

Shelby craned her neck back and glared at BJ, "Traitor!" she said, sticking out her tongue.

Of the three children, BJ was usually the most outgoing. He had an adventurous spirit which rarely needed stoking. No one wanted to dig in the sand for buried treasure any more than he did.

"Sorry, Momma," BJ said, "but it is boring. I wanna go swimming."

"It's okay, honey, I understand." Shelby said, with a reassuring smile. "You'll get to swim soon enough. Perhaps the next bank will be the one, okay?"

"Okay, Momma," came the reply from her middle child.

Jesse pulled into the next bank parking lot on the list. "Here we are, dear."

Shelby climbed out of the van. "Wish me luck, y'all."

"Good luck, Momma," they all said in unison, with little conviction backing their words.

A few moments later, she left the bank and climbed back inside the minivan.

Reaching for her makeshift map she said, "Okay, so this part of the adventure isn't as much fun as I thought it would be. But how can we start digging if we don't find the safe-deposit box?"

115

"Understood, dear," Jesse replied, all but rolling his eyes.

"Why don't we get some lunch. I'm hungry," Shelby said.

"Okay, dear."

All throughout lunch, Shelby felt her heart palpitating in her chest, but kept it to herself. Stuffing a fork full of lettuce in her mouth, it dawned on her that the one thing she'd greatly miscalculated at the outset was the amount of time it would take to drive from one bank to the next. Once they arrived, she was usually in and out in no time. But getting there was the problem!

According to her, they should have visited more than 60 banks by now, instead of just 30, including the 13 the day before.

Even her new and improved script didn't stop some from glaring at her like some crazed lunatic. But Shelby understood. Had she been in their shoes, her reaction would be very similar to theirs.

Perhaps Martin and Jake were right. Maybe I do need help if I have any shot at finding it...

At four that afternoon, most banks were closing for the day. Except for the nagging and bickering common with being siblings—mostly stemming from utter boredom—Trevor, BJ and Brooke were well behaved. It was time to reward their good behavior and drop them back at the hotel for a swim in the pool.

As appealing as going for a swim sounded, especially in this unrelenting heat, Shelby needed to remain focused and finish this not-so-pleasant part of the job by herself.

Shelby dropped her family off at the hotel and went in search of any bank that was still open. Hopefully she would have good news to share when she got back.

Once she found the safe-deposit box, their excitement would intensify again. But right now, they wanted nothing to do with this so-called fabulous adventure.

Shelby didn't blame them. With so many failures already under her belt, it was difficult even for her to remain upbeat much longer.

She looked in her rear-view mirror and sighed. Seeing her reflection staring back at her, she said, "You better find something soon!"

116

23

AFTER ANOTHER DAY FULL of endless disappointment, Stuart Finkel and his three partners met at the 7-11 on Colonial Boulevard at 4:30 p.m. Morale was at an all-time low. Even Ricky Clemmons seemed ready to throw in the towel.

"Why do we always have to meet back here each day after work?" Chris Watkins snapped. "It makes no sense. I'm sick and tired of dodging traffic and wasting so much gas for nothing."

Finkel's expression changed as he considered the question. "What are you getting at, Chris?"

"Don't expect me here tomorrow morning! I'll be at the Ford Street location at eight-thirty. If I find her, I'll call you. If not, you won't hear from me. Got it?"

"I understand how you feel Chris. We're all a little tired, man."

"It's beyond being tired, Stuart." Watkins had an angry scowl on his sunburned face. "Can't you see we're making no progress? How do you expect us to stay motivated under such conditions? How can you assure us that we'll eventually find her?"

Finkel took a deep breath, "I already told you Sunrise Savings and Loan is the only bank my grandfather uses. I'm positive the safe-deposit box is at one of those locations."

Chris Watkins glared at Stuart angrily, then lowered his head in defeat.

"I'm starting to see South Carolina license plates in my sleep," Jed Ashford said, hoping to break the tension. "It's making me crazy!"

Stuart said, "I know, pal. It won't be too much longer." It was time to motivate the troops again. "I think now's the time to share my rock-bottom plan with you. But first, who wants a Slurpee? My treat."

All three men nodded yes.

Stuart exited the store a few moments later with four raspberry Slurpees. "Gather around, fellas," he said.

Handing a frozen drink to each partner, Finkel suddenly became frighteningly even, stoic. He closed his eyes and let the darkness of his dastardly thought totally envelop him.

Opening his eyes, he leaned forward. His brown eyes were noticeably a shade darker, possessing that shifting nature of those not belonging to God. It was evident he'd crossed over into uncharted territory inside his mind; extremely dangerous territory.

They were about to see just how dangerous their leader really was! Stuart took a sip of his Slurpee and lit a cigarette, blowing the smoke skyward. "Here's the deal; if we don't find Shelby by the close of business Saturday afternoon, I'll force my grandfather to take me to the buried treasure, at gunpoint, if necessary.

"Surely he knows where it's buried. If not, his partner, Bob Schuster knows. One way or the other they're gonna spill their guts, if you know what I mean."

All three men stared blankly at Stuart, completely blown away by the words that came out of his mouth.

After a long silence, Chris Watkins finally said, "Are you saying what I think you are?"

"Yup. If I have to shoot them to get them to speak, I'll do it."

"As in kill?"

"Hopefully, not. The first shot will be in the leg or foot or something."

"What if they still won't speak?"

"I'm prepared to use any method of torture to get them to speak. One way or the other, we're finding the buried treasure, boys!"

"But they'll have you arrested. Us too."

Flashing his three partners a quick murderous glare, Finkel said, "First off, no one knows you're involved. And second, dead men tell no tales!"

"Are you serious?"

"As a heart attack, Chris!"

"You would kill your grandfather for money?"

"If push comes to shove, yes."

"That's low man," Watkins said, losing even more respect for the man. "Even for you it's low!"

"Come on, Chris, doesn't it prove how committed I am to your future?"

"No. All it proves is that you're criminally insane!"

"Can't argue with you there," Finkel replied, chuckling without humor.

Try as they might, Jed and Ricky were unable comprehend how Stuart could be so cold and calculating.

It was downright evil.

But Finkel wasn't concerned about what they thought of him. Desperate people tended to take desperate measures and do desperate things. And Stuart was incredibly desperate.

Not finding the buried treasure meant he wouldn't have the $3K interest payment due by tomorrow's deadline. The more Vinnie and Carlos threatened him, the more of an option taking his grandfather and even Bob Schuster hostage would become.

Gruesome as it was, having a rock-bottom option to fall back on gave Finkel a delusional sense of security. This was his one big chance to start anew. And his two options for succeeding were glaringly obvious; find Shelby and steal the treasure from her or kidnap his grandfather and his partner and force them both to speak.

One of those two options needed to be exercised soon, before Vinnie and Carlos found him. It was that simple!

Finkel took a long drag from his cigarette. "Okay Chris, you win. Tomorrow we'll go straight to our designated bank locations at eight-thirty sharp. You'll be at the Ford Street location, right?"

Chris Watkins shot Stuart another nasty look, "Isn't that what I already said?!"

"Okay, man. Geez, calm down!"

"Don't tell me what to do, Stu!"

Stuart managed to bite his tongue. He understood Chris' frustration. He took a deep breath and refocused, "What location will you be manning tomorrow, Ricky?"

"The one on Edwards Street."

"Jed?"

"North Tamiami."

"I'll be at South Tamiami," Stuart said. "Any questions?"

Ricky, Jed and Chris all remained silent.

"Okay then." Stuart took one last drag from his cigarette and flicked it to the ground. "Let's relax and recharge our batteries. I'll call you once I'm settled at my post in the morning. If we don't find her tomorrow, let's meet here one last time to make sure we're on the same page come Saturday morning when I confront ol' Gramps. Hopefully it won't come to that. If we find Shelby first, that can all be avoided."

No one replied to his outlandish comment. Jed and Ricky sucked their Slurpees, beyond convinced their leader really was a madman after all. Both were chilled to the bone.

Chris Watkins, on the other hand, was still too angry and frustrated to feel anything, except a deeper hatred for Stuart Finkel.

Jed, Chris and Ricky left for Jed's place to watch the Rays game on TV. Unmarried, with extremely limited girlfriend potential, the three men practically spent all their free time together.

They halfheartedly invited Stuart to join them, but Finkel declined. Going back to Jed's apartment every night and getting drunk was taking a toll on him. He was tired and had a throbbing headache to boot.

And with Vinnie and Carlos soon to be on his tail again, he needed to remain razor sharp from this point forward.

SHELBY WAS BACK AT the hotel just after 8:00 p.m.

After nearly 10 hours of fruitless searching, she was tired and understandably moody. How could she not be, after visiting 64 banks since arriving in Fort Myers, and still having nothing to show for all her effort except a tired mind and fatigued body?

She changed into her swimsuit and joined her family at the pool. After a quick swim, she dried herself off and sat on a lounge chair next to Jesse. Watching her children splashing around in the water, Shelby decided she would proceed with an idea that had been marinating in her head the past few hours.

Without a new approach, she feared the unpleasant feeling of 64 failed missions under her belt would be so much worse if she was unsuccessful again come tomorrow. That thought acted as a stimulant, which finally tilted her thinking in favor of going to Flamingo Club Condominiums first thing in the morning, to pay a visit to her grandparents' good friends in life.

Perhaps Hank Cavanaugh, Mort and Sophie Kellerman and Jim and Claire Montgomery knew something about the buried treasure hunt. Technically, meeting with them would go against her late grandfather's wishes. But with only three days left to find her inheritance, the desperate woman needed a push in the right direction.

It was settled then. But if her late grandparents' friends couldn't shed light on where her grandfather did his banking, Shelby silently feared she would never find her buried inheritance.

She fought hard to keep these debilitating thoughts to herself…

24

FRIDAY JUNE 24 - DAY 14

SHELBY MCKINNEY WOKE STILL achy from the wear and tear her body had absorbed the past four days. She climbed out of bed and stretched the kinks out.

First it was the long drive to Florida, followed by a full day at Disney World. Then the long drive to Fort Myers, followed by the constant getting in and out of the car each time she pulled into a new bank parking lot. Combined, it had taken a toll on her fatigued body.

What started out as a family adventure full of fun and sun had turned into hard work. Each time she crossed a bank off her list, part of the limitless enthusiasm she harnessed at the outset was lost in the process.

It was impossible at this point to ignore the many condescending looks she got from bank employees at most locations. While some thought it sounded exciting, most glared at her as if she'd lost her mind. Each denial left her feeling a little less optimistic about the buried treasure hunt altogether.

Perhaps I really am insane!

At any rate, Shelby believed she had good reason to feel optimistic this day. "Every day's a new day to a wise person!" she told herself, looking in the mirror.

"Have fun with the kids," she whispered, kissing Jesse on the cheek. "I'll be back as soon as I can."

"Okay, honey," he said, still half asleep. "Take your time."

Shelby knew exactly what he meant: "Leave us alone! Call only if you find it, and we'll come running!"

Hopefully today will be the day, she thought, walking the hallway down to the elevator.

STUART FINKEL WAS OFFICIALLY on-duty, manning the South Tamiami bank location.

Miraculously, his three partners had all reported for duty. Probably because of his little speech the night before when he disclosed his rock-bottom option to them.

121

Even so, Stuart knew Jed and Chris were but a breath away from quitting, if something good didn't happen soon. *Hopefully soon, I'll no longer need those three losers!*

In a way, Finkel was glad they didn't meet at the 7-11 convenience store earlier. Up to this point, the two words that were always at the forefront of his mischievous mind, were "buried" and "treasure". Now that it was Friday, those two words were replaced with *Vinnie* and *Carlos*.

Finkel didn't want Jed Ashford, Chris Watkins and Ricky Clemmons to see the mounting fear in his eyes. He needed to find the buried treasure soon; before the money collectors found him. It was that simple.

SHELBY PULLED INTO HER late grandparents' last residence on earth, the Flamingo Club Condominiums.

If there was one thing she knew about her grandparents' friends, it's that they always had morning coffee together by the pool.

Not knowing where any of them lived, Shelby hoped that tradition had been carried on now that her grandparents were no longer among them.

If Mort and Sophie Kellerman, Jim and Claire Montgomery and Hank Cavanaugh weren't poolside, Shelby was resigned to camp out there until one of them showed up. This was infinitely better than bank hopping.

Shelby parked the minivan in her late grandfather's parking space, then walked the short distance to the pool. Many were milling about, mostly seniors. She rejoiced when she spotted Sophie Kellerman. It was impossible not to notice her dyed bright red hair.

Before Shelby could utter a word, Sophie Kellerman raised an eyebrow. "Shelby, is that you?"

"Hi, Misses Kellerman. Nice to see you again."

Sophie gingerly rose from her chaise lounge chair wearing oversize sunglasses. They embraced. "How are you, my dear?" she said in her annoying high-pitched New York City accent.

But to Shelby, after the week she was having, her voice sounded just perfect. "Fine, thanks. And you?"

"Hard to stay motivated these days without your grandfather being here. This place is so boring without him. When he left us, a great ball of energy left with him."

"I know. Still hard to believe he's gone."

"It sure was a beautiful memorial service."

"Thanks again for coming. It meant so much to my family."

"Your grandparents were very special to us."

122

"They felt the same about you." Shelby scanned the pool area and realized all eyes were glued on her.

"Don't worry about them, Shelby. Gossip and eavesdropping are frequent occurrences among us seniors. They mean no harm. They're just curious."

"It's okay. I understand."

"Why are you here in Florida? Vacation?"

"Sort of, yes." Sophie's question all but confirmed to Shelby that she knew nothing about the treasure hunt.

"Where are Jesse and the kids?"

"Back at the hotel on Fort Myers Beach."

"Would you like some coffee or juice?"

"Juice sounds good."

"Please help yourself. Then come join us."

After pouring herself a glass of orange juice, Shelby listened as the seniors recounted many fond memories with Luther. She wanted to hear everything they had to say about her late grandfather, just not now. The clock inside her head kept ticking louder and louder as the minutes passed.

When there was finally a break in the action, she said, "I was wondering if y'all could help me with something?"

"What is it?"

"Would any of y'all know where my grandfather did his banking?"

Her question generated a bunch of confused looks on their wrinkled faces.

"Why do you wanna know that?" Mort Kellerman asked, rather precariously.

"Apparently y'all are unaware of my situation."

"I'm afraid so, Shelby," Sophie Kellerman replied.

"How can I say this?" Shelby sighed. "For whatever reason, Grandpa purposely left me out of his will..."

Sophie Kellerman covered her mouth with her hands. "What?! You must be kidding me! I won't believe for a second that your grandfather would do that to you! He simply adored you."

"Well, he did. As you can imagine, I was devastated at first." Her voice trailed off.

"You poor thing," Claire Montgomery replied, her eyes projecting pure concern for Luther's granddaughter.

Shelby took a sip of juice. "There's more. A few days after the reading of the will, I received a certified letter from Grandpa informing that he hadn't forgotten about me after all."

"Really? That's terrific, Shelby!" Jim Montgomery exclaimed.

123

"Yes, but if I want my inheritance, I first need to find it. Grandpa buried it somewhere here in Florida." Shelby was barraged with another round of confused looks.

"He did what?!" Hank Cavanaugh was completely blown away by this outrageous statement. "She must be kidding," he whispered softly to himself, hoping Shelby didn't hear him.

"The only clue I have to work with is this key," she said, pulling it out of her shorts pocket. "It's to his safe-deposit box in Florida. Inside are a few brief clues to further assist me. The problem is he didn't provide the name of the bank or the location.

"I've been searching all over Fort Myers the past two days, and still haven't found it. Been to more than sixty banks so far. You can imagine the looks I get from bank employees at most locations."

Mort Kellerman wondered if this had anything to do with the project Luther was always so busy working on before his death? He kept this thought to himself.

"The worst part is we're leaving first thing Monday morning, and I still haven't found the safe-deposit box. I don't think I'll have enough time to find it now." Shelby's voice trailed off again.

Luther's friends of eight years were beyond shocked that he would do this to the one family member they all knew he cherished the most. It was unthinkable.

Sensing what they were thinking, Shelby said, "Please don't be mad at Grandpa. He did it for my own good."

"How could this possibly be for your own good, Shelby?" Claire Montgomery asked, ever so skeptically.

"Grandpa wanted to reinvigorate my sense of adventure, by challenging me to live each day with unbridled passion, like I did in the past. Sending me on this buried treasure hunt has served to awaken me from within. But right now, I'm sort of stuck."

The looks on their faces told Shelby they weren't convinced.

There was an awkward silence, until Hank Cavanaugh decided to weigh in, "I believe your Granddaddy banked at Sunrise Savings and Loan."

Shelby sat straight up in her chair. Her eyes lit up. "Hmm, never heard of that place before." *Why didn't I see it during my many online searches?*

"It's a small bank here in Fort Myers with only a few locations. I don't even think they advertise. They're more of a word-of-mouth type of bank," Hank Cavanaugh exclaimed proudly, knowing he'd just made Shelby's day. It felt good.

Widowed and alone for 10 years now, Hank was a kind and gentle man who was starved for companionship. As the years passed, it seemed no one cared to listen to what he had to say. He was more than happy to be offering advice to someone again.

Said he, "If your grandfather had a safe-deposit box, I'm sure that's where you'll find it."

Shelby's heart raced. "Where can I find this bank?"

"There's one less than a mile from here, just south on Tamiami. If you want, I can take you there."

"That won't be necessary, but I appreciate the kind offer. Just directions will do for now." Shelby was astonished. Having driven Tamiami Trail more than any other road the past two days, especially in this neck of the woods, she thought she'd located every bank within a five-mile radius. *Apparently not!*

"It's so simple you won't even need to write it down," the plump older man said. "When you leave this place, take a right. At the first light, take a left. That's Tamiami. It'll be a half mile down on your left-hand side."

"Thanks so much, Mister Cavanaugh. I really appreciate it."

"My pleasure, Shelby. Hope it helps."

Shelby finished her orange juice. "I'd love to stay, but I'm up against the clock right now."

"We understand, dear. Just go," Sophie Kellerman said, motioning to Shelby with her hands.

"I promise to keep y'all posted."

"Please visit us again soon," said Claire Montgomery.

"I'll do my best."

Shelby left Flamingo Club knowing she'd just provided the retirees with a new juicy topic of discussion for the day. In fact, Luther's misgivings would undoubtedly be the only thing discussed until Shelby found the buried treasure. She just hoped they wouldn't lose respect for her grandfather in the interim. If that happened, she would regret coming here for the remainder of her life.

Shelby pulled into the *Sunrise Savings and Loan* parking lot. For whatever reason, after 64 failures, this felt like the place. Her heart raced. She wondered again how many times she drove past this place without ever seeing it. Perhaps the huge banyan tree outside the bank was responsible for obstructing the view, she thought, completely unaware that it had been supernaturally hidden from her all this time.

Just as Shelby was about to go inside the bank, she stopped dead in her tracks and reached for her phone.

After three rings, Jesse answered. "Hello?"

"Hi honey! I think I'm onto something..."

"Oh, yeah? What?"

"Do you remember the Kellermans, Montgomerys and Hank Cavanaugh from Grandpa's funeral?"

"Yeah. What about them?"

"I just met with them at the pool at Grandpa's condo. When I told them about the buried treasure hunt, they were shocked to say the least."

"And?"

"Anyway, Hank Cavanaugh gave me the name of a bank called Sunrise Savings and Loan. I don't remember seeing it online. I really feel this is it! I'm here now, but was wondering if you want me to come fetch y'all first before I head inside?"

"Yes! Come get us. We'll be ready when you get here."

"See y'all in fifteen minutes."

"Okay." Jesse replaced the phone. "Wake up kids. I think Momma found the bank."

"Awesomeeeeeeeee," BJ shouted at the top of his lungs.

"Get dressed. Momma will be here soon!"

"Woo hoo!" Trevor said.

25

STUART FINKEL WAS NEVER more desperate for a miracle in his life.

Just as he was about to use the *Burger King* restroom across the street, that miraculous break unassumingly pulled into the parking lot of Sunrise Savings and Loan. At least he hoped so.

As the minivan displaying South Carolina tags inched closer toward him, Finkel spotted a woman in the passenger front seat.

Could that be Shelby?

Stuart lit a cigarette and once again considered the many "What If" scenarios, never taking his eyes off the minivan. A young family piled out of the car and hurried inside the bank.

Taking one last drag from his cigarette, Finkel flicked it to the ground without stomping it out with his foot. He was too focused to think about trivial things like that. He went inside the bank sweating profusely trying to remain calm.

If someone approached him, he would inquire about opening a checking account. Of course, if they knew he didn't have two cents to rub together, they'd probably laugh in his face and send him on his way.

In the competitive world of commerce banking, unlike his grandfather, Stuart Finkel was a complete nobody. The only time he came to this place was when his grandfather foolishly scratched out checks to him in the past. He always cashed them at this location.

Hope no one remembers me.

Stuart took a seat. He looked more prone to robbing the bank than anything else. But he wasn't concerned with the looks he got from bank employees and customers.

He was on a mission. It wasn't to rob this bank. Shelby, yes. The bank itself, no. *If that's even her*, he thought.

Finkel scanned the bank again to make sure no one was monitoring him, then returned his gaze to the family in the corner office. He couldn't help but wonder what they were discussing.

Whatever it was, the woman was quite animated as she spoke to a female bank employee. Her husband, or whoever it was, patiently listened.

"Is anyone helping you, sir?" Stuart was caught off guard and nearly jumped out of his skin.

He drew a deep breath. "I'm interested in opening up a checking account."

"Have you ever banked with us before?" the rather tall dark-skinned woman said, towering high above him.

"Uh, no," came the reply.

"Someone will be with you shortly," she said, glaring at him suspiciously.

"Okay."

Finkel leaned forward in his seat when the two women left the corner office and walked into what appeared to be the bank vault.

The man remained in the office with his children, who sucked on lollipops.

Knowing that was where they kept their safe-deposit boxes, Finkel's excitement level reached a new high. He leaned back in his seat and gulped in some air. "Try to remain calm," he told himself, under his breath.

Suddenly the female bank employee frantically emerged from the vault without the woman Stuart hoped was Shelby. She checked something on her computer screen in her office before rejoining her customer inside the vault.

A few moments later, they came out looking ever so jubilant, especially the woman holding the manila envelope. Whatever they were looking for, apparently, they'd found it.

Must be the treasure map! Stuart was convinced it was Shelby. His heart raced. He reached for a magazine and pretended to read it.

When the kids in the corner office saw the manila envelope, the two boys fist-bumped each other. Everyone stood to leave, smiles on their faces. The bank employee walked them to the door.

Stuart placed the magazine back on the table and stood to leave. At the absolute worst possible time, the same tall woman approached again. "Okay, now, where were we?"

No, not now, lady. Not now! "Uh...I'm interested in opening a checking account?"

"Business or personal?" She eyeballed him carefully.

"Uh...personal?" Stuart replied, without taking his eyes off the jubilant family by the front door saying bye to the female bank employee.

"I'd be happy to help you. By the way, I'm Sonya Haynesworth."

Finkel's expression changed as he considered his next move. "Uh...Joel...Yes, Joel Spencer."

"It's a pleasure meeting you, Mister Spencer." Sonya Haynesworth extended her right hand to greet him. *Why are his palms so sweaty?* This aroused suspicion in her.

"Likewise," Stuart lied, his heart racing. He needed to get out of here.

"Follow me, please." Sonya turned and went to her office.

128

"Uh, I changed my mind. I gotta go," Finkel said, hoping to avoid making a scene.

"It won't take but a few moments, Mister Spencer," the bank teller said.

"Another time. I forgot about another appointment I have."

"Would you like to reschedule?"

Come on lady, give it a rest! "Uh, no. I'll come back when I have more time."

An alarm went off in Sonya Haynesworth's head. Something wasn't right. Joel Spencer's behavior was too irrational. A restless, driven energy reverberated all around him. And why was he so interested in the family talking to Susan Fernandez?

Spencer stopped at a cork board hanging on the wall by the front door and pretended to read the business cards posted there. Haynesworth narrowed her eyes at him accusingly. She watched him like a hawk. *Is he looking to rob them or perhaps even the bank?*

"It was so nice meeting you, Trevor, BJ and Brooke," the bank manager said.

"You too, Miss Fernandez," Trevor and BJ both said at the same time.

"Thanks for the lollipop," Brooke said, with a warm smile.

"You're most welcome, Brooke." Shifting her gaze to Jesse and Shelby, Susan Fernandez said, "Mister and Misses McKinney, it was a great pleasure meeting you both. Good luck, guys."

"Don't worry, we'll find it," BJ exclaimed proudly.

"I'm sure you will, boys," Fernandez said. "But, shhhhhhh, we don't want any pirates to overhear you, right?"

Stuart Finkel's pulse raced in his ears. *Yes!*

"Arghhhhhh. Let them try to mess with us, right Trev?"

"Right!" Trevor said, to his little brother.

"I dare you to mess with this pirate, boys!" Stuart mumbled under his breath.

Totally oblivious to Finkel's presence, Susan Fernandez giggled. She was the only bank employee to know what was going on. Not only did she know about the buried treasure, she was one of *Shelby's Saints*. This was a time of great rejoicing.

"Hope you enjoy the rest of your stay here in Florida, Mister and Misses McKinney."

"Thanks, Susan," Jesse replied. "But please call me, Jesse."

"Okay, Jesse." Then to Shelby, "I wish you the best of luck, Shelby. Godspeed."

It's her! Stuart's pulse raced even faster. *Yes!*

129

"Thanks, Susan. With only three days left, I'll need all the luck I can get."

Stuart gulped hard, unable to believe his sudden good fortune. His ship had come in after all! *Remain calm!*

"You'll be fine, Shelby. Just take it one step at a time."

At that, the McKinneys left for the hotel. It suddenly felt like a treasure hunt again.

Bells started going off in Stuart Finkel's head, but certainly not alarm bells. These were the kind heard ringing on slot machines inside a casino, signaling someone had just hit the jackpot!

Someone did hit the jackpot—he did!

Stuart slid behind the wheel of his truck, jotted down the names Jesse and Shelby McKinney on a piece of paper, and drove off to follow the unfortunate family from South Carolina.

Susan Fernandez went back inside with a jovial expression on her face. It faded when Sonya Haynesworth informed her about Joel Spencer, and the great interest he had in the family she just parted company with.

Fully mindful of what was at stake, Fernandez called the local authorities.

"Open it now, Momma," BJ all but shouted.

"Wait till we get back to the hotel."

"Patience, y'all, we'll see it soon enough," Jesse said. Even he was having difficulty containing his excitement.

Stuart Finkel did his best to remain five car lengths behind the minivan at all times. Now retired from his job of surveilling bank parking lots, and very grateful to be, his task now was simple: never let the McKinney family out of his sight.

The first step was to find out where they were staying in Fort Myers. Finkel took a long drag from his cigarette.

Life can be so funny at times. A half-hour ago, he was down in the dumps. Now he was back on top of the world again. As far as he was concerned, finding Shelby was the most difficult part of the job. Putting the remaining pieces into place should be easy.

"Should be all downhill from here," he shouted. "Yes!"

Gripping the steering wheel ever so tightly, Finkel crossed over into dangerous territory again inside his mind. No one gets to this point and reaches this pinnacle of evil without being a cunning and ruthless person. Stuart was always fraternizing with his inner demons, always doing his best to keep them on the fringe.

Eventually, however, the demons always caught up to him, as evidenced by the murderous thoughts invading every square inch of his mind. But this was infinitely worse than all other past thoughts, because women and children had just been entered into the grim equation.

Once the McKinneys unearthed the treasure chest, Finkel would use whatever force necessary to see that it ended up in his hands. If he needed to do the unthinkable, he wouldn't think twice.

There was too much at stake to be denied this time. This was his only chance to fix his financial woes.

With that mental justification, he wouldn't let anyone come between himself and the buried treasure, not even women and children. He was so close now!

Finkel followed the McKinneys into the parking lot of the Outrigger Beach Resort on Fort Myers Beach. Both vehicles were traveling under a canopy of demons. This was the first meeting between Stuart's demons and Jesse's and Shelby's.

The children, still unaccountable for their actions, didn't have demons assigned to them at this time.

There wasn't the slightest trace of camaraderie among them. The hatred they shared for one another could never be measured in human terms.

Even so, all demons assigned to this crucial mission remained united in their cause, to do whatever it took to deliver victory into their commander's blood-soaked hands.

Hopefully soon...

If they could somehow force the vehicles they were following to collide into one another, killing everyone in the process—including all three children—no command would need to be given.

It would already be done. But they didn't have that power...

26

THE MOMENT JESSE CLOSED the door, loud thunder broke directly above the hotel, followed by a soaking rain.

Knowing they were safe, Brooke and Shelby both let out anxious screams at the same time.

"Whoa!" said Jesse. "That was close!"

Trevor and BJ looked at each other with the most amazing expressions on their faces. "Isn't this cool, BJ?"

"Yeah! It feels like we really are pirates!"

"I'm Captain Jack Sparrow!"

"I wanna be Jack Sparrow," BJ declared. "You got to be him last time!"

"Since this is a special occasion," Shelby said, "why don't you both be Jack Sparrow?"

"Okay, fine," BJ said.

Everyone huddled around the small table near the window. The lights flickered off and on due to the storm outside.

"Here goes nothing, y'all!" Shelby tore open the manila envelope and, with Brooke's assistance, emptied its contents onto the table. The first sound they heard was the unmistakable clanking sound of a metal key hitting the wooden table.

"Sounds like a treasure chest key to me!" Jesse said.

"Really, Daddy?" Brooke said. Excitement pulsated through her tiny body.

"Awesomeeeeeeeeeeeeeee," BJ shouted.

Shelby paused to take it all in. This was one of those incredible family moments she wished she could freeze in time. The boredom they'd battled the past couple of days was replaced with sheer jubilation. By far, this was the most excited any of them had been since arriving in Fort Myers.

"Can I open it, Momma?" said BJ.

"Go right ahead, honey."

BJ retrieved the key from inside the small envelope. "Look, Trev!"

"Wow! Looks like a real *Pirates of the Caribbean* treasure chest key! Let's go find it now, Momma!"

"Slow down, Trev, let's see what else is inside."

"Okay, Momma."

If anyone expected to find a map of the state of Florida with an "X" marking the exact spot, or a hand-drawn treasure map with the name of the beach written at the top, they found neither.

There wasn't even a letter enclosed this time. The only other item inside the envelope—besides the key itself—was a thick scroll-shaped, brown piece of hard-pressed paper.

Jesse looked at it rather quizzically. "What in the world could the three 'one-eleven' clues possibly be?"

Shelby had no answer, only a mild look of confusion on her face. Even so, the treasure hunt had officially begun. *Yes!* She read aloud what was written on the scroll, so everyone could hear...

THREE "111" CLUES
TO ASSIST IN FINDING YOUR BURIED INHERITANCE:
First "111" Clue = Numeric Equation
Second "111" Clue = Beachfront Landmark
Third "111" Clue = The Ultimate Payoff!
Decipher all three "111" clues
and you'll find your buried inheritance,
and hopefully so much more!

FURTHER DESCRIPTION OF CLUES

The first "111" clue, once deciphered, will reveal the exact beach in which the treasure chest has been buried. The total sum of this numeric equation equals "111", that is, after you subtract two vowels from one of the words. And here's a clue within a clue; you'll need to have a good attitude in order to succeed with the task at hand. And in this case, attitude really does equal a perfect "100!"

The second "111" clue represents a magnificent landmark that's completely overlooked by most who pass by it. Your inheritance is buried 50 steps due west of it. And here's your clue within a clue; this landmark represents three objects, all of which provide shelter and safe refuge for so many. Once you locate it, count off 50 steps and start digging. Six feet beneath the surface will be the buried treasure chest.

The third and most important "111" clue also represents three things that are so out of this world yet are so much closer than anything you could ever imagine—even if you don't realize it yet! And here's your clue within a clue; these three things really are three-in-one. They are completely inseparable and represent everything. My prayer is that they will be revealed to you soon after you find the buried treasure chest.

133

Oh, and one more thing. Regarding the first two clues, all I can say is there are NO FREE RIDES! Only the third one is FREE! Other than that, there are no other clues or secret decoders to further assist you—only your mind and imagination. Always do your best to keep it very simple! Happy digging!

"Interesting," Trevor said. His thinking cap was already on.

"What's it mean?" BJ asked, a confused look on his face.

Jesse sighed, "Good question, son. Perhaps the first clue is a mile marker on a road or highway. But that wouldn't explain the subtraction of the two vowels, whatever that means."

"Hope we'll find out soon enough," Shelby replied.

Thirty minutes later, it was still raining. BJ and Brooke were getting antsy and wanted to go swimming. They stared out at the pool intently, as if their positive energy would somehow blot out the rain clouds.

As the noon hour approached, Jesse, Shelby and Trevor still hadn't deciphered a single clue. Everyone was hungry.

Twenty minutes later, the McKinneys were seated in a booth at a Friendly's Restaurant wearing swimsuits, just in case.

Trevor and BJ looked like two surfer boys wearing tank tops and knee-length bathing suits, sporting identical patterns, only different colors. Trevor's was brown. BJ's was green.

Jesse wore a blue, knee-length swimsuit and gray muscle shirt.

Shelby and Brooke wore matching colorful beach dresses Shelby purchased in Orlando to cover their swimsuits.

Seated quietly at a table in the far corner of the restaurant was Stuart Finkel. Before venturing inside the restaurant, he called his three ex-partners. As usual, all three were downtrodden.

As they kept roasting in the hot Florida sun monitoring bank parking lots, Finkel celebrated his success by ordering steak and eggs, coffee, and a strawberry milkshake. *Suckers!*

Stuart blinked his now three ex-partners out of his mind and focused his attention on the reason he was at the restaurant.

So far, the family he was staking out was unaware of his presence. It had to remain that way. He was so close now!

In his mind, he was swimming in an ocean full of hundred-dollar bills. Not even the deadline with Vinnie and Carlos mattered to him. Soon those two goons would be out of his life for good!

Meanwhile, a waitress approached the McKinney table. "Welcome to Friendly's. What can I get you to drink?"

134

Seeing Shelby was a million miles away gazing at the scroll in front of her, Jesse did all the ordering.

"The first 'one-eleven' clue is a numeric equation," Shelby said, more to herself than anyone else. "The second is a beachfront landmark. And the third is the ultimate payoff!"

Shelby sighed. "The second clue seems the simplest one. I mean, after all, it's a beachfront landmark, right?"

Jesse rubbed his hair-covered chin, "Yeah, but didn't it say many pass by it without noticing it?"

"Guess we'll find out soon enough. On the surface, the third clue also seems obvious. Probably represents the buried treasure itself."

"Could be," Jesse said.

"Perhaps the 'three-in-one' part represents three items stashed inside the treasure chest; perhaps money, jewelry and rare collectibles."

"Sounds logical to me. But we better find out soon. Time's running out on us."

"We'll be fine, Jesse," Shelby said, confidently.

"I think we should focus on one clue at a time for now."

"I agree." Shelby took a sip of water and read the description of the first clue again for everyone to hear. "The first 'one-eleven' clue, once deciphered, will reveal the exact beach in which the treasure chest has been buried. The total sum of this numeric equation equals 'one-hundred and eleven', that is, after you subtract two vowels from one of the words. And here's a clue within a clue; you'll need to have a good attitude in order to succeed with the task at hand. And in this case, attitude really does equal a perfect 'one-hundred!'"

Jesse weighed in, "I'm sure the attitude equaling a perfect one-hundred part means we always have to have a good attitude no matter what happens, right?"

"I dunno, Jesse. Sounds a little too simple to me. Grandpa said we'll need to have a good attitude *before* saying it equals a perfect one-hundred. Something tells me there's more to it than that."

"Just thinking off the top of my head. That's all."

"Me too, honey. But isn't it exciting?"

Jesse nodded yes. His big blue eyes were full of anticipation.

BJ and Brooke were busy scribbling on their activity menus provided by the restaurant to keep children entertained until their food arrived.

Trevor remained focused, listening and watching his parents ever so astutely, trying his best to help solve the first clue.

Suddenly a light bulb went off inside his head. He scribbled something on his paper menu using a green-colored crayon. A few moments later, he looked up from his menu; "Mom, Dad!"

"Not now Trev, we're trying to concentrate here."

"I think I know what GG meant by attitude equaling a perfect one-hundred."

Shelby stared at her son blankly; "Okay then, what is it?"

Trevor flipped his menu around for his parents to see. "The first clue is a numeric equation, right?"

"Yeah," Jesse and Shelby both said at the same time.

"There are twenty-six letters in the alphabet, right?"

"Yeah..."

"If the letter 'A' is the number 'one', and 'Z' is 'twenty-six', using that formula, I added it all up and it's a perfect one-hundred!"

"Are you serious, Trev?"

"Yes, Momma."

Jesse grabbed a crayon and wrote the word "attitude" on a piece of paper, then added the numbers for himself.

$$Attitude\ 1 + 20 + 20 + 9 + 20 + 21 + 4 + 5 = 100!$$

"Well, I'll be..." Jesse scratched his head in amazement. "Good job, Trev. It's nice to know we have a genius in the family!"

"Thanks, Daddy..." Trevor's face turned various shades of pink.

"How'd you do that, Trev?"

"It's simple, BJ. Anyone could do it."

"Even me?" asked Brooke.

"Yes, Brooke."

Brooke smiled, warmed by her big brother's words.

Though Shelby watched Jesse do it, to be sure, she borrowed Brooke's menu and wrote the word "attitude" on the back, then applied the proper numbers to each letter before adding it all up.

A smile curled onto her lips, "I'm so proud of you, Trev! Thanks to you, we can focus on finding the beach that adds up to one-hundred and eleven. But let's really make it fun and do one beach at a time. Since we're already here, I'll begin with Fort Myers Beach."

Shelby wrote Fort Myers Beach on the back of the menu. The first thing she noticed was the word 'beach' had two vowels, while 'Fort' and 'Myers' had one vowel each. "I think the word we're looking for is, 'beach'. There's an 'e' and 'a'. Makes sense, right?"

"Way to go, honey!" Jesse's excitement level reached a new echelon. "Think I'll try Miami Beach."

"I'll start with Daytona Beach," Trevor replied.

"Where can I start, Daddy?" said BJ.

"Just pick any beach, BJ." Jesse was too focused to give his youngest son his full, undivided attention.

"Try Clearwater Beach, BJ," Trevor opined to his younger brother.

"How do you spell that?"

Trevor rolled his eyes, then wrote *Clearwater Beach* on BJ's menu. "Once you apply all the numbers, I'll add it up for you."

BJ got to work.

Shelby added the numbers for Fort Myers Beach. "One fifty-seven! One fifty-one, minus the 'e' and 'a' in the word 'beach'. Not Fort Myers Beach, y'all!" But she wasn't overly surprised. She never thought it was buried here in the first place.

$$Fort—6 + 15 + 18 + 20 = 59$$
$$Myers—12 + 25 + 5 + 18 + 19 = 79$$
$$Beach—2 + 5 + 1 + 3 + 8 = 19 - 6 = 13$$

Glancing at her menu, Jesse followed his wife's structure. A few moments later, he said, "Not Miami Beach either. Not by a long shot! Only adds up to sixty-four. Fifty-eight minus the two vowels."

$$Miami—13 + 9 + 1 + 13 + 9 = 45$$
$$Beach—2 + 5 + 1 + 3 + 8 = 19 - 6 = 13$$

"Not Daytona Beach either," said Trevor, anxious to try another beach.

"What did it add up to, Trev?"

"Ninety-nine. Ninety-three without the 'e' and 'a'".

"We're getting closer, Trev," said Jesse.

"Not sure it works that way, Daddy."

"Just kidding, son," came the reply with a goofy smile. Trevor cracked up.

"Finished Trev," BJ said to Trevor.

Before adding the numbers, Trevor double-checked to make sure his little brother had properly applied them. He was impressed that he had. "One twenty-five. One nineteen minus the 'e' and 'a'. Close, but no cigar. But good job, BJ."

BJ smiled proudly.

"Okay, time for the next round," said Shelby.

"I wanna help, Momma," Brooke declared.

"Sure, sweetie. Brooke and I will do Sanibel Beach."

"Yeah, we'll do Sabinel Beach."

"It's Sanibel Beach, not Sabinel."

"That's what I said, BJ."

Everyone smiled and left it at that.

"I'll try West Palm Beach," said Jesse.

"Think I'll try Treasure Island!" Trevor exclaimed. "After all, that's what we're looking for!"

Island? Jesse scribbled the word onto a napkin. "The word 'island' also has two vowels—'i' and 'a'. Good thinking, son. You may be onto something. If that's the place, we'll buy it and rename it 'Trevor Island', deal?"

"Ha ha ha, very funny, Daddy!"

"I thought it was," he said, quickly refocusing.

"What beach can I do next, Trev?"

"Try Fort Lauderdale Beach." Trevor wrote it down on BJ's menu.

Shelby finished adding the numbers. "Not Sanibel Beach. Only adds up to seventy-five."

$$Sanibel—19 + 1 + 14 + 9 + 2 + 5 + 12 = 62$$
$$Beach—2 + 5 + 1 + 3 + 8 = 19 - 6 = 13$$

"Not West Palm Beach either," said Jesse. "One twenty-two."

$$West—23 + 5 + 19 + 20 = 67$$
$$Palm—16 + 1 + 12 + 13 = 42$$
$$Beach—2 + 5 + 1 + 3 + 8 = 19 - 6 = 13$$

"One sixty-six. One fifty-six minus the two vowels. Looks like we're not buying Trevor Island after all, Daddy," Trevor said with a smirk.

$$Treasure—20 + 18 + 5 + 1 + 19 + 21 + 18 + 5 = 107$$
$$Island—9 + 19 + 12 + 1 + 14 + 4 = 59 - 10 = 49$$

Trevor added BJ's numbers for Fort Lauderdale Beach. "Not Fort Lauderdale Beach either. One thirty-six without the 'e' and 'a'".

The waitress approached. "How's everything?"

Jesse said, "Can you tell us the names of some of the local beaches around here, besides Fort Myers Beach?"

"Sure. Well there's Sanibel and Captiva Island. And just south of here there's a nice beach called Bonita Beach. And down by Naples is Marco Island. Those are the most popular beaches around."

"Thanks a lot," Jesse said.

"Brooke and I will take Bonita Beach," said Shelby, when the waitress left them.

"I'll take Marco Island," said Jesse.

"Looks like I got Captiva Island," Trevor declared.

"What about me, Trev?"

"Let's do Captiva Island together, BJ," said Trevor to his little brother.

"Okay."

138

"Seventy-four, minus the 'e' and 'a'. Not Bonita Beach," Shelby said, shoveling a handful of French fries in her mouth.

$$Bonita—2 + 15 + 14 + 9 + 20 + 1 = 61$$
$$Beach—2 + 5 + 1 + 3 + 8 = 19 – 6 = 13$$

Jesse sighed, "Not Bonita Beach. Thought I had it for a second there. One-oh-nine. So close!"

$$Marco—13 + 1 + 18 + 3 + 15 = 50$$
$$Island—9 + 19 + 12 + 1 + 14 + 4 = 59 – 10 = 49$$

"Not Marco Island either. One twenty-one, minus the 'i' and 'a'." Trevor took a bite of his hot dog and washed it down with a spoonful of macaroni and cheese. He was fiercely determined to solve the first piece of the puzzle all by himself.

$$Captiva—3 + 1 + 16 + 20 + 9 + 22 + 1 = 72$$
$$Island—9 + 19 + 12 + 1 + 14 + 4 = 59 – 10 = 49$$

"Nor is it Captiva Island..." Trevor scratched his head.

"Why don't we take a break and finish our lunches," Jesse said, taking a bite of his chicken sandwich.

"Good idea," said Shelby, taking the first bite of her lukewarm bacon cheddar burger. It still tasted good.

Stuart Finkel ate his steak and eggs very slowly, savoring each bite, each morsel. Even 30 feet away, he could feel the excitement being generated by the McKinney family. It practically wafted in the air and permeated every inch of the restaurant.

They were doing all the work, but only he would get rich from their efforts. Stuart Finkel finished his meal but had no plans of leaving anytime soon. Not until his employees left.

The waitress dropped the check.

"Refill my coffee cup. I'm going out for a smoke. Be right back."

"Sure thing," she said, a little too cautiously.

Stuart knew what she was thinking and dropped a $20 bill on the table. "Like I said, refill my coffee cup."

"Yes, sir. Be right back with more coffee and your change."

Stuart said nothing but headed outside. *If you knew I'm about to become a wealthy man, that smug look on your face wouldn't be there now. You'd respect me then!*

Trevor took another bite of his hot dog and was struck with a sudden thought; "Momma, did you try Sanibel Beach or Island?"

Shelby looked at her list. "Beach, Trev, why?"

Trevor said nothing. A few moments later—proud smirk on his face—he turned his menu upside down, so his parents could see it. "Have a look..."

139

Sanibel—19 + 1 + 14 + 9 + 2 + 5 + 12 = 62
Island—9 + 19 + 12 + 1 + 14 + 4 = 59 – 10 = 49
111!

Shelby's jaw dropped, "I can't believe you solved it. Good job, honey!"

"Thanks, Momma…" Trevor stiffened up proudly. His hazel-green eyes were fully aglow.

Jesse scratched his head in amazement, "Trevor, my boy, I think you really are a genius!"

"Thanks, Daddy." Trevor was unable to remove the smile from his face.

BJ and Brooke looked at their big brother in total awe. They were so proud of him. It was written all over their faces.

27

"FINISH EATING, Y'ALL," SHELBY ordered. "We gotta go."

"Did you bring your pirate sword BJ?"

"It's in the car, Trev."

"Mine too." This was one of the coolest moments of their young lives.

The McKinneys took U.S. 41 to Cypress Lake Drive and turned left. They reached Summerlin Road and turned left again, then drove straight toward Sanibel Causeway. They pulled up to a toll booth.

As Jesse reached inside his pocket for toll money, Trevor was the only one to connect the dots. "Momma, this is even more proof that we're at the right place."

"What do you mean, Trevor?"

"GG said no free rides, right? Think about it; we need to pay a toll before entering the island. No free rides."

"Wow, Trev, I think you should work for NASA someday," Jesse declared.

Shelby turned around and high-fived her eldest son.

Trevor said, "This is even more fun than going to Disney World!"

"Woo hoo!" Shelby was so excited to the point of bursting open. "Finally, we're making progress!"

Three cars behind the McKinney's minivan was Stuart Finkel, smoking one cigarette after another. He paid the $6 toll and kept following the McKinneys. Upon reaching Periwinkle Way, they turned left and followed the signs leading straight to Sanibel Beach.

They arrived at the Old Town section on Eastern Sanibel Island a few minutes later. Jesse parked the van in the main parking lot, not too far from the Sanibel Beach lighthouse. Finkel parked a few spaces from them.

"Let's see how long it takes for our boy-genius to decipher the second clue."

Trevor reached for his sword, "I'll do my best, Daddy."

BJ already had his sword and was wearing his pirate eye patch.

"First things first; time for sun block, y'all!"

"Okay, Momma," said Brooke.

With everyone doused in sun block, Jesse retrieved the bag in the back of the minivan, containing five small shovels, three of which were mini garden shovels for the children.

Shelby grabbed towels and a blanket before closing the hatch and locking the car doors. This was the first time any of them had stepped foot on Sanibel Island.

"Time to put your thinking cap on again, Trev."

"It's already on, Momma!" he exclaimed, with authority. "Let's go find it!"

Shelby took out the scroll and read the second clue again. "The second 'one-eleven' clue represents a magnificent landmark that's completely overlooked by most who pass by it each day. Your inheritance is buried fifty steps due west of it. And here's your clue within a clue; this landmark represents three objects, all of which provide shelter and safe refuge for so many. Once you locate it, count off fifty steps and start digging. Six feet beneath the surface will be the buried treasure chest."

"I think it's safe to assume it's not the lighthouse over there," said Trevor. "Too obvious."

Jesse sighed. "I agree, son. What is it then? A hotel? Hospital? Church? Restaurant? Homeless shelter? It could be anything."

Shelby put an arm around each of her two sons. "Isn't this exciting?"

"Yes!" said Trevor.

"Awesomeeeeeeeeee," said BJ.

"We're so close. I can just feel it."

"Me too, Momma," Trevor exclaimed.

"Me too, Trev," BJ said, getting more amped-up with each step he took.

Jesse and Brooke followed close behind hand in hand. "Will we find it today, Daddy?"

"That's the plan, sweetheart."

"I'm so excited," Brooke said, trying to keep pace with her father. Her big blue eyes were so alive. Her light brown hair bobbed up and down with each step she took.

For the next three hours, Stuart Finkel sat beneath a shady pine tree watching the McKinneys scouring the beach, fully determined to find the buried treasure. It was nice to see so much dedication coming from his employees.

As much as he wanted to keep monitoring them, he needed to leave so he could meet with Ricky, Jed and Chris. This would be the last time meeting with them.

BJ grew weary of searching, opting for a swim in the Gulf of Mexico. Brooke joined her brother. Jesse spread a blanket out on the beach and watched BJ and Brooke, as Shelby and Trevor continued searching for clues.

It was as if Trevor and BJ had switched personalities. Suddenly Trevor was the ultimate adventurer, not BJ. *Go figure*, the father of three thought to himself.

But Shelby wasn't discouraged. She kept reminding herself that the landmark they were looking for was widely overlooked by most. Not only that, this was only a small part of Sanibel Beach.

Just knowing her inheritance was buried someplace on this beautiful island thrilled her to no end.

The question was, where?

AT 4:30 P.M., STUART Finkel pulled into the 7-11 parking lot back in Fort Myers to meet with his three partners.

Not even a strong dose of truth serum could force him to disclose what he'd just found. Who, rather. As far as he was concerned, it was no longer any of their business. He was sick and tired of their constant complaining and moping around.

When he pulled into the parking lot, all three had slumped shoulders and red faces from the oppressive heat.

Their overall demeanor screamed, "We quit!"

Finkel took their negativity as a huge slap in the face. But it did serve one good purpose; it eliminated the slight pang of guilt he felt knowing he was about to leave them high and dry without paying them anything!

"Anything of interest today, fellas?" Stuart said, halfheartedly.

"Nope," said Ricky.

Chris Watkins watched Finkel carefully with growing suspicion. "How 'bout you, Stu?"

"No, but there's always tomorrow, right?" he replied with a half-smile.

"Hmm."

"What do you mean, 'hmm'?" Stuart waited for a response, but Chris remained silent. "If you wanna quit, quit! See if I care!" he hissed. "I'm sick and tired of trying to keep you motivated each day! All you ever do is complain. If you don't wanna show up for work tomorrow, see if I care!" *One thing's certain; I won't be here!*

"Work! Ha, what a joke!" Chris said in disgust, still upset about the cigarette incident earlier that week.

143

Stuart calmed down. "Sorry for my outburst, fellas," he lied. "I'm frustrated too, okay? But we still have one more day of bank surveillance. If we don't find Shelby McKin..." Stuart froze, then gulped hard.

"What did you say?" An alarm went off inside Chris Watkins' already suspicious mind. Finkel's explanation had been too clumsy.

"Shelby! I said Shelby, okay?" There was a three-second stare down, before Chris finally looked away. "Like I was saying," Stuart continued, "if we don't find her by tomorrow, you all know what the next step is. We're finding the buried treasure with or without Shelby, boys."

Ricky Clemmons and Jed Ashford never picked up on it.

Jed was replying to a text message on his cell phone.

Ricky was too busy thinking about Stuart's next move. "Do you really plan to harm your grandfather?" Ricky blurted out, disappointment on his face.

"You already know the answer, Ricky. Nothing personal. It's just business."

"Nothing personal?! It doesn't get any more personal than that, Stuart." Ricky took a deep breath and exhaled, "The moment you decide to do that is the moment I'm out. I don't want that on my conscience, man."

Of the four men, Ricky Clemmons was the least dangerous. He wasn't a ruthless person. He just had a bad habit of associating with the wrong people, those who came disguised as friends.

If Stuart hadn't already found Shelby McKinney, he would be scheming for a quick retort. But no such retort was needed. "Let's just let tomorrow take care of itself, okay Ricky?"

Ricky looked down at his feet and remained silent. He feared for his friend. *You really do need psychiatric help, Stu!*

"Listen, I can't handle this right now. My head's throbbing. I need to catch up on my sleep. See you all tomorrow." Stuart pulled out of the 7-11 parking lot without confirming each man's location.

Chris Watkins knew something wasn't right. Stuart was acting far too strangely. Had he already forced his grandfather to take him the buried treasure? Did he have it in his possession? After all, he seemed to know Shelby's last name.

"I have a very bad feeling, guys," Chris said softly to Jed and Ricky. His mind raced with a million thoughts; none of them good.

"Me too," Jed and Ricky both said at the same time.

144

28

STUART FINKEL STAGGERED UP the steps leading to his apartment in a drunken stupor. This wasn't the first time and certainly wouldn't be the last. Normally Finkel was a miserable drunk. And an angry one.

Instead of providing a temporary release, like the consumption of alcohol did for many, being drunk always forced Finkel to realize how pathetic his life had turned out to be. But not now.

Stuart Finkel was the jolliest drunk in America this night.

The air was drenched with humidity. A few stray thundershowers were in the area, but nothing too threatening; just some distant thunder and a few flashes of lightning in the distance.

Moths and mosquitoes crowded the light fixture above Finkel's front door. Crickets chirped in the grass below, holding a concert of sorts for all to hear. But the frogs in the small pond behind the old rundown apartment complex stole the show.

There had to be hundreds of them communicating in a language only they understood, without the slightest regard for the mass of humanity trying to sleep at this ungodly hour.

Also hovering in the darkness were the demons assigned to Finkel. They followed his every move like an invisible shadow, growling and snarling and screaming in his ears, "You're a nobody! You're a loser! You're worthless! God hates you!"

Their grossly misshapen faces were mere inches from his face. Their snakelike tongues slithered, licking his cheeks everywhere, wishing it was his soul instead. Their jaundice eyes burned spiritual holes in his body, but Finkel was totally oblivious to it all.

They weren't the only demons present. Others were fast approaching...

In Stuart's condition, it could have been 3:30 in the morning, not 1:30. The clock inside his old pick-up truck stopped ticking years ago. And he didn't own a watch. Not including his cell phone, the only other clock he owned that still worked was on the other side of the door on a small wooden table beside his unkempt bed.

But Finkel didn't care what time it was. He was drunk and tired and just wanted to sleep it off.

After leaving his three ex-partners at the 7-11 parking lot, he purchased a six-pack of Budweiser beer and celebrated his victory alone, poolside at the Outrigger Beach Resort, where the McKinneys were staying.

Before going to the pool area, Stuart searched the hotel parking looking for their minivan. He didn't see it but wasn't overly concerned. He figured they were still out scouring Sanibel Beach.

One way or the other, he knew they'd be back at some point. Hopefully with the buried treasure! That would be just perfect!

Finkel was finishing his third beer when the McKinneys finally arrived, looking sunburned and exhausted. He watched them swim in the pool together, followed by a short stroll on the beach.

They seemed like such a nice family. *Oh well, such is life. Survival of the fittest.*

Finkel remained poolside long after the McKinneys were tucked away for the night. After the beer was gone, he left for home. This was the best day he'd had in a very long time.

In a perfect world, he would have a room at the Outrigger, so he could monitor the McKinneys' every move. But he wasn't about to spend 120 bucks for a hotel room. If he did, he'd be out of money in no time. What little he had left needed to last until the treasure was located and he stole it from Shelby at gunpoint.

But there was another reason Finkel chose to celebrate his great victory at the Outrigger Beach Resort. If he went to one of his favorite watering holes, chances were good he would have run into Vinnie and Carlos! His deadline passed at midnight, and that meant they were out looking for him.

Not only did he not have the $3,000 interest payment due, he never bothered to call asking for an extension. *Definitely not smart,* he thought. *They'll get their money soon enough!*

Finkel had done a good job of dodging them up to now. His luck was about to run out. Fishing inside his pocket for his keys, he felt a thump on the back of the head and fell hard to the ground.

When he finally came to, he saw stars. He rubbed the back of his head, thankful it wasn't bleeding. But he writhed in pain. Once the alcohol wore off, he would really feel it.

Looking up through blurred vision, Stuart saw Vinnie and Carlos glaring back at him. Vinnie's slicked back, jet-black hair was dimly illuminated from the light fixture above his head.

The demons assigned to both men swarmed about, wrestling mightily with Stuart's demons.

146

Vinnie and Carlos weren't handsome men. Their faces were too harsh for that, their cheeks too gaunt, their eyes too fierce. Both men had noticeable beer bellies, but still maintained hardened upper bodies, which was necessary in their line of work.

The two thugs grabbed an arm and lifted Stuart to his feet. "So, you thought you could get away from us again, huh, Stuey?" said Vinnie.

"No," Stuart lied. "What makes you think that?"

Carlos ignored his meaningless words. "Where were you tonight, Stuey?"

"I didn't have the money."

"Yeah. You even quit your job. How convenient." Vinnie grabbed Finkel by the nape of his neck and pulled him close enough to guess the brand of beer he drank. "Did you really think you could disappear without paying us?"

"I have every intention of paying back every cent."

"You got that right," Carlos barked. "For your sake you better have the three G's on you now."

Finkel's eyes grew wide with fear. Beads of sweat formed on his forehead. "I need a little more time. Just a few more days even."

"Sorry, Stuey, time's up!" There was this twisted look on Vinnie's face that would frighten even the most hardened criminal. His nose was irregular, and many who met him wondered in silence if it had ever been broken. His eyes projected an unyielding nature that could love or hate with equal ferocity.

"I'm so close to paying back every dime I owe. And not just the interest. Honest!"

"Yeah, yeah, yeah." Vinnie never believed his clients. They weren't the trusting sort. All they did was lie.

"I'm serious, Vinnie." Stuart was never more terrified for his life.

Vinnie rolled his eyes as if to say, "Here we go again." He released his grip and played along. "Okay, Stuey, indulge me."

How much should I tell them? "This is gonna sound a little far-fetched, but here it goes. Last Friday I happened to be at the right place at the right time. My grandfather had a client who died."

The two men looked at each other totally unamused. "And your point?" Carlos said.

"My point is," Finkel said in a whisper, trying not to wake his neighbors, "the man left a huge inheritance to his granddaughter. I'm a day or two from finding the exact location. Once I do, I'll pay back every cent I owe."

"Not good enough, Stuey," Vinnie and Carlos both said in unison. It had long become their custom.

"It's gonna have to be." Stuart winced at his own words, fully expecting another backlash from the two thugs. It never came. He took it as a good sign.

147

He continued, "Finding this money is the only chance I have of paying you back. If you break my legs, you'll never see your money."

"Oh, we'll see it, Stuey. One way or the other, we'll get our money. You have my word on that." Vinnie inched in closer, "Never forget; we know where your mother lives. Surely you don't want to see her get hurt because you're such a loser, do you?"

"That's not fair, fellas. Leave my mother out of this."

Vinnie poked Stuart hard in the chest. "You're in no position for fairness! We should break you into a million pieces right now, you lowlife!"

"I should've called. I'm sorry. But you know I'm good for it. I always pay you back…"

"Yeah. But only after we threaten to break your legs!" What Carlos saw in Finkel's eyes told him his words had landed hard.

He did have a point. "The reason I quit my job is that I'm looking at such a huge payoff. But it's a twenty-four-hour surveillance job. Once the money's mine, I plan to pay back the entire ten G's."

"It's thirteen G's, you moron!" Vinnie was growing angrier by the minute.

"That's what I meant."

Vinnie and Carlos were tired of Finkel's empty promises. Carlos nodded, and Vinnie threw their client to the ground hard, pinning him down on the cement with the old knee-to-the-gut move.

Removing a cigarette from the pack in Stuart's shirt pocket, Vinnie lit up and blew the smoke directly into his face. He took another long drag and reached for the pistol underneath his shirt.

"Open wide, Stuey!" The gunman jammed the 9mm Beretta in Stuart's mouth and moved it around briskly. It made a distinct clanking sound when touching his teeth.

Finkel's eyes grew as wide as silver dollars.

Cocking the trigger, Vinnie said, "I'm sick and tired of your games, Stuey! And your lies!" He took another long drag from the cigarette. "You have three days, THREE DAYS, to come up with the money! Don't mess up. You won't get another chance…" he said, poking Stuart in the chest with his free hand. "You hear me?"

Finkel nodded yes. He was too petrified to speak. Had he tried, his words would have been unintelligible anyway, with a gun shoved inside his mouth.

Vinnie mercilessly pulled the gun from Finkel's mouth, chipping one of his upper front teeth in the process. "You better understand!" the money collector said, with a seriousness Stuart had never heard uttered before.

Stuart let out a deep, rasping gasp and sucked in a lung full of air.

The gunman wiped Finkel's blood off the tip of his pistol without breaking eye contact with him. He stood and looked down at his deadbeat client. The spineless weasel.

"If we have to come looking for you again, you better pray we don't find you. Am I making myself clear?"

Finkel didn't respond. Eyes full of pain, his mind was incapable of forming any sort of response.

"I said, am I clear?" Vinnie kicked Stuart in the ribs as hard as he could with his right foot. He wondered if he broke a rib or two in the process.

"Owwwwwwwww!" Finkel curled up tightly in anguish, writhing in severe pain. "Yes!" It came out of his mouth in a pained grunt. His coffee and nicotine-stained teeth had a fresh coating of blood on them. Some of it trickled out of his mouth and slowly dripped onto the concrete.

"That's better," the gruff-talking man said. "See you in three days, Stuey."

Vinnie's demons glared at Finkel, snarling and slobbering all over themselves.

Before leaving, Carlos did his customary pocket search for money. Experience had taught him nine times out of ten, their clients usually had something on them. He removed everything from inside Stuart's short pockets.

Sure enough, he found almost $300 in cash. Carlos pocketed it, leaving Finkel with nothing.

Worse, Stuart knew it wouldn't go toward paying off his debt. It was more of a "three-day grace period tip" to Vinnie and Carlos for sparing his ridiculous life.

At least for three more days...

Finished with Finkel, the money collectors left him twisting in pain on the ground and rushed down the stairs, taking them two at a time. They pulled away just as a nosy neighbor, awakened by the commotion, opened her front door, "Get out of here, you hoodlums, or I'm calling the police! People are trying to sleep here!"

"It's okay, they're gone now," Stuart whispered to the older woman.

"I wish you would leave too!" she said, slamming the door.

Finkel wiped blood from his mouth, "Soon enough..."

Stuart picked himself up off the ground using the railing for support. His ribs weren't broken, but they were severely bruised. He had difficulty catching his breath. Even drunk, he knew he wouldn't forget this frightening encounter come morning time.

149

He was in serious trouble. The only way out of this mess was to find the buried treasure before Vinnie and Carlos found him again. If he didn't come up with the $3,000 in three days, the pain he felt now was a mere hiccup, compared to the next round of pain.

Finkel needed to stop drinking alcoholic beverages for the time being. The next time he'd have a beer would be after he found the money and paid his debt to Vinnie and Carlos. Then he would celebrate. Until then, he would go cold turkey. Besides, he didn't even have money for food, let alone beer. *Should have slept at the hotel. I'd still be broke; but at least I'd be pain free.*

"It's amazing how far a man will actually go to lie," Carlos said to Vinnie, en route to meet another client whose deadline expired at midnight.

"That Stuart is something else!"

"Do you believe his bogus story?"

"Come on, Carlos. Are you serious?" Vinnie shot a quick glance at his partner. "You're still high, aren't you?"

"How can you tell?" Carlos burst out in laughter. The dark-skinned man always wore a bandanna on his head. And his face was usually covered with patches of scruffy hair.

While Vinnie was more clean cut than Carlos, his heart was infinitely more wicked than his partner's. If ever crossed, which happened on occasion, Vinnie's dark, piercing eyes produced pools of malice, rage and hatred, to the point of murder toward the poor soul who'd foolishly crossed his path. It was enough to send shivers up one's spine, including Carlos'.

Vinnie snorted. "For starters, your eyes are glassy. And your pupils are dilated. Which leads me to conclude that you must still be in la-la land if you actually believe Finkel's bogus story."

Carlos cracked up, very much sounding like a hyena. "I'm still high, bro. Not gonna deny it," he said. "But come on, Vinnie, let's just pretend..."

"You know how it is when the Stuart Finkels of the world are desperate! They make up the wildest stories!"

"Yeah, but who would have thought old Stuey could think so quickly, with a gun in his mouth and all." Carlos lit a cigarette and took a long drag. "Some imagination he has! He should have been a playwright or something."

"Playwright, ha! I think it was more desperation on his part than imagination!"

"You're probably right. But what if there really is a buried treasure to speak of?" Carlos took another drag from his cigarette and decided to protest a little more. "What if he's really onto something?"

"Okay, Carlos, I'll play along." Vinnie lit a cigarette. "If there really is a buried treasure to speak of, the answer's simple; why should that lowlife have sole access to it! That's not fair, is it?"

"Not at all. Especially since it's not even his to begin with. We have just as much right to it as he does."

"Yup," said Vinnie, now thinking a mile a minute.

"If there's a treasure to speak of," Carlos said, taking another drag from his cigarette and blowing it outside the car window, "why can't we cash-in on it instead of him?"

"What are you saying, Carlos?"

"We already gave him three more days, right?"

"Yeah..."

"Let's follow him around and see if he's telling the truth or not. I mean, what can it hurt?"

"You do have a point..." Taking a few moments to think things through, Vinnie decided against all logic to buy into Finkel's ridiculous story for the time being. "If there's a treasure to speak of, one thing is certain; Finkel will never see a dime of it!"

Fully aware of the big picture, the demons assigned to both men were determined to do all they could to help them succeed with this crucial mission. The more people involved, the more difficult it would be for Shelby McKinney to walk away from this adventure with her buried inheritance once it was unearthed.

If successful, Luther Mellon's granddaughter would never know about the second safe-deposit box, which was the main reason Satan assigned so many demons to this mission in the first place.

If the bad guys ended up killing each other in the process that would be perfect, because any human being leaving Planet Earth without first placing their complete trust in the Lord Jesus Christ for their eternal salvation, were doomed for all eternity, equating to the ultimate accomplishment for Satan's side...

Vinnie said, "We'll pay off his thirteen-grand debt to Bossman, then split the rest fifty-fifty."

"Sounds like a winner. And Finkel won't be in any position to negotiate. He'll just have to accept our terms, or else. Oh well, that's life."

"At least he'll be free of Bossman. He should already be thanking us!"

The way Vinnie said it made Carlos laugh like a hyena again. Part of it was the drugs, he knew. Vinnie shot a greedy grin at his stoned partner and cranked up the music full blast, totally unaware that the devil himself was staring at them both with his mouth wide open. If God would only allow it, the two money collectors would be quickly swallowed up, forever lost.

The demons assigned to them followed their every move. If only they could materialize for the human world to see, it would look like they were flapping, clawing and whirring in sync to the beat of the vulgar rap music screaming from the speakers in Vinnie's car.

The two thugs were totally unaware of their presence. All Vinnie and Carlos knew was the physical world—a world that was rough and tough at times, especially for those who owed their boss money and told numerous lies to buy a little more time.

But compared to the always active and extremely dangerous spirit world, which occupied every inch of the universe, the rough and tough world they knew was like *Romper Room*.

29

SATURDAY JUNE 25 - DAY 15

"I'M GOING FOR A walk," Shelby said softly to Jesse. "Be back a little later."

"Where you going?"

"Sanibel Island to get a better lay of the land. I want to be prepared when we go there later."

"Good thinking, babe," Jesse said, still half asleep.

"Like you said yesterday; time's running out." Jesse didn't need to remind her of this. The time factor was starting to consume Shelby from within. "Besides, I always do my best thinking when strolling the beach alone."

"Just don't start digging without us."

"I won't."

"Be careful," Jesse said, his mouth stretched into a yawn.

Shelby kissed her husband on the cheek and left. She grabbed a cup of coffee in the hotel lobby, then took U.S. 41 to Cypress Lake Drive, and turned left. When she reached Summerlin Road, she took another left and headed straight onto Sanibel Causeway.

She pulled up to the toll booth, paid the $6 toll then drove three miles until she reached Sanibel Island. Before parking her vehicle, she drove up and down West Gulf Drive hoping that something would jump out at her. Nothing did.

But one thing was certain; this was a beautiful island. With so many overhanging trees dotting the landscape, it reminded her of Charleston, South Carolina, except it was more tropical and much less congested. Even at peak season, Sanibel Island boasted a population of only six-thousand people.

But the biggest difference between the two locations was that there were no tall buildings, hotels, or high-rise condominiums here. Not counting the lighthouse, it seemed there wasn't a single structure on the island taller than five stories. This could pose a serious problem when looking for significant landmarks.

Not only that, though Sanibel Island was situated three miles out in the Gulf of Mexico, most of the roads didn't offer prolonged views of the Gulf of Mexico, only a few glimpses here and there.

With the second "111" clue being a beachfront landmark, Shelby realized she might do more walking on this beach than originally planned.

153

The McKinneys had toured the lighthouse before leaving the island the previous night and learned it was constructed back in 1884. Not only was it Sanibel's most famous landmark, it was the oldest structure on the island. With so many visitors, it could never be considered as overlooked by anyone.

Definitely not the second "111" clue!

Shelby parked her vehicle at the Old Town section of Sanibel Island, near the lighthouse, and started walking the beach. She was fiercely determined to succeed this time.

Following from a distance in a very foul mood—every step a new adventure in pain—was Stuart Finkel. Every breath he took was a stark reminder of what Vinnie and Carlos did to him the night before. He never bothered combing his hair this morning. His head hurt too much from being popped by Carlos.

And thanks to Vinnie, the inside of his mouth was shredded in so many places, after Vinnie ripped the gun out with brute force, causing him to lose part of a tooth as a result. It was sensitive to the touch. The gentle sea breeze wasn't helping matters much.

In short, Stuart Finkel was in agony. To make matter's worse, he was hung over, broke and never more fearful for his life. Before leaving his apartment, the battered man packed five peanut butter and jelly sandwiches for lunch and dinner, a half-empty box of Ritz crackers, and filled a jug with water from the kitchen faucet.

Finkel then rolled coins on the bedroom floor for toll money. If there was one thing he was thankful for, when he purchased the six pack of beer the day before, he also filled his gas tank full of gas and bought a carton of cigarettes. He had plenty of both for now.

But with sore ribs, inhaling and exhaling cigarette smoke was extremely unpleasant.

Walking the beach with a severe limp wasn't good in the spying business. Too many people took notice. But at least Shelby wasn't among his many gawkers. She still had no idea who he was or that she was even being followed.

"Come on, Shelby, you need to find it today! I desperately need this money!"

Stuart was struck with a thought; he remembered Shelby telling the bank manager something about only having three days left to work with. Did this mean they were going back to South Carolina soon? He prayed not.

Meanwhile, the clock inside Shelby's head kept ticking louder by the minute. As much as she was enjoying herself, she would enjoy it so much more once she deciphered the second "111" clue.

154

All she knew for now was that it represented some magnificent landmark which was overlooked by so many passersby each day. It also represented three objects, all of which provided shelter and safe refuge for so many, whatever that meant. Fifty steps due west of it, buried six feet beneath the surface, was her inheritance.

Other than that, Shelby McKinney was totally clueless...

After two hours of scouring Sanibel Beach, back and forth, up and down, Shelby made no progress whatsoever. It would have been so much easier had her late grandfather included a list with Sanibel Island's top 100 landmarks on it. Had he only done that, they could visit each landmark and cross them off the list, one by one, until they finally found it, much like she did with each bank location.

But there was no such list.

Did this small island even have 100 landmarks dotting its landscape? Shelby seriously doubted it.

Were there 50 landmarks? She wondered.

Shelby walked back to the van, slightly dehydrated from the hot sun and all that walking. She needed a shower or a swim in the pool.

The only real productivity on her part so far came in the form of exercise. As her family slept soundly she burned calories, which was good. But she would gladly trade all those burned calories straight up for the meaning of the second "111" clue.

Hopefully I'll have better luck later with Jesse and the kids, she thought, starting the engine.

Stuart Finkel picked himself up off the beach and limped back to his pick-up truck ever so gingerly, wincing in pain every step of the way. When he saw Shelby's face up close, the pain worsened.

It was evident she was no closer now than when she first took to the beach two hours ago.

Finkel gulped hard. He, too, had a clock ticking inside his head. No, it wasn't ticking. Thanks to his painful encounter with Vinnie and Carlos, it was screaming nonstop, torturing every fiber of his being. Not even Tylenol was helping.

It felt like his brain had jarred itself loose inside his head. He tried massaging his scalp using all ten of his fingers, but it didn't help. The pain was so excruciating he couldn't think at times.

Stuart Finkel felt like he wanted to die. The only remedy to nurse him back to good health was to find the buried treasure chest. More to the point, steal it from Shelby, at gunpoint, the moment it was finally unearthed.

155

Once he did that, to avoid capture from the police, he would take I-75 north to Panama City for a few days and think things through before making his next move. He was already prepared to go to Mexico or Canada, if need be.

Before leaving the island, Shelby stopped at the visitor's center, to see what she could learn about Sanibel Island—especially its landmarks, whatever they were!

Stuart pulled in behind her and remained inside his vehicle. He lit a smoke—only his third of the day—and called Ricky Clemmons but got his voice mail. "Hey, Ricky, just calling to see what's going on there. Call me if you have exciting news to share with me."

Twenty minutes later, Shelby McKinney left the visitor's center a little more educated on Sanibel Island. She made sure to grab a brochure from each slot in the rack on her way out the door, hoping that something on one of the brochures would jump out at her.

One brochure that sparked her interest was a place called, J.N. Ding Darling National Wildlife Refuge. Its 7,000 acres of mangrove estuary was used to house more than 200 different species of birds, alligators, otters and various other wildlife species.

Refuge, hmm. Could it be buried there? Not only was it a refuge, an admission fee was required to tour the grounds. The second "111" clue fell under the "no free rides" umbrella...*Could it be?*

"One way to find out…" Shelby left at once and steadied the van across the causeway back to the hotel in Fort Myers Beach.

After a quick swim in the hotel pool and a fast-food lunch, the McKinneys were back on Sanibel Island.

The first place they visited was J.N. Ding Darling National Wildlife Refuge Educational Center.

Jesse perused the map. "They have kayak and canoe trails here."

"Can we go canoeing, Daddy?" Trevor said. He and BJ went canoeing with Uncle Jake the previous summer and really enjoyed themselves.

"Sure. Let's do it." Jesse said to his eldest son.

"Why don't you take them. I want to take a good look around."

"You won't join us?" Jesse wanted to protest more but saw the desperation in his wife's eyes. "Let's go kids."

In the 90 minutes Jesse and the kids canoed up and down the river, Shelby was able to explore a good portion of the wildlife refuge. But the more she walked the grounds, the more burying it there made no sense to her.

156

Not only that, it wasn't located directly on the beach. B Shelby wouldn't rule it out just yet. Nothing could be considered outside the realm of possibility on this wacky adventure.

The McKinneys left the wildlife refuge and scoured the beach for three hours, hoping to solve the second "111" clue, but still found nothing. Even Trevor the boy-genius wanted to throw in the towel.

They took a break from walking in favor of driving the island. After three trips up and down the island, Jesse was getting frustrated. "Why don't we try our luck on Captiva Island?"

"Sure, why not," Shelby replied, also losing a little more hope as the minutes passed.

Thirty minutes later, Jesse steadied the van onto Captiva Island, as Shelby and the kids looked at brochures, hoping to find anything that might help the cause. Everyone was hungry.

Jesse pulled into the parking lot of the Bubble Room Restaurant. They waited 15 minutes before being seated.

"If we had a little more to go on, like a treasure map, for instance," Jesse said, twirling Chicken Alfredo on his fork, "or even a few more clues, it would certainly help. It's like we're totally blindfolded, with no compass to guide us. How could anyone succeed under such conditions?"

Shelby tried ignoring her husband's growing skepticism, so she could enjoy her shrimp and scallop scampi, but it was impossible. She was unaware that she had demons assigned to her life, and that they were behind the wheel of the ship called, "Despair". They were doing all they could to crash her ship of dreams into a deadly iceberg.

The remaining sand inside the hourglass was rapidly falling to the bottom.

Shelby glanced at her children; the exuberance they felt at Friendly's was gone. Their faces once again screamed, "Find it yourself, Momma! Once you do, we'll dig the hole for you! Until then, leave us alone!"

After a nice meal, the McKinneys were back on San-Cap Road, headed southeast toward Sanibel Beach.

Nearing the causeway, Jesse said, "What do you say we head back to the hotel for a quick swim before it gets too late?"

"Sure, whatever," Shelby said, the feeling of despair intensifying. *Why can't I find it?*

Jesse looked at his wife of 10 years. "Hey, don't look so down. We still have tomorrow, right?"

When Shelby didn't reply, Jesse turned on a country music station to hopefully break the somber mood inside the minivan.

Fifteen minutes later, the McKinneys were back on Fort Myers Beach.

157

30

AT 10:15 P.M. THE next night, as Jesse spent the last night of his summer vacation swimming in the pool with Trevor, BJ and Brooke, Shelby, took one last walk on the beach. She decided to go alone so her family wouldn't see her crying.

She felt like a complete and total failure. How could she not, having walked so many miles on Sanibel Beach and Captiva Island (where she spent most of the day as Jesse remained on Fort Myers Beach with the kids), and digging dozens of holes in the sand?

She had blistered hands and feet to prove it.

Even more debilitating was that she felt certain at some point that she'd walked near or even directly over top of her inheritance. Perhaps many times over! As exciting as being so close without finding it may have sounded on the surface, it only increased the awful dread she felt inside.

Shelby looked up in the evening sky and saw many low-lying clouds steadily passing beneath the moon. Yet the moon stood firm, unchanged, unmoved. Even the dull pulse of flat stars sprinkled throughout the dark evening sky glimmered softly, showing some form of movement. But not the moon. It remained stoically silent.

But why? What was its purpose for being? Was it there only to provide light for Planet Earth in the darkness?

Shelby honestly didn't know. For the first time in her life, she wondered what it all meant. Was there a Source in the universe that remained calm and unchanged—much like the moon—despite the constant chaos humanity wrestled with on Planet Earth? Why were those rain-less clouds even there? What purpose did they serve? Especially at nighttime! Were they even necessary?

Shelby felt just like one of them—an aimless drifter, a rain-less cloud, purposeless. She, too, was moving ever so quickly in life, but where was she going? Why am I even here on this crazy planet? Is there some unknown purpose for my life that stretches beyond being a wife and mother like Grandpa said in the letter? Is there Divine Order in the universe or just random semi-organized chaos?

Shelby wondered why it took 33 years to finally contemplate such things. After a moment's reflection, it was starting to freak her out. She blinked these troublesome thoughts away and looked out across the Gulf of Mexico.

Seeing Sanibel Beach lit up from a distance, despair washed over her again. *What's wrong with me? Why can't I solve the second "111" clue?*

Shelby burst out in tears. A few moments later, she dried her tear-swollen eyes and had a sudden thought; why not call Bernie Finkel and offer him a portion of her inheritance, if he would only agree to decipher the second "111" clue for her?

Better yet, if he cut to the chase and revealed the exact location, she would sweeten the pot even more. Then she could dig all night, if need be, and unearth it before leaving Florida in the morning.

As tempting as it sounded, it wasn't part of her late grandfather's plan. Shelby already felt guilty for calling the Florida lawyer last week, not to mention her visit to Flamingo Club Condominiums.

Even if her intentions were motivated by more by desperation than greed, the guilt still lingered. Was Bernie Finkel an honorable man? Even if he was, he didn't offer to assist her last time.

Why would he suddenly change his mind now? Shelby knew the answer; money. Even so, she couldn't bring herself to call him...

STUART FINKEL LOITERED THE beach at a safe distance behind Shelby, limping ever so gingerly.

With the passing of 48 hours, the bump on the back of his head felt somewhat better. But the same couldn't be said about the rest of him. The bruised ribs and lacerations inside his mouth still hadn't healed. It felt like he had piping hot pizza stuck to the roof of his mouth for too long.

Finkel still couldn't eat solid foods. The only way he was able to eat the PB&J sandwiches was by taking small bites and letting them dissolve in his own saliva—sometimes mixed with blood—until he was finally able to swallow.

With his three-day grace period set to expire, Vinnie and Carlos would be looking for him again. He observed Shelby standing down by the water's edge. Judging by her slumped shoulders, he sensed she wouldn't be finding the buried treasure anytime soon. *Not good!*

Even worse, after overhearing her two sons at the pool earlier, Finkel knew they were leaving for home in the morning. And who knew what that meant? Would it be the end of the treasure hunt?

Stuart certainly hoped not. As pathetic as it sounded, stealing the buried inheritance once Shelby found it was the only future he had to look forward to. Which meant he needed to continue monitoring the McKinneys at all costs, no matter what! But how?

Suddenly a light bulb went off inside Finkel's still-throbbing head. Not only would this plan allow him to keep monitoring the McKinney family up close and personal, it would give him a much-needed break from Vinnie and Carlos.

Once the family from South Carolina were bedded down for the night, he would pay a quick visit to his mother's house. *Time to ask for another favor*, Finkel thought, suddenly energized again.

SHELBY LEFT THE BEACH and rejoined her family by the pool. "I think it's time to call it a night, y'all."

"Why, Momma?" BJ was splashing around in the pool with his two newest best friends, two boys his age from Virginia.

"We have a long drive home tomorrow, son."

BJ looked into his mother's tear-swollen eyes and knew now wasn't the time to protest her command.

"Are you okay, honey?" Jesse said.

"I'm fine..." Shelby became teary-eyed again and looked away, "I'll see y'all up in the room."

"We'll stay a few more minutes, so you can have a little more time to yourself."

"Okay," Shelby said, slowly walking away.

Jesse got out of the pool and dried himself off. Seeing his wife so upset pierced him deeply. "Twenty more minutes, kids, then it's time for bed."

"Okay, Daddy," came the reply from Trevor.

An hour later, everyone was sound asleep, everyone except Shelby. Even with Jesse's arms wrapped ever so tightly around her, she couldn't sleep.

The way she felt, she'd be lucky to get two hours of sleep this night, if that...

VINNIE AND CARLOS WERE seated at a Tiki bar at a hotel adjacent to the Outrigger, chugging beers, monitoring things from a distance. After following Stuart Finkel the past two days, both men were convinced he was onto something after all.

Vinnie spotted Stuart walking to his truck in the Outrigger Beach Resort parking lot. He and Carlos finished their beers and left at once to see what Finkel would do next. They followed him straight to his mother's house. He spent 30 minutes there before heading home.

160

"Man, oh man, Vinnie, you really did a number on him," Carlos said, watching Finkel limping to his truck, still wincing in pain.

"He'll live." Vinnie couldn't help but wonder why Stuart looked so energetic, despite his current predicament. Something wasn't right. "I think it's time to involve our contact in Port Charlotte."

"Why's that?" said Carlos, a little confused.

"Just a hunch I have." Vinnie sent a text message to Mark Chong, their surveillance contact in Port Charlotte, then dropped Carlos off at home. "Be ready any time tomorrow, Carlos."

"You know I'm always ready, Vinnie," he said. "Just call me!"

"Okay, bro. See you in the morning." Vinnie left for home still trapped beneath a canopy of demons...

31

MONDAY JUNE 27 - DAY 17

THE UNMISTAKABLE LOOK OF devastation, despair and failure, were clearly chiseled onto Shelby's face—much of it demonically induced—as the McKinneys began the long trek back to South Carolina.

Shelby wanted to plead with her husband to turn the car around, that if they'd just had a little more time, a few more days in fact, she felt certain she would have found the buried treasure. They were too close to give up and go home now.

But Jesse couldn't turn the car around. He wanted to find the buried treasure as badly as everyone else did, but he had a job to go back to in the morning. Jesse sympathized with his wife, he really did, but vacation time was over. It was time to get back to reality.

Shelby wasn't mad at him. It wasn't his fault they were leaving. She knew all along she only had one week with which to work. Besides, how could she possibly be mad when he did a marvelous job all week encouraging her and shielding the children from the many shortcomings this adventure had presented?

Even with the many ups and downs, mostly thanks to him the kids still had a nice vacation. Though a little unorthodox, to say the least, they swam each day, played on the beach, and went bike riding and canoeing. Most importantly, they went to Disney World.

For all intents and purposes, it turned out to be a pretty good vacation for them. Only they wouldn't get to come home with the buried treasure.

Whereas Jesse thought that nothing went according to plan, aside from the day spent at Disney World, Shelby begged to differ. Even with the many shortcomings, they found the safe-deposit box and deciphered the first "111" clue, greatly narrowing the search from just under 1,200 miles of Florida coastline to just twelve.

To Shelby, this was a significant achievement. Even so, she failed to come home with the prize.

Driving north on I-75, conversation between the married couple was minimal. They reached I-4 two hours later and traveled eastbound.

Sure enough, as they neared Orlando, Trevor, BJ and Brooke saw the many billboard signs showcasing Orlando's many theme parks and

162

attractions, and their childlike depression returned, knowing they wouldn't be stopping this time.

Once Orlando was behind them, the children settled down again.

They reached I-95 and proceeded north. Two hours later, after nearly six full hours of driving in the state of Florida, they reached the Georgia state line.

Shelby saw the *Welcome to Georgia* sign and a teardrop rode down her cheek. Then another. Then, for the hundredth time since receiving the news that her grandfather had died, the faucet inside her head was turned back on full blast. She wept uncontrollably.

Brooke started sobbing too, as if to comfort her mother.

It didn't help.

Jesse got off at the first exit and pulled into a gas station. He would kill two birds with one stone. Three birds, actually. He would gas up the van, comfort his grieving wife and daughter, and eat lunch.

Everyone got out to stretch their legs, except Shelby. She needed time to collect herself.

While fueling, Jesse gathered Brooke into his arms. "You okay, sweetie?"

Brooke nodded yes, still teary-eyed.

"You okay, boys?"

"Yes, Daddy," Trevor and BJ said in unison. But Jesse knew what they were thinking; would Momma revert back to how she was before receiving GG's letter? He could see it in their eyes.

Gathering his three children into his arms, he said, "Momma'll be fine. She just needs a little time to accept it all. Besides, the search isn't over. There's still plenty of time. For now, we must remain strong for her, okay?"

"Yes, Daddy."

"Yes, Daddy."

"Yes, Daddy."

"I'm so proud of y'all," he said.

All three children half-smiled.

After quick lunch at a *Taco Bell*, the McKinneys were back on I-95 headed north. Even without taking the much longer U.S. 17 this time, the drive home seemed so much longer than the ride down.

Shelby wondered for the thousandth time where she possibly could have miscalculated, and what more she could have done to maximize her time in the Sunshine State. It sounded selfish, she knew, but part of her regretted the time spent in Orlando.

An extra day and a half was like gold in her hands now...

Perhaps if she had two more days on Sanibel Island, they'd be driving home with the treasure chest, instead of coming home empty handed. Before leaving Fort Myers, as her family slept, Shelby drove to the island one last time looking for something, anything, hoping for a last-minute miracle, but it never materialized.

She silently feared she may never know what her grandfather had left there for her. On the drive down to Florida, everything looked so beautiful; so promising. Now it was one big blur again.

Shelby knew the reason; mental stimulation versus mental torture. It really was that simple.

They arrived home at 7:30 p.m. with a Chinese take-out order Jesse picked up on the way.

At 9:00 p.m. everyone was exhausted. Once the kids were bedded down for the night, Jesse was next.

Shelby halfheartedly said she would join him shortly, but Jesse knew better. Even exhausted, there was no way she could sleep.

It was forecast to dip into the low 60's. With the slightly cooler temperatures, Jesse felt no need to turn on the AC.

Opening a window in the master bedroom, he noticed a red pick-up truck slowly drive by the house. He gave it a quick glance, but nothing more. Cars and trucks drove by all the time, day and night.

Jesse felt no need to worry. He had no idea it was the tenth time the red truck had passed by the house. Nor did he know the driver of the truck was a man he never met before, but who'd followed his family all the way from Florida.

Jesse hit the shower totally unaware that they were being stalked by a ruthless psychopath.

Shelby, too, had no idea that a man named Stuart Finkel was parked one-tenth of a mile from her driveway, or that he'd followed them all the way from Florida.

Shelby made herself a hot cup of tea and sat at her computer desk. Now that she was back home, she felt even more trapped, even more powerless.

What could she possibly do in South Carolina to help the situation now? The answer was dreadfully obvious; nothing!

It was a bitter pill to swallow. *Will I ever find my inheritance?*

Shelby didn't know.

All she knew was that she would never stop searching...

164

32

MEANWHILE, STUART FINKEL WAS quite proud of himself.

He felt certain the McKinneys had no idea they'd been followed. Had they known, he'd surely be facing tough questioning from the South Carolina police or possibly sitting in a jail cell.

A smile broke across his face, as he savored this small victory of sorts.

Stuart was thankful that his old Chevy pick-up truck survived the 400-mile trip, but not without a few anxious moments along the way. At one point, he smelled something burning underneath the hood. Light smoke poured out from the sides of the truck and the *check engine* light went on.

When the McKinneys stopped in Georgia for gas, Stuart checked the oil level in his truck. Sure enough, it was two quarts low. Adding oil seemed to do the trick. The *check engine* light went off and the acrid smell of burning oil, and whatever else had contributed to the toxic aroma, slowly dissipated.

Even with 180,000 miles on it, his old truck had always served him well. Still, as soon as the money was in-hand, he would upgrade to a newer vehicle.

Now parked for the night, Finkel shifted in his seat trying to find the most comfortable sleeping position. But with bruised ribs it was next to impossible. Staying at a cheap hotel would have been nice, but it was entirely out of the question for two reasons; 1) he didn't have the money and 2) he wanted to be ready in the morning in case something happened at the McKinney residence and he needed to move fast.

The biggest problem with sleeping in the truck, besides the total lack of comfort, was the bright moonlight. It seeped through the front windshield silhouetting his body like a massive floodlight.

Anyone within close-proximity could easily notice someone sleeping inside. But Stuart wasn't overly concerned. He'd proved to be quite the super spy outsmarting the McKinneys the way he had.

Perhaps I really did miss my true calling in life. Maybe I should have been a detective, instead of a crook.

"Yeah right," Finkel said with a hearty laugh, until it hurt his ribs too much.

Once convinced the McKinneys were sound asleep in their hotel room the night before, Finkel drove to his mother's house and somehow managed to swindle his mother out of yet another loan, only $100 this time.

"This is the last time, Stuart. Please don't ask me again!" Millie Finkel had said, handing the money over to her son. "I'm an old woman living on a fixed income. I'm not a bank!"

Stuart shrugged off the threat like it had never been made. It was nothing more than angry words coming from a lonely, emotional woman. She helped him last night, and Stuart was certain his mother would be there the next time he needed her as well.

That's just the way she was wired.

Millie wanted to toughen up and cut him off—much like her ex father-in-law, Bernie, had done—but she could never bring herself to do it. Stuart Jr. was eleven when Stuart Sr. left his mother for a younger woman in Arizona, turning Millie Finkel into a loner. She rarely left the house these days.

What Millie didn't know was when she went upstairs to fetch the money, Stuart reached into her handbag and snatched one of her rarely used credit cards. He justified this theft by promising only to use it for fuel and any unforeseen emergencies he might encounter along the way.

The cash would be used for cigarettes, food and drink...

Stuart shifted in his truck again, hoping he wouldn't have to stay in South Carolina for too long. Once the money ran out, he'd be forced to use his mother's credit card or head back to Florida.

Unless, of course, he robbed a local convenience store or gas station in Summerville. And there was always the McKinneys house to fall back on. He could be in and out in minutes. He wouldn't need much money, perhaps just a few hundred bucks to hold him over. Judging by the neighborhood they lived in, they wouldn't miss it.

But no matter how badly he needed the money, robbing a bank was entirely out of the question. The price of getting caught was just too high. Hopefully that could all be avoided.

With so much time and effort vested into this project, Finkel now believed he was entitled to Shelby's inheritance. He wasn't merely getting something for nothing anymore. He'd worked so hard up to this point, even suffering a nasty beating at the hands of his two money collectors along the way.

With his three-day grace period expiring, Stuart was certain that Vinnie and Carlos were out searching for him again. Being two states away comforted him greatly.

"Try to find me here, morons!" he said giggling, until it hurt his ribs too much.

Stuart envisioned them going from one joint to the next and leaving each place a little more frustrated than the last.

166

They'd undoubtedly questioned Jed Ashford, Chris Watkins and Ricky Clemmons by now. But even they had no idea where he was or that he'd even left the state of Florida.

All they knew was he never showed up for surveillance work on Saturday morning. They hadn't heard from him since.

After reading the latest note found taped to his apartment door—the third note this week—he knew his three ex-partners were furious with him! Finkel easily recognized the handwriting. It came from the hand of his best friend, Ricky Clemmons, basically accusing him of finding Shelby and ditching them, leaving them high and dry.

Stuart rolled it up into a ball like he did the other two notes and threw it in the trash can. He also received dozens of threatening voice messages from the three men, and a few from Vinnie and Carlos as well, all of which he ignored.

With his mind finally winding down, Finkel decided to let tomorrow take care of itself. Another hour passed before he was finally able to reach a tolerable position in his old truck and he slowly dozed off.

As long as the police didn't become suspicious with his vehicle being parked where it was—especially displaying an out-of-state tag—he didn't see any problem with it being parked where he was.

If local authorities or a nosy neighbor chose to inquire, Stuart would say his truck had overheated, he was low on cash and didn't want to leave it unattended. Compared to Vinnie and Carlos, dealing with the local authorities would be a walk in the park.

With those two dummies hundreds of miles away, Stuart was safe and secure for the evening. Or so he thought...

What Finkel didn't know was that he, too, had been followed and that Vinnie and Carlos were also in Summerville, South Carolina. Once convinced Stuey was parked for the night, the two money collectors checked into a hotel less than a mile from the McKinney residence.

Learning Finkel's whereabouts was no matter of sheer luck on their part. Carlos planted a GPS transponder beneath the bed of his truck, then hired Mark Chong, Bossman's freelance computer geek in Port Charlotte, to monitor his coordinates and contact them immediately if Stuart ever left the Fort Myers area.

A 50-mile radius was programmed into the GPS locator. Though Vinnie and Carlos had never met Mark Chong in person, their boss had retained his services numerous times for situations like this. They promised to pay him double his usual fee if he did a good job and kept his mouth shut. Not even their boss could know about it.

167

Mark Chong rolled his eyes on the phone but agreed to maintain a strict code of silence. After all, he needed the money. It always came down to the money. And this was easy money.

When Stuart reached mile marker #180 on I-75 north early this morning, Chong was alerted. He sent a text message to Vinnie, informing that Finkel was on the move.

But it wasn't until he reached Sarasota, 40 miles further north, that Vinnie was fully alarmed and told Carlos. He then told his boss he received a tip on Stuart's whereabouts, cleared their schedules for the day and raced north, then northeast, then north again, to monitor things up close and personal, only in invisible mode.

According to Mark Chong, by the time they reached the Georgia State line, they were only 50 miles behind Finkel. But even long before then, the two money collectors started piecing things together. Stuey was following that sweet, but unfortunate, family back to their home state of South Carolina.

Where else could he be going? Certainly not to dig up another beach in Florida. The fact that he was in Georgia confirmed that much. Old Stuey wasn't so dumb after all. But he wasn't intelligent enough to know they were spying on him as diligently as he was spying on the family from South Carolina.

As Vinnie and Carlos settled into comfy beds, both men felt confident their plan was working nicely.

Even better, while Finkel was certain to wake up with a stiff neck in the morning, to go along with his severely bruised ribs, the two money collectors would be well rested.

Much like Stuart, they had no idea what the sunrise would bring. They just hoped it would be something good.

But what they did know was, unlike Finkel—who was accountable to no one—they had Bossman to deal with. And this meant they were on a very strict time limit. Otherwise, he might catch on and demand to know their exact location, and possibly send in reinforcements. Maybe he'd be so furious that he'd take the next flight to Charleston, South Carolina, to deal with Stuart personally.

If Finkel thought they were lunatics, Bossman was infinitely worse. He would beat him senseless for ten minutes or so before asking questions and demanding payment. Then he would add the cost of his plane ticket and all other expenses he and his two hired guns had incurred to Finkel's constantly growing debt.

Finally, he'd send a message by breaking a few bones in Stuart's already frail body.

Vinnie and Carlos wanted to avoid this at all costs. "How crazy that we're trying to protect a man we both hate with a passion," said Carlos.

"Yup. For better or worse, we need to protect the moron a little longer."

Before calling it a night, Vinnie called Mark Chong in Port Charlotte.

"Hello?"

"Yeah, it's me," Vinnie said, as if he was Chong's only business contact.

"What can I do for you, Vinnie?"

"If Finkel leaves the Summerville vicinity, I want to be notified immediately. I don't care what time it is. Even if he travels five miles, I wanna know about it. Okay?"

"Yes, sir," came the reply. Chong hated calling either of them, "sir" but they were his bosses, at least temporarily.

"By the way," said Vinnie, "good job today. Your surveillance was right on the money."

"Thank you, sir." Chong ended the call and adjusted the radius on the hidden GPS locator, from 50 miles down to five. Then it was off to bed. If Finkel moved outside the five-mile radius, an alarm would go off and Chong would send a text message to Vinnie.

Vinnie and Carlos both knew if Finkel moved, it would be for good reason. If so, they'd be right behind him again, without his ever knowing...

"It's nice having Stuey do all the dirty work for us," Carlos said, his mouth stretched into a yawn. "I mean, here we are sleeping in comfy beds, while he's sure to wake up feeling like a human pretzel in the morning. Maybe he isn't such a bad guy after all..."

Vinnie turned out the light next to his bed. "It is kinda funny..." There was a brief silence before Vinnie burst into laughter.

Because Vinnie was always so serious, whenever he laughed, it forced Carlos to laugh even harder, cackling and snorting in his customary high pitch tone. In the darkness, the two men practically laughed themselves to sleep.

If the people in the rooms next to theirs could hear all the commotion, they might think the laughter was coming from some kook and his pet hyena!

If Stuart Finkel only knew...

169

33

TUESDAY JUNE 28 - DAY 18

AT 7:30 A.M. JESSE smelled the fresh coffee brewing. In an hour, it was back to work. He begrudgingly got dressed and went downstairs to find Shelby seated at the kitchen table. He knew his wife hadn't slept much, if at all. There was no need to ask why.

"Good morning."

"Morning, honey," Shelby replied, wearily.

"Did you sleep?"

"A little, I guess," came the reply.

Jesse poured two cups of coffee. "You know, honey, I've been thinking."

Shelby looked up from the scroll in her hands, with the three "111" clues displayed on it. "Yeah?"

"Perhaps you should go back to Florida."

Shelby raised an eyebrow, "Me? As in by myself?"

"You and I both know you'll never forgive yourself if you don't keep searching. Besides, not to add anymore unwanted pressure, but I was mulling things over in my mind and something occurred to me."

"What?"

"The letter stated you have ninety days, right?"

"Yeah."

"Well then, that gives you until September eighth to find it instead of the tenth."

Shelby shot Jesse a confused look.

"You received the letter on the tenth, right?"

"Yeah..."

"There are thirty days in June. Since you received the letter on the tenth, that gives us twenty days for this month. But there are thirty-one days in July and August. Add them all together and it comes to eighty-two days, leaving eight days left in September to work with. September eighth, to be exact."

Shelby peeled back the months of June, July and August on the calendar hanging on the kitchen wall. September tenth was circled in big bold strokes. She took a pen and made September eighth look just like the tenth.

170

"If I go back to Florida, what about the children?" Shelby tried sounding like a responsible parent, but deep inside she felt like a child again; a child who'd just been granted her wildest wish.

"I'm sure your mother won't mind watching them during the day. I'll fetch them each night after work."

"Are you sure?"

"We'll find a way to manage without you here," he joked.

"Oh, Jesse, thank you so much."

"I took five-hundred dollars out of the safe and left it on the bureau upstairs. That should hold you over for a while. If you run out of cash, you can always use your credit cards."

Shelby wrapped her arms around Jesse's neck and kissed him on the lips.

"I guess you'll be leaving today?"

"No time like the present, right?" A new surge of excitement flowed through Shelby.

"Will you be okay driving alone?"

"I'll be fine, Jesse."

"How much sleep did you get last night?"

"Not much, but I promise to make up for it at the hotel."

Jesse searched his wife's eyes, "Fair enough."

"How long can I stay?"

"For as long as it takes." His voice was calm, emanating unwavering support for his wife.

"Thank you, Jesse." Shelby's eyes welled up with tears.

There was a short pause. "Where will you stay?"

"Somewhere on the island if it's not too expensive. This way, I won't have to travel back and forth each day and pay the six-dollar toll. Hopefully I'll find a reasonable room online."

Jesse looked at his watch. "Well, what are you waiting for? You'd better get packing!"

"Still have laundry to do. And I need to call my folks. But I'm sure they'll be happy to watch them."

"Call me before you leave so I know what's going on."

"You know I will." Jesse's words breathed new life into her fatigued body, new energy. She was ready for Round Two.

Shelby prepared breakfast then woke the children. "Momma has something to tell y'all."

"What is it?" asked BJ.

"I'm going back to Florida. Alone this time."

"Why, Momma," Brooke replied, with a noticeable sulk.

171

"To search for the treasure again. It won't be a vacation this time. I plan to spend all my time on Sanibel Beach until I find it." Shelby took a small sip of coffee. "Daddy will pick you up at Grandma's and Grandpa's each night after work."

"We'd rather go back to Florida with you, Momma," said Trevor.

"I understand that, sweetie, but it has to be this way for now."

"Oh, alright," came the reply.

At 10 a.m., everything was set. Shelby's suitcase was packed with more than enough clothing to last a week or so. After searching online for hotel rooms in Florida, all hopes of staying on Sanibel Island were squashed. It was too pricey for her budget. Thankfully, she was able to secure another room at the Outrigger Beach Resort.

Fueling at the gas station, Brooke looked out the window. "There's that man again, Momma," the youngest member of the family said, matter of factly.

"What man, baby?" Shelby paid her daughter little mind at first.

"That one, right there in the red truck!" Brooke pointed her little forefinger directly at Stuart Finkel.

Shelby gave the man a good looking over. He quickly looked away. *Hmm.*

"Have you seen him before, honey?"

"Uh-huh."

"Are you sure?"

"Yes, Momma, I'm sure," Brooke said evenly.

"Hmm. Where did you see him, sweetheart?"

"At the pool."

"In Florida?"

"Uh-huh. He waved to me."

Shelby winced, "Are you sure, baby?"

"Yes, Momma, I'm sure."

But Shelby wasn't so sure. She remembered her daughter waving to someone from across the hotel pool the other day. When she inquired, the man turned and quickly left.

Shelby only saw the back of his head. *Could that be him? If so, what's he doing in Summerville of all places? Had he followed us? Does he know about the...?*

Shelby spotted the Florida license plate displayed on the back of his truck and felt a slight panic inside. Her heart rate increased drastically. Euphoria was quickly replaced with slight trembling.

Shelby pulled out of the gas station and drove north on U.S. 17. Her eyes were practically glued to the rear-view mirror.

172

Sure enough, the man in the red truck did the same.

Less than a mile away, Shelby pulled into the driveway of her parents' house, stopping in front of her mother's prized crepe myrtles, now in full bloom.

The red pick-up truck slowly drove past. The creepy man behind the wheel was staring in their direction, lit cigarette in his mouth, a mischievous smirk on his face.

Shelby's heart raced even faster. She gulped in more air. This man, whoever he was, looked very dangerous. She thought to call 911 but decided against it for now. If she told Jesse, he would urge her to go straight to the police, especially now that he knew where her parents lived. *Does he know about the buried treasure?*

John and Trudy were already outside waiting for them to arrive. It didn't take long to suspect something was wrong. "Are you okay, honey?"

"I'm fine, Daddy."

"Are you sure? You look like you just saw a ghost."

"Yes, Daddy, I'm sure," she said, nervously glancing out toward U.S. 17.

Trudy noticed but kept it to herself. "How was Florida, kids?"

"Awesomeeeeeeeeeeee," said BJ.

"We had a great time, Grandma," Trevor said.

"Did you see Cinderella, Brooke?"

"Yes, Grandma," she replied, "She's so pretty."

"Just like you, sweetheart."

"Uh-huh," came the reply.

John and Trudy both knew something was bothering Shelby.

"What's the matter, dear?" said Trudy, looking quite concerned.

Shelby shot a quick glance at Brooke, hoping she wouldn't say anything. "I'm fine, Momma, really. By the way, I'll be staying at the same place in Fort Myers again. Do you still have the number?"

"Yes, of course," Trudy said, "It's on a post-it by the phone."

"I wanted to stay on Sanibel Island, but the only available rooms I could find are almost three-hundred dollars per night."

"Do you need money?"

"No, Daddy, but thanks for asking."

"Be careful driving."

"I will. Promise." Shelby squatted down, "Okay kids, time for Momma to leave. Be good for Grandma and Grandpa, you hear?"

"Yes, Momma," said Brooke, already sniffling.

Shelby gathered her daughter into her arms. "Don't worry, I'll be home soon enough."

"Okay, Momma."

This would be Shelby's first time ever leaving her children like this. She felt like crying but, because of the man in the red truck, was able to control herself for now.

"Group hug time," Shelby said.

"I'll miss you, Momma. Good luck down there."

"Thanks, Trev. Momma's gonna miss you all so much. I'll call every day."

"They'll be fine after a while," Trudy said, whispering softly to her daughter. Shelby climbed back inside the minivan, "Love y'all very much!"

"Let's go inside, kids. Grandma and Grandpa can't wait to hear all about Florida." Trudy wondered yet again why her father had put Shelby through all this nonsense. It was pure insanity. "Have a safe trip, darling."

As Brooke slowly climbed the three steps leading to the front door of her grandparent's house, her little neck was craned back the entire time to catch one last glance of her mother. It was gut wrenching, to say the least.

Shelby dried her eyes, blew kisses to her children and with a nervous twitch in her stomach drove off. She had no plans of taking U.S. 17 this time. She just wanted to get to Florida.

Though she dreaded the very thought of seeing the creepy man in the red pick-up truck again, part of her needed to see him. She needed to know he had no interest in her children or her parents.

Sure enough, he was parked in a vacant driveway a half-mile from her parents' house. Shelby watched him pull out a few car lengths behind her. She gulped hard but was also relieved knowing he wasn't interested in anyone else in the family, only her.

"Who are you and what do you want?"

Shelby was tempted again to call 911 but instead was thinking of the best way to lose him. She turned onto I-26 westbound and set the cruise control at 70 miles per hour.

If she didn't encounter road construction along the way, she should reach the Florida border by 3 p.m., and Fort Myers by 8:30 p.m.

Shelby had a sinking feeling that if she didn't find a way to put distance between herself and the man in the red pick-up truck, he would follow her all the way to Fort Myers.

The very thought nearly sucked the life out of her body...

174

34

VINNIE AND CARLOS WERE watching *Sports Center* in the hotel lobby, finishing breakfast, when Vinnie's mobile device vibrated.

"Who texted you?" asked Carlos. "Our boy in Port Charlotte?"

"Yup. Stuey's on the move again. Headed westbound on interstate twenty-six."

Vinnie replied to Mark Chong: *If he heads southbound on I-95, text me immediately.*

Shelby reached I-95 and drove south.

The driver in the red truck did the same.

Vinnie received another text message: *He's on I-95 now!*

The two money collectors threw on baseball caps and were out the door in ten minutes.

Thanks to Shelby's daughter, Stuart was certain she was aware of his presence. *Not good!* What was good, however, was that she was driving south on I-95, which meant she must have found a significant clue at home. Even better was that she was all alone this time, which meant less sets of eyes potentially staring back at him.

In the spying business, this was a good thing. Even so, his carelessness nearly cost him. He needed to be more careful from here on out. But at least Shelby was going back to Florida again.

"Yes!" Stuart pounded the truck dashboard. He could feel his severely bruised and damaged body healing a little more.

Though Shelby still had two and a half months to find her inheritance, thanks to Jesse's latest calculations, it felt more like two and a half days. At any rate, if it took driving back and forth from South Carolina to Florida fifty times to finally find her inheritance, she was resolved to do just that.

At least that's how she felt now. Who knew what thoughts would ensnare her tomorrow? Especially with this maniac following closely behind her...

Stuart lit up a cigarette and had a sudden thought. He turned on his cell phone and called directory assistance. "What city please?"

"Fort Myers, Florida."

"Business or residence?"

"Business."

"Name of business?"

"Outrigger Beach Resort on Fort Myers Beach."

"One moment please. Would you like me to connect you?"

"Yes!" There was ringing. "Thank you for calling the Outrigger Beach Resort on Fort Myers Beach. How can I help you?"

"Uh, yes, I'm calling to see if my wife's checked in yet?"

"May I have her name?"

"Shelby McKinney."

"I'll check for you, sir," the girl said in a friendly tone of voice. After a few moments, she said, "No sir, she hasn't. According to the reservation, she won't be here until early this evening."

"Okay, thank you very much."

"Oh, you're wel..." She heard the disconnect.

Somewhere in the middle of Georgia, Stuart eased up on the gas pedal. There was no need to tail this woman too closely. He knew exactly where she was going.

Finkel began daydreaming again, spending large amounts of money inside his head, totally unaware that two dream stealers were quickly gaining on him, hoping to turn their dreams into Stuart Finkel's nightmare.

Shelby checked into the Outrigger Beach Resort a little after 8:00 p.m. She was exhausted and had no plans of driving to Sanibel Beach until morning time.

She reached for her cell phone. "Hi baby, I made it."

"Glad you arrived safely."

"It was a piece of cake," she said.

"Good luck down there. I hope tomorrow's the day."

"Me too. I miss y'all so much already."

"We miss you too."

"It was sweet of you to call the hotel earlier."

"What?" Jesse said. "I didn't call there."

"When I checked in I was told you had called," Shelby said, regretting it. "Must have been the wrong room."

Jesse thought back to something Brooke had said at the dinner table. "What's all this about some man Brooke saw at the gas station? She's convinced she saw him at the pool in Florida the other day."

Shelby almost swallowed her tongue. "You know how kids are, Jesse. They have such vivid imaginations."

"I didn't take her seriously until you thanked me for the message. Are you sure you're okay?"

"I'm perfectly safe, Jesse." *Am I really?*

"That's what I wanna hear!"

As always, just hearing her husband's deep, gentle airplane pilot voice soothed her nerves. "I'd like to go for a swim in the pool before I eat. Then it's off to bed. But I'll call before I go to sleep."

"Enjoy your swim."

"Thanks, Jesse."

After her swim, Shelby showered then called home.

While talking to Brooke, she pulled back the curtain in her room and her heart nearly stopped beating in her chest. Parked outside was the creepy-looking man in the red pick-up truck.

Shelby muffled a scream and dropped her cell phone to the floor. She picked it up and sat on the bed to stop her knees from trembling.

"Are you okay, Momma?" said Brooke.

"Momma's fine, sweetie. Just dropped the phone, that's all."

"Good luck tomorrow, Momma," Trevor said. "Love you."

"Love y'all too," said Shelby.

The call ended, and Shelby peeked through the curtain again, this time a little more cautiously.

The creepy-looking man was still there smoking a cigarette, blowing smoke straight up toward her room, staring at her with an expression on his face like he hadn't a care in the world.

Fear snaked through her. *Why is this man following me?* Her gut told her he'd somehow found out about the buried treasure. But how? Yes, he had to know about it. What else could it possibly be?

"Enough is enough!" She reached for the phone.

"Front desk, how may I assist you?"

"I'm calling to report a strange-looking man out in the parking lot in a red pick-up truck."

"Has he been there long?"

"I think so."

"I'll send someone out there immediately."

"Thank you."

"You're welcome, Misses McKinney."

It didn't take long for a security guard to appear, flashlight on, ambling toward the red pick-up truck. The driver started his truck, gazed up at Shelby angrily and drove off.

Fear twisted through her again. Which could only mean one thing; he knew about the buried treasure. Shelby was 100-percent certain of it now. But how did he ever find out?

Shelby spent the next few minutes debating whether to turn this into a police matter or not. But how could she prove this strange man had followed her all the way from South Carolina? She had no proof, no footage. Why would they believe her?

If she involved the police now, they'd surely agree to check into it, but they'd also remind her that this man had done no wrong, that it was a free country, and he had as much right to travel the many highways and by-ways of America as she did, and so on.

Shelby was never more conflicted. Knowing the police were monitoring things would help her feel more protected.

But following him meant they would follow her too.

Shelby didn't want or need that kind of attention.

Besides, just because someone wore a badge didn't necessarily mean they could be trusted. After all, greed was greed, and since the dawn of civilization, humanity had great difficulty with this sin, regardless of profession. And this meant, for now—police officer or not—the least amount of people involved the better...

Shelby grimaced, after realizing she was being greedy herself, by risking her own personal safety and well-being just to find her inheritance.

Though she promised Jesse that she would catch up on her sleep, thanks to the strange man in the red pick-up truck, sleep would come hard again, if at all. *Who is this man?*

Shelby couldn't help but wonder if he would follow her to Sanibel Island in the morning and monitor her every move.

She feared the answer was yes.

She also feared she wouldn't sleep again until convinced the man in the red pick-up truck was completely out of the picture.

"HELLO?"

"Hey, Mark. It's me."

"Hey, Vinnie," Mark Chong replied in a tired voice.

"I need you to readjust the transponder again," he said, to the techno-geek in Port Charlotte. "The moment Finkel leaves his apartment, I wanna know about it!"

"Okay, sure."

"Good work again today, Mark."

"Thanks, Vinnie."

"Don't mention it." The call ended.

He turned to Carlos. "Now we wait..."

35

SUNDAY JULY 2 - DAY 22

THE BOAT WAS ANCHORED 500 feet out in the Gulf of Mexico, just off the coast of Sanibel Island. Even anchored in relatively calm seas, the Pro-Line fishing boat had no choice but to bob and weave to the water's unpredictable rhythm; up and down; back and forth; left to right, rendering the 26' fishing vessel completely powerless against the mighty gulf waters.

The Gulf of Mexico truly was a fisherman's paradise. More than 200 species of saltwater fish loomed beneath the surface, challenging anglers to give it their best shot. It was difficult for many fishing these waters to decide which was more therapeutic; being on a boat in paradise sniffing in the salty sea-air or catching a fish.

It was probably too close to call for most.

It was another beautiful day with hardly a cloud in the sky. Stifling as it was on land, the gulf breeze felt nice out on the water.

The two men on board the boat were both shirtless, gradually adding another layer of tan to their already sun-darkened, heavily-tattooed bodies. Whenever one of them got a new tattoo, the other rushed off to the tattoo parlor to even the score. Beer bellies protruded from their mid-sections, covering the tops of their colorful knee-length swimsuits.

They looked like two tourists on vacation catching dinner. But Vinnie and Carlos weren't tourists. Nor were they locals out taking a break from everyday life to go fishing.

The two money collectors were all about business now. Using binoculars, they carefully staked out Sanibel Beach doing their best to follow every move Stuart Finkel made, as he stalked the fairly-attractive woman from South Carolina from a distance.

The only time either man went below deck was to use the restroom or to refill their drinks, and only one at a time. If they took a break from watching Stuey for even a minute, both feared the little weasel would slip away.

After monitoring his every move the past four days, Vinnie and Carlos now believed his story, hook, line and sinker. Either there was a buried treasure to speak of, or Finkel was doing a magnificent job convincing himself and the two thugs that one existed.

179

Which is why Vinnie and Carlos finally decided to cash in on one of their few company perks and take Bossman's boat out for a day of fishing. At least that's what they told him.

With Sanibel Island being so difficult to navigate at times, by foot or car, the two money collectors figured it would be easier to monitor Finkel and the woman from South Carolina from out on the water. As it turned out, they were right.

They dropped lines in the water to look the part, but always with a keen eye toward the coast. If anyone cared to investigate, they would find two buddies spending a day at sea together.

But, in truth, Vinnie and Carlos were pirates hoping to steal a buried treasure from yet another thief—Stuart Finkel. Yes, they were on a mission, as evidenced by the two 9mm handguns, just in case. Hopefully, there would be no need to use them.

According to the weatherman, they still had two, perhaps three, hours of nice weather left before the rains came. A 50-percent chance of thundershowers was called for early that afternoon. But during summer months in the state of Florida, a 50-percent chance was almost as good as saying 100-percent.

"As soon as the storm clouds begin forming," Carlos said, "we're outta here until the rain subsides."

"Agreed."

The two money collectors weren't seasoned boat enthusiasts by any stretch of the imagination. Combined, they had very little boating experience between them. Carlos was the better of the two.

If they decided to brave the storm and stay out on the open waters, both men feared the fierce winds and rain would stir up the waves like a soup spoon in a kettle of soup and, in the process, toss the boat around like a cork in a Jacuzzi turned on full-blast.

It was just too risky.

Carlos said, "I must say, Stuart's made a believer out of me. He's working himself senseless. Guess he's not so lazy after all."

Vinnie took a swig of Pepsi, "I'm impressed, too. Keep up the good work, Stuey. We really need this money."

Both men laughed.

Though the three-day grace period ended nearly a week ago, Vinnie and Carlos were prepared to give Finkel all the time he needed. Crazy as it sounded, they needed to protect him; at least until the buried treasure was located.

180

But they still left threatening text and voice messages each day to keep him motivated and always on full alert. They couldn't afford for him to get lazy at this point.

Once the treasure chest was found, it was every man for himself. Finkel would walk away from this heist debt-free to their boss.

But that's all he would walk away with...

Carlos lit the half-smoked Cuban cigar dangling from his mouth, "Let's talk about how we're going to spend all that money again,"

"Once the money's ours," Vinnie said, leaning up in his chair, "we'll clear Finkel's debt to Bossman, then take a week-long cruise to the Bahamas. After that, we'll buy two brand new Mustang GTs and totally upgrade our bling and wardrobes."

Carlos adjusted the straw Bermuda hat covering the red bandanna on his head, "Sounds good, bro. Soon, we'll be stylin' and profilin'."

"If there's enough left over, we'll buy a condo on South Beach, in Miami, overlooking the ocean."

"Wouldn't that be awesome!"

"Imagine how many chicks we'll pick up then."

"Si, señor!" Carlos fist-bumped Vinnie.

"Maybe there'll be enough to start our own bookie business."

"Maybe we can hire Stuey boy to be one of our money collectors!" Carlos replied, with a chuckle.

"Yeah right! Stuey couldn't intimidate a flea, let alone someone owing us money!"

"You make a good point there, Vinnie."

"All I can say is there'd better be millions stashed inside that chest, because we already spent more than a million bucks just out here on the boat!"

Carlos scanned the beach with binoculars, "If Stuart only knew."

"Who cares what he thinks!"

"Think there will be enough to retire on?"

Vinnie took a long drag from his cigarette, "Time will tell..."

"Just hope Bossman never finds out we're making a little something extra on the side."

"Don't make too much of it, Carlos. We're allowed to pursue personal endeavors on our own time, right?"

"True. But we're using his boat to spy on one of his deadbeat clients, so we can turn a profit for ourselves. I don't think that would make him very happy."

"The only reason Bossman let us use his boat in the first place is because we're the most loyal men he has."

"Yeah, but come on, Vinnie, if he knew the real reason we're using his boat—good soldiers or not—you and I both know he'd want a piece of the action, plus a stiff penalty for our dishonesty."

Vinnie grunted, "That's why he can never find out. You and I both know what he's most concerned about is that Finkel's on the run with thirteen-thousand of his dollars!"

"Yeah, I never saw him looking so angry."

Vinnie clenched his fists, "We're putting our necks on the line for Finkel! If that lowlife walks away from this score free and clear of his debt to Bossman, it'll be a blessing for him. After all, we could have, should have even, broken both his legs the other night for nonpayment of debt. But we let it slide, right?"

"Yup!"

"Well then, like I said before; if he walks away from this score no longer indebted to Bossman, still in relatively good health, it'll be a good day for him. But that's all he'll walk away with. Just hope Bossman doesn't find him before he finds the buried treasure."

Seeing his partner gritting his teeth, Carlos knew it was time to lighten things up a bit. He said, "Perhaps in time his grandfather can lead him on another buried treasure hunt."

Vinnie burst into laughter, "Good one, Carlos!"

Using binoculars, they scanned the beach looking for anything out of the ordinary, namely the woman from South Carolina frantically digging up the beach looking for buried treasure.

They knew Finkel was also watching a safe distance away.

On at least 30 occasions this week, they watched the woman counting off steps at various locations on Sanibel Beach, then digging holes in the sand. Which could only mean one thing; the treasure must have been buried someplace on this beach.

But where? She'd already dug four separate holes in the sand this morning, doing her best to look inconspicuous.

Each time she started counting, Vinnie raised the anchor and Carlos inched in as close to the shoreline as he could, before dropping anchor again. They wanted to be ready the moment she found it. So far, nothing. But one thing was certain; this woman was fiercely determined to succeed.

"What is she waiting for this time, bro?" Carlos said.

"Don't know. But she better start digging soon before the rain comes."

"The moment she unearths it, you'll swim to shore to finish the job up close and personal."

"Thanks for telling me what I already know, bro."

182

"Just make sure there are no holes in the plastic bag holding your gun."

"I'm not worried about my gun getting wet, Carlos. I'm not stupid enough to fire a gun on a crowded beach! It'll only be used to scare her just enough for me to grab the treasure chest and make a quick getaway. No hard feelings. It's just business."

"Just hope everything goes according to plan."

"I heard that, Carlos."

Since the dawn of civilization, thievery had always been big business. Regardless of merchandise, crooks generated billions of dollars annually by way of theft. For those who were really good at it, it was a lucrative, tax-free way to make quick cash.

Naturally, the downside was in getting caught. Once caught, a thief was usually forced into early retirement. At least for a few years.

Contrary to public belief, thievery by way of piracy on the open seas wasn't mere folklore fantasy. Not only was it still big business, piracy was on the vast increase again. But unlike those caught in the act of stealing on land, most pirates caught on the open seas never stood trial for their crimes. At least not in a courtroom.

Instead, many were executed on the spot for their heinous crimes and unceremoniously dumped into the vast expanse of the ocean, where they ended up as fish food for the many species patrolling that part of the ocean below.

Though Vinnie and Carlos weren't looting treasure out on the open seas, per se, being on a boat made it feel that way. Their minds were full of wild and adventurous thoughts, like two kids living out childhood fantasies.

With one stipulation; the guns and bullets were real, as was the penalty if caught.

At 12:30 p.m., the two men watched the woman from South Carolina leave the beach, get in her car, and drive off.

"Probably going back to her hotel on Fort Myers for a bite to eat," Carlos said, not overly concerned.

"Speaking of hungry," Vinnie said, "I'm going below deck to prepare lunch. How's the mackerel you caught sound?"

"Good. Just not too spicy for me, bro. Not good for my ulcer."

"Come on Carlos, live a little, man."

"Will you drive me to the emergency room if my ulcer acts up?"

"Okay, not too spicy."

Vinnie returned top deck carrying two plates full of freshly-caught fish—cooked in lemon garlic butter with a dash of Cajun seasoning he found in a cabinet above the small stove—steamed rice, mixed vegetables, and two more Pepsis.

Today wasn't a beer day. Both men needed to be vigilant.

"Hope you're hungry, mi amigo."

"Looks good, bro. Bravo!"

Vinnie took a bite of the fish, "Now this is living the life!"

"The only way it can possibly improve is when we steal the treasure from Finkel, the moment he steals it from that poor woman! No, no, no, wait," Carlos said, now thinking a mile a minute, "better yet, I'd love to see you snatch it from her hands just before Finkel lays his filthy hands on it. Imagine the look on his face when he sees you suddenly appear out of nowhere, gun in hand, to steal the treasure chest from her."

The way Carlos said it made Vinnie laugh hard again. He was taking a bite of his food and nearly choked on it.

Carlos went on, "Before you rush back to the boat, you can cold cock him for good measure and leave him writhing in pain on Sanibel Beach, for all to see."

Vinnie laughed even harder this time. "Stop man, I'm trying to eat!"

"Then, when you're safely back on the boat, you can wave to him saying, 'And remember Stuey, crime doesn't pay!'"

Vinnie burst into laughter again, "Stop, Carlos. You're making my stomach hurt."

"Plenty more where that came from, bro," Carlos said, Mr. Hyena once again surfacing.

"Let me finish eating first." Vinnie took a few bites of his mackerel. It literally melted in his mouth. Taking the next bite, he grew serious again. "How much cash do you have stashed under your mattress at home, Carlos?"

"Why do you ask?"

"Until Bossman gets his three G's from Finkel, he'll keep pressuring us to find the little weasel. What if he sends in reinforcements to help us? If so, bye-bye treasure hunt."

"What are you getting at, Vinnie?"

"We're both certain there's a buried treasure to speak of, right?"

"Yeah..."

"If we're able to raise the three G's ourselves, I say we give it to Bossman and tell him we finally collected it from Finkel."

"I don't know, bro. It's kinda risky."

"Sure, but it's a risk worth taking if it gets Bossman off our backs regarding Finkel. This way, when we're not out collecting, we can monitor Stuey, without Bossman constantly freaking out on us."

"If you think that's what we should do, I'm with you, bro."

"I have just over eleven-hundred bucks at home. What about you?"

"I have enough to cover the rest," Carlos said, bursting with pride. "Once we steal the treasure, we can square up."

"Thanks. I really appreciate it."

"De nada, Vinnie."

"So, it's agreed then?"

"Sure, let's do it."

"We better find the buried treasure now! If not, I hate to think what I'll do to that pathetic lowlife!"

"Calm down, bro. It looks like your eyes are about to pop out of your head again."

"I'm fine, Carlos."

"If you say so," Carlos said, taking the last bite of his fish.

Vinnie grunted and left it at that.

36

AFTER LUNCH, VINNIE AND Carlos continued surveilling Sanibel Island, but saw nothing out of the ordinary.

There were plenty of people digging holes in the sand, but that was to be expected. It was normal beach behavior. Most were under the age of twelve. Nothing newsworthy there.

Since returning from lunch, the woman from South Carolina had yet to dig any new holes. She looked tired and frustrated, but still determined as ever to find it.

As the day dragged on storm clouds started gathering. Using his binoculars, Vinnie looked to the south and saw dark rain clouds down in Naples, roughly 25 miles south of them.

When he checked ten minutes ago, it was perfectly clear down there. Now it was as if the clouds had completely gobbled up the normally sun-drenched city. Earth and sky blended together as one.

Vinnie looked to the horizon out west and saw dark rain clouds gathering. And the wind was starting to pick up. There was distant thunder in the background.

"Did you see that lightning?" Carlos asked, with a nervous twitch.

"Yup. I say we head back."

"I agree, bro. Too many a foolish boat captain waited until the last minute only to destroy their vessels. I'm good, but not that good. Neither of us has a hundred and fifty grand to buy a new boat if we destroy this one."

"Yeah. If we destroy Bossman's boat, he'll destroy us too!"

"I heard that!" Carlos replied soberly.

Vinnie and Carlos were debt collectors, under-the-table debt collectors at that. They could never afford a boat like this. According to the U.S. Government, they were either trust fund babies, dead or dead broke, because neither had worked a single day in their lives.

Everything they purchased was paid for in cash. And thirty grand a year only went so far. But at least it was tax free. As non-taxpaying citizens, they would never qualify for a boat loan or any other type of loan for that matter.

"Hopefully soon we'll be able to buy our own boats! Wouldn't that be awesome?"

"We can play bumper yachts out on the open sea!"

Vinnie burst into laughter, "Whatever you're taking to make me laugh is really working. Keep taking it!"

"Like I said, there's plenty more where that came from, bro!"

Whenever Carlos wasn't out collecting for Bossman, his healthy sense of humor was usually put on full display. He could be a real practical joker at times.

Vinnie, on the other hand, didn't have much of a sense of humor. Even when he wasn't collecting for Bossman, he looked angry. He could easily scare most people—even his most violent adversaries—with little more than a glance. His eyes were uncomfortably intense.

Being around Carlos so much was good for him. No one understood Vinnie or feared him any more than he did. Carlos knew how to keep him from exploding like a volcano on any given day.

On the way back to the marina, the waves were getting noticeably bigger. The boat started bobbing up and down in a desperate, but fruitless, attempt to smooth itself out.

"I'm feeling a little queasy, Carlos. If you don't want to see my lunch again, take it easy."

"Doing my best, bro. Why don't you clean up the mess below deck, while I concentrate on getting us safely back to the dock."

"Sounds good," said Vinnie.

"What, no aye-aye. Captain?"

"I'll aye-aye, Captain you!"

"See, Vinnie, you have a sense of humor, after all."

"Once in a while, man," he said going below deck, hoping only to clean the dishes and not his own personal mess as well. The more the boat rocked the more he felt like vomiting.

Carlos maneuvered the fishing vessel into the boat slip as gently and carefully as he could, without hitting the buoys there for added protection when docking.

Both men secured the boat to the dock with relative ease using two thick ropes, then rushed off to where Finkel and the woman from South Carolina were last seen scouring the beach.

Vinnie parked his vehicle in the rear of the hotel parking lot—as far away from Stuart's jalopy of a truck as possible—then walked to the pool area. The rain was but a breath away from coming down in buckets. Winds were already gusting at 40- to 50-miles per hour.

Sure enough, sitting on a stool at the pool bar a mere stone's throw from the beach was Stuart Finkel. He took a long drag from his cigarette and looked in their direction.

Vinnie ducked behind a wall.

Carlos turned around hoping he didn't notice him.

"This is ridiculous! Why are we hiding from that loser?"

"So we don't blow our cover, bro," said Carlos.

"This is nuts!" Vinnie was growing angrier by the minute. "Not only does he owe Bossman a boatload of money, soon he'll owe us three G's. Yet here we are hiding from him!"

"I think it's funny, bro."

"I'm glad someone thinks it's funny, 'cause I sure don't!" Vinnie bit his tongue and let it go at that.

SHELBY CALLED JESSE ONCE the storm clouds gathered, saying she was leaving Florida come sunrise.

With Independence Day two days away, she was anxious to get back home so they could watch the fireworks in Charleston, as a complete family, like they did each fourth of July.

But Jesse knew the approaching holiday was only part of the reason she was coming home. The past four days in Florida were just as fruitless as the last trip had been. Her tone of voice lacked the enthusiasm she was always known for. She sounded tired, depressed even. Even two states away, he sensed his wife was growing tired of searching for her elusive buried inheritance.

What he didn't know was the man Brooke saw at the gas station really *was* the same man at the pool last week in Florida. Not only had he apparently followed them to Summerville, he followed Shelby back to Florida the next day. Even worse, he'd followed her every move the past four days in the Sunshine State.

Thanks to him, Shelby didn't want to spend another day in Florida alone. Yes, it was time to make her getaway from this lunatic before something bad happened to her. She'd already decided that if he dared follow her back to South Carolina this time, she wouldn't hesitate to turn it into a police matter, no questions asked.

Enough was enough!

188

37

JULY 26 - DAY 46 (The Halfway Point)

SHELBY MCKINNEY SLOWLY STEADIED the minivan out of her parents' driveway. Her mother was in the passenger front seat. Trevor, BJ and Brooke were in the back seat. They were en route to Florida for a brief three-day trip. After two unsuccessful trips alone, this was Shelby's fourth time traveling to Florida in search of buried treasure. This was her kids' second trip and Trudy's first.

Trudy insisted that she come along for the ride this time. At the very least, she could babysit the children as Shelby scoured the beach looking for her elusive buried inheritance.

Jesse wanted to join them but was too busy at work.

Trudy's husband, John, also wanted to come, but was going on a business trip to Minneapolis.

At 10 p.m., they reached mile marker #131 on I-75—Daniels Parkway—and exited. An hour later they were at the Holiday Inn Hotel on Sanibel Beach. Trudy insisted on paying for the room and wouldn't take no for an answer. It was the least she could do.

Once they were checked in, Shelby said, "Why don't we take a quick stroll on the beach before calling it a night?"

"Can we go swimming, Momma?" BJ said, yawning.

"It's too late now, honey. Just a walk for now, okay?"

"Okay," he said, long faced.

"Cheer up, BJ, tomorrow you can swim all day."

"It's so nice being back here again," Trudy said, sniffing in the salty sea air. "It's been a while."

This was Trudy's first time back in Florida in more than a year. Fond memories of her parents washed over her. She couldn't wait for her husband to retire so they could take more trips like this together.

Now back on the island, the yoke Shelby felt from her past three failures weighed heavily upon her again. As much as she tried suppressing it negative thoughts had already resurfaced, and she hadn't even started digging yet.

Noticing, Trudy said, "It's here somewhere. Just remain patient."

"I sure hope so. I feel like I've checked everywhere."

"Like Grandpa said, we need to keep it simple, right?"

189

"Wish I still had your same level of enthusiasm." Shelby looked out at the waves gently breaking on the shore, greatly illuminated by the bright moonlight. "This is a relatively small island. If my inheritance was buried on Fort Myers Beach, I could understand the many setbacks. There are so many landmarks there. But not here."

"Try not to think about it too much. You drove all day. Take a few deep breaths and enjoy the moment, okay?"

"I'm sleepy, Momma," Brooke said, yawning.

"Let's head back and get some rest."

When the kids were bedded down for the night, Shelby and Trudy sat on the lanai sipping Ginseng tea.

Once the teacups were empty, Trudy said, "Let's get some rest. Shall we?"

"Sure Momma, I'm bushed."

Shelby woke early the next morning to find her mother sitting out on the lanai still in her pajamas. She opened the door and her nostrils were treated to a pleasant coffee aroma. "Morning, Momma."

"Would you like some Kona Coffee? I brought it with me." Always the thoughtful one, Trudy brewed it outside so the rich aroma wouldn't wake anyone.

"I'd love a cup."

Trudy poured a fresh cup for her daughter. "No matter what happens let's make it a good day, okay?

"I'll do my best, Momma."

There was a certain expression on Shelby's face that made Trudy's mind race back 30 years to when her daughter was Brooke's age. Her face glowed in the memory of it all. In the blink of an eye, her little girl was married with three precious children of her own. *Where did the time go?*

"I think someone slept soundly last night."

"Whatever you put in the Ginseng tea really did the trick," Shelby replied, jokingly. "How 'bout you?"

"I slept just fine." Trudy looked out at the Gulf of Mexico and smiled, grateful to be here with her daughter and three grandchildren.

"After I finish my coffee, would it be okay if I strolled the beach before the kids wake up?"

"Go right ahead."

"Hopefully something will jump out at me. If not, after breakfast, would you mind taking the kids to the pool, so I can keep searching?"

Trudy nodded yes.

190

"Don't worry, Momma. I promise not to go to Ding Darling National Wildlife Refuge without y'all. I know how much you love that place. The kids too."

"I've been wanting to go back there for quite some time."

"I know." Shelby sighed. "Even though wildlife refuges make up more than one-third of Sanibel Island, who in their right mind would bury a treasure chest full of money or whatever else is stashed inside, at a wildlife preserve? Doesn't make much sense."

Was Daddy in his right mind? Trudy kept it to herself. She took a sip of coffee. "But you will you be back in time for breakfast?"

"Yes. Just call me when the kids wake up. We can meet downstairs in the restaurant for breakfast."

"I will. Enjoy your walk."

Shelby hit the beach to begin her diligent pursuit of the buried treasure.

An hour later, Trudy called saying the kids were awake.

After enjoying a nice breakfast together, Shelby left them again. After giving it her all for nearly 10 hours, it turned out to be another day full of disappointments.

Shelby walked at least three miles on Sanibel Beach, shovel in hand, and another mile on Captiva Island.

Each time she thought a certain landmark could possibly be the one, she foolishly counted off 50 steps toward the coastline, then dug six-foot holes in the sand, wishing, hoping, half-expecting to find her inheritance. But it never happened.

Against her better judgment, she even visited a half-dozen wildlife refuges. It was a total waste of time.

For the first time since this bizarre adventure began, the words "give up" surfaced in Shelby's mind.

She was still unaware that she had demons assigned to her, sent by Satan himself, or that they were at the helm of the ship she was presently sailing on called, "Confusion".

Just like the "Despair" ship she'd traveled on last time, her demons stirred her mind like a blender turned on full speed, tearing her up inside. *Perhaps Martin Hightower and Jake were right all along. I really am looking for a needle in ten haystacks!*

At 8:00 p.m., Shelby went back to the hotel and changed into her swimsuit, then joined her family poolside.

"Did y'all have fun today, kids?"

"Yes, Momma," Trevor said cautiously, noticing the defeated look in his mother's eyes. She didn't find what she spent all day looking for.

Shelby glanced at her mother, "Sorry for being out all day, Momma."

"It's okay. We had a great day together, right Brooke?"

"Yes, Grandma."

"You know, I've been thinking," Shelby said, "tomorrow should be a vacation day for all of us."

"Really?"

"Yes, Trev. Momma needs a break from all this searching for buried treasure stuff. Let's have fun tomorrow, and lots of it, okay?"

"Yippie," Trevor exclaimed.

"Awesomeeeeeeeeeee," BJ said, submerging himself beneath the water.

"Hurray, Momma," Brooke said, her face lighting up.

"Come join us in the pool, Momma." said Trevor.

Trudy watched her daughter and grandchildren splashing around in the pool. The stress lines on her daughter's forehead were clearly visible. "Why'd you do this, Daddy?" she said skyward, soft enough that no one heard it.

At 10:00 p.m., Shelby ordered everyone out of the pool.

"Thanks for providing the day's best moment for me, Momma. I look forward to coffee on the lanai with you again in the morning."

Trudy smiled and nodded yes.

"Yes. And after that, let's have fun. I don't even wanna think about the buried treasure."

"I understand, dear…" Trudy flashed a reassuring smile for her daughter to bask in. But behind the smile was a look emanating more concern for Shelby than anything else.

Shelby noticed but ignored it for now. Now more than ever, she needed her mother to remain the tower of strength Shelby had always known her to be. One negative glance from her could send her spiraling again. *Help me, Grandpa…*

192

38

THE KIDS WOKE THE next morning to find Shelby and Grandma on the lanai having morning coffee.

Shelby took the kids for an early morning swim before breakfast. After that, they visited Ding Darling National Wildlife Refuge and went canoeing together. The mother of three made sure to take plenty of pictures.

From there, they went shelling on Captiva Island and enjoyed a nice dinner at *The Bubble Room Restaurant.*

By far, it was the best day she'd had in a long time.

With a full day to recuperate, Shelby took to the beach the next day fully energized and raring to go. Her pace was brisk, and she felt pretty good about her chances. But as the hours passed, the same heavy yoke of failure and disappointment smothered her again.

She halfheartedly dug holes in the sand up and down Sanibel and Captiva Island, frequently closing her eyes and foolishly counting off 50 steps west from any beachfront location she could find.

Even when she found what she thought could be a possible landmark, she was then faced with another challenge.

Should she count off steps at its center or at either end of it? Trying all three would take forever. Shelby didn't know. But The very thought of it dashed her hopes even more.

For whatever reason, she always chose the middle, then counted off 50 steps west toward the water, shovel in hand, feeling a little more foolish each time. Her children and mother accompanied her a handful of times, but more times than not, Shelby dug holes in the sand alone. The fact that it took 45-minutes for each six-foot hole to be dug made it even more grueling.

At 8:00 p.m., Shelby felt fairly-certain she'd located every so-called landmark on Sanibel Beach, and most on Captiva Island. She was beginning to wonder if the landmark was real or metaphorical?

She knew the buried treasure chest was buried someplace here on this relatively small island. But where?

It was the worst kind of torture to be so close, yet so incredibly far away. Her head hurt from too much thinking.

At 9:00 p.m., Shelby walked to the water's edge feeling completely broken inside. They were leaving in the morning and she was no closer now to deciphering the second "111" clue than when she first started searching.

For the first time since this adventure began, Shelby couldn't fight her ongoing depression. Nor could she stop the flood of negative thoughts from crashing on the shores of her confused mind.

She was tired of walking Sanibel and Captiva Islands all for nothing; weary of driving Periwinkle Way and all other roads on the island. She dreaded seeing the lighthouse she'd walked by a million times in her fruitless attempt to find the buried treasure chest.

The paradise island that had so captivated her seven weeks ago now felt more like a prison than anything else. Or more to the point, her own personal insane asylum. The magnificent landmark her late grandfather seemed to cherish so much never showed its face to her in seven weeks' time, equating to four wasted trips.

She didn't want to spend another day here. *Yes*, she thought, *it really must be more metaphorical than physical.*

Aside from the time with her family, the only other good thing to happen on this trip, was that she never saw the creepy man in the red pick-up truck. Other than that, this trip, too, was full of endless disappointments.

Shelby didn't know what to do or where to go from here. She wondered again if Bernie Finkel and his partner, Bob Schuster—whoever he was— really were the charity to be named later.

Against her better logic, she dialed Bernie Finkel's home number.

"Hello?"

"Hi, Mister Finkel, it's me, Shelby McKinney."

"How are you, Shelby?" Bernie Finkel rubbed his forehead. He was surprised to hear her voice again.

"I'm back in Florida."

"Can't say I'm surprised. Hope you're enjoying the nice weather." Bernie didn't need to ask why she was calling. The Florida lawyer knew she hadn't found her buried inheritance and was desperate for more clues. What else could it possibly be? If she'd already found it, her tone of voice would be so much different.

"Just wanted you to know I'm no closer now than I was at the beginning. Since we're leaving in the morning anyway, I was just wondering..."

"About what?"

"Did my grandfather forget to include something in the second 'one-eleven' clue?"

"I don't believe so, why?"

194

"I'm completely stuck. For the life in me, I can't figure it out. I feel so stupid. We solved the first clue the same day we found the safe-deposit box. I was convinced we would decipher the second clue that same day, or the following day at the latest.

"Yet here I am seven weeks later, and still nothing. I'm sure it hasn't escaped your attention that I'm at the halfway point. Part of me wants to give up."

Bernie grimaced. "I wish I could help you, Shelby, but you know I can't. Even if I wanted to, I couldn't."

"Why's that?"

"Truth is, I never wanted to know the exact whereabouts of the buried treasure chest."

"Why's that?"

"Personal reasons, I suppose."

Hmm... "How many others know about it?"

"I'm not at liberty to discuss that with you. Sorry."

There was a prolonged silence until Bernie heard sniffling.

Finally, Shelby said, "I understand, Mister Finkel. Sorry for disturbing you. Hope you have a pleasant evening."

The line went dead, and Shelby exploded into tears. Again.

The demons assigned to her were mere inches from her face. Their jaundice yellow eyes were blood red. They breathed onto her face, each exhale sending sulfuric brownish-green smoke in her direction. "Give up, Shelby!" they hissed. "Go home! It's a lost cause! God hates you!"

Bernie Finkel felt a sharp pain in his heart. He called Bob Schuster. *This is crazy!*

"Hey Bernie, what can I do for you?"

"Shelby McKinney just called me," he said glumly.

Bob gulped hard, "What did she want?"

"She's back in Florida and completely stuck. Since solving the first clue, she's made no other progress." Bernie sighed. "She wanted to know if Luther forgot to include something important regarding the second 'one-eleven' clue."

Bob Schuster felt a slight panic brewing beneath the surface. Bernie didn't need to tell him Shelby was back in Florida. He already knew. In fact, all 140 of *Shelby's Saints* knew it. They also knew about her last three failed trips to the Sunshine State, and that she was still stuck on the second "111" clue.

The reason they knew was each time she came back to Florida, Bob and Ruth Schuster were camped beneath the magnificent landmark overlooked by so many, hoping and praying that she would finally notice it. They watched

Shelby walk by the pelican trees numerous times without noticing them. It was as if the trees weren't even there.

"Did she sound like she wanted to give up?"

"Most certainly," Bernie said. "Even said it, in fact."

"I see."

"Is there any way we can help her, Bob?"

"As much as I'd love to say yes to your question, I'm afraid we can't offer any assistance."

"I feel like weeping for her. I can't take this much longer, Bob. I'm at the point now that if she calls again, I don't think I'll have the strength to even answer the phone."

Bob Schuster sighed, "I understand how you feel, Bernie."

Luther Mellon did a remarkable job planning this amazing adventure for his beloved granddaughter. The only potential roadblock Bob ever saw was the second "111" clue: he thought it might be too vague for Shelby decipher. He even told Luther on a few occasions. But Mellon seemed content to leave it the way it was. Bob now had all the proof that he was right all along.

Seeds of doubt were starting to take root in Bob Schuster's increasingly troubled mind. In order to find the second safe-deposit box—which was the whole point of this treasure hunt adventure—Shelby first had to find her buried inheritance.

Part of Bob wanted to knock on her hotel door, introduce himself and take her straight to the buried treasure. He refocused. "As much as it hurts me to say this, Bernie, we need to remain patient."

"Wanna know what I can't figure out?" Bernie said, softly.

"What's that?"

"Why Luther left us both a hundred-thousand-dollars, for doing absolutely nothing, yet decided to put his own granddaughter through all this personal torture. It's totally beyond me!"

"Luther left a hundred-thousand-dollars for you too?" Bob was completely shocked.

"I assumed you knew that, Bob."

"I had no idea!" Bob was completely taken aback by this new revelation. "Well then, I can give you a hundred-thousand-reasons why you must maintain your strict code of silence." Bob winced at his own words.

"Are you suggesting it was bribery money, Bob?"

"Come on, Bernie. You know Luther wasn't the type to bribe anyone. I'm convinced it came straight from his heart, with absolutely no strings attached."

"That's what I always thought too. But why did he do this to Shelby? I feel guilty just looking at the check." Bernie grimaced. "Are you sure Luther was of sound mind when he hatched this crazy plan?"

"I'm one-hundred percent certain of it, Bernie."

"Can I ask you something?"

"Sure," said Bob, bracing himself.

"Why do you seem okay with all of this?"

"I'm not as okay as you might think. I'm just waiting for God to answer the many prayers being offered up for Shelby each day. We all have faith she'll find it soon enough."

"How many days have you been praying for her success?"

"Since the very beginning when Luther first hatched the idea. Why?"

"With all due respect, a lot of good your prayers are doing!" Bernie immediately regretted his insensitive comment. "Sorry, Bob, I shouldn't have said it."

"It's okay. I understand your frustration. I can assure you that many are just as frustrated as you."

Bernie shook his head. In his opinion, praying to some invisible Being, hoping that something good would eventually happen in the end, was a classic case of shallow thinking. In Bernie Finkel's world, sound planning is what got things done, not mindless praying to a faceless, faraway God, hoping that the roll of the dice would eventually turn up in your favor. It was childish thinking at best.

"I don't know about you, Bob, but I still haven't deposited the check. I feel too guilty. The day Shelby finds her inheritance will be the day I deposit it. Just hope it's soon. Not for my sake. For hers."

"Very noble of you. Let's just pray for everyone's sake that she finds it soon enough."

"You pray, Bob, while I remain worried. I think we will both get the same result in the end."

"Sorry you feel that way, pal."

"You believe what you believe and vice versa. That's why they make chocolate and vanilla, right?"

"I suppose so, Bernie." Bob left it at that. "Let me know if you hear anything else."

"You got it."

As much as Bob Schuster's heart ached for Shelby McKinney, it ached even more for Bernie Finkel. Their friendship was solid, but spiritually speaking Bernie was lost. The only major disagreements they'd had in their long partnership stemmed from Bob's unwavering faith in God.

Bernie knew Bob's compass was pointed straight toward Jesus.

Bernie, on the other hand was a staunch atheist whose compass was pointed toward science and humanity.

Whenever Bob tried redirecting Bernie's spiritual compass toward Jesus, Bernie made it crystal clear that he wanted nothing to do with his so-called Savior.

Now that they were getting up there in age—Bob was 68 and Bernie was 67—Bob's overall concern for his partner's soul deepened more and more. The last thing he wanted was for Bernie to die still in his sins, without first trusting in Christ for his salvation.

The moment they became business partners, the Schusters started praying for Bernie Finkel each day without fail. Bob never told anyone, including Ruth, but he was starting to think God wasn't listening to their prayers on his behalf.

How could he think otherwise when, after so many years, Bernie still hadn't taken the smallest step toward God?

Bob Schuster sighed. With time slowly winding down on this little adventure, he needed to remain focused on Shelby for now. Compared to the 37 years he'd prayed for Bernie, the 18 months of praying for Shelby seemed like nothing. But longsuffering was still longsuffering, despite the amount of time involved.

Knowing what was at stake, for the first time since this little adventure began, Bob was starting to wonder if he needed to make a slight revision to Luther Mellon's plan.

Not a revision, per se, but more of a tweaking, to redirect Shelby's compass a bit without giving it all away. Just the thought of changing what Luther had worked so hard on before his death filled Bob with great remorse.

But if Shelby wasn't reinvigorated, and soon, this adventure might come to an end long before the 90-day time limit came to pass.

Though everything inside Bob told him to leave things alone, he was already thinking of how to keep Shelby in the game without giving it all away.

But how? It was a question that would dominate his thinking more than any other thought for weeks to come...

39

JULY 27 - DAY 47

BOB AND RUTH SCHUSTER called an emergency conference the next night at 8:00 p.m., to update key members of *Shelby's Saints* on her great lack of progress down in Florida.

Pastor Paul Jamison and his wife, Trina, were both online, along with Pastor Mike Cantrell, his wife Alexandra, and Mabel Saunders. Everyone logged onto Skype from home, except for Pastor Paul Jamison; he was at Grace Bible Church in Summerville preparing a message. He listened from inside his small office.

Bob wasted no time coming straight to the point, "Good evening everyone. Thanks for taking time out of your busy schedules to listen in. The reason Ruth and I called this meeting is to inform you all that we believe Shelby's on the verge of quitting."

"Why's that, Bob?" said Pastor Jamison.

"Well, for starters, she called my business partner last night saying she was completely stuck and didn't know where to go from here. Bernie told me she's seriously considering quitting."

Bob Schuster sighed. "I don't need to remind anyone of the time factor. We're now past the halfway point and she's still stuck on the second clue. We need to pray she perseveres until she finally finds it." *If she finds it*, he thought to himself.

"Of course, we'll keep praying, Bob," said Pastor Cantrell calmly, "but there's still plenty of time."

"According to the calendar you would be correct, Pastor. But Ruth and I both saw how defeated she looked the past three days. I can assure you there's cause for concern. You know I'm not one to easily jump the gun, but after four wasted trips, I don't think she has many more trips left in her. All that endless disappointment is weighing heavily on her. Each time we saw her pass by the pelican trees, she looked even more distraught."

Bob sighed, "For the life in me, I can't understand why they never jump out at her like they do for so many others. Ruth can attest to the many people we saw the past three days stop everything they were doing just to marvel at the pelican trees. Many even took pictures. Am I right, Ruth?"

199

"Yes, dear," Ruth replied, softly. "But Shelby never once glanced at them. It's like Satan's supernaturally blinded her view, making them appear completely invisible to her. It's mystifying."

Bob Schuster scratched his head, "You've been there, Mabel. You know how difficult it would be to *not* notice them; especially after passing by as many times as Shelby has."

"I wholeheartedly agree, Bob." Mabel was just as mystified as them.

"Of course, not everyone appreciates the three trees," Bob went on, in a tone of voice rarely heard coming from his mouth, "but almost everyone notices them. Everyone but Shelby, it appears. I can assure you no one's walked past them more than she has the past three days. I'm talking easily a couple dozen times. Ruth is right; it's like there's some huge veil covering the trees, completely obstructing her view. It's almost unexplainable."

Ruth shook her head, "Each time we saw her approaching them, we hoped that would be the time. But it never happened. She kept walking each time. After a while, I stopped counting how many times she walked right over the buried chest." Ruth's voice emanated the same concern as her husband's. "She looked at the condominiums behind the pelican trees where we're staying once or twice, but nothing sparked her interest enough to take a closer look. It was frustrating to watch."

"Well Ruth, as you know," Mabel Saunders said, sitting in a forest green leather reclining chair in her living room, "because of our overall involvement as intercessors, Satan's unleashed his full arsenal on Shelby. If she succeeds in finding the buried treasure chest, the possibility exists that she'll find her salvation."

"Can y'all imagine how furious Satan was the day he lost Luther and Eleanor to Christ?" Pastor Paul Jamison interjected. "Hell's future suddenly became less populated by two."

"Indeed, Paul," Mabel replied. "I'm sure there was a time when Satan felt reasonably certain they would both go to their graves without first trusting in Jesus. When the Most High changed their hearts and rescued their souls from eternal damnation, it must have incensed Satan to no end."

Mabel paused to draw in much needed oxygen to her lungs. The 79-year-old woman's chronic heart condition kept worsening. "God's ultimate enemy will do anything in his power to prevent it from happening again with anyone else from the Mellon clan.

"If Shelby finds redemption at the end of this treasure hunt, it could thwart Satan's plan to keep them all living in spiritual bondage. When it comes to the human soul, just like God, Satan doesn't want to lose anyone."

"That would be correct, Mabel," Pastor Mike Cantrell declared. "Nothing would please the demons assigned to Shelby more than to see her join them in hell someday when her time on earth comes to an end. With that in mind, we can't expect the enemy to give a single inch."

"And we mustn't be naive, y'all," Pastor Jamison said, "Satan knows Mabel wants Shelby to replace her at Operation Forgiveness in the future. That should tell us all we need to know. Satan feels threatened."

"Agreed," Pastor Mike Cantrell opined. "Because Shelby isn't a believer, we can expect supernatural protection to be severely limited. Until she places her complete trust in Jesus, the demons assigned to her will keep tormenting, tempting and deceiving her."

"The more I think about it," said Bob Schuster, "I wouldn't be surprised if Satan's actually pulled demons from other important missions around the globe and reassigned them to this one. Sure, on the surface it looks like a harmless buried treasure hunt. But Satan knows God often works best in simple situations.

"Seeing how blinded Shelby's been regarding the pelican trees, perhaps we've underestimated just how interested Satan really is in this Mission. I think it's time for us to double-up on our efforts."

"I couldn't agree with you more, Bob," Pastor Jamison declared. "We must never lose sight that, from a human standpoint, we're the biggest cogs in Satan's problematic wheel. If the devil loses Shelby to Christ and she ends up replacing Mabel in the future, think of how many could potentially be plucked out of his vast webs of deception and be forever comforted in the arms of Jesus."

"Good point, Pastor," said Mabel. "I agree the spiritual warfare will only get worse and much more intense as we enter into the final weeks. By not being a born-again believer, Shelby's certain to face even greater danger from this point forward. Even we should expect to come under increased spiritual attack, much like Luther did at the outset."

Mabel Saunders paused a moment to formulate her next thoughts. She uttered a simple "Thank you, Lord," skyward, then spoke into her phone, "Pardon me for saying this, brothers and sisters, but aren't we starting to sound as if Satan was in control of the situation instead of God?"

Bob Schuster said, "What are you getting at, Mabel?"

"We mustn't forget that God is sovereign and in complete control of all things at all times. This includes the buried treasure hunt."

"That goes without saying, Mabel…"

"I hear what you're saying, Bob. But if we truly believed what we proclaim about God being sovereign, wouldn't we approach the situation a little differently?"

"In what way?"

"Instead of praying that Shelby finds the buried treasure chest, let's start praying first and foremost that God will change her heart and open her eyes and ears to the Gospel of Jesus Christ beforehand.

"Once that happens, there will be nothing Satan can do to stop Shelby from becoming a believer. We must never forget that God does the calling, not us humans. And certainly not Satan!"

"Amen to that! When you're right, Mabel, you're right!" Ruth Schuster shouted.

Bob Schuster said, "Brothers and sisters, let us pray…"

Shelby's Saints spent nearly an hour praying for each member of the Mellon clan by name. But mostly they prayed that God would rescue Shelby before it was too late...

40

IT WAS A BEAUTIFUL sunshiny day in Summerville, South Carolina. Shelby McKinney was grateful to be back home with her family, far away from Sanibel Island. She didn't feel foolish or vulnerable at home like she did so many times in Florida.

Walking the dirt and gravel driveway leading up to their beautiful house, Shelby drank it all in. The massive oak trees lining the driveway soothed her weary senses. The crepe myrtles looked remarkable.

The flowers and rose bushes she'd planted all throughout the acre and a half of land they owned—not to mention the carpet of finely manicured green grass Jesse worked so hard to maintain—looked and smelled spectacular.

The three broad steps leading up to the white double doors forming the main entrance to the house looked so inviting. Everything looked picture-perfect.

All these things made perfect sense to her, comforting Shelby greatly, making her feel safe and protected.

She went to the garden in the backyard and plucked a few ripened tomatoes off the vine.

Brooke was playing with the little girl next door, Tessa. The two took turns swinging on a large worn-out truck tire hanging from a branch jutting out from the huge live oak tree draped with Spanish moss. The two were connected by a thick rope.

A smile formed on Shelby's face. All these things had been a huge part of her life the past seven years. They were things she could see with her own two eyes and touch with her hands.

Even better, the man in the red pick-up truck couldn't torment her here. At least she hoped not. Though she hadn't seen him since the last day of her second trip to Florida, his image still loomed large in her mind, constantly haunting her.

Shelby needed this time to recharge her batteries—physically, mentally and emotionally. But most of all, she needed time to reconnect with her family.

She yearned for Jesse, Trevor, BJ and Brooke, and was desperate to spend quality time with the four of them again.

The great and daring adventure she was so excited about suddenly became the one topic she wanted to avoid like the plague.

Besides, with Trevor's birthday just three weeks away, and with the new school year fast approaching, Shelby needed to focus on mailing party invitations and shopping for school supplies and clothing for the kids.

Yes, it was time to start acting like a responsible parent again. Jesse and the kids deserved that much.

But even being surrounded by those she loved most in the world, she felt this invisible force separating her from everyone else. She didn't know what it was or from where it came. All she knew was it was there, and she couldn't suppress it or escape from it, no matter how hard she tried.

The one question she kept asking herself more than any other since this insane journey began was, "Why am I here on this crazy planet?" It was a question she never asked prior to going on the buried treasure hunt. It was something she now contemplated on a daily basis, along with a myriad of other "meaning of life" questions.

For the first time ever, Shelby felt the need to take a personal inventory of herself. Yes, it was time to reevaluate everything in her life. But just knowing her inheritance was buried two states south of hers, just waiting to be unearthed, made it impossible to ignore the clock inside her head.

It kept ticking—tick tock, tick tock.

Her mind forwarded to this upcoming November. BJ's birthday was on the nineteenth, two and a half months after the September eighth deadline. Shelby couldn't help but wonder whether she or her grandfather's church in Florida would be in possession of what was still legally hers. It was a sinking feeling, to say the least.

Shelby decided to stop thinking about her buried inheritance for the rest of the day. One day turned into two. Then three. Then a week passed. Then two weeks. Miraculously, save for a few minor mental flare ups, it got to where she barely thought about it at all.

Midway through August, however, the day after Trevor's birthday on the thirteenth, she traveled back to Florida a fifth time.

After three more fruitless days in the Sunshine State, she went home empty-handed again feeling even more foolish.

The good news was that she finally felt she had gotten it out of her system. But then, just as she was coming to grips with her routine life again, September slowly crept in and her thoughts returned to the September eighth deadline.

On September first, her mind went into hyper-speed again. She did all she could to fight the overwhelming urge to travel back to Florida a sixth time.

No matter how hard she tried, she was powerless to overcome it. *Here we go again*, Shelby thought to herself, already trying to think of the best way to tell Jesse that she'd changed her mind once again...

41

SEPTEMBER 2 - DAY 84

"IT'S OKAY, SWEETIE, WE'LL be fine. Just go," Jesse said, trying to conceal this new level of concern in his wife's presence. The smile on his face was somewhat reassuring, but the eyes never lied.

The message they conveyed was altogether different. They screamed, "Give up, Shelby! You're wasting your time!"

Those seven words had loomed large in Jesse's mind ever since her second failed mission back in late June. But they were seven words he would never dare utter to her. Especially now!

Up to this point, Shelby had done a remarkable job of masking her true feelings of mounting despair, but Jesse saw through it all. He knew his wife all too well. She was extremely fragile—on the verge of coming apart at the seams, in fact. Even without saying a word, he believed one more blow might shatter her completely, irreparably.

But Shelby also knew her husband of 10 years enough to know that he, too, was masking his true feelings. She knew what he was thinking; *here we go again!*

To Jesse's credit, he was doing a marvelous job playing the role of supportive husband, keeping his negative thoughts and comments to himself. He would never win an Oscar for his performance, but at least he was trying. Even so, she couldn't ignore what she saw in his eyes. It was anything but encouraging.

Shelby dreaded to think what would happen if he ever knew there was a madman down in Florida following his wife's every move. Though she hadn't seen him on her past three trips there, he still frightened her to no end. If Jesse ever found out, he would be furious with her for withholding this important tidbit from him.

She just hoped that—excluding the three-day trip to the Sunshine State in the middle of August—the six weeks away from Florida had totally thrown him off her scent.

With only six days left to find the buried treasure chest, he was the very last thing she needed now.

206

All these thoughts rendered Shelby vulnerable. She felt like a scared little girl leaving home for the first time. Part of her didn't want to go. She willed herself to remain strong in front of Jesse.

"I'll call the moment I check into the hotel."

"Okay, dear. Be careful driving." Jesse embraced his wife again.

Shelby climbed into the car and pulled out to the edge of the driveway. She looked both ways before proceeding onto U.S. 17, northbound.

Before reaching I-26, she pulled into a Dunkin' Donuts drive-thru and ordered an extra-large coffee and an apple-cinnamon muffin, all the while wondering why in the world she was going back to Florida again, with absolutely no new clues to go on.

Without a doubt, this trip was more "deadline" induced than anything else. It no longer felt like an adventure, but a job; a job she disliked a little more with each passing day. Even the extended break did little to rejuvenate her. It's like her heart was no longer in it.

Shelby unceremoniously reached I-26 and headed westbound. There was no excitement this time. The intrigue was gone. She was somber, stoic. Her vehicle traveled 70 miles per hour, but she felt like she was going nowhere fast. No, she corrected herself, she wasn't going nowhere fast. She was sinking in quicksand.

At least her body was.

Her mind, on the other hand, raced faster than her vehicle traveled at times—her negative, self-defeating thoughts providing the necessary fuel her mind needed for such speed.

The first five trips to Florida felt so much different than now. Even though she came away empty-handed each time, she was always excited beforehand. There was no motivation this time.

How could she be excited when the only assurance she had upon arriving in the Sunshine State was knowing the hotel she would be staying at? Other than that, she was totally clueless. Again.

Shelby knew her inheritance was buried somewhere on Sanibel Island, 50 steps west of the second "111" clue.

But where in the world was it buried? She knew it was a magnificent landmark that was completely overlooked by most and that it represented three objects, all of which provided shelter and safe refuge for so many. But where was it?

She couldn't help but wonder again if her grandfather had mistakenly left out an important element pertaining to the second "111" clue. He must have, because after wracking her brain senseless for nearly three months, she still couldn't figure it out.

And each day that passed brought her dangerously closer to the deadline. Shelby reached I-95 and drove south. Up until now, she'd always viewed I-95 as the main road leading to the end of the rainbow, her inheritance. Now it looked more like a long and winding road that seemingly went on forever and led to nowhere. It was a road that wasted so much time, money and energy.

Try as she might, she couldn't flush these negative thoughts from her mind. They kept haunting her, torturing her.

If she only had something else to go on, it would be enough to totally reinvigorate her again. But she didn't. Even the final "111" clue wouldn't be revealed until she turned into a rocket scientist and miraculously deciphered the second clue.

Having walked Sanibel Beach so many times the past few weeks, she knew it would take a million people a million lifetimes to dig up every square inch of the twelve miles of beach on that island, including Captiva Island, which, in her mind, still couldn't be removed from the equation.

What could she possibly do to make the slightest dent in Sanibel Beach all by herself? The answer was glaringly obvious; not much!

Yet here she was driving back to Florida totally blindfolded with her hands tied behind her back, with no one to free her.

With only six days left and 84 days of disappointment already behind her, how could she remain positive now? Perhaps she really had been walking a plank all this time, which ultimately led straight to the bottom of the ocean. It sure felt that way.

Shelby reached the Georgia state line and pulled into the welcome center to use the restroom. She also needed time to think without her surroundings passing her by at 70 miles per hour.

In short, she needed to be still for a while.

After using the restroom, she stared out the front windshield of her car, trying to decide what to do next. Back and forth she went inside her mind. She had a sudden urge to get out of the car and run.

"What am I doing here? I don't belong here," she cried. "I should be at home with my family. They need me more than Florida needs me!"

The demons assigned to her hovered above and even inside her vehicle, screaming at the top of their lungs, "Stop wasting time!" they hissed. "There's nothing for you in Florida! Go back home! Your grandfather was insane! God hates you!"

Their snakelike tongues slithered and licked her face everywhere, wishing it was her soul. They breathed and slobbered onto her face, each exhale sending sulfuric brownish-green smoke into the air.

208

With the decision made, Shelby reentered the highway and went south. Upon reaching the first southbound exit, she got off. With tears in her eyes, she made a U-Turn and headed north on I-95.

Yes, it was time to go home.

She arrived home at around six p.m. As expected, everyone was shocked to see her walking through the kitchen door, just as they were about to eat dinner. By looking into her eyes, everyone knew not to ask questions. Her face said it all; total failure. Again.

They were just happy she was home.

At four a.m., the distraught woman was still tossing and turning in bed. Even the hot bath didn't help. She still felt restless.

How could she possibly sleep with six wasted trips to Florida—five and a half trips, she corrected herself—constantly toying with her mind, tormenting her nonstop?

It seemed for each step she took forward, she was forced to take two steps back. At least that many! It was getting old. She was getting old. At least she felt older now. And foolish, for attempting to go to Florida a sixth time. And for what? Another misadventure? Another failure?

It was time to accept that she would never find her inheritance and finally give up on this silly little pipe dream. Yes, it was time to accept her great misfortune and move on with her life.

In the back of her mind, she feared her children now harbored ill-feelings toward their late great grandfather. Shelby knew they blamed him, and him alone, for their mother's misery of late, which had taken a severe toll on the entire family.

"Momma was never like this before GG died," she could almost hear them saying in unison, "Never!"

Shelby managed to sleep three hours before Brooke woke her. She was hungry and wanted breakfast.

Jesse offered to feed her, but Brooke said, "I want Mommy to do it."

Shelby climbed out of bed with a throbbing headache from total sleep deprivation, and from being so emotionally unbalanced the past three months.

She went downstairs and put waffles in the toaster for Brooke and made coffee. As it brewed, she moseyed out to her garden to check on her crops and plants. Plucking a few near-ripened tomatoes off the vines, she placed them in a plastic bag.

She pulled out a few pesky weeds here and there, but quickly grew bored and went back in the house. Shelby put the tomatoes on the window sill in the kitchen, poured herself a cup of coffee and sat on the front-porch swing.

That didn't help either.

209

Though emotionally drained, she needed to do something productive, but didn't know what to do. She was stuck in quicksand again and couldn't move. If this little journey did anything, it made her feel completely aimless at times, purposeless.

Prior to going on this adventure, she felt she had everything pretty much under control. Sure, life was hectic at times, especially raising three children, but it was still simple enough to manage.

Three turbulence-filled months later, and she wasn't sure of anything anymore. She found herself questioning everything.

Was there Divine Order in a world so full of chaos and uncertainty? Shelby was still unsure.

Even so, the one question that kept resurfacing in her mind was, *why am I here on this planet?* It was a question which begged an answer. But try as she might she still had no answer, no matter how deep she dug for one.

But Shelby was starting to think it was more than just being a wife and mother.

Later that morning, she walked the short distance to the mailbox at the front of the property to see what Charlie the mailman had left for them. She retrieved the mail and saw a postcard stuffed inside, addressed to her, from Florida. Sanibel Beach, Florida, to be exact.

On the back was written:

> *Greetings, Shelby!*
> *You're so close. Closer than you think!*
> *You've already located the beach. Congratulations!*
> *Here's a bonus clue to reward your great effort!*
> *Find the Pelican Tree. Then, like your grandfather said,*
> *count off 50 steps due west and start digging!*
> *The Pelican Tree is situated **directly** on the beach,*
> *offering a spectacular oceanfront view of paradise.*
> *Find the Pelican Tree and you'll find the buried treasure.*
> *Hopeful that you'll find it, Sincerely, A Friend!*

Shelby raced back to the house. Trevor and BJ were playing catch in the backyard with the boys next door. Brooke was riding her battery operated pink *Barbie* Jeep.

Jesse was relaxing on the couch watching college football on TV. It was opening weekend.

Shelby said nothing but dropped the postcard onto his lap.

"What's this," Jesse said, noticing her complete change of posture.

210

"Read it," she said, beaming inside.

"Hmm," *Here we go again!* Jesse thought. "The Pelican Tree? Is this the elusive landmark you've been searching for all this time?"

"Yup." Shelby dashed to her desk and Googled the *Pelican Tree.* Nothing! She tried four other search engines and still found nothing. The roller coaster ride continued.

She rejoined her husband on the couch.

Jesse didn't need to say a word. It was written all over her face.

"No such place," she said, "At least not online. What kind of landmark goes completely unadvertised like this? This is too strange!"

"You're right. It is strange," came the reply. "But your grandfather did say it went unnoticed by most, right?"

"Yeah. Especially me..."

"What do you plan to do?"

"I don't know." Shelby burst out in tears.

Jesse gathered her into his arms.

"If I knew where the Pelican Tree was located, I'd leave right now," Shelby said. "But with no solid location, I don't think I have the strength to go back again. I'm totally spent. The very thought of coming back empty-handed again fatigues me to no end."

"Would you like me to go for you?" Jesse said, already knowing the answer.

"No. Besides, you know we can't afford another trip to Florida."

"We'll be fine. We still have our credit cards. We'll manage somehow."

Shelby smiled through her tears. Jesse still had faith in her. "What are you suggesting?"

"Could you really live with yourself knowing you gave it your all for eighty-five days, only to quit with five days left?"

"Hmm..."

Jesse reached for the remote. It was halftime. He turned on the Weather Channel. They were charting a fast-developing hurricane projected to make landfall within the next couple of days.

Hurricane expert Susan Pamplona said, "Tropical Storm Gertrude has just been upgraded to a hurricane and is currently three-hundred miles east of Cuba, with sustained winds of eighty-three miles per hour. It's continuing to strengthen.

"Our latest tracks suggest two probable scenarios; either it will strike Cuba then proceed due west toward the Mexican Peninsula, or it will head northwest toward Florida. I believe the latter is the best possibility so far."

"Great," Jesse said, "just great."

Shelby was too numb to comment.

"If Florida ends up in Hurricane Gertrude's path," the meteorologist said, cautiously, "it should make landfall either Wednesday or Thursday, possibly as a category three or even a four..."

"Isn't Thursday the deadline?" Jesse asked.

Shelby didn't reply. Her shoulders slumped, and her head fell downward.

Jesse changed the channel. He wanted to take away his wife's pain but didn't know how. "I don't know what to say, honey, I really don't. Whatever you decide to do, I'm behind you all the way."

"I need a day to rest and think things through. Besides, it's Labor Day weekend, which means I'll never find a room anywhere near Sanibel Island. Not in our price range, anyway."

"Understood," was all Jesse could think to say.

"In the meantime, I'll continue searching for the Pelican Tree online, before even thinking about driving back to Florida again." Shelby leaned into her husband.

Jesse held her without uttering another word. But inside it was like a swarm of bees had invaded his brain. The constant buzzing was starting to make him crazy.

Jesse knew it had to be twice as bad for Shelby.

At least that much!

42

SEPTEMBER 5 - DAY 87

IT WAS LABOR DAY in America, the unofficial end of the Summer season. Tomorrow it was back to school for all kids who hadn't already begun the new school year.

While most American families spent the day having barbecues, going to the beach, attending various sporting events, and a myriad of other family activities, Shelby McKinney begrudgingly decided to travel back to Florida one last time, despite her strongest inner protests.

Not only was she unable to locate the Pelican Tree online, she made dozens of calls to perfect strangers and business owners on the island, using an online directory.

The few she contacted said they had never heard of such a place. *Landmark—what a joke,* she thought in disgust.

In any event, with a full day of rest and a new sense of desperation, Shelby was raring to go again.

Even if no one on Sanibel Island had ever heard of the place, having something new to go on was far better than nothing at all. Had she not received the postcard two days ago, there's no way she'd be going back to Florida now.

Shelby was driving south on I-95 in the state of Georgia listening to an all-news radio station. Not surprisingly, the big story on all stations was the fast-approaching hurricane.

Thirty-eight miles north of the Florida state line, she could already see the growing congestion on I-95 northbound. Most folks had adhered to the strong urging to leave the Sunshine State.

Yet here she was driving directly into harm's way. If everyone got to experience one moment of temporary insanity in life, without a doubt, this could go down as Shelby's defining moment!

Although predictions still varied slightly from one meteorologist to the next, the one thing in which they were all agreed was that Hurricane Gertrude would strike just south of Miami on Wednesday shortly before midnight.

From there it would continue northwest toward the Naples-Fort Myers vicinity, making impact early Thursday morning, at around 3:00 a.m. *At least I'll have two days of decent weather,* she thought, trying to remain upbeat.

Shelby arrived on Sanibel Island just after 8:00 p.m. and checked into the same Holiday Inn she stayed at with her mother and children back in July. Had it not been for the approaching hurricane, she would have never found a vacant room on the island.

Her brother, Jake, insisted on paying for her lodging this time and, like his mother back in July, wasn't about to take no for an answer. Shelby gratefully accepted his generous offer.

Once inside the room, she changed into her swimsuit and took a quick swim in the hotel pool. After showering, she ate a quick meal and called it a night. She wanted to be awake at the crack of dawn, so she could fully maximize her final three days on Sanibel Island.

Shelby woke the next morning at 7:00 a.m. and turned on the TV. All talk was focused on the hurricane. She turned it off and looked outside the window. She was relieved that the man in the red pick-up truck was nowhere to be seen.

Perhaps with so many setbacks and disappointments, he finally grew bored and gave up. Or perhaps the extended break had thrown that maniac off her trail for good.

From a physical standpoint, he wasn't all that menacing; perhaps five-ten and on the thin side. But the scowl on his face and evil look in his eyes more than made up for his lack of physicality.

After a quick breakfast, Shelby hit the beach, postcard in card, determined as ever to find it this time. Up and down the beach radios blared stern warnings for everyone to vacate the area immediately.

Shelby did her best to ignore it all and remain focused. *Perhaps I really am losing my marbles after all!*

She was a little surprised to see many still out collecting seashells. Situated three miles out in the Gulf of Mexico, Sanibel Island was considered one of the best shelling locations in the western hemisphere. Many came for the sole purpose of scouring the beach collecting bags and buckets full of pristine seashells.

As guests slept in comfortable beds each night, they waited expectantly for the newest arrival of shells to wash ashore like clockwork.

Once the hurricane arrived, no one would be shelling here for at least a day or two.

Perhaps even longer than that.

Shelby overheard an older woman tell a family of six that the best seashells were found at Blind Pass on the northern tip of the island. It sounded like fun, but she couldn't think about collecting seashells; she needed to remain focused on the task at hand.

Thanks to the postcard, there was no need to travel back to Captiva Island this time. Shelby could focus all her time and energy on Sanibel Beach. Which was a blessing.

Even so, the thought of aimlessly digging holes in the sand again and still finding nothing provided little motivation. Especially being alone. When Trevor, BJ and Brooke dug holes in the sand with her, many marveled at how great a mother she was being to her three children. But digging holes in the sand without them caused some to raise eyebrows and shake heads.

For the next 10 hours, Shelby walked up and down the sandy white surface too many times to count. Even the bonus clue brought her no closer to locating the second "111" clue, which she now knew to be the Pelican Tree, whatever that was!

To the best of her knowledge, she felt certain she'd checked every possible beachfront landmark on the island, just as the postcard had stated. And still nothing!

Before calling it a day, she walked out to the water's edge and looked skyward. "Come on Pelican Tree, where are you? What are you? Please show yourself! Make yourself known to me. Are you a hotel? A church? A wildlife preserve?"

Shelby sighed, and her shoulders slumped. "Well Grandpa, here I am again. I've done everything you've asked of me, yet I'm still completely stuck. Please help me. Show me the way.

"I'm two days away from losing my inheritance. I need your help now more than ever. Did you forget to include something for me? If so, please reveal it to me. I'm begging you. Please help me. I miss you so much."

The demons assigned to her attacked her mind with wave after wave of self-doubt. They screamed into her ears, "Your grandfather lied to you! He's crazy! Go Home!" they hissed. "God hates you!"

Shelby wanted to weep but amazingly no tears came. She was too numb to cry. She already had a sinking feeling that tomorrow would be a repeat performance of today.

The next morning, like a robot obeying a command, Shelby reluctantly took to the beach, clearly in another self-induced fog.

The only thing she could think to do was aimlessly stroll the beach, up and down, back and forth, shovel in hand, hoping something would jump out and ignite her senses so she could finally locate the Pelican Tree. She refused to visit another wildlife refuge!

After walking dozens of miles of beautiful pristine beaches the past two days, and pushing her mind and legs to the limit, Shelby still had nothing to show for all her efforts.

She wondered for the millionth time if the Pelican Tree even existed, at least from a physical standpoint. She seriously doubted it. *It really must be a metaphorical place*, she thought again.

Perhaps this little adventure really was a lost cause all along. She could almost see Martin Hightower pointing his finger at her saying, "See? Told ya!"

Shelby couldn't help but wonder again if Bernie Finkel and his partner really were out to steal from her.

With the deadline fast approaching, had they purposely sent the postcard to keep her off track? Sure, Bernie sounded like a nice man on the phone, but did that mean he could be trusted?

Shelby knew nothing about his partner, Bob Schuster. Was he really a bad guy in disguise?

At any rate, if there really was a place called the Pelican Tree, business had to be terrible. How could anyone possibly remain in business if not even Sanibel's own residents had ever heard of the establishment? After diligently searching the past two days, practically nonstop, she still couldn't find it! *This is nuts!*

If there was a consolation prize for all her effort, with so much exposure to the sun, Shelby was well-tanned with wisps of blonde streaking all throughout her long brown hair. And all that walking and constant stress had served to shave twelve pounds off her fatigued body.

Combined, the loss of weight, blonde streaks and tanned body made her look much younger than 33. From a distance, one might think she was in her mid-twenties. But up close, mostly because of the deep, dark eye-bags chiseled underneath her eyes, some might think she looked ten years older than that. At least that much.

Shelby stood at the water's edge. With no more clues at her disposal and a little more than 24 hours with which to work, why continue the endless torture? Add the approaching hurricane into the mix, and it was easy for anyone to understand her growing sense of hopelessness.

As the waves splashed gently on her feet, she decided against all logic that she would give it one last shot tomorrow.

If she didn't find it by sunset which, at this point, she didn't expect to, she would leave Florida the moment the sun finished setting in the early evening sky, also setting on her buried treasure hunt adventure once and for all...

43

SEPTEMBER 7 - DAY 89

WITH EXCEPTION TO THE 30-minute break Shelby took for lunch, a Subway sandwich she ate inside her air-conditioned hotel room, she spent the rest of the day walking up and down Sanibel Beach hoping for a last-minute miracle, something that would help her finally locate the Pelican Tree.

Even the bonus clue didn't bring her any closer to finding her buried inheritance. And that meant after one more breathtaking Florida sunset, it was back home to South Carolina.

But at least it would be the last time going home empty-handed. Though her hotel room was already paid for, she saw no point in staying the night. The last thing she needed was to bask in her misery in a hotel room in a category three hurricane.

Sorry for wasting your money, Jake, she thought.

Roughly a quarter mile from her hotel, Shelby sat on the beach and stared out at the Gulf of Mexico.

The winds were noticeably stronger, offering the only proof that a fierce storm was fast approaching.

Shelby breathed in the salty sea air. In a few minutes, everyone would marvel as the majestic setting sun graciously turned the early evening Florida sky into a spectrum of breathtaking colors—white, pink, red, orange, yellow, purple, and various shades of blue—before gently and gracefully dipping behind the placid gulf waters.

As an avid picture-taker, Shelby would normally have her camera ready for this instant photo-op session to commence. But not now. She wasn't in the mood. It was time to accept and let go. A time of resignation. A time to finally put this crazy little adventure behind her once and for all, and head back home.

The sooner the better. Her suitcase was already packed. All she had to do was mentally prepare herself for the long drive home in a few minutes.

Just like the past two days, there were no tears. She was all cried out. She had fought the good fight. It was what it was.

It was time to resettle back into her role as wife and mother to her husband and three precious children.

The phone rang. It was Jesse.

217

"Hi, honey." Shelby stood and brushed sand off her tan shorts. She was totally unaware that 140 Christ followers—a.k.a. *Shelby's Saints*—were fervently praying for her this very moment, prompting God to get her to stop at this precise location on Sanibel Beach.

The demons assigned to her hovered above with a growing sense of desperation and paranoia. They knew how dangerously close Shelby was to the buried treasure.

They couldn't discern her thoughts, but the brilliant white Light high above told them all they needed to know. It started pulsating more brightly and brilliantly, which meant God was moving in this matter. Satan's demons suddenly feared a tragic outcome.

"What's going on down there?" Jesse said, trying his best to sound upbeat.

"I was just about to call you. I'm heading home as soon as the sun sets."

Jesse didn't have to ask why. He knew. "Are you sure that's what you want to do?"

"Yes."

"Everyone knows you gave it your best shot. We're all so proud of you, especially me!"

"Thanks, Jesse."

"I know it hurts, honey, and it'll take time to accept," Jesse said, softly, "but life must go on."

"I know. And you're right, Jesse! I've had three days to think and process it all. I'm okay now. Really."

"Hey, you didn't find your inheritance, but so much good has come from this adventure. For one thing, it's made us a better family. And a closer one! And we have Luther to thank for it. We've already won, Shelby."

Shelby just listened. Deep down inside she still wanted to fight, search, locate and dig, but didn't know where else to turn, where else to look. She was all out of options.

Hence, this feeling of deep resignation. "I hope to be home before sunrise."

"Just take your time and be careful on the road."

Shelby sighed, "Time for me to head back to the hotel and check out. I'll call once I'm on the interstate."

"Hope you can stay ahead of the traffic. Be careful."

"You know I will."

"I love you, Shelby."

"Love you too, Jesse."

The demons assigned to Shelby did all they could to distract her, but to no avail. The blinding white Light high above—created by the many prayers

218

offered up to God by *Shelby's Saints*—was too brilliant, too blinding, which meant their prayers were about to be answered.

Shelby turned to head back to the hotel. Mostly due to the sun's trajectory, she saw it; a large tree with pelicans perched on nearly every branch. There were three trees, in fact.

Is that the Pelican Tree? The roller coaster ride continued.

Shelby wanted to race toward the trees, but the beach was still too crowded. Tears formed in the corners of her hazel-green eyes after a three-day drought.

She ambled in that direction trying hard to maintain her composure, all the while wondering how many times she'd walked past those trees the past couple of months without ever noticing them. "Remain patient," she told herself, under her breath.

Satan's demons were beyond frantic. Up to this point, they'd successfully blinded Shelby from noticing the three trees. Now that she'd finally located them, they banded together one last time in a hopeful attempt to keep her from taking another step in that direction.

Their snakelike tongues slithered and jabbed at her face everywhere, trying to pierce her skin, so they could ultimately attack her heart. Their jaundice yellow eyes were glowing and vibrating as if to lull Shelby into a trance.

They turned blood red when their assignee walked straight through their latest smokescreen. They breathed on her face, each exhale sending sulfuric brownish-green smoke all over her. "Stay away!" they hissed. "Don't go there! God hates you!"

But nothing could stop Shelby from reaching the pelican trees. Also due to the sun's trajectory, once she arrived there she instantly noticed an inscription carved into the largest tree saying, *"You found it, Pumpkin! Woo hoo!"* It was too much to absorb.

Shelby fell to her knees and nearly collapsed on the beach. "I did it!" she exclaimed victoriously. She covered her face with her hands, sobbing tears of joy and relief. "No wonder I couldn't find it online. It really is a tree!"

Many nearby looked concerned for her but left her alone.

Shelby picked herself up off the beach, feeling ever so triumphant. She wanted to count off 50 steps and start digging, but now wasn't the time. The beach was still too crowded with last-minute stragglers wanting to witness one last Florida sunset, before Hurricane Gertrude invaded the region.

But time was of the extreme essence...

Shelby pulled her cell phone out of her pocket.

"Hey, baby. Don't tell me you're on the road already," Jesse said jokingly. There was total silence. Then he heard weeping on the other end. "What's wrong, Shelby? Are you okay?"

After a moment she was finally able to speak. "Jesse, you're not going to believe it."

"What is it?" *What's gotten into her?*

"I found the pelican tree!"

"Wow! Where? How?"

"Just like the writer of the postcard said, it's directly on the beach. It's a real tree full of pelicans! Three of them, in fact; not too far from the hotel I'm staying at. As I turned to head back to my room, I saw the three trees with hundreds of pelicans perched atop them. I'm here now.

"Grandpa even carved an inscription into one of the trees for me saying, 'You found it, Pumpkin! Woo hoo!' "This really is it, Jesse," Shelby said through her tears. "All I need to do now is count off fifty steps due west and start digging."

"Guess what kids? Momma found the pelican tree!"

"Really? Awesomeeeeeeeeeeee!" said BJ. "Where is it?"

"I'll let Momma tell you." Jesse put the speaker on.

"I found it kids! I really found it!"

"I wanna see it, Momma!" said Brooke. "Let's face time."

"Okay, sweetie. Call you right back."

A moment later, Shelby's image appeared on Jesse's cell phone. Her hair blew wildly in the wind as she showed her family the inscription on the middle tree.

"I'm so proud of you!" Trevor said, getting teary-eyed.

"Thanks, Trev." Shelby took a deep whiff of the salty sea air. "Daddy and I are both so proud of the three of you, for being so good the past three months."

They were all smiles.

"When you gonna start digging, Momma?" asked BJ.

"Beach is still too crowded," she said in a near whisper. "As soon as it clears out, I'll begin."

"Wish we could be there," Trevor said.

"Me too, sweetie. But y'all have school in the morning, and I'm almost out of time. I need to find it before the storm hits."

"We know, Momma."

"Thanks for understanding, kids. And thank you too, Jesse."

"Just glad you finally found it, baby," Jesse said.

"Needless to say, I won't be home tonight."

220

"You better not come home," Jesse said with a chuckle.

"Good thing I didn't check out of the hotel. I'm sure the few remaining hotels not yet boarded up due to the storm are sold out by now."

"Sounds exciting."

"Should be all downhill from here, right?"

"Just be careful, okay?"

"You know I will, Jesse." Then to her children, "Time for Momma to get busy. Don't forget to brush your teeth and thank God for this awesome adventure GG blessed us all with."

"Okay, Momma," said Trevor.

"Hurry home, Momma," said Brooke.

"Okay, sweetheart. See y'all tomorrow. Hopefully with our inheritance."

"Bye, Momma, love you," Trevor said.

"Love you too, son."

"Love you, Momma," said BJ. "Can't wait to see the treasure chest!"

"You'll see it soon enough."

"I love you, Mommy," said Brooke.

"And Mommy loves her precious angel so much!"

Brooke's face lit up.

"Hey, what about me," Jesse said, jokingly.

"Of course, I love you!" Shelby took another deep breath. "How could I not? You've been so amazing throughout it all."

Shelby tried to hold back more tears but simply couldn't. "I just hope someday I'm able to express how much I appreciate your undying support these past three months."

"My pleasure," Jesse said. Not wanting to get overly emotional in front of the children, he refocused. "Just don't forget to keep me posted, you hear?"

"I'll do my best."

Jesse knew what his wife meant. If she didn't lose her signal due to the storm. "Good luck, Shelby. Please be careful."

"I will, Jesse."

The call ended.

Shelby looked out at the Gulf of Mexico. Even with blurred vision from this new batch of tears, everything looked spectacular again. She walked south on the beach toward the hotel with an excitement she hadn't felt since this adventure started.

Instead of checking out, it was time to brew a pot of coffee.

As bone-tired as she was, she knew she would need it.

221

44

BOB AND RUTH SCHUSTER watched Shelby leaving the pelican tree area looking ever so jubilant. This was a time of great rejoicing for them. They, too, were forced to ride the oftentimes turbulent roller coaster of emotions this little journey had created for everyone involved.

Camped out near the pelican trees all week, they prayed nonstop that Shelby would appear one last time. Then Ruth spotted her down by the water's edge wearing tan shorts and a yellow shirt.

Bob called Pastor Cantrell. "Shelby's here! She just located the pelican trees! The moment we stopped praying for her on the conference line, Ruth spotted her. It's a miracle! God answered our prayers. Spread the word! Get the troops praying again."

"You got it, Bob," Pastor Cantrell replied, joyfully.

Bob then called his business partner of 37 years. But with Bernie Finkel, it was more of a business courtesy call rather than out of spiritual conviction. "Looks like you'll be cashing that check soon enough, old pal."

"Really?"

"Yes! Shelby just left the pelican trees! I suspect she'll start digging soon enough."

"That's terrific, Bob. She'd better hurry. Storm's almost here."

"Precisely."

"Please keep me posted."

"The moment I hear something, Bernie, I'll let you know."

"I'll look forward to your next call."

Bob Schuster was considered by many to be a man of great faith. But until Shelby arrived 30 minutes ago, even he had all but lost hope. Watching the minutes tick off his watch, his mind was more focused on reclaiming the treasure for the second time this week, and the ninth time since this adventure began nearly two years ago.

But the Florida lawyer was determined to wait until the very last moment before digging it up again.

All that thinking went out the window the moment Shelby miraculously appeared and plopped down by the water's edge, just as the Schusters were about to call it quits and head back to their condo on Sanibel Island, a condo that was owned by Luther Mellon.

The seniors bubbled over with anticipation and excitement.

That is, until Shelby started pacing the beach a few moments later, looking ever so somber. She was on the phone with someone. Her walk was slow, and her head remained down the entire time. She had no idea she was a few feet away from the buried treasure.

Ruth said nothing, but her heart continued to ache for Shelby. She dropped her head and started praying again for Luther's granddaughter, until Bob interrupted her: "Look Ruth!"

Ruth looked out at the coastline and saw Shelby's eyes narrow as she gazed in their direction, after apparently spotting the pelican trees. When she fell to her knees underneath them, the Schusters were moved to tears. Relief flooded them both. By far, it was one of the most satisfying moments of their lives.

Hallelujah! Finally!

Bob Schuster had a sudden urge to run to Shelby and introduce himself, then help her dig up Sanibel Beach like crazy before the storm approached but knew he couldn't.

At the very least, he wanted to congratulate her on a job well done, but it was too soon for all that.

SEVENTY FEET OR SO away in the opposite direction, just north of the pelican trees, Stuart Finkel watched it all unfolding and rejoiced. After following Shelby's every move the past three days—without her knowing this time—he was certain she had found what appeared to be an extremely significant clue.

Even from a distance, he saw her countenance had changed. This was the happiest he'd seen her since he started following her a few months back.

The demons assigned to Stuart Finkel met with the demons assigned to Shelby McKinney, to coordinate their next steps. They needed to band together and remain focused on the task at hand, despite their total hatred for each other.

Knowing what a failed mission meant, their hatred needed to be put aside for now, in the name of solidarity.

Much like Bob Schuster, Stuart had all but given up and was once again rehearsing Plan B inside his diabolical mind. After talking himself out of it many times, he was desperate enough to do it now, no questions asked.

Vile as it was, driven by the extremity of his need and the desperation to which it pushed him, he was ready to confront his grandfather at gunpoint, and force him to speak or else!

His plan was simple: After unearthing the buried treasure, he would tie his grandfather to his bed at home, duct tape his mouth shut and leave Florida, never to return.

Once he was safely out of the state, Stuart would call Bob Schuster and tell him what he'd done to his grandfather.

Thoughts of Canada or Mexico loomed large in his mind, especially knowing it would put great distance between himself and Florida authorities, not to mention Vinnie, Carlos, and his grandfather. His thinking quickly changed when Shelby McKinney miraculously found what appeared to be the final clue, thus sparing his grandfather any potential harm.

Hopefully there would be enough money from this score to start a new life elsewhere. Finkel's gut feeling was that he would know soon enough. Perhaps even tonight! *This is it!*

VINNIE AND CARLOS WERE also camped out on Sanibel Beach, watching everything unfolding from a distance.

Thanks to the GPS transponder mounted underneath Finkel's old pick-up truck, they knew every move he made. Each time he drove to Sanibel Island, during business hours, one of them monitored Stuey up close and personal while the other collected for Bossman.

Finkel now owed their boss $16,000, with another $3,000 due at the end of this month, plus the $3K payment they made for him in June. Stuart still knew nothing about it.

Perhaps tonight they could settle all scores. Hurricane or not, with a potentially huge payoff coming, the two thugs were once again spending large amounts of money in their minds...

"AS EXPECTED, HURRICANE GERTRUDE was just upgraded to a category two, and could become a category three hurricane before reaching Fort Myers in less than two hours," Weather Channel meteorologist, Susan Pamplona said to her many viewers.

With an uneasy tension in her voice, she went on, "The eye is expected to reach the Naples-Fort Myers region at around three a.m. Widespread power outages are already being reported and phone service is severely limited. For those of you who were unable to evacuate, it's time to batten down the hatches."

"Are you okay, Shelby?" Jesse said.

"I can't believe I fell asleep," she replied angrily, listening to the meteorologist's grim forecast.

When Shelby arrived back at her room, she had started a pot of coffee and stretched out on the bed. Before it even finished brewing, she was out cold. Jesse called at least 20 times, but her cell phone was on vibrate mode and Shelby never heard it. The strong winds and fierce rain pelting her window is what finally woke her.

"It's getting worse, Jesse. I should go." The mental clock inside her head was ticking, screaming. She was almost out of time.

Jesse was also watching the Weather Channel and felt sick to his stomach. Having endured his share of hurricanes in the past, he knew how quickly things would deteriorate down in Florida.

Part of him wanted to tell his wife to forget about the buried treasure and head home. He felt so powerless being two states away from her. "If you lose cell service, how will I know you're safe?"

"I'll be fine, sweetie."

Jesse wasn't convinced. "I should be there now."

"Hey, if you can get here, by all means, come. I would love to have you here with me. But like you said, by the time y'all got here, the deadline will have already passed...."

"Just please be careful."

"I will, Jesse, I promise." Shelby's voice trailed off.

"Good luck."

"Thanks. I'll need it."

Shelby McKinney ended the call and went outside in the driving rain, totally unprepared for what she was about to encounter...

45

SEPTEMBER 8 - DAY 90

SHELBY TURNED ON THE flashlight and aimed it at the largest of the three pelican trees, the banyan tree. The bright beam of light illuminated her grandfather's chiseled inscription.

Even carved into a tree, she easily recognized his penmanship. She wondered if it could be called "penmanship", since a pocket knife had apparently been used.

Shelby pushed that thought out of her head and pointed the flashlight skyward. Whereas hundreds of pelicans were perched on these branches just a few short hours ago, there were none now.

Sensing impending danger, they probably flew the coop at dusk seeking safer refuge. Shelby wondered what could be considered a safe refuge for any animal in a hurricane. She dismissed that thought, too, without ever venturing a guess.

She needed to remain focused. It was crunch time.

The air was breezy, dark and humid. Despite the deteriorating conditions, just knowing she was a few feet away from her inheritance filled her with great anticipation.

Even so, with only eight hours of sleep the past three days, including the brief nap earlier, she also felt a little discombobulated.

After experiencing so many peaks and valleys on this journey—mostly valleys—Shelby was physically and mentally fatigued; mental fatigue clearly the front runner.

But with a new burst of adrenaline she was raring to go again, especially knowing with absolute certainty that she was at the right place this time. It was time to put all past failures behind her and unearth the buried treasure, even in this weather.

Shelby began the difficult challenge of counting off steps due west from the pelican trees. The rain and wind kept intensifying, churning up the Gulf of Mexico, blowing wet sand into her face and mouth, stinging her. Even with her hair pulled back in a ponytail, stray wisps of hair constantly broke free and slapped her face.

The unmistakable sound of wind rustling palm trees petrified her. At times, she was forced to walk backwards to avoid getting sand and other wind-blown debris in her eyes.

Meanwhile, Bob Schuster was completely beside himself. For the past few hours, he stared out the window of Luther's beachfront condo, unable to comprehend why Hurricane Gertrude arrived long before Shelby had. With conditions worsening by the minute, what sense did that make? What was taking her so long?

Finally, she appeared on his radar screen. At least he hoped it was Shelby. Then again, who else in their right mind would have any interest in the pelican trees in this storm? *Yes, it had to be her*, Bob thought anxiously, knowing she was just moments away from unearthing the buried treasure chest.

Per Luther's precise instructions, he and Ruth stayed at the condo each time Shelby traveled back to Florida. Whenever Mabel Saunders got word that she was en route again, she contacted the Schusters who, in turn, loaded a suitcase and the treasure chest into their car and left for Sanibel Island.

And just like clockwork, at 3:00 a.m. Bob would dig a six-foot hole in the sand and bury it. This same routine was repeated six days ago.

Early on the second day, as they sipped morning coffee, Mabel took the wind out of their sails, when she called saying Shelby never made it to Florida. For whatever reason, she turned the car around and went back to South Carolina.

Bob and Ruth Schuster were totally dejected. They felt certain she'd given up this time. But with the deadline fast approaching they remained on Sanibel Island, just in case.

They rejoiced three days later when Mabel declared to all of *Shelby's Saints* that Shelby was en route again to Florida.

Bob and Ruth believed they knew the source of her sudden change of heart but kept it to themselves. Apparently, she'd received the postcard...

Having spent so much time on this island the past three months, the Schusters hated to think that this adventure was coming to an end, whether Shelby found the buried treasure or not.

What the Godly couple didn't realize was that it was God's will that they be there now, not Luther Mellon's.

Using night vision binoculars, which Bob was amazed still worked so well, with no moonlight or starlight to draw upon, he strained hard to monitor her every move. His gray eyes were calm and probing. Bob was grateful to be inside with a warm cup of coffee, instead of battling the elements outside like Shelby.

The vibrant senior felt an equal mixture of tension and excitement building inside. Excitement because she was oh so close; tension because of the undesirable elements and the deadline.

Bob took a short break to massage the bridge of his nose with his thumb and forefinger. According to the calendar Shelby still had 24 hours with which to work. But thanks to Hurricane Gertrude, that deadline would be scaled back considerably.

Bob figured she had two hours, if that! He took a sip of coffee and chuckled to himself. Luther would have wanted it this way.

"As long as she finds it without being injured," Bob envisioned Luther saying, "it'll only add to the adventure."

And Luther would be right. Even at 68, this project had totally revived the Schusters in so many ways, by helping them recapture a childlike sense of adventure they hadn't felt in many years.

Thanks to Luther Mellon, Bob felt like a young lad again. But due to the fierce storm, Bob was forced into total seriousness.

Shelby needed to find her inheritance tonight. The storm surge alone would prevent her from coming back at daybreak. Hence, the growing tension on his part.

If she didn't succeed, Bob would have to brave the elements once she left and dig like crazy to reclaim the treasure chest before the storm surge swept it out to sea. If that happened, beneficiary number two—Luther's church in Fort Myers—would also lose out.

The cashier's check inside the buried chest in the amount of $400,000 could easily be replaced, but the $100,000 in cash and the $50,000 in rare coins and fine jewelry, could potentially be lost.

While the money would greatly benefit the church, more than anything, Bob wanted Shelby to find it instead.

In fact, all 70 of *Shelby's Saints* at Grace Evangelical Church in Florida wanted her to find it. If anyone deserved it, it was her. She'd earned it many times over the past 90 days.

And besides, Luther had already left a sizable amount to the church, $700,000 to be precise.

But Bob Schuster was thinking far beyond the money and valuable material items stashed inside the chest.

If Shelby didn't find it, the greatest tragedy was that she'd never know about the second safe-deposit box. Everyone praying for her knew the contents stored inside box number two is what had spawned this wonderful idea in the first place.

Yes, she needed to find it at all costs!

The Florida lawyer watched Shelby counting off steps, arms spread out for leverage. After ten steps Bob Schuster gasped, when a strong gust of wind blew her over. She landed face down with a mouth full of wet sand.

Being so emotionally involved in the "Mellon Project", when Shelby fell, part of Bob fell with her. He reached for his slicker, doing his best to remain calm. But inside he was screaming.

Ruth was startled when she heard the front door open. "Where are you going, dear?"

"To the beach," he said. "To take a closer look. Be back shortly."

"I don't think that's a good idea."

"I'll be fine. Besides, Shelby doesn't know who I am."

"Be careful. It's getting worse out there."

"Yes, dear."

Bob Schuster had been so careful up to this point. Shelby had no knowledge of his involvement, or that he'd been spying on her all this time. It had to remain that way for now.

Then again, in these elements, she wouldn't recognize her next-door neighbor let alone a perfect stranger.

"Grrrr! Why didn't I start digging before the hurricane arrived?" Shelby was still mad at herself for falling asleep. She reached for her water bottle, took a swig, gargled and spit it out. It took three attempts to completely rid her mouth of the bothersome sand.

She picked herself up, dusted off as much of the wet sand from her shorts as she could and counted off steps again toward the coastline, wobbling every step of the way. The whitecaps were more noticeable, more pronounced, more unrelenting.

The clock inside her head was taunting her, teasing her, annoying her. Ticktock, ticktock!

After 15 steps, another strong gust of wind knocked her over again. Shelby sat on the wet sand and burst into tears. Rain and sand pelted her face. Her chin sank to her chest as a horrible depression dropped solidly on her shoulders. The 90-mile-per-hour winds pinned her down on the beach. She couldn't move.

"Are you okay, ma'am?" Bob Schuster shouted at the top of his lungs to be heard.

Shelby looked up and saw the older man, "In all honesty, I don't know how to answer that." Even wearing protective gear, her white shorts and dark colored tee-shirt were soaked all the way through. The disposable raincoat posed no challenge to Hurricane Gertrude.

Bob extended a hand and helped the young woman to her feet. "Is there anything I can do for you?" It was time to see what she was made of.

"Yeah, pray for me."

"And just why do you need prayer?"

"Well, I..." Shelby started crying again.

Instinctively, Bob wrapped his arms around her. Shelby couldn't see it, but Bob was also sobbing. Even if she could see his face, it would be difficult to discern the rain from his tears.

In a silent whisper, he prayed, "Lord, please give me the strength to remain silent. I know my role, Father, but my heart aches for her. She can't quit now. She's too close. Please grant her the necessary strength she'll need until she finally finds it. I ask this in Your Precious Name, Amen."

Bob released his grip and looked deep into Shelby's moist eyes. "May I ask why you're out in these dangerous elements? And why the shovel?"

"I could ask you the same thing."

"Thought I'd take one last look at the beach before it's completely gobbled up by the storm surge," Bob said. Seeing her shoulders slump, he realized his comment had taken even more wind out of her sail. He backpedaled, "But we still have a couple hours left, I suppose. So, again I ask, what are you doing out here?"

"I'd rather not say..." Shelby felt a little more panicked with each passing second.

"Must be something very important."

"You could say that."

"Are you sure I can't be of any assistance?"

"I wish you could, but you can't."

"Okay then. Please be careful. It's getting worse out here."

"I'll do my best. Thanks for your concern."

"I hope you find whatever it is you're looking for. God be with you, ma'am."

"Name's Shelby. God be with you, too, uh..." She hesitated.

"I'm Bob."

"Thanks for your kindness, Bob."

"My pleasure, Shelby. Nice meeting you," Bob said smiling.

Even in the darkness, there was this comforting glow and sincere kindness in Bob's eyes. It strengthened Shelby, even if only slightly.

She had no idea Bob was the second of the unmentionables in Florida. Nor did she know he was the one responsible for burying the treasure chest in the first place.

Bob looked skyward, "Time for me to get a move on. Please be careful, Shelby."

"You too, Bob."

Bob nodded, then hurried back to his room as quickly as someone his age could hurry.

"Any luck?" Ruth asked, the moment her husband returned.

Bob removed his slicker. "Not yet. But I spoke to Shelby."

"You did what?"

"I had to, Ruth. She looked so defeated sitting on the wet sand sobbing like a baby. I wanted to encourage her. Hope it worked."

"I'm sure your very presence comforted her greatly."

"Let's hope so." Bob reached for his night vision binoculars. "She's quite a remarkable woman. Even with the deadline and fierce conditions, she remained loyal to Luther's wishes and never spilled her guts. Nor did she ask for my assistance. I can't help but marvel at her. She's just like Luther was."

The sea was growing angrier by the minute, tossing huge unrelenting waves at the shrinking beach, churning up more sand with each rotation. Shelby was becoming less and less of a person, and more and more of a distant silhouette.

Bob wondered how much time she still had before the sea gobbled up the remaining coastline, and with it her inheritance.

It was starting to get dicey. Too dicey.

Scanning the beach with his night vision binoculars, Bob saw a man hiding in a mangrove bush facing Shelby, hanging on for dear life, apparently monitoring her every move.

Bob gulped hard and was suddenly fearful. The equal mixture of tension and excitement he felt a few moments ago, quickly tilted in favor of full-blown tension. "Who in the world is that?"

"Who, dear?" asked Ruth.

"There's someone hiding in the mangrove bushes over there."

"Are you serious? Can't be good."

Bob now had two people to monitor. Shelby and this stranger. One good. The other potentially bad. No, he corrected himself, not potentially bad, definitely bad!

Who else would hide in a mangrove bush in the middle of the night in a hurricane? Only someone who knew about the buried treasure chest. Had Shelby foolishly told someone about it, someone unworthy of such knowledge?

Suddenly Stuart Finkel came to mind. Bob thought back to his surprise visit at his office two weeks into this adventure.

Stuart said he was there to visit his grandfather, but he was acting far too suspiciously. Was that him hiding in the mangrove bushes? Had he somehow found out about the buried treasure?

If so, how? Bob was certain Bernie didn't tell him. There wasn't a chance of it! "Is the land line phone still working, Ruth?"

Ruth checked. "Yes. There's still a dial tone."

"Good. We may need to involve the police."

"Want me to call them now?"

"Not yet. Might generate too much attention. By the time they wrapped up their investigation, the storm surge could potentially sweep the buried chest out to sea."

"Shelby's safety must come first, Bob!"

"I'm monitoring things very closely, dear."

Bob prayed again, "Lord, please protect Shelby from the elements, and from this stranger!"

The godly senior needed to be twice as vigilant now. He scanned back and forth: Shelby, stranger, Shelby, stranger.

Unbeknownst to him, two FBI agents were also monitoring both subjects from inside the villa next to his.

And two more sets of eyes, courtesy of the local police, were keeping a very close eye on Vinnie and Carlos, as they discreetly monitored Stuart Finkel, who was monitoring Shelby, and all this in a category three hurricane!

It was pure insanity!

The FBI agents were mindful of everyone's overall involvement. They knew the Schusters were on their side. Soon they would order the two on-call police officers monitoring Vinnie and Carlos, to place both men under arrest.

But as of right now, they had nothing solid to pin on Stuart Finkel. They needed to catch him in the act of doing something that would hold up in court before they could arrest him and the others.

Until someone made a significant move, the agents needed to remain patient and continue their silent eavesdropping on everyone.

They just hoped they wouldn't lose power, or that the Schusters wouldn't hear the loud squawking from their walkie-talkies, as they maintained contact with local authorities.

The stage was set, and everyone was in place.

It was showtime...

46

"FORTY-SEVEN. FORTY-EIGHT. Forty-nine. Fifty!" Shelby turned around to make sure she was still in line with the base of the banyan tree. Satisfied that she was, she dropped to her knees and looked skyward.

"Finally! Thank you, Grandpa!" She did her best to mark a three-feet-wide perimeter in the wet sand. With sustained winds approaching 100 miles per hour, it was extremely difficult.

"Close enough," she said, just as a strong gust of wind knocked her over again.

Shelby retrieved the shovel she'd mounted in the sand and began her onslaught on Sanibel Beach. The storm continued intensifying, but she was in a zone and almost couldn't feel it.

She threw heaping piles of wet sand over her shoulders at a very brisk pace, only stopping when wind gusts became too fierce and she was forced to cover her face. Each time she tossed sand from her shovel, the strong hurricane winds blew a portion of it back into her face, stinging her everywhere.

After forty minutes of constant digging, her shoulders were burning. At any rate, she managed to build a bunker of sand around the hole she was digging. Once inside the hole she still battled the heavy rains, but the winds were a little easier to cope with.

Despite all that, she couldn't ignore the raging sea slowly but surely creeping up on her. It was dangerously close.

She couldn't stop now, not even for a short break. Another round of adrenaline kicked in and Shelby intensified her efforts.

Twenty minutes later, the shovel struck something hard, roughly six feet below sea level.

"Definitely not a seashell!" Her excitement level reached a whole new level. Shelby doubled-up on her efforts and cleared a pathway around her discovery. *Could it be?*

Shelby turned on her small flashlight. The bright beam of light exposed the top of the buried chest. "Yes!"

When Bob Schuster saw the beam of light stabbing wildly at the darkness, he got excited. When Shelby hoisted the buried chest to the surface, he was laughing and crying at the same time.

This was an incredible moment for him. That is, until in his peripheral vision he saw the stranger from the mangrove bush approaching Shelby, holding something in his right hand.

"Is that a gun?" Bob was panic-stricken.

"What dear?"

"Call nine-one-one immediately!" Bob shouted to Ruth. He tried his cell phone. There still was no signal.

"Oh my, there's no dial tone," Ruth replied.

Bob's pulse raced in his ears. He reached for his slicker again.

In this storm, Shelby wouldn't hear a pack of charging elephants coming her way, let alone a gun-wielding stranger coming from behind. Bob was frightened for Luther's granddaughter.

Finkel startled her with a loud growl, nearly causing her to jump out of her skin.

"Slowly climb out of the hole and keep your hands where I can see them at all times!" he hissed, trying to steady himself.

Shelby obeyed and climbed out of the hole she'd just dug, just as the seawater invaded. Without even looking, she knew it was the man in the red pick-up truck. Who else could it be?

She was too frightened to reprimand herself for letting her guard down enough to think this madman was out of the picture. She would reprimand herself later, if she lived through the night.

"Who are you?" she said, in a panicked tone. "What do you want?"

"We finally meet face to face, Shelby."

Shelby squinted and wiped rainwater from her eyes. "How do you know my name? And why have you been following me all this time?" Her knees grew weak and she collapsed to the wet sand. Her shorts were soaked all the way through with rainwater. When she saw the gun, she started hyperventilating. She reached for her water bottle.

"Not so fast," barked Finkel.

"I need water. Please!"

"Okay, but don't make any sudden moves. I will *not* hesitate to shoot you."

"Why would you do that?" Her voice trembled in sync with the rest of her body. "What have I ever done to you? I don't even know who you are."

"I know about the buried treasure."

"How'd you find out about it?" Shelby took a large gulp of water.

"That's not important. What's of vital importance is that you don't make any sudden moves or try to scream. Actually, scream all you want! No one can hear you anyway!" Stuart looked skyward and howled insanely, like a wolf in the driving rain, terrifying her all the more.

Shelby peered into Finkel's eyes and saw nothing. Terror hardened and banged at her chest. *This man really is a maniac!*

"It's just you and me here, babe," Finkel said. "Now that you've found the treasure, killing you would be the best possible outcome for me. You already dug the grave. In these conditions, I won't even need to throw sand on top of your corpse. The surge will carry you straight out to sea. No one will ever find you. You'll be fish food! Weather couldn't be more perfect!"

There was an unmistakable greed in his eyes. Shelby looked beyond the greedy glint and was chilled to the bone. For the first time in her life, she knew what it felt like to be on the receiving end of a murderous glare. This man was deadly serious.

"Now give me the key to the chest."

Why now? Tears streamed down Shelby's cheeks. She'd come so far, overcoming so many obstacles the past three months, only to lose her inheritance at the very last moment to this lunatic. It wasn't right. Nor was it fair!

Shelby hesitated and Finkel aimed the gun at her chest and cocked the trigger. Her eyes grew wide with fear.

"The key, Shelby! I'm not playing games!" he snapped.

Seeing Shelby was trembling too much, Finkel reached inside her pocket and fished around for the key. He removed what appeared to be an authentic treasure chest key. *Yes!*

"Now slowly back away and do not leave my sight! Do you hear me?"

Shelby nodded. She was trembling too much to utter an audible reply.

Finkel put the key inside the lock. "Open Sesame," he shouted. His long curly hair was blowing wildly in the wind. Rainwater dripped off his nose. With his right hand, he opened the chest with caution, so the wind wouldn't blow anything away. With his left hand, he reached for Shelby's flashlight and turned it on.

"Wow!" Stuart's eyes nearly popped out of his head. It was loaded with stacks of hundred-dollar bills, rare coins and jewelry, just like he'd imagined inside his mind a million times! *Easily a six-figure score*, he thought, closing the chest. *At least now I won't have to harm my grandfather!*

Finkel's gaze returned to Shelby. Fear snaked through her. Now that this deranged psychopath who'd followed her for many weeks finally got what he wanted, Shelby knew he wanted to kill her.

She could see it in his eyes. A distinct air of murder was present that not even the strong, relentless hurricane winds could blow away. *Instead of coming home with my inheritance, I'll return to South Carolina much like Grandpa did a few months ago, in a casket!*

Another thing the punishing winds couldn't blow away was the demonic presence hovering above, greatly anticipating a favorable outcome for their side. They wanted Stuart Finkel and Shelby McKinney dead, so they could hand-deliver their souls to Satan.

If God would only relinquish His grip, both would quickly descend into the bottomless pit, with nothing between them and hell but the air.

Satan's demons stabbed at the darkness with razor-sharp talons. Their midnight black chiseled wings were long and fierce, flapping and flexing to remain airborne, as if flapping with such velocity would somehow extinguish the bright Light above them, created by *Shelby's Saints* in the form of incessant prayer.

Mindful that the Light could destroy them at any time, even so, they never stopped spewing blasphemous hatred in that direction with deafening shrieks and moans.

Sadly, there was no such Light for Stuart Finkel. Not even a flicker! Satan's demons knew how much it hurt God's heart that not a single Christ follower in all the world cared enough to pray for Stuart by name, as evidenced by the total absence of Light on his behalf. The demons assigned to him were fiercely determined to keep it that way.

As the sustained winds reached 100 miles per hour, the demons assigned to Shelby cackled and hissed, slobbering black saliva all over themselves. It quickly smoldered into foam. Their grossly contorted faces were just inches from her face. Their snakelike tongues licked her everywhere trying to locate and destroy her soul.

Sensing victory, their jaundice yellow eyes became blood red.

Meanwhile, the demons assigned to Stuart Finkel hissed in his ears, "Shoot her! Kill her! Stop wasting time!"

Finkel's murderous glow intensified. Pointing the gun at Shelby he said, "Sorry it has to end like this, but you leave me no other choice. You saw my face."

I'm not being buried in that hole! Mustering what little strength she had left, Shelby lunged forward and kicked him in the right kneecap with the heel of her right foot, karate-chop style. She then kicked him in the groin. Finkel, who already had two bad knees, buckled-over and fell to the surface, wincing in pain.

"Run, Shelby," Bob Schuster yelled. He was close enough to hear the man from the mangrove bush moaning in agony.

Shelby recognized Bob's voice from earlier and ran as quickly as she could toward him. But with sustained winds reaching 100 MPH, it felt like she was running in place at times, going nowhere, as if caught in quicksand again. It felt like a dream. No, a nightmare.

According to the Saffir-Simpson Hurricane Scale, once the wind speed reached 111 miles per hour, it would be upgraded to a category three hurricane. But right now, it felt more like a thousand miles an hour, instead of a hundred.

Stuart shielded his face with his left hand and aimed the gun at Shelby with his right hand. She was 20 feet away. He fired off a shot in the darkness that just missed her. It ricocheted off a palm tree less than a foot from her head, before burying itself in the wet sand. The sound was deafening.

Shelby screamed in terror and dove head first to the ground. She pressed her body as flat to the surface as she could, hoping that the wet sand would protect her from this monster. Her body shut down.

"Please help me!" she screamed as loudly as she could, hoping Bob Schuster heard her desperate plea.

Bob also fell to the surface when the shot was fired. He picked himself up off the beach and ran toward Shelby as fast as he could. He needed to do all he could to save her now. Even Luther would agree enough was enough!

"Let's move," barked FBI Agent Curtis Watson, hearing the gunfire.

Stuart did his best to steady the gun again, as the wind-swept sand maliciously attacked his eyes, mouth and nostrils. He fired off another shot. It, too, just missed. Shelby remained frozen on the surface still unable to move.

Finkel picked himself up off the wet beach, steadied himself as best he could, and limped toward her. He wanted to see the fear in her eyes when he pulled the trigger again.

How dare she kick me there!

Shelby rolled onto her back. She covered her face, her heart pounding through her clothing.

Finkel steadied the gun at her chest and cocked the trigger.

Bob was close enough to see that it was his partner's grandson. "Stuart, no!"

Stuart was shocked. "What are you doing here, Bob?"

"The real question is, what are *you* doing here?"

Shelby wanted to say, "Y'all know each other?" but she remained silent.

"None of your concern, Bob. Stay out of it." Stuart cleared more sand and rainwater from his eyes. "Actually, you just made it your concern. Now get down on the beach and don't try anything foolish. We both know I won't hesitate to kill you, too!"

"Why, Stuart?"

"I'm a desperate man, Bob," Finkel barked, "I need this money to bail me out."

"But it was never yours to begin with."

Stuart laughed. "And your point?"

"Do the right thing, Stuart."

"I plan to, Bob. Sorry to say but that treasure chest is more important to me than you'll ever be!" Returning his gaze to Shelby, he said, "As for you, you just happen to be a victim of circumstance. Now, who wants to go first?"

"Please don't kill us!" Shelby screamed through her tears.

"I regret to inform you that I'm unable to accommodate your request." Finkel's eyes expanded for a moment. Then it was as if something behind them exploded. "Think I'll kill you first," he said, pointing the gun at Shelby's chest. "Best to ease your suffering as quickly as possible. But hey, no need to thank me."

Shot number three didn't miss. It came from FBI Agent Curtis Watson's gun, ripping straight into Stuart Finkel's right shoulder.

Even in the driving rain and fierce sustained winds, the seasoned agent still managed to hit his target from 50 feet away. He was good. Real good.

Stuart dropped the gun and fell to the sand. "Who shot me?" he hissed.

Fiercely determined to exact a more permanent level of revenge on his two prisoners, using his left arm, Finkel clenched his teeth and crawled to retrieve his gun. He aimed it at Shelby, who was still too paralyzed with fear to move.

Stuart felt a second shot rip through his flesh, once again from Agent Watson's gun. This time in his left shoulder. He fell to the sand writhing in pain.

Within seconds, Finkel was surrounded by the two FBI agents. Meanwhile, the two on-duty police officers arrested Vinnie and Carlos. Carlos wasn't laughing like a hyena now.

Shelby watched her assailant twitching violently in agony and disgust, as he was handcuffed. It was finally over. But nothing could stop her from shaking uncontrollably.

"Are you okay, Shelby?" said Bob Schuster.

"No, I'm not," she screamed, trying to catch her breath.

"Breathe in and out, dear. You're safe now."

"Why are you back? And how do you know that maniac? Are you involved in all this?"

238

"Not exactly. Allow me to reintroduce myself. I'm Bob Schuster."

As soon as Shelby heard his last name, she knew he was the second "unknown" man in Florida.

"You're Bernie Finkel's business partner?"

"Yes, I am. Your grandfather and I were very close friends. We attended the same church. He was one of the finest men I've ever had the privilege of knowing. Until just now, I felt so honored to be involved in this project. At least you finally found your inheritance," the older man with the kind eyes said.

Pointing his finger at Stuart, Bob said, "I can assure you *that man* wasn't part of the overall plan!"

"I was almost killed, Bob," Shelby said yelling, still shivering.

"Also not part of the plan." Bob rubbed at his throbbing head to release more pressure. "So many from our church have been praying for you nonstop. They will rejoice knowing you finally found it!"

"Why are y'all so concerned with me finding my inheritance?"

"We knew how much your grandfather wanted you to find it. It was an obsession of his, in fact."

Shelby was still too numb to try wrapping her mind around his comment.

Clearing his throat, Bob yelled as loudly as he could so Shelby could hear him above the fierce winds, "Unfortunately, the culprit is none other than my partner's grandson."

"And just how did he find out about my inheritance?" she said, growing more angry, furious even.

"I don't know." Bob sighed. "But I promise to get to the bottom of it. One way or the other, I'll find out."

Shelby didn't reply. She was too busy breathing in and out.

"You won't get away with it this time, Stuart," said Bob, angrily. "You're finally where you need to be, in police custody!"

"Whatever," Stuart growled, clenching his teeth. The pain was getting worse.

Bob looked into Shelby's eyes. "My partner's grandson is always in trouble. Finally, he'll get what he deserves—prison. Hopefully for a long time. With your blessing, I'd like to press full charges."

Shelby nodded yes.

"I feel awful about how it all ended. You know your grandfather would never willingly place you in harm's way like this."

"I know that, Mister Schuster." Shelby was suddenly furious with Martin Hightower for leaving the names on her kitchen table way back when. Had he not done that, she would have never contacted Bernie Finkel, and his grandson

239

would have never known about the buried treasure. But Martin never forced her to take the piece of paper. The choice was completely hers to make.

Once Stuart was led away by local Florida police, a female FBI Agent approached. "Shelby McKinney?"

"Yes?"

"I'm FBI Agent Gloria Sanchez," she said, flashing her badge. "I'm going to need you both to come with me for questioning."

"How do you know my name?" Shelby felt even more violated now.

"Everything will be explained to you inside. Now please come with me."

"Where are you taking us?"

"Inside where it's dry," the female agent replied, in an assuring voice. "It's okay, Shelby, you're safe now."

Shelby looked at Bob Schuster. He shrugged his shoulders, totally unaware that the FBI was involved. Like everything else that happened over the past few hours, this wasn't part of the plan.

"What about my..."

"Please, ma'am, just follow me."

"With all due respect, Agent Sanchez," Bob Schuster yelled above the strong winds, "I don't want that chest to leave Shelby's sight. If it needs to remain here for investigation purposes, I'm willing to stay and safeguard it for her. You can always question me later."

Bob noticed Shelby's discomfort, "Relax, my dear. Why would I want to steal it from you when I'm the one who buried it in the first place? Many times, in fact! It's an amazing story that I look forward to sharing with you sometime."

Shelby shot a quick glance at FBI Agent Sanchez. "It's true. We've been watching Mister Schuster for many weeks from the villa next to yours. He's a good man. We appreciate all your help, Bob."

Now Bob Schuster sort of felt violated himself.

"There's no need to stay out here in this storm," Agent Sanchez looked skyward. A strong gust of wind nearly knocked her over. "Removing evidence from a crime scene prematurely isn't typical FBI procedure, but under the conditions I'll let it pass. After everything you've already endured, I'd hate to see it swept out to sea."

"Thank you, Agent Sanchez," Bob replied, gratefully.

"Agent Watson, would you carry the chest to the villa for me?"

"Sure thing," he said, to his female counterpart.

Bob looked at Shelby, "Everything's going to be fine now."

"Thank you, Mister Schuster," she said, wanting to smile but still unable to.

"No, Shelby, thank you..."

"Why are you thanking me?"

"I don't even know where to begin, dear."

Noticing the sincere kindness in his eyes, she said, "You're welcome."

They followed the female FBI agent to the villa.

Agent Watson tucked the treasure chest into his mid-section, lowered his head, and hurried to the villa as quickly as he could, without being blown over by the 100-mile per hour winds.

Once inside, he hoisted the wet, sandy chest onto the small table.

Just then the power went out.

But even in the darkness, for the first time in a long time, Shelby McKinney felt safe...

47

AFTER NEARLY TWO HOURS of questioning by local authorities and FBI agents, Shelby's nightmarish ordeal was finally over.

With everything finally coming to a screeching halt, a subdued calm overtook her. Yet, despite her best efforts, she couldn't stop her hands from trembling.

The interview process began inside the villa in which the FBI had been staked out the past three days. It quickly shifted next door to the Schuster's villa, because they had plenty of candles to provide much-needed light.

With Stuart Finkel in police custody (albeit handcuffed to a hospital bed), and the two bad guys Shelby knew nothing about being booked and processed at the Lee County Jail, she was finally able to relax.

It was the eighth of September. Shelby's deadline. Her *Big Day* was almost her last day on earth.

Had someone told her at the outset she'd be inside a candlelit villa on Sanibel Island in a category three hurricane, being questioned by the FBI without her family beside her, she would not believe it. Or she would have flat-out rejected her grandfather's challenge to go on this crazy adventure in the first place.

Ironically, now that it was behind her, Shelby felt stronger for having overcome so many obstacles.

Bob and Ruth Schuster were equally relieved to finally have this nightmare behind them. The constant threat of Stuart Finkel lurking in the darkness all these years was finally over. Hopefully for a long time. He had tormented too many unfortunate souls for far too long.

Bob wasn't the least bit surprised that his partner's grandson was capable of spearheading something so monstrous. He never felt comfortable in his presence.

Then again, not even his own mother could tolerate being in Stuart's presence for extended periods of time. Bob and Shelby got to see firsthand just how dangerous he really was, especially when pushed to the limit.

Bernie often told Bob how unnerving it was sharing his last name with his trouble-laden grandson, not to mention his only son, Stuart Sr., whom he hadn't heard from in nearly two decades. It always came back to bite him at some point.

242

Much like a seismologist preeminently bracing for the big quake, Bernie anxiously braced for Stuart's big quake to strike at any time. Though he hadn't yet felt the trembling caused by his grandson's actions, Earthquake Finkel had indeed joined forces with Hurricane Gertrude, striking unimaginable fear into the hearts of two people, Bob Schuster and Shelby McKinney.

Bob just hoped Bernie would survive the strong aftershocks sure to follow in the days ahead. He needed Jesus in the worst way.

Bob thought to call his partner to inform him of what had just transpired but, for starters, it was three in the morning. And with all modes of communication disrupted, it would have to wait until sunrise at the earliest.

Besides, with the storm now here in full force, why ruin his evening by adding to his troubles?

Not exactly one to roll with the punches, Bob didn't want Bernie to have a heart attack if authorities came knocking on his door in the morning asking questions about his grandson. And he certainly didn't want Bernie to read about it in the newspaper or watch it on the local news before Bob had a chance to speak to him.

It was just a matter of time before reporters came sniffing around. It was too juicy a story not to! Yes, it would surface at some point. And the Finkel name would once again be dragged through the mud; this time on a much larger scale.

Bob dreaded it, but knew he had to be the one to tell his partner that his worst fears had unfortunately come true. It would then be up to Bernie to inform his ex-daughter-in-law, Millie Finkel, before police came knocking on her door too.

Though they'd all but lost contact as the years passed—mostly due to two men, Stuart Junior and his father, Stuart Senior—Bernie always thought Millie was a kind and decent woman.

After suffering years of physical and emotional abuse at the hands and mouth of her ex-husband, Stuart Senior did Millie Finkel a huge favor 20 years ago by moving to Arizona, leaving her and Stuart Junior behind.

No one had heard a word from him since, not even Bernie.

Bernie and Millie were good citizens who just happened to have two bad eggs sandwiched in between them.

Millie didn't deserve this any more than Bernie did. In any event, she, too, would be completely mortified in the coming days and weeks, due to her son's vile actions.

Hopefully prison life would have a profound positive impact on Stuart Finkel's, right now, rather pathetic life.

That was already Bob Schuster's prayer for the man who surely would have killed him, had he only been given the chance.

To avoid facing felony charges themselves, after enduring hours of intense questioning, Stuart's three friends, Jed Ashford, Chris Watkins and Ricky Clemmons all admitted to their involvement in Finkel's diabolical plan. They confessed to staking out the bank's four locations for five straight days until Stuart stumbled upon Shelby McKinney and ditched them.

Plea agreement or not, Jed, Chris and Ricky—still enraged by Stuart's disloyalty to them—willingly agreed to testify in court against him. All three were on record as saying in no way was this a random act of robbery. It was all premeditated by Stuart Finkel, from start to finish. He was even prepared to kill his own grandfather, if need be, just to find the buried treasure.

The interview process with FBI and local authorities began a week after Finkel found Shelby and quickly ditched them. All three were prohibited from calling Finkel, sending text messages or visiting his residence.

The Feds wanted Stuart to feel like he'd outsmarted everyone, including his three friends—which according to the agent in charge, wasn't all that difficult to do—and continue with his plan.

Finkel now faced a long list of charges, the most serious being the two counts of attempted murder. Odds were good that their old pal would be spending many years beyond prison bars.

Good riddance!

48

"SHELBY, PLEASE STAY WITH us tonight," said Ruth Schuster, after the interview process had ended. "It's too dangerous out there."

"Really? I can stay with y'all?"

"Why, of course."

"Last thing I want now is to be left alone."

"Your grandparents had so many nice things to say about you. We'd love to get to know you better."

"Would it be okay if I showered first?" Shelby sighed. "I don't have my things here."

"Where are you staying," FBI Agent Curtis Watson chimed in, already knowing the answer. The FBI knew exactly where she was staying the past three visits, in fact.

"The Holiday Inn just up the beach."

"I know where it is," he replied. "If you'd like, I'll swing by your hotel and grab your things for you."

"You would do that for me?"

"My pleasure, Ma'am."

"Thank you, Agent Watson." Shelby flashed a weary smile.

"Please, call me Curtis."

"My suitcase is already packed so it shouldn't be too difficult. You can be in and out in no time."

"I'll try my best not to let you down..." Watson flashed a quick smile trying to ease the tension on Shelby's face. It didn't work.

"I'm in room three-twenty-three," she said, handing her room key to Agent Watson. "Please be careful out there, Curtis!"

"I will. Thanks for the concern." Curtis Watson left at once for the hotel.

Hurricane Gertrude was at full peak now, causing power to be lost on the entire island. It felt as if the fierce winds would soon tear the roof off or shred the villa to pieces. According to local meteorologists, the eye would soon pass over Sanibel Island, allowing for a temporary reprieve from the torrential rains.

"Once the massive storm taps the warm gulf waters," a meteorologist warned on a transistor radio, "much like the consumption of caffeine energizes the human body, the warm gulf waters will provide much added strength,

245

making the tail end of the hurricane far more punishing than what we've already encountered so far. Whatever you do, seek safe shelter immediately."

Shelby was desperate to contact Jesse but knew it would have to wait until tomorrow at the earliest. She was tired and dirty and needed a good night's rest.

She showered in near darkness. A scent-free candle rested on the bathroom sink, flickering dimly, providing the only source of light.

Shelby thought it ironic to be showering in a hurricane, but the warm water soothed her fatigued, sandy body. That, plus the sound of the water inside the shower helped drown out the brute-force hurricane winds wreaking havoc outside.

When Agent Watson returned with Shelby's belongings, Bob handed him a box full of candles, a flashlight, food and water. "This is in appreciation for everything you did for Shelby. Thank you, Agent Watson." Bob sounded like an overprotective grandfather.

"Just doing my job, Bob. But thanks for this," the FBI agent said, gratefully.

"It's the least I can do, Agent Watson."

"Please, call me Curtis. I'm off duty now."

"You got it, Curtis."

"Time for me to set up camp next door."

"We're here if you need anything."

"Likewise, Bob."

Shelby slipped into her pajamas, then sat on the couch in the living room staring at the dim candlelight as it softly flickered.

She was nowhere near ready to sleep. Her gaze shifted to the treasure chest sitting on the coffee table. It was opened.

The jewelry and rare coins glistened in the dim candlelight. She saw stacks of hundred-dollar bills. The ambiance alone screamed full-blown adventure, much like she'd drawn up in her head at the outset.

She just never expected to encounter so much danger along the way; the three bad guys and dangerous hurricane topping the "danger" list!

As alluring and inviting as the treasure chest looked, without her family here, she couldn't fully appreciate it. They were her true treasures in life, not the contents staring back at her inside the chest.

Yes, more than anything else, she wanted them here now.

Shelby retrieved the scroll she wanted to shred into a million pieces so many times from her suitcase. Once she returned to South Carolina, she would frame and hang it on the wall above her desk. It would serve as a memento and stark reminder of what a little persistence can do.

Feeling ever so triumphant, Shelby read each clue in the dim candlelight with a victorious expression on her face. *I did it!*

THREE "111" CLUES
TO ASSIST IN FINDING YOUR BURIED INHERITANCE:
First "111" Clue = Numeric Equation
Second "111" Clue = Beachfront Landmark
Third "111" Clue = The Ultimate Payoff!

Decipher all three "111" clues
and you'll find your buried inheritance, and hopefully so much more!

FURTHER DESCRIPTION OF CLUES

The first "111" clue, once deciphered, will reveal the exact beach in which the treasure chest has been buried. The total sum of this numeric equation equals "111", that is, after you subtract two vowels from one of the words. And here's a clue within a clue; you'll need to have a good attitude in order to succeed with the task at hand. And in this case, attitude really does equal a perfect "100!"

The second "111" clue represents a magnificent landmark that's completely overlooked by most who pass by it. Your inheritance is buried 50 steps due west of it. And here's your clue within a clue; this landmark represents three objects, all of which provide shelter and safe refuge for so many. Once you locate it, count off 50 steps and start digging. Six feet beneath the surface will be the buried treasure chest.

"I thought I'd never solve you," Shelby said to the second "111" clue in a calm whisper.

The third and most important "111" clue also represents three things that are so out of this world yet are so much closer than anything you could ever imagine—even if you don't realize it yet! And here's your clue within a clue; these three things really are three-in-one. They are completely inseparable and represent everything. My prayer is that they will be revealed to you soon after you find the buried treasure chest.

Oh, and one more thing. Regarding the first two clues, all I can say is there are NO FREE RIDES! Only the third one is FREE! Other than that, there are no other clues or secret decoders to further assist you—only your mind and imagination. Always do your best to keep it very simple! Happy digging!

247

Shelby shook her head in bewilderment. *Ninety days*, she thought. Ninety turbulent days were needed to finally find it.

This adventure nearly cost Shelby her life. But even with the many ups and downs experienced along the way—physically, mentally and emotionally—Shelby couldn't remember feeling any more alive than she did right now.

Amazingly, though she'd pretty much tapped every emotion along the way, the only time boredom had entered into the equation was on those handful of occasions when she wanted to give up and quit. Even at four a.m., this came as a startling revelation to her.

"How was your shower, dear," said Ruth softly, breaking her from her reverie.

"Refreshing, thanks."

"Mind if we sit down?"

"Not at all. I'm grateful for the company." Shelby sighed. "Just wish I could call Jesse. Under normal conditions, I can send a text message halfway around the world in just seconds.

"Now I can't even call the room next door, let alone my husband in South Carolina. Just goes to show that even the world's most amazing technologies can't compete with nature's fury."

"Don't worry, you'll speak to your husband soon enough. Just do your best to remain patient a little longer." Ruth's calm, gentle voice washed over Shelby, soothing her nerves all the more.

"Treasure chest sure looks inviting," Bob said, joining the conversation.

"Sure does..." Shelby pressed her legs up against her chest and hugged them.

"Have you sorted through it yet?"

"Too exhausted. I'll look at everything tomorrow."

"Do you even know how much money you've inherited?"

Shelby smiled wearily. "Nope. Guess I'll find out soon enough. Looks like a lot though."

"As I was saying earlier, I actually buried it nine times before you finally found it."

"Really?"

Bob nodded yes. "First two times were test burials, so to speak. Your grandfather and I came here late at night when the beach was deserted. When we came back a few days later to retrieve it, though it was completely empty inside, we rejoiced knowing it was safe and sound exactly where we'd buried it. That's when I started getting excited about this adventure!"

"Are you the one who sent the postcard?"

248

"Guilty!" Bob smiled. "I know I overstepped my bounds, but you were so close, and I didn't want you to give up. I always knew the second 'one-eleven' clue would be your greatest challenge. Even told your grandfather that. Looks like I was right, after all."

Shelby didn't know this man's age but would be hard-pressed to believe Bob was 68. Even in the dim candlelight, his near-perfect smile was infectious. His full head of salt and pepper colored hair was messy from being out in the storm, but his warm gray eyes were calm and assuring.

"Had you not sent the postcard, I never would have come back to Florida. I was completely out of options. And hope. I was just about ready to give up." Shelby shook her head, "And that wasn't the only time I felt like quitting."

"I can't tell you how relieved I am to hear you say that," Bob said. "I purposely wrote 'Pelican Tree' singular instead of 'Pelican Trees' plural. I wanted to reinvigorate you without giving it all away. I figured the Pelican Tree could be one of many things—a local business, restaurant, hotel, or a wildlife refuge. The goal was to readjust your compass a bit, but also keep you on your toes, so to speak."

"Well, you've succeeded wonderfully, Mister Schuster! You nearly drove me insane, I'll have you know," Shelby said, finally able to display a slight sense of humor. She paused to let his words sink in. "Wow, come to think of it, you're right! One letter really did make all the difference. Had you written 'trees' instead of 'tree', I think I might have found it rather easily."

"Just glad you found it. But talk about waiting 'til the last minute. Man, oh man!" Bob said, trying to make light of it all.

"Just glad it's finally over."

"Almost," Bob said cautiously.

Shelby gave Bob a sideways look, "What do you mean almost?"

"You'll see after you sort through your inheritance chest."

Shelby stiffened up, "Hmm."

"Don't worry, Shelby, you've already done all the hard work. No more wild goose chasing for you. It should be all downhill from here on out."

"That's what I said after I discovered the pelican trees, and I still almost got myself killed."

"Trust me, you're safe now."

Tension built on Shelby's face, "What's in the chest, Bob?"

Ruth placed a hand on Shelby's left shoulder. Her face was aglow, "I can assure you, Shelby, it's all good."

Bob Schuster smiled. One thing he loved most about his wife of 46 years was the calming effect she had on others. He often said the strongest muscle Ruth possessed was her giant-size heart.

She didn't have a mean bone inside her five-three, petite body. Her soft brown eyes reflected that much. They were kind and engaging. When it came to living life to the fullest, no one tried harder to meet that objective than Ruth.

Even emotionally drained it could wait no longer. "No time like the present, right?"

The moment Shelby got up off the couch, the dark, chiseled wings on the demons assigned to her started whirring with the strength of a million dragonflies. The constant buzzing noise their wings generated echoed throughout the densely populated spirit world. If Bob, Ruth and Shelby could only hear it, their eardrums would explode.

On either side of the treasure chest were their Heavenly assailants, sent by God Almighty Himself, to protect Bob and Ruth Schuster and the treasure chest.

God's mighty warriors were totally silent. They stood firm and were stoically calm and resolute, always observing, always ready.

They would never back down from Satan's demons!

As their evil adversaries flitted this way and that looking for comfort, looking for peace, God's warriors remained perfectly still. Whenever they moved it was for good reason.

The only right Satan's demons had to be there was that Shelby had yet to surrender her life to the One who created her 33 years ago and saw her unformed body long before the foundations of the earth were set in place. Because of the sin nature she inherited at birth—like all other humans on the planet—Shelby McKinney needed God's forgiveness for her many sins in life.

Until she received Jesus Christ as Lord and Savior, she would continue to have demons assigned to her sent by Satan himself!

They screamed into her ears, "Don't look inside that chest! There's nothing of interest in there for you! Stay away! God hates you!"

Their jaundice yellow eyes turned blood red, after being swatted away by the blades of God's two mighty warriors, for inching too closely to their holiness. The impact sent them spiraling backwards out of control, until they were finally able to stabilize themselves using their long black wings.

But knowing their Heavenly assailants couldn't run their blades clear through them, sending them into utter blackness, until their assignee's name was first found written in the Book of Life, they constantly cursed the Most High, filling the air with unspeakable profanities.

Totally unaware of the invisible activity taking place all around her, Shelby removed a stack of hundred-dollar bills from inside the chest, then two more stacks, before finally seeing it; a small envelope addressed to her.

250

She tore it open to find a one-paragraph handwritten letter inside, once again from her grandfather, and another key which looked identical to the one she received with Luther's first letter. She read and soon learned why.

Greetings, Pumpkin! The fact that you are reading this fills my heart with great joy! But your search isn't over yet. There's one more thing you need to do. In my opinion, it's the most important part of this great journey. It's time for you to discover the third "111" clue! This key is to another safe-deposit box.

But unlike last time, I won't make you search all over the state of Florida looking for it. In fact, it's right next to the first box you've already located. All you need to do now is go back to Sunrise Savings and Loan and open it. I'm so proud of you, Shelby. Bravo! Hope to see you again someday. God bless you. All my love, Grandpa.

"Hmm. I thought the third 'one-eleven' clue was the buried treasure chest."

"Surprise, surprise," Bob Schuster exclaimed, with a hearty chuckle.

What is it then? Hmm, here we go again...

251

49

AT 11 A.M. THE next morning, Hurricane Gertrude was finally out of the region, headed straight toward Louisiana. She was expected to make landfall as a category four, possibly even a category five hurricane, after traveling over the warm gulf waters.

Louisiana residents were already evacuating the area.

Bob and Ruth Schuster were out on the porch fronting Sanibel Beach, sitting in wooden rocking chairs. With power still out, instead of having morning coffee together, they sipped water.

"Good morning, Curtis," Bob said, seeing the FBI agent emerge from the villa next door.

"Good morning, Mister and Misses Schuster." From a physical standpoint, Agent Curtis Watson was an imposing figure. He stood a well-toned 6'2" and weighed 220. His father was black; his mother was Filipino. While he resembled both parents, his facial features more resembled his mother's Asian heritage. Back in the day, Watson played football at the University of Georgia, as a second-string running back. Now 40, he looked like he could still play.

Bob took a gulp of water. "Some storm we had, huh?"

"Very impressive indeed. How'd y'all manage last night?" Curtis Watson was casually dressed, wearing black khaki shorts and a white tee-shirt.

"We managed just fine, thanks," Ruth replied softly.

"How's Shelby?"

"She finally fell asleep at around seven this morning," Ruth replied. "We have no plans of waking her."

"Were you able to sleep?"

"Truth be told, we barely slept at all. But not to worry, we'll make it up later. How about you, Curtis?"

"I slept soundly for five hours."

"How'd you manage that?"

"I always sleep soundly after catching the bad guys," he said, flashing a friendly smile.

Ruth smiled back.

Looking out at the horizon, the tail end of Hurricane Gertrude was still clearly visible. Even from a distance, she looked angry, dangerous. The beach was completely deserted. Most homes and hotels had plywood covering all doors and windows.

There couldn't have been more than a few hundred people left on the island, if that. The smarter ones evacuated.

"You'd think there'd be so much more visible damage," Bob said. Except for a few tipped over trash cans, lifeguard stands, and various debris scattered about—mostly paper, leaves and palm branches blown off trees—there wasn't much other damage to speak of.

Curtis nodded agreement. "Just the winds alone were nerve-wracking enough. I thought the roof was coming off a few times, before I finally fell asleep. I'm sure a considerable amount of damage was done in some places. Once power's restored, we'll see just how bad it really was."

They were all startled when a man suddenly approached with three small children. "Good morning," he said a little discombobulated, a confused look on his face. "I'm hoping this is the right place. I'm looking for my wife. Her name is..."

Bob cut him off, "You must be Jesse..."

"I am." Jesse reached into his pocket for the piece of paper with the names of the two men from Florida written on it. "Are you Bernie Finkel or Bob Schuster?"

Bob extended his right hand. "I'm Bob Schuster. And this is my wife, Ruth, and our new friend, Curtis Watson."

"Nice to meet y'all." Jesse wore a Carolina Panthers baseball cap and sunglasses. He looked completely exhausted.

Bob wondered if he knew what had happened to his wife last night. If so, it would explain the tension on his face. Bob shifted his focus to the children. "Hi, kids! Welcome back to Florida! What are your names?"

"I'm BJ," came the reply from the middle child with the tired eyes.

"I'm Trevor."

Both boys had messy hair from sleeping in the car.

"And what's your name, sweetheart?" Ruth said, smiling warmly.

"I'm Brooke." She was still wearing pajamas.

"What beautiful hair you have, Brooke."

"Thank you." Her mouth was stretched wide in a yawn. "I wanna see Momma."

"Don't worry kids," the kind older man said reassuringly, "your Momma's safe and sound. She's inside sleeping now." Then to Jesse; "How did you know she was here?"

"I got a call from a police officer at two a.m., informing me of what took place. After much prodding, he finally gave me this address. I programmed it

253

into the GPS, loaded the kids into the car and drove straight through the night. When Shelby wasn't at the Holiday Inn, I figured she'd be here with y'all."

"Good detective work, Jesse," Ruth said. "You must be exhausted."

"You could say that again. But at least my wife's safe. That's the important thing." Jesse took a deep breath and relaxed.

"She's been through quite an ordeal," Bob replied. "She'll be happy to see you all."

"I wanna see Momma, Daddy."

"Momma needs her rest, sweetie."

"I'm sleepy too."

"You wanna sleep with Momma?"

Brooke looked up at her father and squinted due to the bright morning sky. "Uh-huh..."

"I think Momma would really like that. Just don't wake her, okay?"

"Okay, Daddy."

"I wanna see the treasure chest," BJ declared.

"Me too, Daddy."

"We'll see it soon enough, boys."

"It's right inside," Ruth said. "Wanna see it now?"

"Yes!" Trevor and BJ both said at the same time.

The moment BJ and Trevor saw the treasure chest, their eyes nearly popped out of their heads. "Wow," Trevor exclaimed, "Look at all that money! It's more than I ever imagined. We're rich!"

"Awesomeeeeeeeeeeeee!"

"Shhhh. Keep it down boys. Momma's still sleeping," Jesse said sternly.

Brooke glanced at the treasure chest resting on the coffee table but was too exhausted to fully appreciate it. She just wanted her mother.

"Be right back, boys," Ruth said, leading Jesse and Brooke to Shelby's room.

"Don't worry, we'll protect it from any more bad guys!" BJ said, suddenly in pirate mode again.

"Yeah, we'll take it from here!" Trevor fumbled through the chest. Holding up a stack of hundred-dollar bills, he said, "Must be a million bucks in my hands! Wonder what we can buy with this?"

"Let's buy Disney World, Trev!"

"I doubt we're that rich."

Ruth opened the bedroom door and Jesse quietly tiptoed inside, carrying Brooke, careful not to wake his wife. Ruth left them alone and rejoined the boys in the living room.

The vibrant senior considered it a great blessing to hear youthful voices now. It still saddened her to this day that she was unable to have children. By far, it was her greatest disappointment in life.

But watching Trevor and BJ rummaging through the treasure chest with reckless abandon, Ruth couldn't help but smile. Just being with them was therapeutic.

BJ held up a pearl necklace, "Look at this, Trev!"

"Yeah. Look at this!" Trevor held up a pair of diamond earrings.

Back and forth they went; both were in their glory.

Jesse gently laid Brooke down next to Shelby. "Let Momma sleep, okay?"

"Okay, Daddy," Brooke said, softly, unable to stop yawning.

Jesse kissed his two favorite girls in all the world on the cheek then quietly tiptoed out of the room, gently closing the door behind him. He badly needed rest himself, but first wanted to see what was stashed inside the treasure chest.

After all, it nearly cost Shelby her life.

It didn't take long for Shelby to realize Brooke was lying next to her. Her eyes grew wide with excitement. "When did you get here, sweetie?"

"Hi, Momma! Just now. We drove all night."

"Where's Daddy and the boys?"

"Outside looking at the treasure chest. I wanna see the pelican trees, Momma!"

"Sure, but let me wake up first, okay?"

"Okay," came the tired reply.

"I'm so happy to see you, sweetie." Shelby wrapped her arms around her daughter. Within minutes, they were both sound asleep. Two hours later, they awoke and joined everyone in the living room.

"Momma," BJ and Trevor both said at the same time, loud enough to wake their father, who'd dozed off on the couch soon after searching the contents inside the chest. They raced into their mother's arms.

"Hi boys!" They shared a tearful embrace. "What do you think of the treasure chest? Not too shabby, huh?"

"It's awesome, Momma. You did it! We're so proud of you!"

"Aww, thanks, Trev."

Glancing at Jesse, Shelby said, "Welcome back to Florida, honey! I can't tell you how happy I am to see you."

"It's good to be back." They embraced for the longest time. "You had me so worried, baby..."

"All's well that ends well, right?"

"I heard what happened."

"How?"

255

"A police officer on the scene called me at home. Bob and Ruth filled in many of the blanks. I felt so powerless being two states away, and knew I needed to be here. We drove all night."

"Having y'all here now is more important than the treasure chest."

Now wide awake, the treasure chest quickly captivated Brooke, luring her in. She pulled out an expensive-looking beautiful pearl necklace. "Look how pretty, Momma!"

"I saw it earlier. I'm thinking we'll keep it in a safe place for when you're a big girl."

"I am a big girl, Momma," she replied, feeling a little dejected.

"I know, sweetie. I mean when you're even bigger. Okay?"

"What about us, Momma?"

"Settle down, boys," Jesse said. "Let Momma wake up first..."

Bob and Ruth Schuster watched the McKinneys in total silence, savoring each moment, very much feeling like they were among family. It felt good.

Jesse looked outside the window. "Are those the pelican trees out there?"

"Yup. That's them."

"I thought to ask Bob and Ruth earlier, but wanted to ask you first."

Brooke looked outside the window. "Where, Momma?"

"Right out there, sweetie."

Shelby pointed in the direction of the three trees. This was a near-perfect moment, one of the many highs accompanying the many lows this journey had presented along the way.

Her mind raced back to the day they entered Sunrise Savings and Loan together, to retrieve the contents stored inside the safe-deposit box. Her thoughts then shifted to the euphoric expression on Trevor's face, after he solved the first "111" clue at Friendly's Restaurant later that same day. This was right up there with it.

Jesse frowned, "How many times did we walk by them when we were here last June?"

"I don't know. But I'm certain I passed by them at least a hundred times myself."

"Can we go there now, Momma?" asked BJ.

"Sure, why not. Let's go!"

Once they were there, Shelby pointed out the inscription carved into the largest of the three pelican trees.

Trevor read it aloud for all to hear, "You found it, Pumpkin! Woo hoo!"

Shelby did her best to recount the many harrowing moments for her children, greatly downplaying all the dangerous parts.

256

Jesse watched the four of them holding hands walking step-by-step, slowly counting off 50 steps due west, to the exact location of the buried treasure chest.

Shelby was quite animated, even falling onto the sandy surface on occasion, as if battling the fierce hurricane winds all over again. She even spit air out of her mouth, signifying the wet sand she spewed from her mouth just a few short hours ago.

Being kids, Trevor, BJ and Brooke did the same.

"Forty-eight, forty-nine, fifty!"

"Hooray! We made it," Brooke shouted.

"Where's the hole, Momma?" There was a confused look on BJ's face.

"Hmm. Storm surge must have completely covered it up."

Shelby was amazed. There wasn't a single trace of evidence to validate the fierce struggle with her assailant that nearly cost Shelby her life.

It was like last night was only a dream. But it wasn't a dream. The hole she dug was very real. The gun Stuart Finkel brandished was also real, along with the bullets he fired at her.

Just a few short hours ago, this place was anything but tranquil.

Jesse watched his wife and kids from underneath the pelican trees. He was drinking it all in, basking in it. Outside of watching Shelby giving birth to their three children, he couldn't remember being any more-proud of his wife. She really did it!

Jesse read the inscription carved into the banyan tree again and became teary-eyed. "Thank you, Luther," was all he could manage to say.

"Guess what kids?"

"What Momma?" Trevor said glowingly, still so proud of his mother. They were stretched out on the damp beach on their bellies, elbows in the sand, chins resting in their palms, looking like one big awkward square sprouting eight legs.

"We're not finished with this adventure yet. There's still one last thing we need to do?"

"What is it?" said BJ.

"Well, there's a second safe-deposit box."

Trevor, BJ and Brooke all looked at their mother in total silence. The looks on their faces screamed, "Please, Momma, not again!" It was as if she'd just volunteered her children to donate blood.

"It's okay, kids," Shelby assured them, "Momma knows exactly where it's located this time."

"Where, Momma," said Brooke.

"Believe it or not, it's right next to the first safe-deposit box."

257

"Can we go now?" Trevor's excitement was building again.

"Sure, why not? Let's go!"

"Woo hoo," Trevor exclaimed, with a loud shout.

Shelby couldn't help but smile. Even in death, her beloved grandfather still had everyone "woo hooing!" It was a fitting tribute to the greatest man she'd ever known.

From a human standpoint, Sanibel Beach may have appeared tranquil now, but the demons assigned to Shelby were anything but that. They more resembled the fierce hurricane that just invaded the area a few short hours ago.

But they were a million times worse now! They screamed into Shelby's ears, "Don't go there! Stay away! There's nothing there that would interest you! God hates you!" They breathed and slobbered all over their assignee, desperately trying to distract her from going to the bank and opening the second safe-deposit box.

But with so many believers still praying for her, their efforts were completely ineffective.

With Stuart Finkel, and Vinnie and Carlos sitting in jail cells, the demons assigned to the three men were in jail with them, only their assignees didn't know it.

The prison bars, doors and ceilings constructed to keep many of society's worst from escaping, posed absolutely no challenge for Satan's demons. They passed through these man-made objects with the greatest of ease, like they weren't even there.

But one thing they couldn't do was be at two places at the same time. Which meant they were powerless from helping Shelby's demons back on Sanibel Island.

Knowing what was stored inside the second safe-deposit box, they sensed the end was near...

50

THE MCKINNEYS LEFT SANIBEL Island for Sunrise Savings and Loan, in nearby Fort Myers.

Susan Fernandez was sitting at her desk when they arrived. The moment she saw them, she left her small office to greet them.

"Welcome back, guys! It's so nice to see you all again!" Fernandez was bursting on the inside.

"It's nice to be back, Susan."

When Shelby saw her face, her mind raced back to her first visit to this place, when the bank manager left her alone inside the vault a few moments, as she frantically rushed back to her office to double-check something. Now she knew why. Susan didn't want her to prematurely open the wrong box.

"Guess you're here because of the second safe deposit box."

"Yes indeed!"

"Well then, what are we waiting for," Susan Fernandez said, leading Shelby to the vault.

Just like last time, Jesse remained in her office with the kids.

As one of *Shelby's Saints*, this was a time of rejoicing for Susan Fernandez as well. As soon as phone service was restored, she received a text message from FBI Agent Gloria Sanchez, informing that Shelby had found the buried treasure chest.

Now that it had been found, Susan was free to openly discuss the topic with Shelby. It seemed so long ago when Susan Fernandez notified local authorities after her co-worker, Sonya Haynesworth, spotted Stuart Finkel— a.k.a. Joel Spencer—stalking the McKinney family inside the bank.

Since Shelby hailed from another state, the Feds were eventually called in. A week after contacting the police, FBI Agent Gloria Sanchez was sitting at Susan's desk.

During the interview process, agent Sanchez learned that Susan and Luther Mellon were good friends in life, and even attended the same church.

The FBI agent also learned Susan was the only bank employee to know anything about the buried treasure hunt. Agent Sanchez promised to keep Fernandez in the loop to the best of her ability.

The bank manager was aware of some of the hardships Shelby had endured the past three months but had no idea just how traumatic it had really

259

been. But from the little she did know, having endured so much personal tragedy, Susan sort of expected Shelby to be an emotional wreck. But that didn't appear to be the case.

If anything, there was this peaceful smile on her face that was reminiscent of her late friend, Luther Mellon.

Shelby opened safe-deposit box number two and retrieved a large manila envelope, identical to the last one she received from her late grandfather. Fernandez wanted her to open it in her presence, but also understood she would probably want to do it with her family in private. They were back in her office in no time.

Sensing the McKinneys were anxious to leave, Susan escorted them out to their vehicle and they said their goodbyes.

As soon as they pulled away, Susan Fernandez dropped her head and prayed in the bank parking lot, "Lord, thank You for answering our prayers. We rejoice knowing Shelby finally found her buried inheritance. Our prayer now is that she wholeheartedly receives the Message enclosed inside the manila envelope now in her possession. I ask this in Jesus' mighty name. Amen!"

Susan hurried back inside the bank and e-mailed all 139 of her fellow Shelby's Saints, to share the wonderful news. The subject line read: *Package picked up—Woo hoo!* The message was short and simple. *Just wanted you all to know Shelby found the buried treasure last night. So exciting! She just left with the contents from safe-deposit box #2. It isn't Mission Accomplished yet. Keep praying!*

Within 30 minutes, Susan's inbox was flooded with more than 50 replies from some of her fellow *Shelby's Saints.* All were overjoyed and promised to pray for her throughout the day.

The McKinneys arrived back on Sanibel Island totally unaware of it all and went straight to the pelican trees.

The demons assigned to Shelby and Jesse were fully aroused and increasingly fearful. With each step their assignees took toward the Sovereign God of the universe, even if unknowingly, they felt their power dwindling more and more.

They sparred among themselves in mid-air, looking for comfort; looking for peace, but finding neither.

Shelby used her fingernails to catch the edge of the tape and pull it off. With Brooke's help, she tore open the manila envelope.

Stuffed inside was a Bible, two sealed envelopes, and what appeared to be two homemade DVDs.

260

Both were tagged. One said, "For Shelby. Please watch alone." The second post-it tag read; "Also watch alone before sharing with the others. Thanks, Pumpkin!"

"You got it, Grandpa," Shelby said, as if he were here now. Then to Jesse, "Did you bring the charger?"

Jesse looked quizzically at the contents stuffed inside the manila envelope. "It's in the van, why?"

"I need to charge my laptop battery in case power isn't restored to the condo today."

"Good thinking."

The McKinneys walked back to the condo.

Sure enough, power was still out. Jesse grabbed Shelby's laptop and went out to the van, to charge the battery for his wife. He also grabbed the cooler he'd packed at home full of lunch meats, sliced cheese and cold beverages, and took it inside the villa.

While the battery charged, they ate sandwiches with Ruth Schuster.

Bob wasn't with them. Ten minutes after they left for Sunrise Savings and Loan, he left to meet his good friend, Bernie Finkel.

"HEY, BOB, GOOD MORNING," Bernie said, greeting his friend warmly. His windows were covered with plywood. "Some storm that was!"

"Indeed, Bernie. I'm glad you survived it, old pal." *Just hope you survive the next storm!*

"You too, Bob."

"May I come in?"

"By all means."

"It's nice that you still have electricity. Power's still out on the island."

"It flickered off and on all night, but it seems fine now. I checked earlier for any structural damage. Looks like I came away from this hurricane totally unscathed…"

"Well, not totally, my friend."

Bernie looked deep into Bob's troubled eyes and felt his pulse race in his ears. "Coffee?"

"I'd love a cup, thanks."

Bernie led Bob to the kitchen and poured two cups. It could wait no longer, "What is it, Bob?"

"Which would you like first, Bernie, the good news or bad?"

"Since I think I already know the good news, why don't you give it to me first."

261

"Yes, Bernie, you can cash the check now. Shelby found the treasure chest last night."

"Hey, that's terrific," he said. Then it dawned on him; "Are you saying she dug up the beach during the hurricane?"

"Yes. She's quite a remarkable woman, even if she doesn't always think so. She fought hard every step of the way, with a relentless determination only few people possess. She's a real trooper. I couldn't be more-proud of her."

"Same here." Knowing the bad news was coming, Bernie grew more serious. He decided to venture a guess; "Please don't tell me the strong hurricane winds blew her inheritance away."

"No, Bernie, it's nothing like that. Her inheritance is safe and sound." Bob took a deep breath. It was time. "Stuart was arrested last night."

A mild look of shock filled Bernie's face. "What?!"

"Somehow, he knew all about the buried treasure."

The look on Bernie's face shifted from shock to utter disbelief! "What? How?"

"I don't know, Bernie, and I'm sure you don't either."

Bernie thought back to when Shelby first called three months back, the same day his grandson visited him. *Had he overheard something important?* "Oh my. What happened last night, Bob."

"You may want to sit down first."

Bernie obeyed, and Bob told his partner of 37 years everything from start to finish, including his strong premonition that the story might make the local news once power was fully restored.

Though not at all surprised by his grandson's actions, Bernie Finkel felt deeply ashamed, and covered his face with his hands, "You're right. I didn't walk away from this hurricane unscathed, after all."

Bernie was already bracing himself for the vicious storm he'd soon face due to his troublemaker grandson. "Well, I guess that's that then," he said, somberly, with absolutely no emotion.

"Sorry to be the bearer of such tragic news, Bernie, but I felt I needed to be the one to tell you. I'm sorry."

"You're sorry? I should be apologizing to you. My grandson tried to kill you." The shame on Bernie Finkel's face was more pronounced, more palpable. The guilt he felt was overbearing. "I'm finished. My career is over."

"Listen Bernie. You're not finished. You did nothing wrong, okay? Nothing whatsoever. Just because Stuart bears the same last name as you, doesn't mean you're capable of doing such horrific things. You're a good man. Everyone who knows you thinks highly of you. Especially me!

"Stuart is your grandson, but he's still an individual, which means he's fully responsible for his own actions in life. This is not your fault, okay? Sorry to say, but I think Stuart needs to be in prison now. Hopefully it will help him in the long run."

Bernie didn't reply. His head remained down.

"Hey, why don't you come join us on the island? It might do you some good to get away for a couple of days."

"Thanks, Bob, but I need to be alone for a while."

"Are you sure?"

"Yes, Bob. Sorry."

"It's okay, old pal. I understand completely. I want you to know nothing's changed between us. I'm still honored to be your business partner, and I plan to ride out this storm with you all the way. If it ends up hurting our practice, so be it.

"Besides, we're both getting up there in age. This may be a sign from God that it's time for us to walk away and enjoy the remainder of our lives while we still have life left in our bodies. Or perhaps it might be time to pursue something altogether different."

Bernie Finkel remained silent.

Bob stood to leave. "I know the next few weeks will be difficult, but whatever happens, I'm behind you all the way. We've faced so many storms over the years. We'll make it through this storm, too."

Bernie rose from his seat and sobbed on Bob Schuster's shoulders for the longest time, before finally assuring his partner he was okay.

"If you need anything, anything at all, please don't hesitate to call me."

Bernie gazed at Bob with a faint, weary expression on his face. His hands trembled, and his breathing was noticeably heavier.

To Bob Schuster, it looked as though his partner had aged ten years in just ten minutes' time. His facial bones pushed through his skin; his eye sockets were hollow, distant, hopeless, as if his insides were being carved out right in front of Bob's very eyes.

Bob knew what Bernie needed right now—God's peace that surpasses all understanding. But that kind of peace was only available to those who trusted in Christ Jesus.

In the many years they'd been friends, their greatest disagreements in life were always spiritual in nature. Bernie made it crystal clear on several occasions that he wanted nothing to do with Bob's Jesus!

Bob still wondered at times if God was listening to his prayers.

After 37 years, it didn't seem like it.

Otherwise their good friend surely would have taken at least one small step in God's direction by now.

But it never happened. Bernie Finkel remained completely unchanged in his way of thinking as a staunch atheist. By not having God's full protection, Bob feared his partner would never experience true peace on any level, ever again.

Just by looking into Bernie's eyes, he saw someone who was out of hope and wanted to give up. Bernie didn't realize it, but he needed Jesus in the worst way now.

Driving back to Sanibel Island, a teary-eyed Bob Schuster cried out to his Creator, "Please, Lord Jesus, come to Bernie's rescue! I fear for him. Open his spiritual eyes and ears. Change his heart before it's too late."

51

SHELBY GRABBED BOTH DVDS, her grandfather's beach chair, retrieved her fully recharged laptop from the van and walked the short distance to the pelican trees. Alone this time.

Thanks to Hurricane Gertrude, she had the beach all to herself, which was perfect because it allowed her to honor her grandfather's wish to watch both DVDs in private.

Then again, even had the electricity been restored to the condo, for whatever reason, she felt prompted to watch them here instead

Shelby took a deep breath and inserted the first DVD into the laptop. The demons assigned to her were beyond frantic now. They were completely terrified! Knowing many were praying for her, as evidenced by the blinding white Light always hovering high above, they felt their power dwindling a little more as the minutes passed.

They moved briskly over, around and even through the pelican trees, rustling leaves and limbs, but always mindful and ever so fearful of the Light above. It was a Light they detested with murderous vengeance...

Luther's image appeared on screen, looking vibrant as ever and so full of life. Chills shot up and down Shelby's spine when the camera slowly pulled back exposing his location.

Her late grandfather was sitting under the pelican trees in the very same beach chair she was using, wearing flip-flops, white shorts, a bright yellow shirt, mirrored sunglasses and a straw hat.

Luther Mellon was grinning from ear to ear. His silver-white hair glistened in the bright sunshine. His face was well-tanned.

"Greetings, Pumpkin," Luther said to his beloved granddaughter, in a robust voice. "I hope this finds you well. Welcome to the place I affectionately call the Pelican Trees! Not only is this landmark the second of the three 'one-eleven' clues, it also happens to be my favorite place in all the earth. I'm sure you struggled mightily at times trying to find this glorious location. The lesson here is that not all landmarks are man-made.

"In fact, no matter how hard man tries to outdo God, man-made landmarks can never compare to the Most High's glorious creations! Part of this Mission was specifically designed to pull you away from all man-made things and philosophies for a while and get you to focus on all things eternal. But more on that in a bit.

"For now, I want to congratulate you on a job well done. I couldn't be more-proud of you. I never doubted for a second that you'd eventually find your inheritance. I'm sure you were greatly challenged at times along the way. At least I hope you were; that was part of the plan. By persevering to the very end, I'm sure you're so much stronger for it.

"I always knew you had the heart of a champion. It just needed to be re-cultivated, so to speak. In time, I think you'll count the many obstacles faced along the way, both seen and unseen, as valuable life-lessons. I hope this journey has allowed you to get reacquainted with the adventurous woman I always knew you to be!"

Shelby dabbed at her moist eyes with a tissue but kept watching. With this turbulent journey now behind her, it seemed like her grandfather had been gone for three years, not three months.

"So many people have been praying that you would find it. The fact that you're watching this now confirms that their prayers, and mine, were finally answered. Hallelujah!

"Now that the buried treasure is safe in your possession, may you, Jesse, Trevor, BJ and sweet Brooke enjoy it in good health and happiness. But in all honesty, even had you failed to find it within the ninety-day time frame, it was always yours. You were never in danger of losing it."

The look on Shelby's face said it all; complete and total shock!

"Please forgive me for not being totally forthright with you, but it was never destined to go to my church. As you know, I already left a substantial amount to them.

"Not even Bob Schuster or Bernie Finkel, whom I must say are both kind and decent men, knew this part of the plan. Only Mabel Saunders and my pastor here in Florida knew. Come on Shelby, did you really think I'd give your inheritance away to someone else?"

"Grrrr, I'll get you for this, Grandpa!" she said, sort of jokingly.

"Not a chance! But had I just handed it over to you like I did the others, would you feel this fantastic now? I think not!"

Luther paused and looked skyward. "You'll have to forgive the hat. It can be quite messy sitting beneath a tree full of hundreds of pelicans, if you know what I mean. Even living in paradise presents challenges at times," he said, with a goofy expression on his face he was known for.

Shelby burst into laughter and looked up, hoping she wouldn't become a target herself. She was thankful there were far fewer pelicans above her now than when she first discovered this place. But with the hurricane now out of the region, they'd be back soon enough.

Luther shifted in his seat and leaned forward. It was time to get serious with his granddaughter. "Though this is a one-way conversation, it's the most important discussion you and I will ever have together. I wanted to have this conversation with you so many times in the past, tried to even, but you never seemed interested.

"It's okay, Shelby, don't feel bad. After all, it's partly my fault. It took a major jolt to my system before I ever took this subject seriously myself. I came to realize you needed the same thing—a jolt to the system to awaken you from within before we could ever have this talk. I hope this little adventure did just that!"

Shelby exhaled deeply, "You could say that, Grandpa!"

"I certainly hope so, because it's time to discuss the topic I briefly mentioned in my first letter; the thing I said was the most important thing in life, and without it you can never experience true happiness, joy and success in life. Do you remember?"

Shelby nodded yes, as if her grandfather was sitting directly across from her. She clearly felt his presence. She felt something.

"If my plan works to perfection, you'll one day count the items found inside safe-deposit box number two as the most significant discovery, because they have eternal value, whereas the contents stored inside the buried treasure chest are extremely temporal.

"Now that me and Grandma are in Heaven, nothing would please us more than to be reunited with the entire family someday. But after filling your minds with so much worthless philosophy over the years, I fear no one in the family knows what it takes to qualify for Heaven.

"I struggled mightily to find a way to right the ship, spiritually speaking. With Mabel's help, I finally decided the best way to get your attention would be to make it fun and adventurous, something so spectacular you simply couldn't resist."

Luther leaned forward in his chair and looked directly into the camera. "Many changes were made along the way, but the one thing that remained unchanged was *you*! I always knew you were the key to making it happen."

Shelby thought, *Why me?*

"But I'll come back to that. I confess part of this adventure was concocted out of guilt on my part. On far too many occasions, I taught y'all to place 'self' above all other things, including God."

Luther sighed, "I was wrong, Shelby! In fact, nothing could be further from the truth. I also told you on occasion that God was too busy dealing with all the bad people in the world to have time for the rest of us good citizens. Once again, I was wrong."

Luther's face stiffened. He looked troubled. "Please discard any and all past teachings! I've come to realize we're all sinners in need of a Savior. This includes you and I. Contrary to what I said in the past, God never takes a break from you. Never! He is Omnipresent, meaning He's everywhere at all times.

"Remember what I said about the third 'one-eleven' clue? That it represents three things that are so out of this world, yet they're so much closer than anything you could ever imagine? I also said they were completely inseparable and represent everything. They are God the Father, Jesus the Son, and the Holy Spirit.

"Now that you've found the buried treasure chest, my prayer is that all three will be revealed to you soon, even today. Believe me when I say; the attention brandished upon you on this little journey is nothing compared to the constant attention you receive from God Almighty every second of every day.

"Even if you're unaware of it, God is deeply interested in all aspects of your life, sweetie, and longs to fellowship with you always. More than you can ever imagine!"

Luther unfolded a piece of paper and placed it on his lap, so he could exchange his sunglasses for reading glasses. Pushing them up the bridge of his nose, he picked up the paper before him.

"I want to read something to you that's straight out of the Word of God. Hopefully it will help you realize just how much God really loves you, and how close He is to you at all times. Allow me to read Psalm one-thirty-nine for you. Most of it anyway."

1) O Lord, you have searched me and known me!

2) You know when I sit down and when I rise up; you discern my thoughts from afar.

3) You search out my path and my lying down and are acquainted with all my ways.

4) Even before a word is on my tongue, behold, O Lord, you know it altogether.

5) You hem me in, behind and before, and lay your hand upon me.

6) Such knowledge is too wonderful for me; it is high; I cannot attain it.

7) Where shall I go from your Spirit? Or where shall I flee from your presence?

8) If I ascend to heaven, you are there! If I make my bed in Sheol, you are there!

268

9) If I take the wings of the morning and dwell in the uttermost parts of the sea,

10) even there your hand shall lead me, and your right hand shall hold me.

11) If I say, "Surely the darkness shall cover me, and the light about me be night,"

12) even the darkness is not dark to you; the night is bright as the day, for darkness is as light with you.

13) For you formed my inward parts; you knitted me together in my mother's womb.

14) I praise you, for I am fearfully and wonderfully made. Wonderful are your works; my soul knows it very well.

15) My frame was not hidden from you, when I was being made in secret, intricately woven in the depths of the earth.

16) Your eyes saw my unformed substance; in your book were written, every one of them, the days that were formed for me, when as yet there was none of them.

17) How precious to me are your thoughts, O God! How vast is the sum of them!

18) If I would count them, they are more than the sand. I awake, and I am still with you.

23) Search me, O God, and know my heart! Try me and know my thoughts!

24) And see if there be any grievous way in me, and lead me in the way everlasting!

Luther removed his reading glasses and looked straight into the camera. Wiping his eyes, he said, "Sorry, Pumpkin, it gets me every time I read it. If that doesn't prove how deeply interested God really is in His children, nothing will.

"That was written from the hand of someone who truly loved God as intimately as I've come to. Most Christ followers may not be able to write as eloquently as the Psalmist David, but that's how all of us who love and serve Christ feel inside. You either feel it or you don't. There is no in-between."

Shelby felt a deep stirring in her soul. It was a feeling she never felt before. This was the first time anyone had ever read Psalm 139 or any other part of the Bible to her, for that matter.

"Thankfully I learned before it was too late that it's not about 'self' after all. Everything begins and ends with Jesus! Now it's your turn to learn the same lessons Grandma and I both learned on your side of the grave!"

269

Luther took a deep breath. "No one's ever told me this, but after I became a Christian, I always felt certain family members thought I was a little crazy for making a complete turnaround so late in life. Perhaps they thought I was losing my mind, that Alzheimer's started attacking my brain, when nothing could be further from the truth!

"I hope this little adventure has proven to you that my mind is still very much intact! It's as strong as ever! Grandpa still strong like bull," he said jokingly, flexing his muscles.

Shelby burst into laughter.

"So please pay close attention to what I have to say. Nothing could be more important. I'll begin with a few simple questions." Luther shifted in his beach chair again. "If your life were to come to an end today, do you know where you'll spend your eternity? Have you ever pondered the word 'eternity' before?

"Do you have absolute assurance of Heaven like me and Grandma had in life? With the mortality rate on planet earth being one-hundred percent, these aren't unrealistic questions for me to ask, or for you to ponder. No one gets out alive, Shelby, at least not in the flesh. And you know how uncertain life can be at times."

Shelby was totally blown away by that statement. After all, she nearly lost her life twelve hours ago. *Too strange*, she thought.

"If you're blessed to live to see eighty like me, it's something for which to be grateful. Nevertheless, whether you live to be forty, sixty, eighty or even a hundred, it's still but a grain of sand when compared to an endless universe of time known as eternity.

"It would be utterly fruitless to try comparing our mortal lives in the flesh to eternity. And since eternity has no end, where you'll end up after you die is of vital importance, especially since there are only two eternal choices— Heaven or hell!

"With that in mind, the time, effort and enthusiasm you've invested into finding your inheritance is the same manner in which all of humanity should pursue eternity and the afterlife.

"Unfortunately, this isn't the case. Most people could care less about the two! They only want the things they can see, hear, taste and touch. If they can't see it, in their minds it simply doesn't exist."

Luther grew somber. "My fear is that you're also traveling down that same dangerous path without even knowing it. You're too beautiful and precious to be cast into hell. I know it sounds mean, heartless even, but hell really is the eternal destination for each doomed sinner at the time of their death.

"This isn't only my opinion, Shelby, it's straight out of the Word of God. With eternity being humanity's most common link, you'd think it would be the most discussed topic on the planet, even the big story on all major news stations every night.

"But that simply isn't the case. Outside of the church, it's one of the least discussed topics in most circles. Never forget, sweetie, your life will fly by in a jiffy. Once a soul arrives at its final-destination, absolutely nothing can be done to switch sides. Those who end up on the Good side of eternity are eternally grateful.

"Those who end up on the other side are tormented for all eternity. A great chasm will separate both sides, based solely on a single choice, either to receive or reject God's plan of salvation.

"Like I've already said, I needed to have my system completely shocked before seriously contemplating God and the afterlife. My jolt occurred when Vern Saunders was tragically killed by that drunk driver way back when.

"Up until that time, I'd lived my life without giving the slightest regard to eternity. I'm sure you can still recall how difficult it was for me to accept his death. At the time, I was angry, confused and bitter all wrapped into one. I wanted justice! I was angry with God and asked, 'why Vern,' a million times."

Luther took a sip of water before continuing. "I couldn't accept that God would allow something so tragic to happen to the godliest man I'd ever known. It was the most distressing and confusing time of my life. That is, until I watched God moving mightily in the days and weeks following Vern's trial. That tragic incident helped bring so many people face to face with Jesus, including me and Grandma.

"Which brings me back to this wonderful place on Sanibel Island. When me and Grandma first looked at this property, they were being offered as timeshares only. We never had much interest in purchasing a timeshare, but that all changed the moment we laid eyes on this place. It wasn't the property itself that had lured us in. It was these wonderful trees. There was just something about them that instantly comforted us."

Shelby knew the feeling. This place was already growing on her.

"So we became timeshare owners. This place became our favorite location on earth. Some of my fondest memories of Grandma occurred here," Luther said, with a deep yearning in his heart. "Anyway, when they were offered as condominiums a few years later, we were the first ones to purchase. Until just recently, I never fully understood why we never told anyone in the family about this place. But I'll come back to that..."

271

"Shortly after Vern's death, the pelican trees took on an even greater significance in our lives. When the trial had ended, your grandmother and I needed to get away to clear our heads for a while. We booked our two weeks here and invited Mabel Saunders to join us.

"During our two weeks together, we learned firsthand that the way she conducted herself in that courtroom—especially the way she lovingly forgave Vern's killer—wasn't merely an act. It was very real. And genuine."

Luther paused, "Her kind actions forced me to reevaluate everything in life. I came to realize I didn't have as much control as I always gave myself credit for. I came to see just how fragile and uncertain life really was. Grandma and I had plenty of financial security. But because we didn't have Jesus, we had no eternal security. Mabel made us realize we were living life far too dangerously.

"After lunch one day, our eternal destinations were forever changed when, in faith, Grandma and I received Christ as Lord and Savior of our lives right here under these wonderful trees! By far, it was the greatest moment of our lives.

"With the Holy Spirit living inside us and leading the way, God's Word slowly but surely changed us both from the inside out. It would be nice to see history repeat itself again from this place.

"I can assure you that Grandma and I are alive and living on the Good side of eternity. But my fear is that you think we're here because we were good people, or because we left a generous inheritance to our children and grandchildren; if so, you are tragically mistaken.

"Perhaps you think the money we've donated to various charities in the past had something to do with it. Though it's true we did such things, from a salvation standpoint, our good works and deeds did absolutely nothing to save us.

"Getting to the crux of the issue, my dearest Shelby; it's not what we did for God that got us into Heaven, but what Jesus did for us when He nailed our sins to the cross with Him, no longer holding them against us.

"Talk about love! Romans three-twenty-three states, '*For all have sinned and fall short of the glory of God.*' All means all, Shelby! God's Word also states that anyone who commits one sin is guilty of them all.

"In Acts chapter four, verse twelve, which, if you don't already know, Shelby, is one of the sixty-six books in the Bible, it says, '*And there is salvation in no one else, for there is no other name under heaven given among men by which we must be saved.*'

"Of course, the Apostle Paul was referring to Jesus. The moment Grandma and I placed our trust in Christ as Lord and Savior of our lives, God

272

rescued our souls from the clutches of the Master Deceiver—yes I'm referring to Satan—and delivered us into His Kingdom of Righteousness."

Luther looked skyward and was teary-eyed. Raising his hands high above his head, he practically shouted the words, "Thank you, Jesus!"

He took a moment to compose himself, and went on, "I hope someday you'll come to believe that if you only have Jesus, you will have all you'll ever need in this world. On the other hand, if you don't have Jesus, every day you wake up without Him is like walking on eggshells."

Luther took another sip of water. "I hope you'll come to love the pelican trees as much as we have. To help sweeten the deal, I've transferred ownership of our condo over to you. You'll find the deed inside one of the two sealed envelopes enclosed in this package.

"Congratulations, Shelby! And don't worry, this offer won't expire in ninety-days," he said, flashing a goofy smile.

Shelby's jaw dropped open. "Wow! Thank you, Grandpa!" Shelby craned her neck back to take a good look at the condo she'd slept in last night, totally unaware that she actually owned the place!

"In my will, I made sure to divide all my possessions equally among the family. The only thing I left out was this beautiful beachfront condo in paradise. If this little treasure hunt was as grueling and challenging as I planned it to be, I'm sure everyone in the family will agree when I say you've earned this condo many times over! I just hope as the new owner, you'll visit here more often. So, no more excuses, okay?"

Luther winked, then smiled. "Just kidding, Pumpkin."

Shelby dabbed at her moist eyes again with a new tissue.

"Who would have ever imagined fourteen years ago that my last Mission here on earth would be as a seed planter? Certainly not me!"

Looking skyward, the loving grandfather said, "See these marvelous trees?" The camera slowly panned up, but Shelby didn't need to look at the monitor. She simply looked up. "All three began as tiny little seeds. Yet look at them now! Not only are they enormous, they provide shelter for hundreds of pelicans and comforting shade for all who sit underneath them. Hence, the second 'one-eleven' clue!"

How clever, she thought. It certainly didn't seem so clever a few days ago!

"Well, I'm not ashamed to admit the sole purpose of this journey was to plant a spiritual seed inside your heart which, once nurtured, would allow you to grow mightily much like these trees, in the hopes of ultimately impacting the rest of the Mellon family tree as well.

273

"My greatest hope is that you'll come to realize that only by surrendering your life to Jesus can you ever truly be free. Only then can you ever live life with genuine passion and excitement. Don't get me wrong; by no means will becoming a Christ follower remove all problems and challenges from your life. Far from it!

"I've learned that problems and challenges are necessary in life. They serve to test us, challenge us and ultimately strengthen us. After going on this exciting adventure, I'm sure you know what I mean."

"Do I ever!" said Shelby.

"But when problems do invade your life, you'll never have to deal with them alone. Jesus will be with you every step of the way. With His help, you can one day be just like Mabel Saunders. She has an uncanny way of visiting sadness, worry and despair on occasion, without ever moving into those self-debilitating prisons. She's simply amazing!" Luther took a deep breath and exhaled.

"Oh, there's one more thing. I hope you'll take time to read the Bible I've left for you. Some of its pages had to be taped from being so torn. Even so, the Message remains unchanged. I've highlighted some key verses for you that have greatly impacted my life.

"I hope you'll check them for yourself. Believe it or not, this one's not nearly as tattered as the Bible I plan to be buried with. I once read somewhere that a Bible that's falling apart is owned by someone who isn't! Well, I'm happy to say my two Bibles are falling apart, but certainly not me!

"My prayer is that you'll hunger and thirst for God's Word with the same gusto you garnered while searching for your buried inheritance. The treasure you'll find within its Divinely inspired pages is more rewarding than anything else this crazy world has to offer.

"I just hope you'll one day come to consider your life as nothing more than a test for eternity. As long as you have life in your body, the power to choose your eternal destination is still in your hands.

"I pray you make the right choice soon. Once you do, it'll be up to you to get the rest of the family on board. No one else has your charisma, Shelby. Which is why you were chosen for this assignment in the first place.

"Hey, you found your inheritance; now it's time to take the next vital step in your life-journey by choosing Jesus! Once you do that, I promise you'll experience life at the very highest level. How can you possibly refuse that?"

Flashing his very best smile for his precious granddaughter, Luther ended by saying, "Congratulations, again, on finding your inheritance. I never doubted for a second that you'd find it!

"I love you, Pumpkin, and more than anything else, I hope to spend eternity with you someday. Please watch the second DVD now. God bless you."

52

SHELBY MCKINNEY STARED OUT at the water thankful that the beach was still deserted. She took a few deep breaths and slowly exhaled. Her shoulders slumped as relief flooded over her.

She was deeply touched that her grandfather had exerted so much time and effort doing all of this just for her.

Clearly this little adventure stretched far beyond finding buried treasure. At the end of this rainbow was yet another bold challenge from her loving grandfather. More than one, in fact!

The wife and mother of three got up out of her chair and walked out to the water's edge.

The gulf waters were still brownish-gray, from being churned up so much the past 24 hours. The sea floor was still very much unsettled. Hence, the brownish-gray color.

Once the sand resettled on the bottom of the Gulf of Mexico, it would once again recapture it's brilliant greenish, aqua-blue tone, instantly re-captivating residents and visitors alike.

As the waves foamed up on the shore in rapid succession, Shelby's mind raced even faster. The last thing she expected after the most pressure-packed 90 days of her life was yet another bold challenge from her late grandfather.

But unlike last time, this challenge had no time limit. Did that mean a lifetime commitment was required? Shelby was still unsure.

Her thoughts shifted to God: "If You're so mindful of me and know my innermost thoughts like Grandpa said, why can't I feel Your presence? If I can never flee from Your presence, where were You last night when I needed You most?

"In case You weren't watching," Shelby said to the vast expanse before her, "I was nearly killed! If You really love me so much, why did You allow it to happen? And why did You make me struggle so much before I finally found my inheritance?

"Are You really the Source of Divine order on this crazy planet? Do you really have everything under complete control, regardless of how uncertain life seems at times?

"Is it possible for me to feel that same closeness Grandpa felt toward You? If so, please send me a sign or something. If you do, I will surely listen."

Shelby's insides were stirring like never before. She couldn't help but wonder what she would find on the second DVD. Part of her didn't want to know. Would it present a whole new set of challenges? She hoped not, because she was all challenged out and needed a break!

Her curiosity kept gnawing away on her until she finally gave in and walked back to the pelican trees, still under a canopy of increasingly paranoid and agitated demonic imps.

Shelby sat in her grandfather's beach chair again, and hesitantly inserted the second DVD. The tears she shed watching the first DVD paled in comparison to this time. She never felt such raw emotion pouring out of her grandfather before.

Shelby laughed with her late grandfather. She cried with him. And just as she came to expect, she was greatly challenged by him yet again. But unlike the first DVD, this challenge included the entire family, along with so many others as well.

The demons assigned to her couldn't discern her thoughts, but what they saw beyond the confused expression on their assignee's face terrified them!

They suddenly sensed the end was near.

Not for Shelby McKinney, but for them!

53

BOB SCHUSTER ARRIVED BACK at the condo a few minutes after power was restored. The kids were watching TV in the living room. "I see you're making good use of electricity again."

"Uh huh," said Trevor. BJ and Brooke were too engrossed in their favorite cartoon to comment.

Bob signaled for Ruth and Jesse, who were both in the kitchen, to join him outside on the porch. They came outside to find Bob knocking on Agent Watson's door.

"Already left," Ruth said. "But he left his card in case we ever need him for anything."

"How nice of him!" Bob looked at Jesse. "Had it not been for Curtis, Shelby and I might be..." His voice trailed off.

Ruth glanced at Jesse. He seemed fidgety again. Now wasn't the time to relive the mayhem. Time to change the subject. "How's Bernie, dear?"

"Not so good, I'm afraid. I think part of him thinks it's his fault."

"Nonsense! Nothing could be further from the truth." Ruth grimaced. "I don't know how Stuart found out about the buried treasure chest, but I'll never believe for a second that Bernie had anything to do with his grandson's reprehensible actions."

"Of course not, dear." Bob stared out at the deserted beach and saw Shelby down by the water's edge, slowly pacing back and forth. Was she praying? He hoped so. "But I sense Bernie feels guilty by association for being careless at some point, enough for Stuart to pick up on it. Just hope he can rise above it this time."

Ruth felt a sharp pain in her heart. Though Bernie Finkel was lost, spiritually speaking, he was a kind and generous man who certainly didn't deserve any of this to happen to him. Her greatest concern now was that this incident would push him even further away from his Maker. "We need to pray for him like never before."

Whenever Bernie saw great evil being perpetrated in the world, his atheistic viewpoint flared up, which, in turn, hardened his heart toward the Most High all the more. He often said, "Take a good look around! How can you say there's a God amid so much evil?"

To this, Bob and Ruth would say, "God didn't do this to us, Bernie, we did it to ourselves! The reason humanity is in the mess we're in is because we're all self-absorbed sinners who want to make our own choices in life and be in total control of everything. The problem is, as humans, we're greatly flawed, which means the choices and decisions we make are just as flawed."

Bernie was usually the first to change the subject, oftentimes saying, "Once again, we agree to disagree."

But after all this time, something had to give soon. "I never saw him like this before, Ruth. He's a broken man. He had the look of someone who no longer wanted to be alive."

Ruth lowered her head. It was the last thing she wanted to hear. Was Bernie suicidal? She wondered. "I think he should replace Shelby as the sole focus of next week's conference call."

"I agree," Bob said, shooting a cautious look at Ruth, as if to say, "Later, dear. Not in front of Jesse."

Meanwhile, Jesse's mind drifted back to when Shelby first called the Florida lawyer on the phone before all this nonsense began. Bernie Finkel seemed like such a nice man back then.

Thanks to the Schusters, Jesse believed their good friend wasn't involved in any of this. Bernie wasn't the one who tried killing Shelby. It was his no-good grandson, Stuart! Just the thought of another man trying to harm his wife enraged him to no end.

Jesse's face reddened and burned with the same anger he felt driving to Florida. "All I can say is if Stuart thinks lying in a hospital room handcuffed to a bed with two gunshot wounds is bad, it's nothing compared to how he'd feel if I ever get my hands on him!"

Ruth placed her hand on Jesse's shoulder, "You can rest assured knowing he's in police custody now, where he'll remain for quite some time. Let's let the legal system handle things from here on out. Shall we?"

"You're right," Jesse McKinney replied. "But truth be told, if he were here right now, I think I would strangle him!"

"I understand your feelings, Jesse." It was time to change the subject again. Ruth shifted her attention to her husband, "Did you see much damage on the island while you were out, Bob?"

Bob knew she was creating another diversion. *Good job, honey!* "Frankly, not as much as I expected. I saw plenty of downed wires and trees, broken glass, a few tiles blown off a few roofs and scattered debris everywhere. Other than that, there wasn't much significant structural damage to be seen anywhere."

"Did you check on the house?"

279

Bob nodded yes. "Everything seems fine. Power's back on. Bernie's house is fine, too."

"Very good then," Ruth replied, with a sigh of relief.

"Don't think Hurricane Gertrude will make our top ten list." Bob was referring to a list they kept at home, listing the ten worst hurricanes they'd encountered in their 46 years together as husband and wife. "Perhaps the reason it felt so much worse is that our nerves were already on high alert long before Gertrude came steam-rolling into town. But in the end, her bark was much worse than her bite."

A few moments later, they went back inside. Bob turned on the TV in the kitchen to hear one local newscaster apparently in total agreement with his assessment of the storm. "For the most part," said the newscaster, "Southwest Florida really dodged a bullet."

Yeah, just like me and Shelby, Bob thought, just as Shelby walked through the front door.

"Welcome back, baby." Jesse knew she'd been crying. But he expected that much. "You okay?"

"I'm fine, honey," she said. "Really, I am. It was so nice to see Grandpa again, even if only on DVD. I have a warm feeling inside now." She glanced at Bob. "Let me guess, you held the camera for Grandpa, right?"

"That would be correct, my dear. And it was my honor to do so."

Shelby smiled. "Very nicely done."

"Well?"

Shelby knew what Bob meant. "What can I say! It was deeply emotional. So much to absorb all at once. I need time to think things through and process it all."

"Understood."

"But what an amazing experience! I actually felt Grandpa's presence on the beach."

"Your grandfather was a remarkable man. One of the finest men I've ever met."

"Wow! Such high praise, Bob."

"And one-hundred percent true." Bob paused and was suddenly reflective, "Not counting last night's traumatic experience, which wasn't part of the plan, this little adventure would prove to anyone just how much your grandfather truly loved you, Shelby."

"Don't make me cry again, Bob."

"What grandparent wouldn't want something like this for their family? Talk about a legacy!"

Shelby confessed, "It really was a well-devised plan. I can tell he poured his heart into it."

"Your grandfather worked on this project every day for a year and a half, planning, blueprinting, writing and then memorizing both scripts he wrote, until he was finally convinced the plan was sound."

Shelby grabbed a tissue and dabbed at her eyes. She felt entirely unworthy of the attention her grandfather had brandished upon her.

"Luther Mellon was one of a kind."

"Indeed, he was, Mister Schuster." Shelby's hazel-green eyes were fully alive, even if swollen from so many tears.

Ruth said, "Your grandmother was one of my best friends in life. We spent so much time together, mostly at church functions or here at the beach. I miss them both and long to see them again someday. I'm prepared for that day. Are you?"

"Like I said, I'm still processing it all."

"I understand," came the reply. "It's been an emotional couple of months. I'm sure you need time to relax your mind and body."

Jesse remained silent. But his mind was racing. *What in the world are they talking about! Processing what?* He knew he'd find out once he watched both DVDs for himself. He wondered if he wanted to watch them.

Noticing Jesse's discomfort, Bob switched gears. "Now that you're the rightful owners of this place, when do we need to check-out?"

Jesse shot a sideways look at his wife of ten years.

"It's true, Jesse. My grandparents left this place to us. We're the new owners."

"Really?"

Shelby nodded yes.

"Wow."

Shelby's eyes volleyed back to the Schusters. "Please stay as long as you'd like. You're welcome here anytime. In fact, please hold onto the keys Grandpa gave you. If you ever feel the need to get away, don't hesitate to come back, whether we're here or not."

"That's so sweet of you, Shelby," Ruth said. *She really is just like Luther and Eleanor!*

"We just may take you up on your offer," Bob said.

Jesse wanted to speak but didn't know what to say. Everything went from slow as molasses the past three months to hyper-speed, just like that. His head was spinning trying to catch up to everyone else.

"Now that we pretty much have Sanibel Beach all to ourselves," Bob said, slowly straightening up in his chair, "what shall we do today?"

"Anything, so long as it doesn't involve digging holes in the sand!"

Bob Schuster belly-laughed, "Amen to that," the Godly older man said. "The thought of digging another six-foot hole in the sand fatigues me to no end! Nine times was more than enough for me!"

"I heard that," Shelby said glowingly, allowing the Schusters another prolonged glimpse of the endearing sparkle in her eyes Luther was always bragging about.

Sensing she was so close, Bob didn't want the Master Deceiver to push her away again before the seed Luther planted inside his granddaughter's heart had a chance to take root and grow.

He thought about the Parable of the Sower in the Gospel of Mark, chapter four. *A sower went out to sow. And as he sowed, some seed fell along the path, and the birds came and devoured it. Other seed fell on rocky ground, where it did not have much soil, and immediately it sprang up, since it had no depth of soil. And when the sun rose, it was scorched, and since it had no root, it withered away. Other seed fell among thorns, and the thorns grew up and choked it, and it yielded no grain. And other seeds fell into good soil and produced grain, growing up and increasing and yielding thirtyfold and sixtyfold and a hundredfold.*

When Jesus was alone with His twelve disciples, he explained the parable to them, *"The sower sows the word. And these are the ones along the path, where the word is sown: when they hear, Satan immediately comes and takes away the word that is sown in them. And these are the ones sown on rocky ground: the ones who, when they hear the word, immediately receive it with joy. And they have no root in themselves, but endure for a while; then, when tribulation or persecution arises on account of the word, immediately they fall away. And others are the ones sown among thorns. They are those who hear the word, but the cares of the world and the deceitfulness of riches and the desires for other things enter in and choke the word, and it proves unfruitful. But those that were sown on the good soil are the ones who hear the word and accept it and bear fruit, thirtyfold and sixtyfold and a hundredfold."*

Bob Schuster felt a strong inner-prompting and excused himself from the table. He turned on his laptop computer and sent a blast e-mail to *Shelby's Saints*, urgently seeking prayer for both Shelby and for his partner, Bernie Finkel.

Now that the seed had been planted inside Shelby's heart, they needed to pray it would quickly take root before Satan ruthlessly snatched it away, thus keeping her bound and chained in spiritual darkness.

As much as Bob sensed Shelby inching closer and closer to Jesus, he feared Bernie was drifting even further away; if that was even possible. The very thought of either of them perishing in hell for all eternity sent chills racing up and down his spine.

54

THE FOLLOWING DAY

JUST AS THE SCHUSTERS and McKinneys were about to enjoy a home-cooked meal prepared by Ruth, there was a knock on the door.

"I wonder who that could be," Bob said. They weren't expecting anyone. He excused himself from the table. When he opened the door, he couldn't believe his eyes.

Standing outside in the brilliant Florida sunshine, wearing a simple lavender dress and matching hat, flashing a brilliant smile of her own, was Mabel Saunders.

"Mabel! What are you doing here?"

"Did you really think I would let my illness stop me from celebrating with y'all, Bob? Not a chance!" Mabel was wheezing heavily.

Mindful of her terminal condition and not seeing anyone with her, Bob said, "Are you traveling alone?"

"Yes. I took a taxi from the airport. I wanted to bring Richard Klein along with me but felt led in my spirit to take this trip alone."

"Understood," Bob said. "Did you get my messages?"

"Yes, I did. I wanted to call back but didn't want to ruin the surprise. Sorry if I caused you to worry about me."

"I appreciate the surprise and all, but I wish you would have called. I would have gladly picked you up at the airport."

"And miss seeing the surprised look on your face? Not in a million years," Mabel said, with a chuckle that quickly affected her breathing. She started coughing and wheezing again.

"Are you okay, Mabel?"

"I'll be fine, thanks."

Bob went outside to cordially greet the woman whose fingerprints were all over this awesome adventure. "It's an honor to have you here, Mabel."

"Nice to be back in Florida again. Especially here at this place." Taking another deep breath, she said, "Is Shelby still here?"

"Yes. Jesse and the kids are also here. They arrived yesterday morning."

"Well, did she?"

"Not yet," the Florida lawyer said with a sigh. He knew exactly what Mabel was referring to.

Seeing concern in Bob's eyes, Mabel said, "Don't lose hope, my brother. I'm still convinced God wants her to replace me at Operation Forgiveness."

"I haven't lost hope. I know she's so close. The good news is, she's already watched both DVDs." This was said in a near whisper.

"That's great. When?"

"Yesterday. Underneath the pelican trees."

"Really? How interesting."

"Are you aware of what took place two nights ago? This little adventure nearly cost Shelby her life. I could have been killed, too."

Mabel nodded yes, "I received a phone call from authorities. They were kind enough to share some details with me, including the attempted murder charges being filed against Bernie's grandson. You both must have been so frightened."

"To say the least." Bob Schuster sighed and took a deep breath, "I just hope after sustaining so much mental trauma, this incident draws her closer to God instead of pushing her farther away."

"Let's pray that God opens her heart soon!"

"Amen to that," came the reply. "I e-mailed everyone urging them to keep praying around the clock."

"I'm so proud of all of *Shelby's Saints*."

"Yeah, me too. Perhaps today's the day our prayer will be answered," Bob said, excitedly. "Lord willing..."

Mabel smiled. "Wouldn't that be wonderful."

"Indeed, it would. Hey, we're just about to eat lunch. Are you hungry?"

"A little, I suppose."

"Mabel! What in the world...," Ruth said, joining them outside.

"Hi Ruth. I couldn't resist."

"But what about your health?"

"Before too long, I'll get to live in perfect health for all eternity. I can handle this." There was a certain twinkle in her eye.

Ruth expected nothing less from her. By far, Mabel Saunders was the most faithfully optimistic woman Ruth Schuster had ever known. "Won't you please join us for lunch?"

"Sounds good. I think I will."

Bob reached for her suitcase. Mabel latched onto his right arm and they slowly and gingerly made their way to the dining room. She struggled mightily, forcing the old couple to wonder how she had the strength to travel alone.

But they already knew the answer; Mabel was powered from above. But even just walking looked painful for her. Yet the smile on her face told a different story altogether.

"Misses Saunders? Wow! Why shouldn't I be surprised," Shelby said. "I guess I can say I was sort of expecting you." *Is this my sign?*

"Hi, Shelby. So nice to see you again, dear." Mabel looked at her ever so proudly, like she'd just won a gold medal in the Olympics. "You look so much better than last time I saw you at Martin Hightower's office. I can't tell you how much my heart ached for you that day. But at least now you know why it all happened. Praise God!"

Shelby smiled warmly. "It's a great privilege having you here."

Jesse looked at his wife and smiled. After watching both DVDs, part of him also expected to see her here too.

"Hi kids," Mabel said, breathing heavily again. Her almond-shaped eyes were so alive, even if the rest of her body looked completely exhausted. In between wheezes, she said, "Y'all have grown so much over the summer. Are y'all proud of your Momma for finding the treasure chest?"

"Uh-huh," BJ said. Trevor simply nodded.

"I'm very proud of Momma," said Brooke.

"Thanks, sweetie." Shelby said, blowing her daughter a kiss.

"We're all so proud of her, too." There were more heavy gasps. Mabel searched Shelby's eyes and said, "Just glad you found it without my assistance, if you know what I mean."

"Thanks, Misses Saunders," Shelby replied warmly. "Me too."

Noticing the confused looks on Bob's and Ruth's faces, Mabel said, "Shelby was never in danger of losing her inheritance, even after the ninety-day deadline had passed. Only me and Pastor Cantrell knew about it. Sorry for keeping you in the dark all this time. Luther wanted to keep everyone on their toes at all times."

"I should have known," said Bob Schuster, a wry smile on his face. "So that's why he wasn't overly concerned about the second 'one-eleven' clue being too vague. In the end, it didn't matter. It was Shelby's all along. It also explains why Pastor Cantrell was always more relaxed than the rest of us. You got me good, Luther!" he said looking skyward, a mock scowl on his face.

"Thanks for being such a good sport, Bob," Mabel said. Then to Shelby, "The moment I heard you found it, I booked my flight here. I wanted to come yesterday, but all flights were overbooked due to the hurricane. Just happy to be here now."

"Us too," Shelby replied.

"I heard you had quite an experience the other night. But no need to discuss it now." *Not with the children here*, she thought to say, but didn't.

"I'm fine now." Having already watched both DVD's, Shelby knew Mabel was here for a specific purpose. Knowing that *she* was the main-focus of it all, she felt like Kevin Costner in *Field of Dreams*.

"Please sit down, Mabel. Take a load off," Ruth said. "Make yourself comfortable."

Mabel took a few deep breaths before she was able to stabilize her breathing. After lunch, the elderly woman took a much-needed three-hour nap, before rejoining everyone in the living room.

Plopping down onto a reclining chair, Mabel came straight to the point. "Shelby, would it be okay if you and I went for a stroll after dinner?"

"I'd really like that."

"I'd like to go to my favorite place if it's okay with you."

Shelby grinned. "I think I know just the place."

"Can we come, Momma," asked Brooke, her ears perking up.

"No sweetie," Jesse said to his little girl, "I think they need to be alone for a while. Tell you what; after dinner we'll go back to the pool. Fair enough, kids?"

"Yes, Daddy," BJ and Trevor both said at the same time.

"Yes, Daddy," Brooke said, without protesting any further.

Mabel flashed Jesse one of her trademark smiles and left it at that.

55

AFTER DINNER, SHELBY AND Mabel left for the beach. It was still a little on the hot and sticky side, but with the sun now beginning its initial descent, and with a steady breeze blowing, it felt refreshing.

Shelby spread a University of South Carolina Gamecocks beach blanket out on the sand, then helped Mabel get settled onto it.

The elderly woman had beads of perspiration on her forehead but was determined to take care of business now. "Your hair's so much lighter and longer than last time I saw you, dear."

"Yes, from digging up so many beaches."

"I can only imagine," Mabel said, coughing again. Her breaths were raspy and filled with spittle.

"I hate to keep asking, Misses Saunders, but are you sure you're okay?"

"I'll be fine, dear. Thanks for your concern. Just need to catch my breath."

I hope so... Shelby joined Mabel on the blanket.

The demons assigned to Shelby McKinney sensed grave danger. The blinding white Light hovering high above them kept getting brighter. They moved briskly over, around and even through the pelican trees, rustling leaves and limbs.

They flapped and clawed to gain higher altitude, before banking sharply and gliding back to the earth's surface, sweeping just above the landscape at blinding speed mere inches above Shelby's head.

If they could somehow run the sharp blades of their swords through Shelby's flowery cotton dress, slaying her in the process, they would have already done it by now. Nothing would please them more, in fact. But they didn't have that power...

Mabel looked out at the ocean. "Don't you just love the smell of the salty sea air?"

"Yes! Still can't believe I own a condo here. I can see why my grandparents loved this place so much." There was a childlike expression on Shelby's face. She was full of anticipation without knowing why.

Mabel searched her eyes again. "Your grandparents were always kind and generous people, especially to me. So much good has been done with the generous contribution they left to Operation Forgiveness."

"I couldn't have been blessed with better grandparents."

288

"Indeed. They simply adored you!"

"They thought highly of you too, Misses Saunders." Shelby closed her eyes, took a few deep breaths and sniffed in the history of the quaint beach town. The salty sea air and warm breeze washed over her body. "This place is really growing on me. I plan to come back often."

"Your grandparents would be thrilled knowing that."

"Funny thing is, I always thought Beaufort was their favorite place on earth."

"Oh, they loved Beaufort, and you're right; it *was* their favorite place until they discovered this wonderful haven," Mabel said, her breathing a little more stable. There was a pause as both women scanned Sanibel Beach, before Mabel finally came to the point. "What did you think of the two DVDs?"

"Honestly, it's hard to put into words just how I feel. Like I told the Schusters, I'm still processing it all." Shelby sighed. "I actually watched them both right here on my laptop."

"Yes, Bob was kind enough to share that with me."

"The moment I saw Grandpa's face the tears came." Shelby sighed again. "The second DVD, especially, had me all choked up inside. I must have gone through a half box of tissues while watching it."

"I know what you mean, dear. Gets me every time, too." Mabel took a deep breath. "I know you're still processing everything and all, but did you at least understand your grandfather's message?"

"Sort of, yes. One thing I'll say—I never knew God was so intimately concerned for me."

"Yeah, Psalm one-thirty-nine is one of my favorites."

"When Grandpa read it to me, it melted my heart."

"As you know, it took for my husband to be killed before your grandparents finally decided to get serious with God. So much good came from Vern's death. I'm sure you've heard some of the stories."

"I have."

"Then I'm sure you know I eventually became close friends with Vern's killer, excuse me, Richard Klein. I promised myself to never call him a killer again. And guess what?"

"What?"

"I spoke on Richard's behalf at his probation hearing and convinced them he was a changed man for the better, and that he was ready to be returned back to society. Knowing God can do anything with a surrendered soul, I knew he would have a profound impact on God's Kingdom once released back to society. I believed this so much that I told the three-member parole board I'd be proud to have him on my staff. We've been working together ever since!"

289

"I don't know how you do it."

"It's not me, dear. Only by the grace of God can I ever be like this. Once you experience God's transforming power in your life, you'll go out of your way to look for opportunities to do good things for others without expecting anything in return."

Mabel paused to catch her breath, "Including those who are undeserving of it. Think about it, Shelby, it's easy to do nice things for those we love and care about. Where's the challenge there? The real challenge is when we go out of our way to reach out to those who have done harm to us."

"You make it sound so simple. How do you do it?"

"I'm not the only person on Earth who lives this way. It should be the mindset, heart-set rather, of all practicing Christians. Vern was also like me. Because of what Christ did for him, even though Richard took his life, I can assure you Vern will welcome Richard warmly in Heaven someday. Imagine that?"

"Frankly, it's hard to imagine let alone comprehend. I've heard the many stories of your amazing kindness toward Richard Klein, and I still shake my head. But Vern too? It's simply mind-boggling!"

"Your grandfather used to say the same things. He was so angry and wanted Richard to rot in prison the rest of his life. But that was then. Even Luther will embrace Richard in Heaven."

The expression on Shelby's face said it all; total awe.

Mabel remained silent, hoping and praying she was falling under the conviction of the Holy Spirit.

After a few moments, Shelby finally said, "Thanks for having such a profound impact on my grandparents."

"You're welcome, dear. Thanks to them, this little haven is also my favorite place on earth. Your grandparents extended an open invitation for me to come here whenever I wanted. I used to visit at least once a year, beginning the year after Vern was killed.

"It still amazes me that my late husband never got to visit the place I've come to love so much. Life can be so unpredictable..."

"Please don't think anything's changed. You're always welcome here whenever you want."

Mabel gazed deep into Shelby's warm hazel-green eyes and smiled. "Your generous nature reminds me so much of your grandparents. It's refreshing to see the fruit didn't fall too far from the tree."

"Thanks, Misses Saunders. That means a lot to me."

"However, I can't accept your generosity."

"Why's that?"

"My days on earth are extremely numbered. This will undoubtedly be my last visit to Florida. Too tired to travel these days."

Shelby lowered her head. "Sorry to hear that."

"Please don't feel sad for me. I'm so ready to leave this old, sickly body behind and finally meet my Savior face to face. What a glorious day it'll be! I get excited just thinking about it. And I can't wait to be reunited with Vern. As wonderful as this life can be at times, as you know, we're forced to suffer many moments of pain, heartache and despair along the way.

"Lord knows you've had your fair share the past three months." Mabel paused after noticing Shelby's downcast expression, "But the good news for all Christ followers is that none of these unpleasant feelings are found in Heaven. This is only one of the countless reasons Planet Earth can never compare to God's eternal Domain."

"You sound just like Grandpa. You both make Heaven sound so amazing!"

"I'm afraid we can't come close to expressing the full majesty of Heaven this side of the grave. How can anyone properly describe something so indescribable? Like I said at your grandfather's funeral, when Vern went to be with the Lord, Heaven suddenly became my number one destination of choice. I read everything I could get my hands on, pertaining to Heaven and the afterlife.

"To be honest, the more I learned about it, the more I wanted to be there. Just knowing it's my final-destination thrills me to no end."

"You make me want to be there now."

Mabel's eyes lit up, "Really?"

"Don't get me wrong, there's still so much I want to accomplish here. I also have children to raise. But I must say, you make it sound like the greatest place ever."

"That's because it is the greatest place ever! After all, Heaven is where Jesus is and that's good enough for me! But Heaven is so much more than just Jesus, Shelby. It's a real place with real people, who all have the distinct privilege of living together in perfect peace and harmony with the Creator of the universe.

"Believe me, child, we won't be turned into angels sitting on clouds playing harps, like so many seem to believe. No, we'll lead very productive lives. Everything in Heaven is completely magnified like your grandfather alluded to on the DVD.

"Imagine everything looking, sounding, smelling, feeling and tasting a million times better than what we're used to here on earth. I can't wait to hear

291

the angels singing in Glory as one! Not even the greatest singing voices on the planet combined could compare to it."

"Will we really eat food in Heaven?"

"Yes, dear. But everything will taste a million times yummier than here on earth. And one-hundred percent pure! I can't wait to experience everything Heaven has to offer. As your grandfather always said, 'Woo hoo!'"

Shelby smiled, all the while doing her best to absorb every one of Mabel's words of wisdom. "I can tell you really love Jesus!"

"With every breath I possess! As much as I long to see Vern again, it can't compare to finally meeting Jesus! Part of me is envious that he's already there, but I'll see Him soon enough. I can just feel it."

"How will you recognize everyone once you're there?"

"Much like your grandfather had alluded to on the second DVD, we'll instantly recognize each other." Mabel grew more serious. "Do you really want to see your grandparents again someday?"

"Of course, I do. That goes without saying."

"Can you imagine how wonderful it will feel to embrace your grandfather again and thank him in person for this amazing adventure he sent you on!"

"That's the first thing I intend to do. Because of him, I'm forever changed for the better."

Mabel flashed a warm smile. As fast as it appeared, it faded just as quickly. "What have you done to prepare for that glorious reunion?"

"Prepare? I'm not sure I understand you, Misses Saunders."

"Remember the question your grandfather asked on the DVD, about if your life came to an end today, what assurance do you have of going to Heaven?"

"How could I forget?"

"Do you even know how to qualify to go to that Glorious Place?"

"Well, I..."

Mabel drew in another big gulp of air. "It's okay, dear. That's why I came to Florida, despite my terminal illness."

"Why's that?"

"To help you better understand what your grandfather was getting at. It's that important!" Mabel paused and looked out at the ocean again.

"I sort of understood what he meant. Much like you, he said it all comes down to having a personal relationship with God through Jesus Christ, right?"

"Exactly, dear." Mabel took another deep breath and exhaled. "So I ask; is Jesus living inside your heart?"

"I think so. At least I'd like to think He is."

"You think so? With eternity at stake, what kind of an answer is that?"

"How can I know for sure?"

The demons assigned to Shelby stopped everything they were doing. They were eerily silent, motionless. The blinding white Light high above them was slowly inching closer and getting brighter. The more it pulsated, the more terrified Satan's demons were.

They screamed, "Leave this place at once, Shelby! Run away! You've already found your inheritance. None of this interests you! Go live your life! God hates you!"

But their assignee remained completely unmoved by any of it.

"I know salvation in Jesus sounds so simple on the surface," Mabel said, "Too simple, that most people fail to fully comprehend the power behind the simplicity. In First Corinthians, chapter one, the Apostle Paul said, 'To those who are perishing, God's Word is utter foolishness. But to those who are being saved, it's the power of God!'"

"I see."

"For many, salvation in Christ sounds too good to be true, and therefore, really must be. The reason it's so simple is because God wants that none should perish, not even one! If this really is true, why would He utterly confuse us all by sending us on wild goose chases to find it? Wouldn't make much sense now, would it?"

"Hmm." Shelby thought about the 90-day wild goose chase she'd just barely survived. "Interesting..."

Mabel knew exactly what Shelby was thinking. "Now that you've been greatly tested at the hands of your loving grandfather, I hope you can better understand what I'm getting at..."

"Not really."

"Think about it, Shelby, if God made humanity jump through as many hoops as your grandfather made you jump through on this journey, many who are now in Heaven might not be there. Your grandfather merely wanted you to temporarily break away from your comfortable life in Summerville, where everything was seemingly perfect before the reading of the will.

"He wanted to get your complete, undivided attention. He wanted you to be tested, really tested, and experience the feelings of desperation, hopelessness, fear and confusion, so you'd better understand just how fragile and uncertain life really is at times.

"Thankfully God made salvation so simple anyone can easily understand it. Anyone who wants it, that is." Mabel took a deep breath, "I sincerely hope you enjoy the nice things your grandparents left for you, especially this condo. I must say I'm slightly jealous," she said, with a wink. "But more than anything, I hope when your time on this crazy planet comes to an end, Heaven will be your final-destination."

"How can I know for sure whether I have chosen Jesus or not?"

"The simple-truth is that we don't choose Jesus. He chooses us! In that light, whenever someone has a life-altering experience with the Son of God, thinking very quickly turns into knowing. I'm 100-percent certain that Jesus is living inside my heart."

"That goes without saying, Misses Saunders. Everyone knows you're a God-fearing woman, and in very good standing with the Almighty."

"Thanks, dear, but with all due respect, we're not talking about my salvation. I'm here to discuss yours."

"I really appreciate it. But in your frail condition, wouldn't it have been best for you to remain in South Carolina? After all, I'll be home in a day or two."

"I must confess part of my coming here was for selfish reasons. I wanted to see this place one last time before Jesus calls me Home. So, in a sense, I should be thanking you."

"We're all so honored to have you here. How can I ever repay you?"

"Repay me? Nonsense child! What I do isn't *for* the blessing of God but *because* of the blessing of God! I'm honored to represent His Kingdom on your behalf. There's no other place I'd rather be right now than here with you."

"How can you say that? We hardly even know each other?"

"Oh, but you see, dearest Shelby, I know you better than you may think. As your grandfather and I set out to put this little adventure into motion, Luther assembled a group of a hundred and forty believers from his church here in Florida, and from his former church up in Summerville, to pray for the success of this Mission. I'm proud to be part of this group. Initially, we called ourselves, '*Mellon's Mission Saints.*'"

Shelby's face lit up. "Wow! I don't know what to say."

"Once your grandfather went to be with the Lord, I changed the name to '*Shelby's Saints*'. Bob and Ruth are also two of *Shelby's Saints,* as well as Susan Fernandez from Sunrise Savings and Loan."

Mabel stopped when Shelby's mouth dropped open and tears formed in her eyes. "We've been praying for you ever since. So, in that light, I feel like I've known you forever. We want nothing more than to spend eternity with you in Heaven someday."

Shelby could no longer hold back her tears. They streamed down her face one after the next. Mabel gathered her in her arms and gently rocked her back

294

and forth. Shelby felt completely broken inside, but in a good way for a change. Her earthly resolve started peeling away, layer by layer, like an onion.

Mabel knew she was ready. *Hallelujah!*

The demons assigned to Shelby were frighteningly still. There was no cackling. No sparring. No shrieks. No moans. They were totally prostrate!

Mabel called Bob's cell phone. He and Ruth were sitting on the front porch praying for Shelby when it rang.

In a whisper, Mabel said, "I think we're about to make the news in Heaven. Come. Hurry! And bring your Bible."

Tears welled up in Bob's eyes. "You got it. Be right there!" The call ended. "It's about to happen," Bob said to Ruth. "Mabel asked us to join them there."

"Praise God!"

A minute or so later, the Schusters joined Shelby and Mabel underneath the pelican trees.

Mabel opened Bob's Bible and started reading from the Gospel of John, chapter six. When she read verses 37-44, Shelby started weeping. Perhaps it was the sheer exhaustion. Perhaps it was due to the deep emotion from watching both DVDs.

Whatever it was, with her heart changed, Shelby suddenly went off on her own, "Please save me, Jesus," she cried. "Come to my rescue! I know my sins are what caused You to die so brutally on that cross! I finally get it now and I'm so sorry. Please forgive me and be my Lord and Savior! I want to be among those You promise to raise up on the last day…"

"Wow!" Mabel shouted, before taking a moment to collect herself. "Thank you, Jesus! We exalt You!"

Bob and Ruth opened their eyes and glanced at each other. Both were deeply moved by Shelby's unscripted words. Joy pulsated throughout their bodies. The hair on the back of Bob's neck stood at full attention.

The Holy Spirit flooded all four hearts. It was an intimately beautiful moment for each participant. Bob Schuster, especially, couldn't stop sniffling. It had been an emotional week. Each word Shelby spoke caused another wave of relief to wash over him.

Mabel prayed in a voice that was glad, "Lord Father God, thanks for allowing us to experience this truly remarkable life-changing moment. Please lead our new sister in Christ down the designated righteous path You have chosen for her to travel.

"Strengthen her daily, especially when dark clouds appear on the horizon from time to time. Be her Rock and Comforter in all situations and grant her the necessary wisdom to do what is just and right in Your sight. I ask these things in Jesus' matchless, mighty name, thanking You again for the wonderful privilege of representing Your Kingdom here on earth. Amen."

"Amen," Shelby all but shouted, just as the sun was setting on the Gulf of Mexico, fully illuminating the majestic Florida sky.

With the decision made and the heart changed, as the angels in Heaven rejoiced on Shelby's behalf, God's mighty warriors representing the blinding white Light quickly swept down from Heaven like a great ball of fire, vanquishing and consuming all demons assigned to Shelby McKinney in the twinkling of an eye, sending them spiraling into outer darkness, never to hover again in the human world.

"How do you feel now, Shelby?" Bob Schuster was fully aglow.

"I feel this incredible peace inside I can't possibly explain."

"I can't tell you how relieved I am to hear you say that. You just made the best decision of your life."

Shelby wrapped her arms around Bob and Ruth Schuster and rested her head on both of their shoulders. "Thanks for being two of *Shelby's Saints*."

Ruth said, "It was our pleasure, dear. We haven't felt this alive in so many years."

"When Mabel told me y'all were praying for me all along, I was deeply touched. I feel so connected to y'all right now. It feels like we're family."

"That's because we are Family—God's Family!"

Mabel looked skyward, "Mission accomplished, Luther! It's so nice to see history repeat itself here again."

"I can almost hear him shouting, 'Woo hoo' in Heaven!" Bob said, joyfully.

Shelby just smiled. There was nothing left to say. She felt weightless, like she was about to float away. The many burdens she'd carried around all her life dissipated into thin air.

In her mind's eye, she saw the hole she dug in the sand two nights ago, and for a moment felt the full weight of the struggle that ensued on that fateful night. Then the hole was completely covered up, replaced with inner-tranquility, as if God Himself had filled all the holes and repaired all scar tissue in her heart, like they were never even there at all.

Shelby then saw the calendar hanging on her kitchen wall back home, and the two dates she'd circled for the month of September; the eighth and the tenth. She didn't hear an audible voice. There was no thunder or lightning. Whatever it was, she quickly identified as God's Holy Spirit living inside her heart for the very first time, ministering to her, communicating with her.

The message was loud and clear, "You were right all along, Shelby. September tenth was the correct date you circled after all! On September eighth, you found your buried inheritance. But on September tenth, you found something far more valuable than earthly riches. On September tenth, you found your salvation."

Shelby was totally floored by this precious revelation but kept it to herself, as she slowly drifted back to Earth. "You're so right, Misses Saunders. There really is no in-between. I can feel the Spirit of God living inside me. And all I can say is, 'Wow!'"

"Welcome to the exciting world of being a spirit-filled Christ follower! I can promise your life will never be the same, child. Sure, it will be wild and wacky at times but, from this moment on, you'll never have to cope with life's many struggles alone like in the past.

"Thanks to Jesus, you're now powered from above! With our loving Savior leading the way, there's no telling what you can accomplish for His glory! The sky truly is the limit!"

"Thanks, Misses Saunders!"

"You're welcome. Now we need to get busy getting everyone else on board."

Hmmm...Here we go again!

56

THE NEXT MORNING THE Schusters were seated at the kitchen table having morning coffee with Jesse and Shelby, as the kids ate pancakes and sausage.

Shelby was still glowing after her remarkable beach experience. Jesse heard about what happened to her the night before but couldn't seem to grasp it, despite Shelby's best efforts. What she didn't know was that her husband's agitation was demonically induced.

Just because she no longer had demons assigned to her life, didn't mean Jesse was in the clear. His demons followed him everywhere he went, even if he didn't know it.

And right now, they were doing all they could to stir things up between the married couple, using Jesse's closed mind to create strife within their marriage.

This was one of the many ploys Satan used against married couples, after one of them suddenly became a Christ follower.

Feeling the need to be alone, Jesse excused himself from the breakfast table just as Mabel sat down.

"Good morning, everyone."

"Good morning, Mabel."

"How do you feel now, Shelby?" Mabel watched Jesse amble out to the front porch. She didn't need to ask what was wrong. She knew.

"Still floating here, Misses Saunders," she said warmly. She was still wearing her pink short pajamas.

"I can still see the glow in your eyes. It's the look of someone who has God's Holy Spirit inside her heart."

"I just wish Jesse understood."

"Sounds like someone I knew just yesterday."

"I know I'll need to remain patient with him."

"And pray without ceasing until he comes to faith in Christ."

"That's the plan."

Bob was flicking through the TV channels and saw Stuart Finkel's face posted on the TV screen.

"Look guys. It's Stuart!"

Everyone watched with great interest.

"Just when you think you've heard it all," said the local news broadcaster, "here's an unlikely story that sounds more like an action and adventure flick. Police arrested Stuart Finkel of Fort Myers late Thursday night, after he attempted to steal a buried treasure from a South Carolina woman at gunpoint. This took place two nights ago on Sanibel Island, at the height of Hurricane Gertrude!"

The reporter was taken aback by her own words. "Apparently, Shelby McKinney was bequeathed a sizable inheritance from her late grandfather, Luther Mellon, a South Carolina native who retired to South Florida a few years ago.

"For whatever reason, Mellon decided to send his granddaughter on a buried treasure hunt here in the Sunshine State. From what we've been able to confirm so far, McKinney searched all over the state before finally narrowing her search down to Sanibel Island."

"According to local police, the reason McKinney dug up the buried treasure on the night Gertrude blew into town, was to avoid losing her inheritance altogether. And not only from the storm surge, although that was a real concern.

"It appears McKinney was given ninety-days to find her buried inheritance. The deadline was set to expire at midnight that night. Had she not found it, her inheritance would have been donated to Mellon's church in Florida."

"Not entirely true," said Bob, in a near whisper.

"And talk about a close call; the moment she hoisted the buried chest to the surface, seawater invaded the hole she'd just dug. A second later and it very well may have swept her inheritance out to sea. That's when Stuart Finkel, who was monitoring her from a distance, stole it from her at gunpoint.

"But Finkel didn't get too far. After firing two shots at McKinney, he sustained two non-life-threatening gunshot wounds in both shoulders, from FBI agents on the scene.

"Finkel was apprehended and taken to Gulf Coast Hospital, where he remains in police custody at this time.

"Charges are still pending, but it's expected the list will be quite long, including two counts of attempted murder. We'll keep you updated as more information surfaces."

Mabel watched, but was more focused on how Shelby bristled in silent annoyance while staring at the TV screen. What Mabel saw in her eyes brought her back 14 years to when Vern was killed. *Not good!*

Ruth Schuster was thankful Jesse wasn't watching for fear that he might become enraged again.

At 10 a.m. Bob carried Mabel's luggage out to the car. Her flight was scheduled for 1 p.m., leaving her an hour before Bob dropped her at the airport.

From there, he would drive to Bernie Finkel's house to try and comfort him. He wasn't answering his phone. And that meant Bernie must have seen his grandson's face on TV with the rest of Southwest Florida.

Bob sent a text message to his old friend saying he would stop by after lunch.

For now, knowing Mabel had one last thing to discuss with Shelby before leaving, he and Ruth took the kids for a stroll on the beach, so the two women could be alone for a while.

Jesse joined them.

Mabel wasted no time, "Operation Forgiveness has many supporters. Many rely on us as a source of spiritual guidance in their day-to-day walk with Christ."

"Can't say I'm surprised."

"My time on earth is extremely limited. But the ministry must carry on after I'm gone. The reason I'm telling you this is that I want you to be the one to replace me."

"What?" Shelby was taking a sip of coffee and nearly spit it out of her mouth. "Me? Wow, I'm flattered that you would think to consider me, Misses Saunders, but I'm not qualified to replace you."

"What if I told you accepting my offer could be fulfilling God's purpose in your life?"

The roller coaster ride continued. "Are you aware that I haven't had a job in ten years? What skills can I possibly bring to the table? I'm just a stay-at-home mom."

Mabel burst into laughter, causing her almond-shaped eyes to sparkle like diamonds. "You're so much more than a stay-at-home wife and mother. You are fearfully and wonderfully made, remember? One in infinity, remember?"

"Point taken," came the reply.

"Do you know what my job was before Vern was killed?"

Shelby shook her head no.

"I was a stay-at-home housewife, just like you. Yet look at what God has done with this surrendered soul. Naturally I had my share of struggles and battles with self-doubt along the way. But I knew the devil was trying to distract and confuse me. I eventually developed the catch-phrase, 'God and I against any other two!'

300

"Been using it ever since. Truth be told, I didn't want to get out of bed the other day, let alone travel to Florida. I prayed and prayed, and God reminded me of my little catch-phrase, and so here I am."

"I can never thank you enough. It's been life-changing to say the least."

"No need to think you have to pay me back, Shelby. At any rate, I hope you'll accept my offer."

"Hmm."

"Please don't let your lack of experience get in the way of your thinking. Sure, it will take time to grow into the position. And you'll make your share of mistakes along the way. One reason I believe you'll be a reliable replacement is your big heart. I got to see just how big it was last night. You're a kind, caring and compassionate woman. And simple! I like that about you."

"Thank you."

Mabel drew in a deep breath. "Did you know Jesus' Twelve Disciples were simple men? They were humble fisherman and tax collectors? Even the Apostle Paul—the greatest Christian who ever lived—was a simple tent maker. Like you, they were kind, caring and compassionate individuals. What set them apart from everyone else was their great faith in their Master. At least most of the time."

"I'm sure they also possessed great leadership skills." Shelby looked down at the table. "Unlike me."

"Not really. They were ordinary men following an extraordinary God! They were flawed and even lacked faith at times, often quarreling among themselves. They made many mistakes along the way.

"Even the Disciple Peter, whom Jesus commended for his great faith, denied his Master three times on the night Jesus was betrayed by Judas Iscariot. Even before then, Jesus needed to ask him three times if he really loved him. Imagine that..."

Mabel took a sip of orange juice. "Before the Apostle Paul's Road to Damascus experience, he imprisoned and even killed Christians because of their faith in Christ. Like I said, they were extremely flawed humans. Yet look at how God ended up using them for His glory."

Shelby wanted to speak but didn't know what to say, so she remained silent.

"The Bible is chock full of examples of how God used flawed men and women to accomplish His purposes. Elijah was suicidal. Jacob was a liar. Isaiah preached naked. Sampson was a womanizer. Rahab was a prostitute. Jonah ran away from God! Martha worried about everything. Thomas was the great doubter.

301

"Even more remarkable, David, known as a man after God's own heart, was an adulterer and a murderer. Yet, despite all this, God used each of them mightily because they were willing to be used!"

"Simply remarkable."

"Those who fully embrace the way God made them are the ones who stand out the most in life and end up doing more for God's Kingdom than the rest! I'm living proof that God can fill anyone with His great power and might. After monitoring you closely the past three months, I know He can do the same with you too!"

"Hmm, I don't know..."

"I don't expect an answer now. Pray about it and discuss it with Jesse. But please don't take too long. I don't know how much longer I'll be here."

"It will be my pleasure to volunteer whenever I can. But how can I possibly replace you?"

"As you contemplate my offer, read the Bible every day. Even if you decide not to accept my offer, never stop reading God's Handbook for humanity. The more you get into God's Word and let God's Word get into you, the better equipped you'll be in all facets of life, including Operation Forgiveness.

"The more you keep growing in God's grace and wisdom, the more the Most High will reveal talents you never knew you had. Test me on this, dear. It's one-hundred percent true!"

"I'm sorry, but this is overwhelming. I feel under qualified having this conversation with you, let alone accepting your generous offer."

"That's to be expected, dear. You've had quite a week. Quite a past three months, in fact. I know you're tired and need ample time to recuperate."

"You could say that again."

"Your grandfather always said you had the heart of a champion. You've certainly made a believer out of me. I can only imagine how many times you wanted to quit the past three months."

"Too many to count."

"The important thing is that you didn't quit. And in my book, that's what having the heart of a champion is all about. Besides, if you accept my offer, you'll never be alone. More than a dozen on my staff are ready to assist you at every turn, until you get your legs underneath you, so to speak. Not to further pressure you, Shelby, but you're the only one I'm considering at this time."

"Why's that, Misses Saunders?"

"I already told you, dear. I believe God has ordained it. If so, accepting my offer will be fulfilling His will in your life."

"I still don't know what to say."

"Long before you went in search of buried treasure, your grandfather and I prayed every day regarding this matter. I confess I was shocked when you kept popping into my mind. Especially since you weren't a believer at the time.

"Now that that's been taken care of, you seem more and more the logical choice to replace me. But if you decide to accept my offer, I have a requirement of my own before you can take my place. It's a simple requirement, but not particularly easy to carry out. The question is, are you willing to do it?"

"And what might that be?"

"You must forgive Stuart Finkel."

57

SHELBY'S JAW NEARLY HIT the kitchen table. "Excuse me?"

"That's all I ask of you, Shelby. I mean really forgive him, not just in your heart, but by going out of your way to shower him with kindness until it brings him to his knees."

The look on Shelby's face told the story. Forgive her would-be killer? It was the last thing she expected from Mabel. Then again, Mabel was only asking her to do what she did with Richard Klein.

But forgive the man who robbed her at gunpoint then tried to kill her? "I have nothing but hatred for that man. He tried to kill me!"

"I understand your feelings, Shelby. Lord knows I do. One of the saddest things I encounter is witnessing someone come to faith in Christ, only to allow the burdens Jesus just removed to slowly creep back in.

"Of course, there's no perfect Christian. We're all flawed and weak at times. And we all sin, even after Jesus saves us. This includes me. But one of the greatest sins Christians commit is our unwillingness to forgive others, regardless of offense, after what Christ did for us on the cross! We, of all people, should know better."

Reaching for another deep breath, Mabel went on, "I can assure you I'll certainly be praying for Stuart Finkel from this day forward. If anyone needs God's healing touch right now, it's him."

Just speaking those words to Shelby added to the small flicker of Light hovering above on Stuart Finkel's behalf, created two days ago when Bob and Ruth Schuster started praying for him in earnest.

Shelby lowered her head in shame but kept listening.

"I know it's a difficult request, especially with everything still so fresh in your mind. When Vern was killed, many months had to pass before I was able to do what I now ask of you."

Shelby's brow furrowed. It was too much to absorb.

"I think it's time you took a walk with me down my Memory Lane. Vern and I were avid churchgoers all our lives. Not to boast, but we were good Christians. Not perfect, but we always kept our eyes focused on Jesus."

Mabel sighed. "I never expected that my husband would be tragically killed. I figured since we were good Christians, we were protected from things like that. What I failed to remember was, yes, we were protected, it was from the second death, which is far more important than the first death, which no human being can escape."

"Second death?" Shelby couldn't have looked any more confused.

"Yes, dear. Revelation, chapter twenty, verses fourteen and fifteen states, *'Then Death and Hades were thrown into the lake of fire. This is the second death, the lake of fire. And if anyone's name was not found written in the book of life, he was thrown into the lake of fire.'* Your grandfather touched on it on the second DVD."

Shelby nodded. It sounded terrifying.

"My point is everyone dies. That's the first death. But only God's children can escape the second death. Yes, I'm referring to hell. The Bible describes those who do not have the Spirit of God within them as clouds without rain, blown along by the wind.

"They are like autumn trees without fruit, and God Himself will soon uproot them, and they will be twice dead! They are like the wild waves of the sea, foaming up their shame. They are wandering stars, for whom the blackest darkness has been reserved forever."

"That's deep! And scary."

"I knew this fourteen years ago, but I was so angry and emotional I chose not to remember it. I didn't want to forgive Richard Klein. It was easier to blame him for ruining my life. But like all things that aren't from God, it didn't last.

"Even after I forgave Richard Klein, I was confronted with another challenge. Some of my friends and neighbors bearing the same skin color as me, were furious with me. They got so caught up in the emotionally charged race issue the trial generated in the press. They wanted justice at all costs.

"Even some of my own children and grandchildren made me feel like I'd committed a crime by forgiving him. Some said I was being selfish and was doing it all for personal gain. The pressure was unbearable at times!

"Not to scare you, Shelby, but it's not always easy being a true follower of Jesus. Nor is it always fair. The more you commit to God's calling for your life, the more trials and persecution you can expect to suffer along the way."

Shelby shot Mabel a quick look that was anything but promising. "Doesn't sound like something I could easily get excited about."

"Let's face the facts; with or without Christ in our lives, we still face our share of trials and tribulations."

"Can't argue with you there."

"That said, give me Jesus any day of the week, in good times and bad."

"You're such a wise woman."

305

"Only because of the Word of God, dear. The more I read it, the wiser I become. It's that simple!" Mabel shook her head, "But back then, I was too focused on my own little world to put God's Word into motion, especially knowing many who were persecuting me were self-professing Christ followers!"

Mabel grimaced, "All that grief simply for doing what God commanded me to do. It was difficult to accept. But I knew Satan was doing all he could to derail what God wanted to accomplish. Praise God, most of my persecutors finally came to their senses after seeing God moving so mightily when the trial came to an end."

Searching her new sister in Christ's eyes, she said, "Playing the role of victim too long can turn anyone into a selfish person. Thankfully God let me see just how selfish I was being, and I finally obeyed and forgave Richard."

"You make it all sound so easy."

"By no means was it easy. Simple, yes, but definitely not easy. We humans often mistake the word, 'difficult' for 'impossible'. It may be difficult to forgive Stuart, especially while it's still raw in your mind, but it's certainly not impossible.

"I'm living proof that it can be done. With God's help, you can do it too, Shelby. On the other hand, if you don't forgive him, not only will it affect you physically, mentally and emotionally, you'll even lose sleep at night. Wanna know why?"

"Tell me."

"Because in the back of your mind, you'll know you have the power to change it all, by forgiving the man who *will* haunt your dreams at night. Truth is, you don't get ulcers from what you eat, but from what eats you. Things like anger, hatred, bitterness, envy, jealousy, and yes, the lack of forgiveness, aren't from God and will tear you up inside.

"Whenever you set out to destroy another person, even if only in your mind, you destroy part of yourself in the process. But when you sincerely forgive from the heart, especially those you feel aren't entitled to it, you'll always give so much more to yourself than you'll give to them.

"Even if Stuart doesn't accept your forgiveness, you'll still feel a tremendous release inside. Try me on this. Look at what a little loving kindness did for Richard Klein."

"I see what you mean."

"Stop by the office when you get back home. I want you to meet the man God placed in my life as a test, before trusting me with even greater tasks for His Kingdom. Thankfully I passed His test by forgiving Richard. I don't need to tell you again what followed.

306

"I walked into that courtroom that day an ordinary housewife just like you. The rest is history. Or shall I say, His Story? After all, it's His story we need to tell! Are you hearing me, Shelby?"

"Loud and clear."

"I did it. You can too. Once you forgive Stuart Finkel, fasten your seat belt because I think God's about to take you on an incredible journey, enough to make the last three months look like a tea party! But you must take the first step in obedience. You and I know what that step is. So, the question remains, what will you do?"

"Hmm."

The front door opened. "We're back!" said Bob Schuster. "Time to head to the airport, Mabel."

"I'm ready, Bob." Mabel returned her gaze back to Shelby, "Think it over, dear. Pray about it. And please stop by my office for a visit."

"I will, Misses Saunders. Promise."

"I'll look forward to that day, dear."

"From the bottom of my heart, thanks for two of the greatest days of my life. I'll never be the same. But I would be remiss if I didn't reiterate that your offer overwhelms me. But I promise to pray about it."

"That's all I ask, dear."

"I hope you have a safe flight back home. God bless you, Mabel."

"God bless you too, Shelby."

As Bob and Mabel left for the airport, Shelby's mind was focused on the despicable man who tried killing her two nights ago. Forgiving him was the last thing she wanted to do.

She just wanted to forget about Stuart Finkel and the buried treasure hunt adventure, for that matter, and do her best to move on with her life. She would soon find out it was easier said than done...

58

JUNE 1 THE FOLLOWING YEAR

MORE THAN THREE HUNDRED of Luther and Eleanor Mellon's closest friends and family members were gathered, not to remember Luther's passing a year ago, but to celebrate his first full year in Heaven.

Wanting to mark the occasion, Luther paid for everything using a slush-fund account he set aside for the occasion. He left all the planning up to Shelby, sparing no expense. The only request he had was that it take place on Sanibel Beach.

More precisely, underneath the pelican trees.

Shelby was determined as ever to make it happen. After carefully weighing all her options, she ultimately opted for a Hawaiian luau as the theme of choice. She then called, texted and e-mailed each person Luther had put on the list she found inside the manila envelope in the second safe-deposit box.

Once contact was made, Shelby cordially invited them to a luau on Sanibel Beach, Florida, to mark Luther's first year in Heaven. "All expenses, including travel have been paid for by my grandfather," she told each person. "And the best part is Grandpa will address us on a DVD he made shortly before his death."

More than 100 plane tickets were purchased for family members and friends requiring air travel, including *Shelby's 70 Saints* in South Carolina, FBI agent Curtis Watson, Martin Hightower and Richard Klein.

Terrence and Audrey Bannister, who were both flown in from Nashville, Tennessee. Shelby's two cousins Charlotte and Morgan were flown in from Raleigh, North Carolina.

Everyone else was flown in from Charleston International. All but one: Mabel Saunders. Though mindful of her deteriorating condition, Shelby purchased a plane ticket for her anyway, hoping she would regain enough strength to make the trip.

But it never happened. Mabel took a trip, but where she went no man-made airplane or space shuttle could transport her. She succumbed to heart disease and finally got to meet Jesus face to face.

According to her physician, she died peacefully.

More than 3,000 mourners attended her funeral. Like Luther's funeral, it was a time of great celebration. Numerous stories were told of how Mabel had greatly impacted this person or that person, or this group or that group, or this orphanage or that.

Up until the time of her funeral, only God was aware of many of these wonderful stories. It was a fitting tribute to the woman who had impacted the lives of so many people worldwide.

Shelby took comfort knowing she was reunited with Vern, her grandparents, and numerous other friends she'd made in life. Most importantly, she was with Jesus living in perfect peace with no more wheezing, no more pain, no more chronic heart disease!

All remaining 139 *Shelby's Saints* were there. Also, there were Mort and Sophie Kellerman, Jim and Claire Montgomery and Hank Cavanaugh, FBI Agent Gloria Sanchez and more than 100 friends Luther had accumulated in his eight years of living in Florida.

Bernie Finkel was also invited but respectfully declined. He said he was still too humiliated by his grandson's recent actions to attend.

Shelby pleaded with him, but his mind was made up. The old man rarely left home, for fear of being gawked at by nosy neighbors all wondering how it went wrong for him.

For a nominal fee, Shelby was granted private access to the pelican tree location for the evening. She hired a Polynesian catering company to provide authentic food and cultural activities, including a hukilau celebration—an ancient Hawaiian fishing tradition dating back many generations—and hula lessons for anyone wanting them.

Lastly, she hired a Hawaiian musical group from the island of Kauai to serenade everyone with authentic Hawaiian music. She purchased matching Hawaiian shirts for the boys and men, matching mu-mu's for the women and Hawaiian grass skirts for the young girls, all compliments of the late, great Luther Mellon.

Three large buffet tables full of mouth-watering foods were set up 20 feet away from the trees. This was to avoid having pelican droppings become part of the delicious Hawaiian entrees the caterers spent all day preparing.

Colorful Polynesian lights were skillfully strung on all three trees. Lit kerosene torches encircled the trees in three-foot intervals.

Much like last summer's luau at Disney's Polynesian Resort, the ambiance served to transcend the 5,000-mile distance separating Florida from the shores of Waikiki Beach, in Honolulu.

But this was so much better because they were celebrating Luther's first full year in Heaven. Nothing could compare to that.

309

Whereas Luther's one request was that the celebration take place beneath the pelican trees, Shelby's request to herself was that the DVD be played as dusk crept its way across the surface of the water, just before the sun gracefully dipped behind the Gulf of Mexico.

It was nearing that time now.

Once everyone had enough food to eat, Shelby asked everyone to gather around the large flat screen monitor provided by the catering company. It was time for the Main Event.

The demons assigned to everyone who weren't children of the Most High God knew the mouth of hell was wide open waiting to receive their assignees. If God would only allow it, the wicked would instantly be swallowed up and forever lost.

There was nothing they wanted more.

There were more demons now than pelicans perched on the trees' many branches. If they could somehow sink their razor-sharp talons or rows of jagged-edged fangs into the mass of weak human flesh below, they would turn the landscape below into a bloody beach massacre, so Satan could become drunk with their blood.

Nothing would please them more.

But they didn't have that power...

Fearing the outcome, they could feel their power dwindling with each passing minute. They did all they could to disrupt Shelby from playing the DVD, but nothing worked. She was fully protected from above and there was nothing they could do to stop her.

They screamed into the ears of those to whom they were assigned saying, "Do not listen to Luther Mellon. He really was crazy after all. Run from here! God hates you!"

Totally unaware of their presence, Shelby inserted the DVD and pushed play. Luther Mellon's image appeared on screen, instantly bringing tears to many eyes. Even one year later, he was sorely missed by everyone.

He looked spectacular as always, sitting on a beach chair under the pelican trees, wearing the same outfit he wore in the first DVD. His full head of silver-white hair glistened brilliantly in the luminous sunshine.

He wasted no time, "Greetings, everyone, and welcome to paradise! I hope this finds you all in God's tender loving care, and that y'all are enjoying your time together on Sanibel Island. This tiny little speck of beach is my favorite place in all the world, especially under these wonderful pelican trees, as I affectionately call them. Just being here fills me with inner-peace. I often come here to pray and meditate on God's Word. I even wrote the script for this DVD from right here."

310

Luther took a sip from what looked like a tropical fruit drink. "Ahh, refreshing!" He took another long sip. "From a human standpoint this place truly is paradise. But ever since God rescued me from hell fourteen years ago, beautiful as it is, this place is paradise with a lower case 'p'.

"If this is God's footstool," he said, looking to his left and right, "can you imagine how glorious Heaven must really be? The fact that y'all are watching this DVD means I'm now in Paradise with a capital 'P'! And believe me when I say, Sanibel Island can never compare to this place!

"Yes, Eleanor is here too. And believe it or not, as irresistibly dashing as I look to y'all right now, I'm a million times more handsome now than when I wore a younger man's face! Woo hoo!"

Everyone laughed. It was so like Luther to say something like that.

"Just kidding y'all." He grew serious again. "The Bible describes life in human form as a mist—here today, gone tomorrow! Poof, just like that!" Luther snapped his fingers to further demonstrate his point.

"Eternity, on the other hand, has no end. Each of us will spend eternity someplace! Not to petrify you, but whoever doesn't belong to Jesus will be sentenced to an eternity in hell. With that in mind, I need to ask; if your life came to an end today, do you have absolute assurance of spending your eternity in Heaven?

"Since no one can live on this planet forever, I want to take a moment to remind you all that once your time on earth comes to an end, your soul will be transported to one of two places, Heaven or hell! Despite what many believe, there's no in-between place. It's either A or B! And once you arrive there, you can never switch sides. It will become your eternal destination.

"Let's briefly examine the bad side of eternity. It truly amazes me how so many describe hell as the place where planet earth's coolest citizens end up when they die." Luther sighed. "I can assure you there are no parties in hell. Nor is it a place of fellowship, like Heaven's inhabitants get to experience in great abundance.

"On the contrary, it's a place full of dreadful isolation and condemnation. The problem for all who end up there is that, by the time they discover this truth, it's too late." Luther hated to think of anyone going there, friend or foe alike. It was evident on his face.

"Let's say four friends took a trip together. Two were saved. The other two weren't. Suddenly all four were killed in one of life's many unexpected tragedies; perhaps an earthquake, hurricane, car or plane crash, whatever.

"Regardless of cause of death, the two whose names were found written in the Lamb's Book of Life were ushered straight into the presence of our loving Savior. According to God's Holy Word, not only will they instantly recognize each other, their friendship will greatly deepen in the most Glorious Place God ever created!"

Luther lit up for a split second until his smile vanished and he became somber again. "By not having their names found written in the Lamb's Book of Life, the other two were ushered to a place called Hades. Hades is sort of like a local jail where prisoners who can't post bail or who are denied bail remain until they have their day in court.

"Those found guilty are sentenced and transported to prison to carry out their sentences, whether it be a few months, years or even a lifetime. Whereas Hades can be likened to a local jail, Hell is like the prison where all sentences are ultimately carried out."

Luther shifted in his beach chair. "Unlike the American judicial system, once a soul arrives in Hades, it can never be bailed out. It will remain there until the Great Day of Judgment arrives. Come that day, after being forced to give an account for every-last sin committed in life and openly acknowledging Jesus as King of kings and Lord of lords, that soul is banished from God's presence and thrown into the eternal lake of fire.

"Yes, I'm referring to Hell. There will be constant weeping and gnashing of teeth. And make no mistake: God's Word clearly states all sentences are final, eternal, without any chance of probation or parole."

Luther had the look of someone who didn't want to continue, but knew he had to. It was that important. "Though the two now-doomed sinners were good friends in life, all time spent in Hades and Hell will be in total isolation. There will be no welcoming committees or reunions with former friends. In fact, there will be no communication whatsoever, only unspeakable suffering.

"Even worse, the mind of each condemned soul sent there will constantly replay each time God's Word was being shared with them back on earth and willfully rejected each time—whether in spoken word, printed form, TV, radio, Internet, whatever—all the while knowing they are without hope."

Luther shook his head. "Imagine looking down the corridors of time and seeing an unlimited length of time and judgment before you. The very thought alone will swallow up the thoughts of each unrepentant soul sent there. They will groan in despair knowing they can never be delivered from that place or receive any reduction of torment. Even after struggling and fighting through millions of ages, they'll realize hardly a second has gone by. An eternity still remains.

"I sincerely hope y'all are getting this. If not, let me put it this way; had God not changed our hearts and breathed His regenerating life into us, Eleanor and I would be in Hades this very minute, terrified and alone, with no way of comforting each other.

312

"While it's true that we donated large sums of money to various churches and charities and performed various good works in life, even so, had we died without first repenting of our many sins and trusting in Jesus, we'd be doomed for all eternity. It's only because of God's grace that we're in Heaven.

"Hey, if what I'm saying is true, which it certainly is, why risk living another day on this crazy planet without trusting in Jesus as Lord and Savior? No one knows the exact day they will die. Regardless of age, tomorrow is guaranteed to no one!

"I envision a huge sign hanging on the walls of hell with the word 'tomorrow' written on it. So many people promise to change for the better *tomorrow*, when the day of salvation is at hand today! Now is the time for you to be bailed out! Not tomorrow! And only Jesus can bail you out! Do you even know Him?

"Only two things will remain for all eternity, the Word of God and the soul of man. With that in mind, God's salvation is, by far, the greatest Gift anyone can ever receive. But like all gifts that are given, a price was paid before God could offer His gift of salvation to humanity. And what a price it was!"

Tears formed in the corners of Luther's eyes. "God loves His children so much that He offered up His only begotten Son to be crucified for their sins. An innocent Man was publicly condemned for our iniquities. Before He was crucified, He was tortured and beaten senseless. They drove nails through his wrists and feet!"

Luther wiped his eyes with his shirt sleeve. Many who were watching started sniffling. "Scores of angels could have come to His rescue at any time, but Jesus remained silent. Wanna know why? Look in the mirror and you will see."

Satan's demons swirled above the crowd trying to create a spiritual vortex, hoping it would suck up the large-TV screen and spew it out in the Gulf of Mexico. But they were powerless from stopping what was happening.

Just hearing the name "Jesus" uttered by any of God's children, packed the power of a million atom bombs going off inside their calloused minds all at once. They growled. They shrieked. They wheezed, and with each exhale, sulfuric brownish-green smoke poured out of their mouths and nostrils. Their eyes were blood red.

The blinding white Light high above continued inching closer, pulsating like a giant heartbeat, as God's mighty warriors prepared for more souls being surrendered, more repentant hearts being changed this night.

Luther collected himself and went on, "Many still debate whether the Jews or Romans put Jesus on the cross. Next time you watch the crucifixion

313

scene on TV, try watching it from a different perspective. Just before the nails are driven into His marred hands and feet, imagine Jesus looking straight at you and saying, 'It's okay. I can handle it.

"The pain is excruciating, but each time I think of *you* being separated from my Father for all eternity, it makes all My suffering worthwhile. Each time they strike Me with their whips and chains, I see *your* face and know the beating must continue. I love *you* too much to have them stop. This is all being done for *you*, and I will let nothing interfere until it is finished!'"

Luther buried his face in his hands and sobbed uncontrollably for the longest time before he was finally able to continue. Many watching also sobbed. "My point is this; God used Roman soldiers and the Jews to carry it all out, but the simple-truth is that *you* put Jesus on that bloody cross," he said, pointing into the camera. "And I did, too, I'm afraid.

"The sooner you personalize Jesus' death on the cross and realize He was pierced for *your* transgressions, crushed for *your* iniquities, and that *your* future death sentence was freely brought upon Him, you'll finally understand what God's amazing grace is all about. It will change your life forever!

"Ultimately, however, you must understand that the One who really put Christ on the cross was God Almighty Himself. In truth, no sinner was ever saved by giving his heart to God. We are not saved by our own giving, but by God's giving.

"While our Maker is holy and just, He is also merciful and gracious. Because of this, He offers complete forgiveness to all who have a saving faith in Christ Jesus. For those who truly repent of their sins and embrace Christ completely, there is forgiveness of sin and deliverance from the penalty of sin. That's the Good news that follows the bad news. What's the bad news, you might be asking?

"There's no way to sugarcoat it. Your sin is the cause of the great separation between you and God. Just like my sin, your sin is an affront to God's holiness. Only the blood of Jesus can make any of us right with God. There's no other way!

"With that in mind, I hope I've made it crystal clear to you this day that the consequences of life without Jesus are very real. And eternal. For those of you who may feel prompted in your hearts to receive Christ as Lord and Savior, there are plenty of God-fearing men and women among you who will be honored to share the Word of God with you until you are fully mindful of what it means to have eternal assurance."

With eyes aglow, Luther finished by saying, "For those of you who already are my brothers and sisters in Christ Jesus, I look forward to seeing

314

you again someday. Can you imagine still knowing each other a thousand years from now? Ten thousand? A million? How awesome is that?

"Until then, may God continue to bless and keep you. Enjoy the remainder of your time together. I love and miss you all."

59

IN ALL, GOD CHANGED thirty-seven hearts underneath the pelican trees. The angels in Heaven rejoiced on their behalf, as God's mighty warriors quickly swept down from Heaven like an unquenchable fireball, vanquishing all demons assigned to Heaven's newest saints, sending them spiraling into outer darkness, never to dwell in the human world again.

All demons representing still unrepentant unbelievers weren't vanquished, but they nevertheless withered in the presence of the Light. Suddenly, as if a bomb had been detonated, they were sent spiraling out of control; some were blown many miles out over the Gulf of Mexico, before they could finally correct themselves using their wings, and racing back to the humans they were assigned to deceive and destroy.

Now that Shelby fully understood the importance of salvation in Christ Jesus, and the eternal power accompanying that decision, she rejoiced for all 37 of her new brothers and sisters in Christ.

Among them were her parents.

"Welcome to God's Family, Momma and Daddy!" Shelby said, sharing a tearful embrace with them. "I can't fully express how thrilled and relieved I am knowing y'all are both Heaven-bound someday!" John and Trudy Ross looked like little children again.

Shelby couldn't help but marvel. It was priceless!

Aunt Audrey was next. "I'm sure Grandpa's joy knew no bounds the moment the angels in Heaven rejoiced on your behalf," Shelby said. Aunt Audrey was too emotional to utter a reply.

Shelby then hugged her uncle Terrence, great aunt Bea and Uncle Sam.

Lastly, she approached FBI Agent Curtis Watson. "Welcome to God's eternal Family! It's only fitting that the man God used to save my life last year made the news in Heaven. Had it not been for my late grandfather, you and I wouldn't even know each other. Talk about paying it forward!"

"You sure throw some luau," the FBI Agent said, with a grateful heart. They embraced again.

Shelby looked skyward. With tears in her eyes, she said, "Mission Accomplished guys! At least partially." Her words were meant for the two most beautiful people she'd ever known in life—Mabel Saunders and her grandfather, Luther Mellon. "I love and miss you both so much and can't wait to see y'all again someday! I love and miss you too, Grandma!"

The Hawaiian group resumed playing song after song, as many took selfies underneath the pelican trees.

Shelby sighed. Incredible as it was, it could have been so much better. For starters, Jesse wasn't among the 37 to receive Christ as Lord and Savior. This came a s a great disappointment to her.

But Jesse was only part of what had blocked her from experiencing the complete fullness of God's joy. Seeing Richard Klein again also had her stomach in knots. She first met him at Operation Forgiveness Headquarters nine months ago, after returning to South Carolina with her buried treasure.

The second time they met was a month ago at Mabel Saunders' funeral. Without even asking, Klein knew the shameful expression on Shelby's face was there because she never got to give Mabel an answer before she died, regarding her involvement with Operation Forgiveness.

Before heading back to his hotel, Klein handed Shelby an envelope. Once the celebration ended and everyone was gone, she walked down to the water's edge alone and removed the letter from inside the small envelope.

Not surprisingly, it was a copy of the same letter Richard gave her at Mabel's funeral, handwritten by Mabel herself.

Drawing light from one of the still-blazing gas torches, Shelby reluctantly read the letter again.

Greetings, Shelby! I hope this finds you well and fully alive in God's tender loving care. I finally achieved the ultimate-goal in life; I'm finally with Jesus! Hallelujah!

Now that I'm Home with my Savior, Richard Klein knows I want you to replace me at Operation Forgiveness. Truth be told, I thought I would have heard from you one way or the other. But it's okay. I understand you, dear.

This letter serves to inform that the offer still stands. But please decide soon. I'm sure everyone involved is waiting and wondering who my new replacement will be.

Richard's doing a wonderful job as acting director, but he's very good at running the ministry's IT department. It would be difficult to replace him in that capacity.

Now that I'm gone, Operation Forgiveness needs a new face. The position will not remain available forever. Though I haven't heard from you, I remain convinced that God wants you to be the one to replace me.

I hope when you see Richard at my funeral, you'll be reminded once again of what a little forgiveness and loving kindness can do in the life of another human being.

Once you make your final decision, please contact Richard either way. He'll know what to do from there. I miss you, Shelby, and very much look forward to seeing you again someday in the greatest Place ever when your life's journey comes to an end. God bless you!

In Him,
Mabel

Shelby grimaced and looked skyward, "Lord, why won't You just let me forget about last September, so I can finally move on with my life? I just want to be happy!"

Lowering her head in defeat, Shelby didn't need an answer. She already knew. It all came down to forgiving Stuart Finkel.

It was like she had a throbbing toothache, but instead of going to the dentist to fix the problem, she decided to leave it alone and do her best to live with the pain.

But in her mind, that man didn't deserve her forgiveness.

As a fairly-new Christian, Shelby knew what God's Word said about the importance of forgiving others. If she didn't forgive, she wouldn't be forgiven. It was that simple!

But Stuart Finkel nearly killed her! That was her major sticking point, and Shelby was fully prepared to fight it every step of the way. Sooner or later, the dreadful feeling she felt would pass, hopefully replaced with comforting peace for a change.

She just hoped it was sooner rather than later.

What Shelby didn't know was God was trying to take her to a whole new level in life, if only she would obey His command and forgive the man who tried killing her nine months ago.

Yes, if she only did that, her joy and happiness would know no bounds. Only she didn't know it yet...

60

SEPTEMBER 10

FIFTEEN MONTHS TO THE day when her treasure hunt adventure began, Shelby McKinney received word that Stuart Finkel's case wasn't going to trial after all. His attorney convinced him to accept the plea agreement being offered to him.

The rebel inside Finkel wanted to fight it all the way, but with so much indisputable evidence stacked against him, and with many slated to testify against him—including Susan Fernandez and Sonya Haynesworth from Sunrise Savings and Loan and FBI Agents Gloria Sanchez and Curtis Watson—Stuart Finkel had no chance of winning his case.

Just the thought of being dragged into court and forced to listen to former friends, Ricky Clemmons, Jed Ashford and Chris Watkins, testifying against him was the last thing he wanted.

On the tenth of June, Finkel was sentenced to 20 years in prison for his heinous actions. With good behavior, he could be eligible for parole in twelve years, but only if he was a model prisoner, which most thought highly unlikely.

Shelby was never more relieved to hear the news that day. She didn't feel she had the strength to see him again, even in a crowded courtroom, where she knew she'd be perfectly safe.

She just wanted to forget all about Stuart Finkel and let him rot away in prison for as long as the system would allow. But forgetting about him meant she needed to block Mabel Saunders out of her mind as well. It was impossible to think about her without being reminded of her bold challenge to forgive the man who kept invading her mind.

Each time Stuart crept back in, anger followed and the small part of her heart that wanted to offer forgiveness hardened like steel again. Mabel warned last year that if she didn't forgive him, it would have a profound negative impact on her walk with Christ.

This was happening with greater frequency. Her defiance of God's command had put her in a spiritual holding pattern.

What ate away at her insides most was that she was ignoring the final wish of a 79-year-old woman who'd traveled all the way to Florida in failing health for her sake.

319

Another thing Shelby wrestled with was in God's eyes, sin was sin, regardless of how great or small it appeared in the eyes of humans. And the Word of God clearly stated that whoever commits one sin was guilty of them all. This meant Shelby was just as much a sinner as Stuart Finkel.

Even so, she still couldn't bring herself to do it. How could she forgive him when he wanted to take the life of a mother still raising three young children?

And Jesse certainly wasn't helping much. He constantly encouraged his wife of eleven years that she was taking the right approach by not forgiving him, especially face to face. No way!

"It's best to just forget about him," Jesse often told her. "Finkel did this to himself! He deserves to rot away in prison. Let's just move on and enjoy our lives together."

Nevertheless, no matter how hard she tried blocking him out of her mind, Shelby simply couldn't do it. Which is why she drove to Union Correctional Institution now, all alone, without her husband's full blessing.

Stuart Finkel was escorted by a prison guard to the visitor's section and ordered to be seated.

A moment later Shelby appeared on the opposite side of the protective glass, wearing black jeans and a white cotton shirt. This was the first time the two had locked eyes since last year on Sanibel Beach. Shelby mentally noted that his hair was much shorter now.

Other than that, he pretty much looked the same. His eyes were still full of rage, malice and hatred, which Shelby surmised was normal for anyone who was one year into a 20-year prison sentence.

"What do you want?" Stuart snapped, still very much projecting the look of someone possessing an empty soul.

"Hmm," Shelby said, wondering if she'd made a mistake by coming here. Just hearing his voice zapped all energy from her body, much like Kryptonite did to Superman. She started trembling, but miraculously kept Stuart from noticing. She didn't want him to use her fear against her.

On Stuart's side of the protective glass, the dark wings on the demons assigned to him whirred with the strength of a million dragonflies. They flitted this way and that, as if caught up in the vortex of a powerful tornado.

They screamed into Stuart's ears, "Ignore her! It's a set up! She's crazy!"

On the other side of the protective glass were their Heavenly assailants, sent by God to protect Shelby. They stood firm and were stoically silent. They were calm and resolute, always observing, always ready.

Their very presence frightened Stuart's demons to no end...

Even so, it didn't stop them from taunting God's warriors with blood-curdling shrieks. They growled and hissed and spewed venomous hatred at them—their razor-sharp talons firmly planted in Stuart Finkel's soul—but God's warriors remained perfectly still.

Each attempt they made to tempt, torment and deceive Shelby's mind was deflected, like a sponge ball hitting a brick wall.

Totally unaware of what was taking place all around her in the spirit world, Shelby took a deep breath and cleared her throat, "I came here to forgive you for what you did to me."

Finkel rolled his eyes and looked away. It was obvious her forgiveness meant absolutely nothing to him. His reaction bolstered the confidence of his demons even more. They snarled and hissed at God's warriors, then sparred among themselves like a pack of wild lions fighting over a fresh kill.

There goes my whole speech, Shelby thought, regarding the mental pep-talk she'd rehearsed in her mind a million times already. The scowl on Stuart's face forced her mind to go completely blank.

Noticing the confused expression on Shelby's face, the vile imps assigned to Stuart Finkel tried once more to invade her mind, but God's warriors swatted them away with the flat of their swords.

Their jaundice yellow eyes turned blood red with anger upon impact. Acrid brownish-green smoke poured out of their mouths and nostrils, as they spun backwards, desperately trying to steady themselves with their wings.

Shelby gulped air into her lungs, "Are you okay in here?"

"Yup," Finkel said, matter of factly, totally unaware of the black clouds of God's wrath hanging directly over his head.

"Have your gunshot wounds healed?"

"I'll live," came the reply. The gaze on his face bored into her like this was all her fault.

Shelby gulped in some air, "I can only imagine how difficult it must be in here at times."

"Have you ever spent time in prison, lady?"

"No, I haven't."

"Well then, you have no idea what it's like," Finkel hissed, a cold and calculating glare on his face.

What Shelby didn't know was that Vinnie and Carlos were also sent to this prison for five years each, for illegal gun possession on the night their paths all collided on Sanibel Island.

Much of the stress Finkel battled stemmed from doing all he could to avoid the two men he knew would surely kill him if given the chance. Not only did he owe their boss a boatload of money, he owed them the three grand they foolishly laid out for him.

Stuart finally became aware of it when the three came face to face a few months back. "You better watch your back in here," Vinnie said, angrily that day. "If I were you, I wouldn't even blink!"

"You're right." Shelby realized the irony of it all. It was as if she'd wronged him and was here to beg his forgiveness, not the other way around. She lowered her head and silently prayed, "Help me, Lord. I can't do this without You." She looked up and gazed into Finkel's unfriendly eyes. "I just want you to know there's someone on the outside who cares."

"Yeah, and who might that be?" Stuart said, slightly humored by her comment.

"Me."

Stuart was clearly suspicious. "Are you being paid to do this?"

Shelby was taken aback by his remark. "Paid?"

"Yeah, by one of those tabloid TV shows."

"No, I'm not being paid. In fact, no one except my family and a few others know I'm here. And certainly no one from the media."

"Does my grandfather know?"

"Not to my knowledge."

Finkel was still suspicious. "I'm still waiting for a cameraman to appear from behind that door to commemorate the one-year anniversary of what happened last year. I'm not in the mood to be interviewed now lady," Finkel snapped. "Besides you're two days late. It was the eighth of September, not the tenth! Get it right next time!"

Shelby ignored his comment. "There are no cameramen with me and you're not being interviewed. It's just me, okay? I'm on vacation with my family." She grimaced. "This isn't easy for me. Visiting a prison while on vacation is the last thing I ever thought I'd do. I tried to talk myself out of it a million times, but you kept popping back into my head. I believe God wanted me to visit you, so I could forgive you face to face, and not just in my heart."

"God, ha! Are you on drugs, lady?"

"I'm perfectly fine. Why do you ask?"

Finkel stared blankly at her, then winced. He shot a quick glance at the prison guard to see if this was some sort of practical joke.

The guard said nothing but monitored him very closely.

Returning his gaze back to his visitor, Finkel said, "Why are you doing this, lady? What's the catch!"

"I don't follow you, Stuart."

"Come on, there must be a catch."

322

"I, uh..."

"Come on, spit it out, lady, I ain't got all day."

"There isn't a catch, Stuart. I already told you, my main reason for coming was to offer my forgiveness."

Shelby shot a nervous glance at the muscular prison guard. He had the look of someone greatly anticipating what would come out of her mouth next. In fact, he seemed more interested than even Stuart.

Stuart opened his mouth as if to speak, but no words came out.

Shelby noticed, took a deep breath, exhaled and continued, "Whenever I think back to the night you tried to kill me, fear and anger always set in. Had you not been stopped, we both know I'd be dead. I still have nightmares about it. I wanted you to go to prison for the rest of your life. Until just recently, the very thought of you made my skin crawl."

"You're not the first person to tell me that, lady," Finkel replied, in a tone one might hear after just being paid a compliment. He still refused to call her by name. It was too personal.

"I never thought the day would come when I could bring myself to forgive you, especially face to face."

"Why the sudden change of heart?"

"Partly for selfish reasons..." Shelby looked down at her hands. "Harboring ill feelings toward you all this time has prevented me from experiencing the true inner-peace and joy I know is possible in this lifetime. I've seen it manifested in others with my own two eyes. I want the same thing."

Finkel had no idea what she was talking about. Nor did he care to know. He just wanted her to leave.

Shelby sighed. "Two days after our dangerous encounter, exactly one year ago today, I became a Christian and everything changed for me. I was fortunate to spend time with a woman who impacted my life in so many ways, especially regarding the topic of forgiveness. One reason I'm here is that I aspire to be just like her."

"And?" Stuart still had no idea where she was going with all this.

"Well, she had a similar experience. But hers was much worse than mine. Her husband was killed by a drunk driver."

Shelby noticed the scowl on Stuart's face soften a bit. "Much time had to pass before she could finally accept it for what it was. Instead of hating her husband's killer, she became his friend and often visited him in prison.

"Because of her, Richard completely turned his life around. Years later she spoke at his parole hearing and told the parole board that if they released him, she would offer him a position with her outreach ministry. Richard was paroled early, and they worked very closely together until Mabel recently died."

Shelby nearly lost it, but somehow controlled herself. "Time truly does heal all wounds. With God's help, I've had enough time to think things through and accept the events of last September. God always reminds me in my spirit that had I been killed that night, I would have died still in my sins, which means I would have been doomed for all eternity.

"But God spared my life by sending that FBI agent to protect me. If God loves me so much that He allowed me to live so I could find my salvation two days later, who am I to not sincerely forgive you in return? Which is why I no longer harbor anger or hatred toward you, only forgiveness."

"Are you sure you're okay, lady?"

Shelby took another deep breath, "I can only imagine how awkward this must make you feel. Believe me when I say, I can only be like this because of He who lives in me."

Stuart couldn't deny the joy on her face. "And who might that be?"

"Jesus! Because He first loved and forgave me, I can forgive you."

Finkel rolled his eyes again. "Listen lady, I got all the religion I can handle here in this hell hole. I don't need any more thank you very much." He grunted sarcastically.

"The last thing I want is to come across as religious, Stuart." Shelby paused. The silence was deafening. "I'm just trying to be your friend."

Friend? Stuart's lewd and crude resolve started fading away. He looked peaceful for a change. "You really want to be my friend?"

"Yes."

Finkel studied her face even more carefully. "Why, after everything I did to you?"

"Again, it's all because of Jesus."

"Hmm." Stuart ignored the Jesus part, but found it impossible to ignore how this woman, of all people, wanted to be his friend. "Do you know how long it's been since anyone's asked to be my friend?"

"Indulge me," she said softly.

"Too long to count," was the reply.

"Finding the buried treasure has changed my life in so many ways. The money I inherited had little to do with it. In fact, the treasure hunt was just a tool my grandfather used to bring me face to face with Jesus! I'm not the same woman I used to be. Not even close! And when I say I forgive you, I mean it sincerely."

For the first time ever, Stuart Finkel felt something stirring deep inside his soul. His demons stopped sparring among themselves, suddenly fearful.

324

How could the woman he tried killing last September act so kindly toward him now?

Stuart was thinking the same thing. It was overwhelming. He looked as if he was about to cry. "You really forgive me?"

"Yes, I do."

"Do you think my grandfather will forgive me?"

"I can't speak for your grandfather. But it can't hurt to ask, right?"

Stuart wanted to speak but remained silent.

"I can't tell you what to do. But I believe seeking the forgiveness of others is a good first step to finding inner-peace here in prison. Even if your grandfather refuses to forgive you, you'll feel so much better for at least trying."

"You really think it's possible for me to find peace here?"

"Absolutely! But if you want to experience the kind of peace that surpasses all understanding, it can't come from seeking the forgiveness of those you've wronged in the past. It can only come from God, through a personal relationship with His Son, Jesus Christ!"

"Do you realize I'm Jewish, and that most Jews don't believe in Jesus?"

"Not to sound insensitive, Stuart, but your being Jewish doesn't change the fact that Jesus really is Israel's Savior. It's all recorded in God's Holy Word. If you'll just read it for yourself with an open heart and mind and receive the message of hope it offers for all who come to believe it, you *will* experience His peace that surpasses all understanding, even in a prison cell."

Stuart didn't reply. He couldn't.

"What I'm trying to say is my forgiveness isn't merely enough. It will give you temporary peace at best. But God's unconditional forgiveness is eternal! Even with the many bad things you did in life, God still loves you and is willing to forgive every sin you've ever committed.

"Even if your grandfather doesn't forgive you, that's between him and God. The important thing is once God forgives you, your sins are removed from His mind forever, never to be counted against you again. Talk about an incredible plea deal! It doesn't get any better than that!"

Stuart leaned forward in his seat. He didn't want word to spread in this place that he was getting soft. You show weakness in here, you're dead. You limp, they trample you. It's that simple.

In a near whisper, he said, "You make it sound so comforting."

"Three more minutes," said the prison guard bluntly, to Stuart Finkel. He glanced at Shelby with a look on his face that said, "Sorry, Ma'am, just doing my job."

325

Shelby understood. It was time to wrap it up. She stood to leave. "I'd like to keep in touch with you if you wouldn't mind. You know, to encourage and remind you that you're not alone in this crazy world."

"That would be fine."

"Would it be okay if I sent reading materials?"

"I suppose."

"I'd also like to send you a copy of the Word of God if you wouldn't mind."

"The Bible?"

Shelby nodded yes.

"I can get that in here."

"That's good to know, but I'd still like to send it as a Gift. You have plenty of time in here. If you come to believe the Message it teaches, it *will* change your life forever, guaranteed!"

Shelby took a deep breath and exhaled. "But only if you apply its many teachings."

"Feel free to send it then."

"Hallelujah!" the toned, bulky prison guard said under his breath. Shelby didn't hear him, but Stuart sure did. He shot him a quizzical look, but the prison guard looked away.

The demons assigned to Stuart started trembling, suddenly fearful.

Awesome! "God bless you, Stuart. Always know that I'm praying for you daily."

When Finkel didn't reply, Shelby turned to leave.

Just before she left the small room, Finkel finally spoke up, "Shelby?"

"Yes?"

"Thanks for coming." Stuart couldn't remember the last time he'd uttered those words to anyone. It felt good because, for the first time in a very long time, he was being sincere.

Shelby flashed a warm smile. "You're welcome. I know it will be difficult for you in this place, but never forget you have a friend on the outside." At that, she left the room.

The prison guard handcuffed Finkel and escorted him back to his cell.

Shelby was totally unaware of the impact her words had on the prison guard. She reminded him again of how Christians were supposed to treat others, by providing the perfect object lesson.

Stuart was the first beneficiary of his new-found kindness. For the first time since being sent to this place, the guard treated him like a human being instead of some worthless piece of garbage.

God saw it all unfolding, and He smiled.

326

Once back inside his cell, Finkel marked this moment as the first time ever feeling comforted in this dreadful place.

Let the healing begin, he thought...

Shelby left Union Correctional Institution feeling high as a kite. She looked skyward, "You're right, Mabel, it does feel incredible! Mission accomplished. I did it! I really did it! Woo hoo!"

Driving back to Sanibel Island, Shelby had plenty of time to reflect upon her visit with Stuart. The one thing she would remember most was how drastically his face had softened in the 30 minutes they were together. There wasn't a trace of anger there when she left. Also gone was the hatred, bitterness and menacing scowl.

It was remarkable. He still had a shocked expression on his face, but it was in a good way for a change. "Thank you, Jesus!"

With a renewed mind, Shelby revisited her last conversation with Mabel Saunders, the day after God changed her heart and granted her the faith and repentance to receive Jesus as Lord and Savior.

Mabel Saunders was right! A little loving kindness toward others really did go a long way in this oftentimes cruel world.

Forgiving Stuart Finkel was one of her most satisfying experiences in life. Another thing Mabel said that loomed large in her mind now was forgiving him would draw her closer to God.

Driving southbound on I-75 to her condominium on Sanibel Island, Shelby was 100-percent certain now that God wanted her to accept Mabel's offer to join Operation Forgiveness.

Now that her mind was clear, it all seemed so exciting...

61

"HI, RICHARD, IT'S SHELBY!"

"Well, hey there, stranger! Long time no hear! How are you?"

"Just great, thanks. And you?"

"It is well with my soul," Richard Klein said. "Believe it or not, I was just about to call you."

"Really?"

"Yup. I haven't forgotten today's a special day for you. Your one-year born-again anniversary, right?"

"Yes!"

"Happy birthday, sis!"

"Thanks for remembering." It sounded a little strange hearing this because her natural birth date was April 15th.

"As I was rejoicing in my spirit on your behalf, I suddenly felt prompted to pray for you."

"Really? That's amazing!"

"Why?" *Is she finally ready to take the job?*

"I'm in Florida. And guess what?"

"What?"

"I visited Stuart Finkel in prison today. Just got back twenty minutes ago."

"Wow, really?"

"Yes, sir."

"That explains the strong inner-prompting I had to pray for you earlier." Klein took a deep breath, "How'd you make out?"

"I was scared to death. When I first saw his face, I felt sick to my stomach and thought I was going to pass out. But with God's help, I was able to overcome it all. And guess what?"

"What?"

"I forgave him to his face!"

"Wow!" Klein's mind raced back to his prison experience with the late Mabel Saunders, 16 years ago.

"It was one of the most incredible experiences of my life," Shelby said.

There was sniffling. "Thank you, Jesus," Richard shouted joyously. "I don't think you'll ever fully know what you did for him today. I speak from personal experience when I say Stuart will never forget your loving kindness toward him. Now I see why Mabel wanted you to be the one to replace her."

"It's not me, Richard, but He who lives in me."

Good student! "Amen to that!"

"Speaking of Operation Forgiveness, I want you to know that I'm finally ready to assume the position if it's still available. More than ready, in fact."

"Truth be told, we were willing to wait until the end of this year before moving in another direction. Just glad you called before it was too late."

"Excellent. I'm plum excited to begin. Of course, I can't replace Mabel. She's simply irreplaceable."

"Indeed, there will *never* be another like her."

"But just like she said, if only I will do my best to be the very best Shelby McKinney I can be, with God's Divine guidance, everything else will take care of itself, right?"

"Yes," Klein said. "I look forward to working with you. Let's meet for lunch when you get back to South Carolina."

"I have a better idea. Why don't we meet in Florida instead?"

Richard paused to let the thought marinate in his mind. "What a wonderful idea! I pray for Stuart every day without fail. In fact, everyone here on staff does. I've been wanting to visit him, but always sensed in my spirit that you needed to be the first. I'm sure you planted a seed today."

"All I can say is I truly felt God's presence with me. Once I remembered I wasn't alone, my fear vanished, and God strengthened me to do what needed to be done."

"Did you touch on my story?"

"I think that's what finally broke the ice. Before that, he seemed edgy and angry."

Klein whispered a soft "Thank You" skyward, then said, "I can't wait to meet him. Hopefully seeing this once-imprisoned man leading a good life as a productive citizen on the outside will encourage him as he serves out his long sentence. Perhaps in time, it can happen to him too."

"I sense that's exactly what he needs."

"Well then, I need to get busy clearing my schedule. How long will you be in Florida?"

"Five more days."

"Okay. After I visit Stuart, we can get together to discuss your role here at Operation Forgiveness."

"I look forward to it."

"Me too, Shelby. Truth be told, I wasn't sure if you'd ever accept Mabel's offer. She would be so proud of you. I'm proud of you, too! You took a huge step today."

"I feel like a new woman."

"Amen to that, Shelby."

"Amen!"

62

THREE DAYS LATER, RICHARD Klein pulled into the parking lot of Union Correctional Institution, in Bradford County, Florida.

Tall and lanky, with long hair and a full beard and mustache, the 42-year-old man received his share of menacing glances from prison guards. But Klein didn't let it upset him. He was on a Mission as evidenced by the radiating glow shooting out from his blazing blue eyes.

After clearing various checkpoints, he was ushered into the visitor's section.

A few moments later, Stuart Finkel appeared on the other side of the glass. He gazed at his visitor blankly. "Are you sure you've got the right person?"

"Are you Stuart Finkel?" At first glance, this man didn't seem capable of perpetrating the kind of evil that had landed him in this place. Nor did he look the slightest bit edgy or angry like Shelby had experienced when she visited him.

"Who wants to know?"

"My name's Richard Klein. I'm a friend of Shelby McKinney."

"I see. You're the one who spent time in prison."

"That would be me."

"What can I do for you?"

"Just thought I'd pay a visit and encourage you to remain strong in here, until this challenging time in your life is finally over."

"That's very kind of you, Richard."

On Stuart's side of the protective glass, the demons assigned to him were terrified. Before Shelby McKinney's visit three days ago, they monitored their assignee more on cruise control than anything else. Every move Finkel made was nearly perfect because he never took a single step toward God.

They were *not* on cruise control now! They were on full alert.

On the other side of the protective glass were their newly assigned Heavenly assailants, there to protect Richard Klein.

Just like the angels who'd protected Shelby three days ago, God's mighty warriors stood firm and were stoically silent. They would never leave Richard's side.

Their evil adversaries couldn't even look in their eyes. The radiant light was too brilliant, too majestic, too blinding, too condemning. If they could

331

somehow rip Richard Klein's tongue out of his mouth, they would do it. But they didn't have that power.

They listened and watched with the patience of a honeycomb being invaded by a swarm of angry bees. "This man's a lunatic!" they hissed into Finkel's ears. "He's a hippie freak! Do not listen to him! Ignore him! God's forgotten all about you! He hates you!"

God's warriors weren't permitted at this time to vanquish Finkel's demons into outer darkness until a decision was first made.

Even as a prisoner in chains, Stuart had unlimited power just waiting to be unleashed in the spirit world, if only he asked for it. But through the constant denial of the ways of God, his heart became wickedly hardened, to the point that he was completely blinded to the Truth. Satan's demons wanted to keep it that way.

One thing Satan's demons knew was that all of humanity would ultimately acknowledge Jesus Christ as Lord and Savior in the afterlife. No one could escape this future appointment—themselves included—regardless of race, gender, social status or chosen religion.

Up until three days ago, the demons assigned to Stuart Finkel thought he would never step foot inside Heaven. He was destined to end up with them, only to be eternally tormented. He'd always been a good soldier for their side. He was almost as vile as they were.

Now they weren't so sure.

"What did Shelby say about me?" asked Richard.

"Basically, that you were driving drunk one night and you killed someone. And that his grieving widow forgave you publicly, and eventually became your good friend."

Richard Klein nodded agreement, "Not only did she forgive me, God used her to share His Word with me, which changed my eternal destination. It's like she was more of an angel than a friend. Definitely the most amazing woman I've ever met."

"Yeah, Shelby told me. Lucky you."

"Not lucky me. Blessed me. Luck is man-made, Stuart, but all blessings come from God."

Interesting, Finkel thought. "I still can't believe Shelby visited me here. She's the last person I ever expected." Stuart squirmed in his seat. Tears formed in the corners of his eyes, "Can't believe I almost killed the one person who cared enough to visit me in this place. Until you, that is."

"I know what you mean. But in my case, though it wasn't premeditated, I did end up killing someone. The last thing I expected was to hear Mabel forgive me on the day of my sentencing."

"Shelby sure gave me a lot to think about the other day," Stuart said calmly.

"Yeah, like what?"

"Life in general. Why I'm here on this crazy planet. It can't be merely to do bad things to others. She also made me question if there really is a God and the role Jesus plays in it all. Things like that."

Good job, Shelby! Richard thought, keeping it to himself. "And what have you concluded?"

"You've been in prison, Richard. You know how hopeless it feels to be stuck on the inside."

"Difficult, yes," said Richard Klein, "but the moment I received Christ as Lord and Savior, I never felt hopeless again. No matter what happened, I knew everything would be okay because God had everything under His complete control. I learned I was safer being locked up in prison being *in* God's will, than at any other place on earth being out of His will. That thought comforted me greatly."

"I hate this place. Nothing but constant doom and gloom! I'm always fearful for my life. I still have a long way to go before they'll release me. Until three days ago, I never felt a moment of peace or comfort in this place."

Klein rubbed his chin, "I remember that feeling all too well. Had Jesus not been walking beside me, protecting me, I don't think I could have survived prison life. I wasn't a hardened criminal. I was just an alcoholic who'd made a terrible decision one night that ended up killing another man. Yet there I was, walking among the worst society had to offer."

A lone tear rode down Finkel's right cheek, "Shelby's kindness toward me made me realize just how out of my mind I really was. Greed was my god. Human life meant nothing to me. All I cared about was myself! No one or nothing else mattered. If I had to hurt someone to get what I wanted, it was all part of the process."

Stuart Finkel exhaled deeply, "Shelby knew this, yet she still forgave me. She even offered to be my friend. Imagine that. She's inspired me to write letters to my mother and my grandfather, asking their forgiveness."

"Wow! That's fantastic, Stuart."

"Just glad I didn't end up killing her. No one else on the planet could have impacted me like she did."

Richard sensed something happening in his spirit. Was Stuart close to being converted? "I still remember to this day how unworthy I felt of Mabel's kindness."

"Exactly. You hit it right on the head. I don't deserve any of it."

"None of us do, Stuart. The first two times Mabel visited me in prison, her focus was on friendship. After her first visit, I started reading the Word of God in my cell every day. On her third visit, it could no longer wait. I needed what she had.

"Mabel took her time explaining the Gospel of Jesus Christ to me. A light bulb went off in my head when she read John fifteen, verse sixteen, and I realized I wasn't choosing God. He chose me! How awesome is that!"

Richard Klein smiled, "By far, receiving Christ as Lord and Savior was the greatest decision of my life. I haven't been the same since. I spent the remainder of my time in prison learning all I could about God's Word so when I was finally released, I'd be fully prepared for successful living on the outside. Praise God, I haven't had a drop of alcohol to drink since being released. Nor do I have the urge to drink. God is so good!"

Stuart sighed, "Are you aware that I'm Jewish?"

"Perfect. So was Jesus! Are you a practicing Jew?"

"Let's put it this way; the last time I was inside a synagogue was for my Bar Mitzvah."

"Listen, why don't you focus less on religion for now and get as up close and personal with the Most High as you possibly can. If you seek Him with everything that's in you, the Bible makes it clear that you'll come to see for yourself that Jesus really is the Son of God, and Israel's Savior. So many Jews have read the Bible from cover to cover trying to dispel Christianity for the fraud they thought it to be. And guess what?"

"What?"

"Many became Christ followers as a result. Praise God!"

Stuart leaned forward in his chair. "I want to tell you something. After Shelby left, that guard over there brought me back to my cell. Soon after, he returned and handed me a Bible. Been reading it ever since."

"That's the best news I've heard all day! What have you read so far?"

"Since Shelby gave all credit to Jesus for visiting me in prison, I decided to check Him out first and see what all the hoopla was about. I started in Matthew. I'm in Luke now."

Richard's heart was flooded with joy, "And what have you learned?"

"I was just reading about Jesus' crucifixion and His resurrection three days later, when the guard brought me here. How amazing that you're here three days after Shelby's visit."

"Really?"

"Yes. I believe Jesus really did rise from the dead and is the Savior of the world." Stuart bit his lower lip, "But why would He want to save someone as wretched as me?"

334

"Because you matter to Him."

Finkel lowered his head in shame. "How can you say that? Sure, I've been good the past three days. But prior to that, I was as vile as they came."

"Yeah, I heard some of the stories about you. But despite what others may think, only God knows your true heart. He knows everything there is to know about you, including the softer, kinder, gentler heart you now possess."

"How can you be so sure? Until three days ago, I was a despicable man!"

"Even with your rough and rowdy past, if God's calling you to salvation, nothing or no one can stop it from happening. And that means, in God's eyes, you're more precious than the rarest diamond on Earth.

"Think about it, Stuart, there are seven billion people on the planet, yet no one walks like *you,* talks like *you,* laughs like *you* or loves like *you*! You're not one in a million, my friend, or even one in a billion. In God's eyes, you're one in infinity."

Richard Klein got choked up over his own words but pressed on, "Not only does God know how many breaths you took today, not a single heartbeat occurred inside your chest without His permission. He even knows the exact number of hairs on your head. Did you know that?"

Finkel nodded yes, "I read something about all my hairs being counted in Matthew, I think it was, but figured it was meant for everyone else, just not me."

"That's just Satan attacking your mind. I stand firmly on God's Word and His authority when I say the wonderful things you're reading in God's Word apply to you, too, my friend, if you come to believe them as Truth."

Richard's cobalt blue eyes filled with tears, "Regardless of your current lot in life, once you receive Jesus as Lord and Savior, you'll truly be free even in this undesirable place. Believe me, I know what I'm talking about!"

Stuart blinked hard. He was too choked up to voice an audible reply.

"If God's calling you to salvation, Stuart, it means He's willing to forgive every sin you've ever committed. And once they're gone, they're gone for good!" Richard Klein said.

The prison guard, now fully caught up in the moment, could no longer contain himself. He shouted, "Hallelujah" at the top of his lungs, loud enough that even Richard heard it on his side of the glass.

Stuart took a few deep breaths, lowered his head again and started weeping uncontrollably. The demons assigned to him felt one of Satan's better students in human form slowly slipping away from their clutches. There was nothing they could do to stop it.

It was the worst feeling for any demon to have someone so deep within their clutches for so many years, only to be ripped away and placed into the loving arms of their most hated enemy, the Lord Jesus Christ! The Light high above kept intensifying and pulsating.

"Jesus loves you, Stuart," Richard shouted above Finkel's loud sobs. "Cry out to Him. He is listening! He wants to give you a fresh start in life. You know, a do-over. But this time with Him leading the way. Not you."

There were a few awkward moments of silence until Stuart Finkel gazed straight into Richard Klein's friendly moist eyes.

With two moist eyes of his own, and a heart forever changed, Finkel said, "Can you please tell me what I must do to make Jesus the Lord and Savior of my life? There's nothing more I want."

"Nothing would please me more," Klein declared.

"Three minutes," said the guard, in a kind and gentle voice. If it were his choice to make, he would ask Finkel's visitor to stay all day to offer hope to everyone housed inside this dreadful place. But he had a job to do.

"Just keep reading the Scriptures and seeking God with everything that's in you. If you'll only do that, like I already said, you *will* find Him, guaranteed! God says in His Word that all who seek Him will find Him. All means all!"

"I admit I feel this deep stirring in my soul to want to know the God who created me."

"I can't tell you how overjoyed I am to hear you say that!"

"Thanks to you and Shelby, I'm convinced this can only be possible by trusting in Jesus."

"There is no other way, Stuart."

Richard Klein watched as Stuart Finkel closed his eyes and cried out to Jesus for forgiveness and redemption. It was an amazing thing to behold. The moment it was confirmed in Heaven, the angels rejoiced and all of hell shook!

God's mighty warriors transformed into two blazing fireballs, generating the light and heat of a million lit furnaces, consuming each demon assigned to Stuart Finkel, sending them into outer blackness, where they would remain until they were cast into the eternal lake of fire with Satan himself, forever doomed!

"I feel so different," Relief flooded Stuart's soul. It was depicted on his face. Even in prison chains, this instance proved that God can do anything with a surrendered soul—anything!

"And just what do you feel, Stuart?"

"I can feel the spirit of God living in me now."

"Hallelujah!" Richard said. "Wish I could reach through this glass and hug you, my dear brother. From this point on, always know that Jesus will be with you. Communicate with Him daily. Read His Word. Hunger and thirst for it. Believe me when I say, it will greatly comfort you in this place."

"How can I ever thank you, Richard?"

"By paying it forward, brother!"

"Brother, I like the sound of that."

"Me too, Stuart. Me too," Richard said. "Whatever I can do to make prison life a little easier for you, just ask and I'll do my best to assist you."

"This has been the greatest moment of my life."

"I know how you feel. I'll be sure to visit you whenever I'm in Florida. You can bank on it, brother."

"I'll look forward to each visit with you."

Richard stood to leave, "By the way, Shelby's still wondering how you found out about the buried treasure. Care to tell me?"

Stuart leaned forward in his seat, "You said God forgives and forgets, right?"

"Yeah..."

"Can you do the same? I just want to forget the past and move on."

Klein chuckled to himself. "Point well taken. You're right, it's not important. We already took care of the most important thing. And when your time on earth comes to an end, there's a one-way ticket with your name written on it, headed non-stop to Heaven."

Stuart shook his head. He was totally astonished.

"Imagine that—two former convicts walking Heaven's streets of gold together, living in perfect peace forever and ever. For now, just hang in there, brother. This isn't our home. We're just visitors. Our real Home is in Heaven with Jesus. Can I get an Amen?"

"Amen!"

"HALLELUJAH!" cried the prison guard. "This beats going to church by a long shot!"

Stuart Finkel's caffeine and nicotine-stained teeth were fully exposed, displaying the most brilliant smile he could possibly generate. What Richard Klein saw on his face was the look of someone who'd been strapped to an electric chair awaiting electrocution, only to be rescued at the last possible moment.

Someone did rescue him and save his soul from an eternity in hell! His name was Jesus! And regardless of what Stuart Finkel's many past victims thought about him, he wasn't the same wretched man they knew him to be. Stuart was Heaven-bound someday, and there was nothing anyone in human form could do to change it!

Richard Klein left Union Correctional Institution feeling the same way Shelby McKinney felt when she left this place—on top of the world. He pulled his cell phone from his pocket.

"Hi Richard," Shelby said, seeing his name appear on her cell phone. "How'd it go?"

"Mission accomplished, sis!" Klein said, triumphantly.

"Are you serious?"

"Yes! We made the news in Heaven today from behind prison walls. I can't wait to tell you all about it."

"Woo hoo!" Shelby said.

The irony was so thick you could cut it with a chainsaw. Irony may be hard to define, but it was easy to recognize. Most would marvel at how Shelby could rejoice for a man who tried killing her last year. Some might even question her sanity. Normal people didn't do such things. But to God's children, it made perfect sense.

"If it's okay with you, I'd rather tell you in person."

"Sure. I understand," Shelby replied.

"All I will say for now is after you left, a prison guard brought a Bible to his cell. He's been reading it ever since. God was already changing his heart long before I arrived. All I did was make sure he had a full understanding of the Gospel then pray with him. You had quite an impact on him. He even said so himself."

"Really?"

"Yup. How's it feel knowing that the Most High used you to start the process of bringing Stuart back to Him?

"Glory to God!" Shelby exclaimed, in a voice that was glad.

"I'm leaving the prison now. Hope to be there in three hours. Where would you like to meet?"

"I know just the place, Richard," came the answer, without hesitation.

"Noted. I'll try to be there before sunset."

Richard Klein ended the call and cranked up his *Mercy Me* CD, singing the lyrics to *I Can Only Imagine* at the top of his lungs, en route to the pelican trees. He felt weightless.

When Klein placed his trust in Jesus in that South Carolina prison way back when, God's grace alone had saved his soul. It had absolutely nothing to do with free will, or because of anything good in him. Nor was it because he was holy, righteous or religious.

The only thing Richard Klein brought to his salvation was his sin. Nothing more. God did everything else. It was 100-percent grace; 100-percent Gift!

The instant his eyes and ears were opened to the Gospel and he surrendered his life to Jesus, he felt the wonder of God's majesty for the first time.

Only those redeemed by the blood of Jesus got to feel this way. To the rest of the world—including Planet Earth's wealthiest and most influential people—it was simply indescribable...

63

SEPTEMBER THE FOLLOWING YEAR

AFTER A FULL YEAR under her belt as Director of *Operation Forgiveness,* Shelby McKinney finally made her first significant contribution to the flourishing outreach ministry.

Until just recently, she'd performed only a handful of menial tasks, as she struggled to get her legs beneath her, so to speak; certainly nothing worthy of her title as Director. Because of this, Shelby frequently questioned her overall involvement, wondering if she'd made a mistake by accepting the position in the first place, especially as Mabel Saunders' replacement!

If ever there was a fish out of water story, this was it!

Believing it was God's will for her to be involved, everyone encouraged her to remain patient, often reminding her that it would take time to settle into her new position.

Richard Klein knew Shelby was putting enough pressure on herself for a hundred people—wracking her brain senseless—trying to think of what she could possibly bring to the table to finally be considered an asset.

She prayed for months on end that God would define her role at this place. When she didn't hear from Him, anguish flooded her weary soul. She even questioned whether Mabel Saunders really heard from God that day. Did He really want Shelby to replace her as director in the future? It sure didn't seem that way.

Everything changed three months into her tenure, when God gave her a clear-cut vision of how she could make her own mark on the ministry.

If successful, not only would it help keep *Operation Forgiveness* in the limelight, the potential was there to turn the tens of thousands of names already stored inside the ministry database into hundreds of thousands, perhaps even millions, within a few years.

Shelby got her answer after reading the Bible her grandfather had left for her, in the eighth chapter of the Gospel of Matthew, when Jesus and His Disciples were traveling in a boat. *Without warning, there arose a great storm on the sea, causing the waves to sweep over the boat. Fearful for their lives they woke Jesus who was sleeping saying, "Save us, Lord; we are perishing." And he said to them, "Why are you afraid, O you of little faith?"*

Then again in chapter 14, Jesus' Disciples saw their Master approaching them walking on water. They were terrified, and feared it was a ghost. *Jesus said to them, "Take courage. It is I! Don't be afraid!" Peter said to Jesus, "Lord, if it is you, command me to come to you on the water." Jesus said, "Come." So Peter got out of the boat and walked on the water and came to Jesus. But when he saw the wind, he was afraid, and beginning to sink he cried out, "Lord, save me." Jesus immediately reached out his hand and took hold of him, saying to him, "O you of little faith, why did you doubt?"*

Those two passages penetrated her heart like a hot knife in butter. Shelby realized she'd turned into one of the many doubting Christ followers in the world.

Even worse, the self-doubt she harbored had created an instant passageway for Satan to invade her mind and constantly attack it. Her lack of faith at times was the chief cause of her self-doubt.

Shelby was too wishy-washy at times. And who wanted to follow a wishy-washy leader?

She decided that day to stop allowing outside influences to control her so much and trust God in all things, not just some. Instead of feeling inferior about the talents and abilities she didn't possess, it was time to utilize the talent she was blessed with at birth.

If she only did that, perhaps she too could do great things for God's Kingdom, just like the Disciple Peter had done; just like Mabel Saunders had done.

Ironically, what God revealed to her that day as her best way to contribute to *Operation Forgiveness*, should have been clear to her all along. But because she was so wishy-washy she never connected the dots, so to speak.

The picture started coming into focus the day she visited Stuart Finkel in prison. When Shelby got home, she felt incredibly inspired and couldn't sit still.

Jesse told her to go for a long walk on the beach to release all that high-octane energy.

Five hours later, Shelby was still walking, her mind traveling light years ahead of her body. By the time she got back to the condo it was after 10 p.m.

Jesse raised an eyebrow, "Training for the Olympics, dear?" he had said.

"Sorry, but you wouldn't have wanted me here earlier. I would have been bouncing off the walls all night."

"Why don't you soak in the tub a while. After that, I'll massage you to sleep. Fair enough?"

Shelby grabbed a pad of paper and pen and started jotting down a few thoughts. She ended up soaking in the tub until 5 a.m. There was a note on her pillow saying, *Rain check good for one massage!*

Shelby showered her husband with plenty of kisses that night. She woke the next day and was just as restless. She grabbed her late grandfather's beach chair and went to the pelican trees.

Sensing her words might inspire others at some point, instead of trying to forget all about the whole treasure hunt ordeal—especially the most frightening parts—it was time to relive it all again.

Shelby picked up where she'd left off the night before, jotting down thoughts on paper, recounting the 90 days it took to finally find her inheritance and, ultimately, her salvation. She made it look so messy on paper but planned to organize it all later.

For now, she needed to get it all out while it was still fresh in her mind. She was mildly surprised that the moment she'd dreaded revisiting all this time wasn't so painful anymore.

Each time she put pen to paper, it was like having a personal therapy session with God. It was as if her Maker was patiently waiting for her to forgive Stuart Finkel before allowing the inspirational floodgates to open.

Writing became a great release to Shelby.

One page turned into two.

Then three.

Then four.

Then five.

As the waves broke quietly on Sanibel Beach that morning and the seagulls chirped high above her, Shelby sat beneath the trees she'd come to love, and the floodgates of creativity opened wide.

With each new written word, she was healed a little more from the inside out. Writing quickly blossomed into a full-blown obsession of sorts for her.

Back home in South Carolina, she organized her messy notes and retyped them onto her laptop computer. In between balancing her home and ministry life, every-last second was spent pecking away on her laptop keyboard. At times, her fingers couldn't keep up with her brain; eight hours passed feeling like only two.

Keeping a promise to honor her late grandparents' wishes, the McKinneys visited Sanibel Island every few months. They loved their Florida beach home.

Shelby always did her best writing underneath the pelican trees, always in her late grandfather's beach chair. The more she wrote the more convinced she became that it had all the makings of a pretty good story. But just to make

342

sure, she asked Bob and Ruth Schuster to read it for themselves, to see if they agreed with her assessment.

They, too, were gripped by the story. The fact that they were part of it brought back so many memories—good and bad—making it an emotional read at times. Both were convinced Shelby's book would be well received in the marketplace.

"Hire an editor as quickly as possible, dear, to dot the *I's* and cross the *T's*," Ruth Schuster declared. "This book needs to be published. The whole world needs to read it!"

In no way was writing the book obstacle-free. There were many moments along the way when Shelby allowed her humanity to rise above her Divine inspiration. Each time she did, self-doubt crept in and Satan attacked, doing all he could to block her creativity; anything to stop her book from being published!

Still enraged for losing her, eternally speaking, God's ultimate enemy sensed great danger for his side if this book ever saw the light of day. It could mean a huge future depopulation of his eternal domain, as countless readers turned their lives over to his arch enemy, the Lord Jesus Christ!

Satan and his hordes of demons did all they could to confuse her mind. They won a few battles along the way, but the problem was that it wasn't Shelby's book to begin with. It was God's book, and His will that it be published.

Six months later—after nine solid months of writing—just like that, Shelby McKinney was a Christian author.

Had someone told her before going on the buried treasure hunt that she had the gift of writing, and that it would eventually lead to all this, she would have laughed at them. With a database full of tens of thousands of names at her disposal, Shelby felt certain that this was her best way to contribute to *Operation Forgiveness.*

The book went to press on June tenth, two years to the day when she received her late grandfather's letter, commencing the buried treasure hunt adventure. When she handed over the final manuscript for publication, it was one of the most satisfying, triumphant moments of her life. It was totally beyond description.

The title of the book was *The Pelican Trees.* By choice, it was released on September tenth, two years to the day she made the news in Heaven underneath the pelican trees.

Though Shelby was the author, the name "Shelby McKinney" wasn't found anywhere on the book cover. She chose instead to use *A Grateful Believer* as her pen name.

Shelby shipped two copies to Union Correctional Institution, one for Stuart Finkel and one for the prison guard who gave him a Bible. Stuart read it in just two days.

To celebrate being a first-time author, there was only one place to mark the momentous occasion—under the pelican trees on Sanibel Island. More than 300 family members and friends gathered to celebrate with her. Each received a copy of her book.

For the 100 or so unbelievers there that night, after reading how Shelby had gone out of her way to offer genuine forgiveness and friendship to the man who tried killing her two years ago, it was the straw that broke their backs.

Realizing Shelby had something they didn't have, they dusted off their Bibles and read all about God's plan of salvation for humanity, and their spiritual eyes and ears were opened.

Now that they finally understood what Luther Mellon had said in his video that it was God's glorious, unmerited, undeserved salvation—which came by grace through faith in Christ alone—they also understood they didn't need to travel to any particular location or recite some memorized prayer to receive this free Gift.

Even so, they wanted to meet again at the pelican trees, so they could pray for each other, fellowship together as new believers, and share the Gospel with those who perhaps still didn't understand it.

There was nothing they wanted more, in fact.

64

TWO WEEKS LATER, SHELBY McKinney was flying back from the West Coast to Fort Myers, Florida, after addressing 7,000 people at a large church conference in Southern California.

This was Shelby's first "official" speaking engagement as Director of *Operation Forgiveness*. Hundreds among the large gathering had already read *The Pelican Trees* prior to her arrival. Thousands of copies were sold at the conference. The one question everyone wanted to know who wrote *The Pelican Trees?*

Shelby replied saying, "Just what the book suggests. The story was written by *A Grateful Believer.*"

She left it at that. But the way she said it with a certain sparkle in her eye made many believe *she* was the author.

As satisfying as the trip to California was, Shelby was even more excited about the next gathering beneath the pelican trees. Just thinking about it flooded her heart with anticipation.

Shelby thought it amazing how the shedding of tears represented so many different things. At first glance, some passengers on this nearly-full flight might think she was grieving, when nothing could be further from the truth. She was simply overwhelmed by God's goodness and couldn't stop praising Him for the many blessings in her life.

Looking out the airplane window from 30,000 feet in the air, Shelby was astonished. Twenty-seven months ago, none of this would have seemed thinkable.

Had someone told her at the outset that all this would happen, her first reply would be, "Come again? I'm going to write a book and address 7,000 people in one setting? Yeah right!"

But that was then. Shelby McKinney was a new woman, and this was her new normal in life. And one thing was certain; she wasn't going back to the life she once knew.

It was all about moving forward...

Shelby looked skyward and smiled.

Going on the buried treasure hunt adventure provided her with this incredible story. Receiving Christ as Lord and Savior had literally saved her soul from an eternity separated from her Creator.

It also led to her forgiving Stuart Finkel which, in turn, opened the floodgates of creativity, allowing her to tap into tremendous amounts of energy and talent she never even knew she possessed.

Knowing that God's sovereign hand was in it all, from start to finish, Shelby McKinney couldn't stop praising her Maker...

65

THE FOLLOWING EVENING EVERYONE reconvened beneath the pelican trees.

There were no lit torches circling the three trees this night. No lights draped along the many branches. Nor were catering companies or musical groups flown in from Hawaii.

It was beyond that point. With so many hearts changed, it was all about business. The mood was joyous.

Much like the last two times—Luther's first year in Heaven celebration, and Shelby's book signing—there were more demons than pelicans perched on the trees' many branches. They were petrified of the outcome.

They sparred among themselves hoping it would help. It didn't. They shrieked and moaned. They moved briskly in the early evening sky, sand and water passing beneath their wings with the quickness of a thought. They raced over, around and even through the pelican trees hoping to knock them over, killing everyone standing underneath them in the process. But they didn't have that power.

The blinding white Light high above in the Heavens was too bright, too holy, too condemning. There wasn't a place in all the universe where Satan's demons could hide to escape the Light.

They were suddenly fearful that those they were sent to deceive and destroy, would soon destroy them in the name of Jesus!

Totally unaware of their presence, Pastor Cantrell took his time walking everyone through the Bible until everyone assured him they had a clear understanding of the Gospel of Jesus Christ.

Said he, "It's essential for everyone to understand that as sinners we cannot save ourselves. Even on our best day, we all deserve hell. Only by repenting of your sins and trusting in Jesus can anyone be spared that awfully dreadful place. Do you all understand this?"

Every head nodded yes. At that, Shelby asked everyone to form small circles and join hands. In all, twelve circles were formed, with at least one designated believer in each circle.

In Shelby's circle were Jesse, her brother Jake, her two cousins Charlotte and Morgan, Martin Hightower, Jim and Claire Montgomery and Hank

Cavanaugh. Her son, Trevor, was also part of the circle. Now ten, after reading his mother's book, Trevor wanted what she had. It could wait no longer.

BJ and Brooke still couldn't grasp what was going on. They played on the beach as everyone formed circles.

In Bob and Ruth Schuster's circle were FBI Agent Gloria Sanchez, Susan Fernandez and her good friend, Sonya Haynesworth, from Sunrise Savings and Loan. After reading *The Pelican Trees* for themselves, three other colleagues from the bank were among them.

Also, in this circle, standing in between Bob and Ruth Schuster, with hands trembling, was Bernie Finkel.

After receiving a series of heartfelt letters from his grandson in prison—each one asking forgiveness for the many reprehensible things he did throughout the years—Bernie sensed his grandson wasn't the same wretched man he was before his incarceration. Stuart seemed calmer, gentler and kinder. And for the first time ever, sincere.

But Bernie never replied to any of his letters. Nor did he accept his frequent collect calls. And there wasn't a chance he would visit his grandson in prison. Especially knowing his own flesh and blood was prepared to kill him if it meant getting his hands on Shelby McKinney's buried treasure. It was an unforgivable act.

Stuart's mother wrote occasionally, but never visited him. It was too far for Millie Finkel to travel alone.

Being locked up the past two years gave Stuart plenty of time to contemplate the bad things he did to so many people, especially his grandfather. Not hearing from him kept Stuart awake most nights, tossing and turning in his cell.

It was torturous at times. He cried a river of tears, wave after wave of deep anguish and sadness nearly drowning him at times. But he never shared these feelings of agony and despair with his grandfather, a man Stuart prayed for every night without fail.

In his latest letter, sent early last week, Stuart was never more desperate to hear back from him:

Please, Grandpa, even just one line from you will make all the difference. I know you have no reason to believe me, but I miss you and need to know you're okay.

I'm not trying to pull the wool over your eyes again. All I want is your forgiveness. Nothing more! I'm not the man I was before coming to this place. The changes in me are real and permanent.

It started after Shelby McKinney visited me last year and forgave me to my face. I believe God sent her, and another friend, to visit me here and introduce me to the Gospel of Jesus Christ. I'm eternally grateful to say Jesus is my Lord and Savior.

Shelby and Richard are so supportive and visit me on occasion. They make me want to be a better man. Both have helped me turn my life around. I don't know what I would do without them!

I know the pain, embarrassment and humiliation I've caused has deeply scarred you, Grandpa. But please tell me what I must do to receive your forgiveness and I'll do it. It's that important to me.

What hurts the most is that you only know the bad side of me. There's also a good side. Believe it or not, many look up to me for spiritual guidance in this place. I even lead a weekly Bible study.

Hearing kind words from so many here gives me hope and strength to continue on. But truth be told, I'd gladly trade it straight up just to hear from you again. I never told you this, but you were always my hero growing up. When Dad left us, you were always there for me and Mom. And how did I thank you? By constantly letting you down. I'm so sorry.

In the Bible it says, "All things are possible with God". Well, I've come to learn that without God all things are possible too, but in a bad way. In my former life, I was a despicable person who cared only for myself.

But thanks to the two most beautiful people I know on this planet, I was finally introduced to Jesus. He totally changed me from the inside out. Had it not been for God's mercy and grace, I'd still be that angry, bitter prisoner I was when I was first sent here.

Even if you never reply to my letters, I'll keep writing asking your forgiveness. God has already forgiven me. I just hope you can someday bring yourself to do the same. That's all I ask. If you got to see the new me, you might even be proud for a change.

I love you, Grandpa, and pray for you every day. God bless you!

Your loving Grandson,
Stuart

P.S. Above all, love each other deeply, because love covers over a multitude of sins (1 Peter 4:8).

Bernie Finkel was deeply touched by his grandson's sincerity, but still couldn't trust anything he told him, especially about all this Jesus stuff. He chalked it up as desperate words coming from a man who'd finally been caught and would be locked up for a very long time.

There are no atheists in foxholes, was the first thing that came to Bernie's mind, after reading the letter, which, coming from the mind of a staunch atheist was rather peculiar. He was relieved that Stuart was changed for the better, but still wanted nothing to do with him. Too much damage had been done to offer him forgiveness.

Then Bernie read *The Pelican Trees,* and everything changed.

In the end, after reading everything Stuart did to Shelby McKinney, including attempted murder, it was her genuine love and compassion for his grandson that finally convicted his heart, pushing Bernie Finkel over the edge.

Pastor Mike Cantrell closed his eyes and said, "For those of you who feel God calling you to salvation, cry out to Him and repent of your sins. The Word of God states that if you confess with your mouth that Jesus is Lord and believe in your heart that God raised Him from the dead and you will be saved. Cry out to Him. He is listening..."

Pastor Cantrell remained quiet among the soft praying, weeping and sniffling. He felt God moving in a very big way.

After a while, he opened his eyes and declared in a joyous voice, "Praise be to the One who has the power to give eternal life. All glory and honor and praise go to Him. For those of you who are new children of God, let me be the first to welcome you into God's eternal Family."

Shelby wrapped her arms around Jesse, shedding tears of great joy. *Finally!* Trevor was next.

Bernie Finkel nearly collapsed in Bob Schuster's arms. Both men sobbed. When Luther Mellon proposed the *Mellon Project* to Bob four years ago, never in a million years did he think it would have a profound eternal impact on his partner.

To finally experience 39 years of constant praying come to pass before his and Ruth's eyes was totally beyond description.

God's mighty warriors swept down like an unquenchable fireball, vanquishing all demons assigned to those who were new children of the Most High God, sending them all spiraling into outer darkness, never to hover in the human world again.

While Heaven's newest saints were promised glorious futures, the only thing Satan's demons had to look forward to, was constant torment in an eternal lake of fire.

Mercifully spared that same wretched destiny, the newly redeemed gathered beneath the pelican trees were eternally grateful.

After a few moments, Bernie was able to speak. "Are you busy tomorrow, Bob?"

"Not at all, Bernie. What do you need?" Bob looked deep into his partner's eyes. Finally, after all those years, there was a spark there.

"I need to visit someone and offer my sincere forgiveness. He's suffered long enough. It's time to mend fences and build a new relationship with my grandson. I also need to ask his forgiveness in return, for being so stubborn and selfish the past two years. It can wait no longer."

Wow! "What time would you like to leave?"

"The earlier the better."

"I'll be at your house come sunrise."

"Perfect!" Bernie Finkel sniffled. His bushy eyebrows shot out above his tear-steamed bifocal glasses. His well-tanned face looked peaceful for a change.

"If it's okay with you, Bernie, I'd like to visit him too. I already forgave your grandson in my heart, now I'd like to do it face to face. I also want to encourage my brother in Christ in prison and assure him he's not alone."

"That's very noble of you, Bob."

"It's time for me to grow up as a Christian and do everything God wants me to do, instead of selfishly picking and choosing according to my feelings."

"What would I ever do without you, Bob?"

"It's not me, Bernie, but He who lives in me."

Jesse McKinney overheard the conversation. With a certain glow on his face that wasn't there a few minutes ago said, "Will y'all have room for one more passenger? After seeing what offering a little forgiveness did for Shelby, I'd like to do the same. I'm sure it'll be difficult seeing Stuart in person, but with God's help anything is possible, right?"

"I'd love for you to join us," Bob said.

"Me too," said Bernie Finkel. A rush of gratitude snaked through him.

Ruth joined them. After so many years of constant praying, her dear friend was finally Heaven-bound when his time on earth came to an end. Ruth couldn't flush the smile from her face.

"How do you feel, Bernie?" she said.

"Simply incredible!" Placing his left hand on Bob's left shoulder, and his right hand on Ruth's right shoulder, Bernie looked deep into their eyes, "I always knew something set you apart from everyone else I knew. Now I know why. Thanks for constantly praying for this stubborn old man all those years. A big part of why I now trust in Jesus is because of the constant example you've both set for me all these years..." His voice trailed off.

"To God be the glory," said Bob.

Ruth was too emotional to speak. Until just now, she never fully understood why "longsuffering" was listed as one of the nine fruits of the Spirit in Galatians 5:22-23, in the King James Version.

Feeling her husband's business partner trembling with joy in her arms, she now understood it completely.

Relief washed over them both...

66

AFTER IT ALL HAD ended, and everyone went home or back to their hotels, Shelby sat on the front porch with Jesse and the Schusters. The kids were inside watching TV.

Now that Jesse was a true child of God, knowing they would spend eternity together flooded Shelby's soul. She took a sip of lemonade, she tallied the numbers of all who received Christ as Lord and Savior. She started doing this after her book was released, so she could pray for everyone each day.

Her heart fluttered when she read, *Trevor McKinney, age 10*, near the bottom of the second page. Watching her husband and ten-year-old son both come to faith in Christ was almost as uplifting as her own conversion two years ago.

Before calling it a night, Shelby strolled down to the water's edge alone. As always, the salty sea air wafting up from the Gulf of Mexico seduced her senses. But in no way could it compare to what took place beneath the pelican trees a short while ago.

It was a priceless moment which yielded a sizable harvest for God's Kingdom. She had a premonition that this was just the beginning of greater things to come.

Looking skyward Shelby prayed, "Thank You, Father, for an amazing evening. It couldn't have gone any better! Please tell Grandpa the seed he planted in me has finally blossomed into a mighty oak tree, forever changing the Mellon family tree. Mission Accomplished!

"Thanks again for loving me so much that You spared my life until I finally saw the Light. I am eternally grateful to You for calling me to Yourself and giving me light for my darkness, sight for my blindness, knowledge for my ignorance and Truth for my deceit.

"You are an amazing God, and I remain dedicated to loving You back for the remainder of my life. Use me any way You see fit. Bless and keep the remaining one-hundred and thirty-nine Shelby's Saints. Thanks for sending them into my life. I love you, Lord..."

As it turned out, Luther Mellon and Mabel Saunders were right all along; Shelby really was the key to making the plan come to fruition. But only because God's hand was in it from start to finish, even when she didn't know it. Knowing God had used her story to deliver the spiritual jolt many needed to finally bring them to their knees and get them to focus on eternity and salvation through Christ Jesus thrilled her to no end.

What started with a brokenhearted woman sitting on a front-porch swing crying out for answers and understanding, was the beginning phase of the two most incredible years of her life.

So much had happened; both good and bad. But it took being temporarily plucked out of her cozy little life, where she felt completely safe in her familiar surroundings, to come face to face with her Lord and Savior and find her true worth in Him.

Shelby also discovered her talent as a writer during this time, which was about to impact so many others worldwide.

They were already planning to have *The Pelican Trees* translated into Spanish, with other languages to follow.

Had Shelby bought into all the negativity surrounding the buried treasure hunt at the outset and decided not to embark on her late grandfather's great and daring adventure, *The Pelican Trees* would have never been written.

She sniffed in the salty night air and smiled, knowing she was finally experiencing what the late Mabel Saunders had felt all those years—the fullness of God's joy. And it felt terrific!

In Shelby's case, it took an alcoholic to strike and kill a good Christian man nearly two decades ago, to finally bring her late grandparents to their knees, which ultimately led her grandfather to send her on a wild goose chase, which led to all of this.

In Bernie Finkel's case, it came down to a little book Shelby was blessed to have the privilege of writing, and a grandson in prison. Had Stuart's past actions, vile as they were, not been part of *The Pelican Trees* story, Bernie Finkel—a staunch atheist all his life—would have never read it in the first place.

Once convinced that whatever Shelby possessed was genuine and real, Bernie Finkel wanted it too. With his heart changed, nothing on the planet could have kept him from plugging into the greatest Source in all the universe—Christ Jesus.

Another thing Shelby learned the past two years was that true forgiveness was giving up one's right to retaliate. Just as there is a circle of life, a circle of forgiveness also existed in the universe.

Once unleashed, the after-effects were beyond description. Shelby was living proof that any person obedient enough to take the first step in forgiveness always received the greatest blessings in the end!

354

Looking up into the pitch-black sky, Shelby saw the dull pulse of flat stars in the bright moonlit sky and felt so incredibly alive and at peace! A small, low-lying rain-less cloud drifted underneath the moon.

Watching it slowly floating in the late evening sky, the "crossroads" encounter she'd had on the beach at the start of this great and daring adventure flooded her mind again.

The cloud very much resembled the one she saw and felt just like that night. Back then, Shelby McKinney was just another aimless drifter, a rain-less cloud moving along in the universe, searching for a true sense of belonging.

Only she didn't know it...

But her late grandfather knew and sent her on the buried treasure hunt. For that, Shelby was eternally grateful. It literally saved her soul from an eternity in hell!

A tear escaped her eye. No longer was Shelby McKinney a small fraction of who she once was. The new Shelby McKinney was a child of the King. And she was on a Mission; to lead multitudes into a personal relationship with her Lord and Savior, Jesus Christ!

With God leading the way, she looked forward to every step along the way. *Hallelujah!*

355

A little forgiveness

really can go a long way!

Question is...

Who do YOU need to forgive?

"The fruit of

the righteousness

is a tree of life,

and he who

wins souls is wise"

(Proverbs 11:30)

Thanks for taking the time to read my book. I sincerely hope you enjoyed it. If so, I would be most grateful if you left a review on Amazon. Even a short review would be appreciated. May God continue to bless and keep you. To contact me personally: patrick12272003@gmail.com

Like on Facebook: https://www.facebook.com/patrick12272003

Follow on Twitter: https://twitter.com/patrick12272003

Be sure to read Patrick Higgins' award-winning prophetic end times series,

Chaos in the Blink of an Eye.

The first five installments are now available.

About the Author:

Patrick Higgins is the author of *The Pelican Trees*, *Coffee In Manila*, the award-winning *The Unannounced Christmas Visitor*, and the award-winning prophetic end-times series titled, *Chaos In The Blink Of An Eye*. While the stories he writes all have different themes and take place in different settings, the one thread that links them all together is his heart for Jesus and his yearning for the lost.

With that in mind, it is his wish that the message his stories convey will greatly impact each reader, by challenging you not only to contemplate life on this side of the grave, but on the other side as well. After all, each of us will spend eternity at one of two places, based solely upon a single decision which must be made this side of the grave. That decision will be made crystal clear to each reader of his books.

Higgins is currently writing many other books, both fiction and non-fiction, including a sequel to *Coffee In Manila,* which will shine a bright, sobering light on the diabolical human trafficking industry.

What readers are saying about The Pelican Trees...

This book has been such a HUGE help to me. You have no idea how transformed I feel right now! After feeling kind of lost the past few months, reading this book was like having a revival in my heart. I cried all weekend, but it was a good healing, forgiving cry. I can only imagine how many lives will be impacted with this new weapon that God's Holy Spirit has blessed our planet with. I see millions of souls being saved after reading this book, as their names are written in the Book of Life!!

Blanca Garcia, Mexico City, Mexico

I thoroughly enjoyed The Pelican Trees. The story was simply amazing. I found myself unable to put it down most of the time. There is mystery, intrigue, evil plots and good plots, with enough twists and turns to keep me guessing right up to the end. Throughout the story, the reader will discover that even our most unimportant choices and decisions can have dire consequences that of which we may never really know. I have never said this about a book, but I believe The Pelican Trees would make an excellent movie and one that would do fairly well at the box office. In the end, the theme of forgiveness and salvation really makes for an enjoyable read. I can see it being used by the Holy Spirit to bring others to salvation in Christ because of the gospel message that is throughout.

Terry Delaney Pastor/Founder of Christian Book Notes

Wow! Words can't express how I feel about this novel. I struggled with forgiveness and grace toward others for years and, again, recently for six long, painful weeks due to a betrayal by two sisters in Christ. This book really touched me to my core. I'm still shedding tears of joy and have goose bumps. Thank you for being a mighty vessel of God's and being obedient to Him. I will be reading this again and again as well as giving copies to family and friends who need God's salvation. God bless you and I have added you to my daily prayer list... God knows who you are.

In Him, Chaplain Lynn Burton

This book was so good. There were times I just couldn't put it down. The best part about The Pelican Trees story is that it has allowed me to forgive one specific person within my family, who has caused me great heartache since my mother's death 10 years ago. I have passed this life-changing book on to other members of our staff, for them to read and also recommend. And I will definitely recommend this book to others. There are a few non-Christians in my life that I will recommend the book to as well. Thanks for the opportunity to read and comment on the book.

Sheila Barber Publications Ministry Assistant
Fort Caroline Baptist Church, Jacksonville, Florida

This is the greatest Christian novel on the market today! When I read the beach scene, especially, I was completely frozen in my seat and couldn't even breathe! And just when I thought the book had fully climaxed, it kept getting better and better. Wow! What an amazing story! It truly is a must-read for everyone!

Karen M. Kouyoumjian - Celebration, Florida

The Pelican Trees touched my heart as it reminded me of my own experience with the four men responsible for shooting and killing my son. I was able to express my forgiveness of all of them in four separate sentencing hearings in Federal Court. I have corresponded with two of them, both of whom have accepted Jesus as their Savior. I am humbled to be used by the Lord to share His love, grace, and mercy with them.

Carol Lewis - Summit Christian Academy Lee's Summit, Missouri

GREAT!!!!!!! Just read the entire book. This is one of the greatest novels ever! I finally understand what forgiveness is all about and its many positive benefits to those who sincerely forgive others. I can't stop reading it over and over again. I believe every woman who reads it will want to be Shelby McKinney! This story will give each reader the warmest feeling inside. It's so amazing!

Jovelyn Dal – The Philippines

This was an excellent book, once I started reading it, it was hard to put down. I really enjoyed it and felt very blessed.

Terrand – Amazon Review

This s a very good book. I have never read a book as awesome as this one. It touched my heart and I found myself close to tears several times. I can't think of the words to say how much I love this book. I highly recommend it to everyone.

Dawn Galloway – Amazon Review

I have now read The Pelican Trees and the first 5 installments of Chaos In The Blink of An Eye. So very inspiring! I was raised in a Christian home, sadly enough I have slipped back many times. Through Higgins' books I now have a much better understanding of God's Word. At 73 years old, I will now be making plans to be baptized. Thank you so very much!

Amazon Customer

Couldn't stop reading! God's love and plan of salvation was beautifully presented throughout the entire story. Even as a long time Christian it still gives you the realization that all are reformed sinners. God bless you as you read and examine your life and Christian walk.

Mary E. – Amazon review

Wonderful story! Patrick Higgins books are so good. I love all his books. This book was really a great read and such a wonderful concept. I wish there was more authors in the world today like Patrick Higgins. The world would be a better place if people read books like this.

GodisGreat – Amazon review

This is the greatest Christian novel I have ever had a chance to read. I am excited to read the rest of his books.

Kindle customer review

Fantastic. Brings out all your emotions in one book. Great read!

C. Nina Farley